The LANE LIGHT

A Christmas Story

CANDEE MACQUEEN

ISBN 978-1-64670-798-0 (Paperback)
ISBN 978-1-64670-799-7 (Hardcover)
ISBN 978-1-64670-800-0 (Digital)

Covenant Books, Inc.
11661 Hwy 707
Murrells Inlet, SC 29576
www.covenantbooks.com

For Alan
My husband and best friend
For your encouraging words
In following my dreams—
I miss you every day

Acknowledgments

I find myself in appreciation of my life experiences, for without them, I could not have written this story.

Many thanks go out to family and friends whose encouragement was heartfelt. To my friends, Marcie Welden, a special thank-you, for the much needed computer help, your honest opinions, and most importantly for standing by me every day, and to Kate Sweeney for her contribution of artwork for the cover.

Many years ago, a passion to write was instilled in me. I told it, "I don't know how."

It answered back, "You will, when the time is right." A lifetime later, the time was right and the words seemed to come.

The entire story is written with lifetime of farming experiences and knowledge, which I have been blessed with. This is strictly a fictional story, in some opinions, the work may not fact check, it was not intended to.

This is a simple Christmas story of fiction from my heart, put there by the Lord.

November 27

*S*teph had been sitting at the desk for over an hour but it felt much longer.

"I'd much rather be sitting on a horse," she said to herself, feeling defeated. The morning had started out on a positive note, until she went on the computer and found an e-mail that she hadn't been expecting. The people who had booked Christmas week were canceling. "We are so sorry for the inconvenience," it read. The deposit was non-refundable, so at least she had that. Her head went straight to panic mode. It was already the weekend after Thanksgiving, which didn't leave much time for her to secure another booking. She stared at the computer screen. Her gut feeling was telling her to upgrade the retreat website, highlighting Christmas week.

"I wish I was better at this. Marketing has never been my strong suit," she said to herself. As she began to get discouraged, she heard Gram's voice ringing loudly in her head, "Never give up, child."

She smiled and whispered, "I won't, Gram!"

She dug through the file drawer until she found the article on the ranch that had been printed in a Casper newspaper when she officially opened her retreat business, earlier this year. She read it again now.

Discovering the Kahler Ranch
by Martha Simms

Driving northwest on Hwy AA, toward the
town of Bethlehem, watch for the grand entrance

to the Kahler Ranch, home to a six-generation cattle and horse business and the new Kahler Retreat. The welcoming lane is ¾ mile long, lined with pipe fencing and young aspen trees. As you head toward the buildings, the heart of the ranch, the first one you come up on, is the "old barn," sitting quietly on the right. This original barn is used for anything and everything, from the newest litter of kittens to a young couple saying their vows standing on a straw-covered floor.

A little ways up on the left you will find the new state-of-the-art equine center which includes a full size indoor arena and stalling for thirty horses. From here, the lane forks left and right. A right takes you to the big cabin, home of the Kahler family and the Kahler Ranch Retreat. Further up this lane you will discover the multi-generation family cemetery and an original log cabin. Behind this is the beauty of the ranch's north open range. Going back now, from the horse barn, take a left. This lane takes you past large equipment barns and toward the cattle operating end of the ranch. Here you will find barns, paddocks, and pastures housing some of the best Angus cattle in the West. To the north are rows of hundreds of tons of stacked covered hay bales. These rows act as a windbreak for the cattle during the severe Wyoming winters.

She stopped reading without finishing the article.

"Does anybody really care where a barn sits or why?"

A voice in her head said, "Some would."

She stayed quiet for a few moments then shook her head to clear it and thought, "Concentrate, Steph!"

"Okay, this sounds like a visitor's guide, so maybe if I steal a few words and pretty them up…," she stopped talking to herself and typed on the keyboard. A few minutes later she read her work, now typing and talking to herself again, "…just maybe I can convince somebody that they really need to spend their Christmas—here!"

Steph read the newly updated website one more time, hoping to sell herself on the wording. Two minutes later, with a confident smile, she said, "Sold." She closed the laptop and gave it a gentle pat for luck. "I'd better get going."

She glanced at the clock. Chip was going to be wondering where his parts were, and she was still hoping for a little time for herself in town.

"Hey, Steph, you out enjoying this amazing fall weather, while it lasts?" Joyce laughed lightly as she cleared off the counter next to the register. The Gold Nugget Antique Mall was Steph's favorite place in town. She loved scanning the shelves and over the years had trained her eyes to do it quickly, but at the same time, miss nothing. Usually Steph's trips to town were hurried, as someone back at the ranch was waiting for that special tractor part or bottle of needed cattle vaccine, but today she had a little extra time and was looking forward to visiting with her talkative friend.

"I don't think I can remember a prettier November and I've seen a lot of them." Joyce laughed. Steph had never asked the woman her age, but she guessed her to be in her early sixties. Steph loved her beautiful long silvery gray hair and secretly hoped she looked that good when she reached whatever age that was. Joyce walked around the counter and gave Steph a big hug, "You haven't been in for a while."

"Oh, Chip's been working me on the ranch, says he can't work cattle without me." Steph laughed, then added, "Sold off some odds and ends, you know, the kind with no size, not taking any chances this year."

"Don't blame you one bit," Joyce replied.

Steph continued, "Any excuse to get me to help, but I don't mind; I like the extra time with him." Steph smiled, thinking of her husband.

"Got anything new?" Steph asked, with her eyes already looking around the store.

"Well, I guess you're just going to have to look for yourself," Joyce teased.

The store was decorated beautifully for the season. It contained a little of something for everyone's taste, from European furniture to barn wood frames. Steph was always on the lookout for things she collected. She decorated her ranch home with farm country that had a rustic flare of Western and cowboy thrown in. Right away she found a plain grapevine wreath she liked. Walking down the last aisle, a wooden box caught her eye. Stopping, she studied it, a simple box made of white pine. She ran her fingers over the nicely finished edges. It measured about two and a half feet wide, three feet long with one by ten sides; the tag on it said twenty dollars. The price didn't scare her off, but she had no clue why she wanted it, but she did. On the drive home, she asked herself, "Any plans for that box lady?" Then answering herself, she said, "Not a one!"

She pulled up to the old barn and unloaded Chip's stuff from the tractor supply and her new box, placing it on a bale of straw next to the wall, where it would stay until it was needed.

As soon as she got back inside, she checked the computer. Steph clicked on the inbox, which contained one new e-mail, and she held her breath.

It was from a Susan Conners of New York City. She mentioned seeing the website and was inquiring about Christmas week. She asked all the normal questions: was it still available, how much, etc. Steph was grateful for the interest, but until she had a deposit check in her hand, she wouldn't let herself get too excited. She answered all of the Conner woman's questions, thanked her for her interest, and hit the reply button. "Now," she thought, "I'll check it in a couple hours."

Steph always tried to get her Christmas decorations up the week between Thanksgiving and the first week in December. She had some big plans this year, this being the retreat's first Christmas. She wanted everything to be "over-the-top nice." There were two other big ranches doing the same thing: one other in Wyoming, right out of Yellowstone, and the other in southern Montana. Both had been in business for at least ten years, were very well established and successful, with holidays being booked a full year in advance. She knew from experience that she had to build her own reputation and that it could take a while. She was secretly hoping she might be lucky enough to pick up some of their overflow business this first year. She was also intelligent enough to understand that she only had one chance to get it right. "Word of mouth could make you or break you."

The old Victorian Steph grew up in was always done up right for the holidays, by Gram's standards. The Kahler family had thought Steph was a little "excessive" with her Christmas decorations when she married into the family, but after seventeen years, nothing surprised them anymore.

Steph checked the computer again before starting dinner—nothing. Oh well, she thought, people who inquired but didn't pan out were referred to as "looky-loos.

Susan waited until Lilly was asleep before approaching Rick with her idea. She didn't need Lilly being disappointed again.

"Rick, I found this, for Christmas," she said, handing the copies of the website that she had printed off to her husband.

"What is it?" Rick scanned the pages. He looked up at her with a stunned look on his face. "You want to go to Wyoming, to a dude ranch for Christmas?"

"It's not a dude ranch, it's a retreat on a cattle ranch," she answered.

He read more, flipping the pages hastily, and without looking up said, "Yea well, it's still a dude ranch!"

"Stay calm, Susan, you can do this, Lilly needs this," she whispered so low that Rick didn't hear. She kept talking to herself, in her mind; this was the only way she could keep her courage up. She knew she needed to get as many words out as she could before Rick shut her down.

"Not this time, Rick," she said a little louder, but he wasn't paying any attention to her as he read.

"You keep promising Lilly, she's not little any more. You can't keep telling her things then letting her down. Rick she's changed. Can't you see the difference in her in the last year?" Susan's voice was quivering now. "If you can't, then you are a fool, you're losing her, Rick!"

"Don't cry, don't cry!" she kept telling herself, her heart was beating hard. All this hurt.

Rick looked up from the pages, "Is it really that bad, Susan?" His voice had that "you're bothering me" tone to it, but she wasn't going to let up this time; she had nothing to lose.

"Yes it is, Rick. I'm serious. I want us to go away for Lilly's sake, Rick. It's only five days. It's Christmas, please." She hesitated a few moments, regaining her courage, then, she laughed, which caused him to look up, directly into her eyes.

"I'm sure your job can do without you physically being there for a few days."

She was afraid to say what she really wanted to about his job.

"You always promise her a vacation in the summer, then you tell her you can't get away. Your words don't mean anything, Rick!" She tried to get ahold of her voice. It was getting too squeaky, which wouldn't help.

"Everyone takes a little time off for Christmas. What good is it to make all this money and then not ever get to enjoy it? Please, Rick."

Rick hated giving in to Susan, for anything. He was raised in a household where the man was the decision maker and begging wasn't tolerated, but at the same time, Rick had memories of his dad taking things too far.

Am I turning into my dad? He quickly dismissed the thought. He had to admit, he had seen a change in his daughter; she was too quiet, she didn't seem to care about much of anything anymore, at least when she was with him. If he was going to admit this, he might as well admit that he hadn't been spending enough quality time with either one of them. He knew she was right; this family was falling apart.

Rick kept reading then laughed, "Wow, for five thousand dollars for a five-night stay, they'd better be feeding us gold at that rate!"

Susan's heart took a leap for a second, "It promises a Christmas experience you'll never forget," using a gentler tone in her voice now. She had a feeling that her next words would make or break her chances and possibly make Rick really mad.

She held her head up high as she said, "Maybe someone keeps their promises!"

Susan held her breath. Rick slowly looked up at her but didn't say anything. The next few seconds felt like a lifetime to Susan as her heart beat in panic mode.

Finally he took a deep breath.

The scared little girl inside Susan's head said, "You're dead!"

Rick exhaled slowly, "Okay, you win, but only five days, no longer, and leave here on the twenty-first that will put us there for Christmas." He didn't look at her as he threw the pages on the desk and got up to walk toward the bedroom. As he got to the door, he turned and said, "I hope you know what you are doing." He didn't wait for an answer as he slammed the bedroom door closed behind him.

Susan didn't move, she couldn't, but she felt the tears running down her face and heard her voice say, "Me too."

At midnight, New York time, Susan sent an e-mail to the Kahler Ranch, booking Christmas week.

Steph checked the computer one last time before going to bed. It was a little after ten in the evening mountain time. The inbox held one new e-mail, from Susan Conners. Steph held her breath as she read. The woman wanted to book two rooms, from the twenty-first to the twenty-sixth or twenty-seventh. She had enclosed a credit card number with a deposit of $1500, three times the required amount. Susan added that she was very excited and would contact Steph in the morning for details and added she couldn't wait to tell her eight-year-old daughter. Steph smiled to herself, "Eight—it will be fun having a little girl in the house for Christmas again." She read the ending of the e-mail, "Good night, Steph, and thank you for our first Country Christmas!"

November 28

*T*he two women walked out onto the sidewalk. The crisp air felt good, especially after the hour of yoga lessons. "Got time for a coffee, Sue?" her friend Madge asked.

The two lived in the same apartment building. Madge was a devoted single and a registered nurse at New York City's largest hospital. The two didn't get much time to visit, normally only on yoga mornings.

"Sure, there's something I've been waiting to tell you about!" Susan replied happily.

The two turned south and walked the half block to the Starbucks. The street was in busy mode as usual, cars honking, people hollering, trying to flag down one of the numerous cabs that turned the streets of the city yellow. Sirens wailed in the distance and the air smelled of exhaust. It was just another normal day in the city.

With coffees in hand, they walked toward the only available table in the place and sat down to chat. For some reason, Susan seemed a little happier today, Madge thought. It had been a long time since she had seen a smile on her friend's face.

Giggling now, Susan couldn't wait any longer, "Remember that Western retreat you told me about?" Susan talked quietly, but her eyes twinkled.

"Yes, did you check it out?" Madge asked.

She was almost bouncing in her chair, like a little kid, "Yes, and I talked Rick into it. I can't believe I did that!" Susan's voice was full of excitement, and she went on, "We're going for Christmas week, really only five days. Rick wouldn't do longer, but I'm okay with that—five whole days." Susan was all smiles, "We'll be there for Christmas, that's what matters, for Lilly." Now she was rattling, "I'm a little scared, no, I'm big time scared. I have no idea what to expect!"

Madge waited for an opening where she could break in.

"Slow down, I don't think I've ever seen you like this before," Madge smiled.

"I know," Susan giggled. "Lilly is so excited. Rick thinks it's a big waste of his time but agreed for Lilly's sake."

Madge stayed quiet and let her friend talk. Susan took a sip of coffee, then continued, "We leave on the twenty-first."

"I'm so happy for you and, of course, Lilly," then with a serious look on her face said, "I hope it helps."

Susan looked down at the cup she was holding in her hands and said, "Me too."

Madge decided she needed to change the mood of the conversation.

"I can't wait to hear about all those cowboys, you know, the ones in those tight jeans with the cute little rears, like in the commercials!"

Susan blushed, "Oh, Madgie!"

More serious now, Susan said, "I've got to get the rest of Lilly's Christmas gifts bought up and mailed to the ranch real soon. Got to make sure Santa finds my little girl!" Then with a smile, "I've got so much to do!"

"Feels good to be busy, in a happy way, right, my friend?" Madge asked.

Susan let out a long breath and smiled, "Yes!"

The two friends rode the elevator to Madge's floor and shared small talk before saying goodbye. They'd see each other one more time before Christmas. Susan continued up to the fifteenth floor. Entering the apartment, she dropped her yoga bag on the floor and placed her purse and keys on the hall table. She walked into the living room and over to the large bay window. The view was of Central Park. Most of the leaves had fallen, leaving the trees barren; they looked cold and lonely. The joyful feelings she had when she was with Madge were gone, a sadness washed over her now. She let her mind wander wherever it wanted to.

She'd married Rick twenty years ago. It had started out okay, she thought. Rick was a good provider and the apartment they owned was amazing. Susan didn't want for anything, but the old saying "Money can't buy happiness" was definitely true. Later, as the years went by, she felt incomplete and lonely. She had talked Rick into having a baby but realized now that she had wanted Lilly for the wrong reasons. Back then, she needed a time-filler, not a heart-filler. She loved her daughter, they both did, but life wasn't the way Susan had imagined it would be. Slowly, their family fell apart until there didn't seemed to be much family left.

Rick had a high-powered job on Wall Street, which engulfed his entire being and left very little for Lilly and literally nothing for Susan. Susan could deal with her own unhappiness, but not Lilly's. Susan's heart was breaking for Lilly. She was only eight—things needed to change.

December 2

"*H*ey, Uncle, why are we doing this?" Marco's arms waved in the air. He had stopped working and thrown the handsaw to the ground. Now he reached for the pack of cigarettes in his coat pocket. The small tree he had been cutting was still standing, the cut incomplete. The two men had been working in a stand of young spruce trees.

Chico looked up at him and in a grumpy voice in Spanish said, "Because this is what Missy Kahler wants," referring to Steph.

"Besides, you get the same pay regardless of what you do!" Chico was getting fed up with the eighteen-year-old. He was his wife's nephew, but he didn't care anymore. The kid wasn't cut out for ranch work. Chico had been covering for him on the workload for a while now and that was going to come to an end. Chico was hoping they could all go home to New Mexico for Christmas and he was going to make sure the lad didn't make a return trip back to the ranch.

Marco broke Chico's thoughts, "Well, you don't have to get mad!" Marco hollered at his uncle, adding, "This is stupid!" under his breath, but Chico heard.

"Missy," as Chico called Steph, was decorating the entrance to the ranch for Christmas. She wanted trees cut at one-foot intervals, starting at two feet and up to five feet, enough for both sides of the entrance. The tallest ones would be tied up, next to the rock columns along the pipe fence and then the trees going down in size along the fence out to the road. She planned to put red bows on the trees. It wasn't very fancy, she had thought, but without any power out there, she couldn't do much. The constant winds also challenged her attempts at decorating the entrance.

December 18

"You see the weather forecast this morning?" Chip hollered in Ken's direction. The two men were working on a tractor. Ken was underneath with wrenches in hand as he tightened down the bolts on the cover plate of the transmission case. Chip was up top adding oil to the engine.

"I don't have to," Ken replied, "I can feel it in the air," and with a slight laugh added, "and my bones. This next one is going to sting!"

"Sting, sting, he says!" Chip laughed full heartily, "It's going to beat the crap out of us!"

His tone of voice relayed the meaning of his statement.

"How much time we got," Ken asked Chip, adding, "according to the educated."

The dolly slid out from under the tractor, straight into the Aussie that was sleeping under their feet.

Her response to being run over by the dolly was heard by both men.

"Well, move then!" Ken hollered at her as she trotted off with hurt feelings.

Chip smiled toward her, "He's sorry."

"Oh, they're saying nine to twelve days out, claiming it's a slow mover, right now anyhow," Chip replied to his brother-in-law's question.

"Well, they are wrong," Ken replied, adding, "we need to be ready in six."

Chip nodded his head in agreement, while his thoughts ran.

"Have they named this one yet?"

19

Chip leaned on the tractor, giving his brother-in-law his full attention.

Ken looked serious, "All these storms are named after women, er, females," stuttering a little, "I just don't think they're all that bad!"

Chip felt himself building with laughter but held it in until Ken was finished.

Laughing out loud now, he said, "Oh, it sounds like someone had a nice evening with his Angie last night!"

Ken wiped his greasy hands on a shop rag in silence. Chip waited with a big grin on his face. Finally, Ken looked up at Chip with a solemn look on his face, then threw the rag at him, turned, and walked off.

Chip doubled over with laughter, "No comment. Must have been a very nice evening!" Chip followed Ken out the door and kept teasing but kept a safe distance behind.

"We can still name her!" Chip was still laughing.

"Think we should call her, you know, the storm, the Wicked Witch from the North." Ken didn't take Chip's bait; he just waved an arm over his head and kept going.

———

"Chip, do you need Chico Christmas week?" Steph asked.

Chip was under the tractor again when Steph appeared in the shop. Without coming out, he asked, "Why?"

"Maria's grandfather is ill and her mother feels they should come home for Christmas."

"New Mexico?" he asked.

"Yes."

Chip was silent. She waited, giving him time to think it over.

"Did he say anything to you?" she asked.

"No, but I'll tell him to take a week off; it can be part of his Christmas bonus." Then he added, "I think they should go."

She smiled, already knowing that he would agree. Family was important.

"Horses are all up, we'll be fine." He added, "Plus Kelly will help, I'll tell him tonight."

Rolling out from under the tractor, she knelt down to his level and said, "Thanks, babe," as she gave him a quick kiss. She jumped on the four-wheeler and headed back to the cabin.

It was the eighteenth of December and starting to feel like winter. She thought about the family that would be there in three days, two adults and an eight-year-old, from New York City. "That should be interesting," she told herself. She had all the decorating and shopping done and she felt fairly content with herself. This was the first year of her retreat business and the first Christmas sharing her home and holiday with strangers. She wouldn't admit it out loud but she was nervous. So many things could go wrong and ruin Christmas for everyone.

December 19

As soon as Maria got Anna settled with her schoolwork, she went upstairs looking for Steph. She found her staring into the open linen closet and deep in thought. Maria instantly threw her arms around her friend and said, "Thank you, Missy, I know it was your doing!"

Pulling back and placing her hands on the small woman's shoulders, Steph answered, "Maria, you all go home and have a wonderful Christmas with your family and your precious granddad."

"We will Missy, I promise!" Maria's voice quivered and tears rolled down her cheeks. She grabbed an armload of folded towels and headed off.

In her heart, Steph was happy. "Merry Christmas, Martinez family," she whispered to herself. Deciding now that the linen closet held everything she'd need for the next week, she closed the doors. With Maria gone next week, she was on her own—housekeeper, maid, cook, and hostess. Steph could hear Gram's words, "You've got this, baby girl." This was Gram's nickname for her only granddaughter.

"I miss you, Gram," she smiled, "and yes, I've got this!"

———————— ✦ ————————

"What's going on with the weather?" Chip asked his dad, who had shown up this morning.

Standing next to the wood stove, with his back to Chip, he didn't answer right away. He was looking out the glass wall in Chip's office that was above the horse stalls and overlooking the arena in the new barn.

"Only getting up to twenty-two degrees today," Chip added, waiting for his dad to engage in a conversation. His dad, a veteran of many Wyoming winters, continued his silence. Chip had inherited this same long thinking personality from his father.

"I hope you are sitting pretty near where you plan to be for this weather coming in," a solemn statement from his father, using the word *weather* instead of *storm*.

Chip looked up from his paperwork, and in a serious tone asked, "You listened to the same forecast I did, you know something I don't?"

His dad cuffed his boot on the wood floor and looked at his son, "It's just a gut feeling, but I think we are going to get slapped in the face hard, around Christmas."

"Ken says the same thing, but kinda early for a blizzard, don't you think?" Chip asked.

"I know, been five years since the last early one. Just be ready." His dad's voice had a defeated tone to it, "We've been here before."

"Cattle are all in the cover, plenty of hay out, just need to keep an eye on water, but temps would have to drop to thirty below and stay there to freeze up that creek, runs too hard. No calves due until the first of April this year, not losing calves again."

His statement referred to the major loss three years ago when an unexpected early spring blizzard hit the upper plain states. Ranchers lost three million head of calves. It nearly wiped out a large percentage of ranches, big and small. The financial losses were huge.

"But you'll take a beating in the fall for their lack of size," his dad said.

"I know, but at least I'll have calves to sell," Chip answered.

Suddenly aggravated, Chip stood up, and looking at his father, said, "Gosh, I hate those gut feelings of yours, and to top it off, Steph has city slickers from New York City coming for Christmas week!"

His dad chuckled lightly, "What we won't do for money!"

Chip smiled, "That's okay, I can play nice for five days—for five thousand dollars!"

His dad whistled, "Must be some real nice rooms!"

"You know Steph. She does things up right, and besides, I don't think the city will want to follow me around much," Chip added, joking.

When Steph decided to start her new venture, she had put a lot of thought into it; could she make it work, would it help the ranch financially, and most importantly, how would it affect their family? It was agreed to be a trial run. Steph felt it needed a full year, encompassing all the seasons and holidays. Chip had put his foot down on two things: he didn't want it called a "bed and breakfast," so the term "ranch retreat" was agreed on, but his opinions didn't end there.

"This is a working ranch of the highest caliber, and I won't have it downgraded in reference to a 'dude ranch,' and secondly, only one family at a time, though more than one generation can be considered as one family. Chip was ready to put up a fight if needed. Steph wasn't arguing with what he was insisting on, in fact, she had some rules set for herself: only one family per month. She had no plans to overwhelm their life. The ranch business came first on all levels.

In the end, Steph was optimistic about the retreat's future, Chip was leery, and Kelly was excited. Being her father's daughter, she fantasized a paycheck for her part, as resident camp counselor and babysitter.

During the planning stages, Ken, Chico, and his wife Maria were brought into the discussion. Chip relied on these two men to help run the ranch and considered them family; of course Ken was. Steph approached Maria about helping in the house. She was an excellent cook and housekeeper and had occasionally helped Steph in the past. Chico and Maria had a twelve-year-old daughter, Anna, who was stricken with muscular dystrophy and was confined to a wheelchair. Steph felt it would be a good fit for mother and daughter. Maria could bring Anna with her and continue her care routine at the cabin. Anna loved Kelly and couldn't wait for her to get home from school when she was at the ranch, and Kelly was equally excited to spend time with Anna. Maria homeschooled her daughter, with Anna's grades being above average for her age. So, with Chico's blessing, Maria agreed to help Steph when needed. Steph had also thought that Maria would enjoy earning money of her own.

Chico was definitely the breadwinner in the family, but with Anna's medical bills, they had to be careful. Steph hoped this might be a way for Maria to have the little things she usually did without. She knew there was no use in trying to help the family. Chico was a very proud man, and he would provide for his family. Steph felt it was important that Chico understand that Maria was helping her, not the other way around.

That night Chip called Ken, "In the morning I want you to go back out to where the cows are and put chains on the bottoms of all the gates. I'm worried they might get a sense of that storm heading this way and start walking fences early."

Ken waited for him to finish, "You know something I don't?"

Chip grinned to himself as he said, "Second time that phrase has been used today. No, just Dad, said he's got a gut feeling we are going to get hit hard, like you said, at Christmas. Weather's weird, don't you think?" He waited.

"Yeah, I do, bulls walking the runs already, wanting out. I'll chain those too, and the horses are getting jumpy. Turning Buck and Brite loose in the horse barn and kenneling the Aussies."

Buck and Brite were the ranch's answer to calming companions for the horses. They were Nubian wethers left over from Kelly's 4-H goat project. Chip had picked up on the trick of running goats in the horse barn while visiting a big quarter horse training stable in New Mexico years ago. That trip had been invaluable to the ranch in more ways than one. He had met Chico Martinez there and offered him a job he couldn't refuse. Chico packed a bag, kissed his wife, and left with Chip for Wyoming. A month later he returned to New Mexico to gather his family. That was sixteen years ago.

"What about closing center gates on the bulls?" Ken asked.

"Yes, good call, and Ken, do the chaining yourself. It's not that I don't trust the others," he said with a long silence, "I don't trust the others!"

Ken laughed, understanding, "Got it, Boss, I'll see to it in the morning."

"Night, Ken." Chip instantly sensed that something was behind him. Turning quickly, he found Steph looking concerned.

"Did I hear you correct, worse than we thought?" she asked.

"Yes, I think the weatherman is playing it down. Going to be bad, honey." Then he added, "Nothing in writing. It's Dad; he's got that dang gut feeling again," Chip said dryly.

"Well, that's good enough for me," she said. "I'll handle everything at the house. Let me know if I can help outside. Oh, and can you have one of the guys bring more wood up to the house, fill the wood room and upstairs?" she asked.

"Yes, and I'll want extra in the old barn too. She's always been the emergency spot on the ranch. Hopefully we won't need to thaw anything or anyone out," Chip said with a nervous laugh and big pit in his stomach.

She rubbed his back, "Let's get to bed. Tomorrow's going be busy and cold."

December 20

*S*usan poured her husband a cup of coffee. It was only six thirty, but Rick's eyes were already glued to his laptop computer, checking e-mails.

"Are you going to the office today?" she asked sweetly.

"Of course, why wouldn't I?" He looked up at her, adding, "We aren't leaving until tomorrow, right?"

She didn't answer, wishing she hadn't said anything.

"Don't push it, Susan," she told herself, "he said he'd go, not that he'd like it."

He kept looking at her, so she said, trying to be cheerful, "That's fine, just asking."

That was the end of the conversation between the two of them. A few minutes later, Lilly walked into the kitchen, sleepy eyed. "One more day, Mommy," then turning to her father, she said, "Are you excited, Daddy?"

"Yes, Lilly, I'm excited," Rick said with clenched teeth and without looking at his daughter. A moment later, he exploded, "I hope you two are satisfied, this really messes things up at work!" His aggravation about the trip was apparent.

"But Daddy, it's going to be a fun Christmas. I just know it!" Lilly said, trying to sound uplifting in an eight-year-old's way.

"Yeah, yeah, yeah," was his response, his eyes still on the laptop.

Susan got mad, "There's no reason to take everything out on Lilly, Rick!" She had more to say, "You owe her this trip." Susan used a voice that told him she was about to cry any minute. Rick hated her crying.

He looked at Lilly without a smile, "I'm sorry, Lil," then turned and stared at Susan. Moments later he closed his laptop, grabbed his coat, and walked out the door.

Susan took a deep breath and walked over to Lilly, sitting down. She hugged her tight.

"It's okay, Lilly, he doesn't mean it. He worries about work too much," she said gently, stroking Lilly's blond hair, hoping Lilly accepted the excuses for her father's bad behavior, one more time.

"I know, Mommy," she said in a sad voice.

Susan took the little girl's face in her hands, "Look at Mom, kiddo. You are going to have the time of your life!"

"You promise, Mommy?"

"Yes, promise, baby girl." Susan still holding her, protectively now, whispered, "I hope!"

The clock on the kitchen wall said four thirty in the morning, hard dark outside, a northern prairie expression for the time of early morning before sunrise. Steph poured Chip a cup of coffee while waiting for the biscuits to bake.

"Is Chico coming out today?"

"Just to get his check, do you need Maria to come out today?" Then he added, "She can probably ride with Chico."

"No, but I do want to send their Christmas gifts with him. I'll bring them out to the barn office," she said.

"I'm going into town at noon, wanna ride a long?" Chip smiled. Riding into town together was something they both enjoyed.

She thought for a moment, "Probably, I'll make myself a list so I don't forget anything. What are you after?"

"I'm low on kerosene and wicks. We'll probably lose power with this storm, so I plan on getting a little more than usual. Ken said he'd clean all the lanterns up tonight." Everyone had talked about getting a couple generators for years. The new barn had one installed when it was built, but it was hard to part with the old ways on some things.

"Okay, going out, see you later then." Chip walked over and kissed her on top of the head as he put his jacket on and headed out the back door.

"It's only eight. Surely she's not drunk already this morning," Molly thought. She was in the bathroom and could hear her mom cussing at someone or something.

Molly took a deep breath and opened the bathroom door, whispering to herself, "Gosh, here we go again!"

Jeanie Thomas sat at the kitchen table, in her undies and bra, hair uncombed, with a beer in one hand and a cigarette in the other.

"Aren't you cold, Mom?" Molly asked. She turned toward her mom's bedroom to go get her robe. A few seconds later she walked back to the kitchen and held it out to her mom. Instantly she grabbed it and threw it to the floor. "If I was cold, I wouldn't be sittin' here like this. It's too damn hot in here," her voice was slurred.

She looked at Molly, "I'm so sick of looking at that damn thing," referring to Molly's stomach. "I thought I told you to get out!" She lit another cigarette, blowing the smoke into Molly's face and waited for Molly to answer her. "Well!"

Molly tried to keep her voice calm, "I told you, Mom, I'll leave as soon as I can. Jamie is still working on his truck." Jamie knew Molly was having a tough time living with her mother, but until his truck was running better, they couldn't go far. Molly's Aunt Jane was seventy miles away and his gramps was three hundred and fifty miles away, down in South Dakota. Those were the only places the kids felt they would be welcomed.

Jamie begged her to stick it out as long as she could. She was trying. She knew he needed time.

"Jamie this, Jamie that, Jamie's baby, I'm sick of all of you and I want you out," her mom was screaming at her now.

"I know, Mom, I know!" Molly said heartlessly. She felt dead on the inside. The heart can only take so much, even if you're only seventeen.

Standing at the big glass wall that looked down on the arena and horse stalls, Ken filled Chip in on what the rest of the men were doing, basically getting ready for the incoming storm.

"Feed bunks for bulls filled to the max, extra hay ready to put in. Horse barn has four days' worth of hay bales set out in the stall aisles. We're leaving the two-wheel drive John Deere in the bull barn, four-wheel JD with the loader in the horse barn. Jack has the big tractor with the snow blower on and front end loader sitting next to it, sitting in the overhang on the south side of the tractor shed. He put a big tarp up to try and keep the snow from blowing in so bad. He was worried about having all the tractors inside and not being able to open doors. I went out early and got everything chained, cattle staying close where we want them."

"Good," Chip answered, "I'd like to check them one more time before it hits."

A moment later, Chip asked, "You see the weather?"

"Yeah, guess it all depends on which side of the Rockies it comes down. Doesn't look good, causing havoc in Canada already. Temp's not too bad, but man, it dumped three feet of snow overnight. Guess it's a slow mover right now," Ken said.

"Yep, all we can do is keep our fingers crossed and pray," Chip stated seriously.

"Think we have at least forty-eight hours or more before it hits," Ken said.

"Steph and I are driving to Casper in the morning to pick up the New Yorkers. You're in charge, get plans made with guys through the twenty-third, pay them and wish them a Merry Christmas, and tell them to stay home until this blows over. You and I can handle this. They're saying it's going to be a thirty-six-hour monster. I guess we'll see. I'd worry more, but it's early in the season and we've got everyone up, and that group of cows on their own will be okay; they're survivors, been through this before."

Chip's voice was staying calm about everything so far.

Ken laughed, "We've definitely taken on worse than this storm!"

Chip knew he was referring to their tour in Afghanistan.

"Oh, before I forget, Kelly's out for Christmas and is staying home tomorrow, wants to take Poco and the dogs out for some exercise. Can you keep an eye on her or maybe, better yet, make up an excuse to go with her. I'd feel a lot better if she wasn't out there alone. Critters are not themselves right now, but at the same time, don't scare her," Chip said.

"Take care of her like she's my own," Ken smiled, adding, "I have vested interest remember, she's my goddaughter."

Chip smiled back, "Yep," then added, "Steph and I are headed to town at noon, need anything?"

"Yup, the biggest bottle of Jack Daniels you can find. We may need it, you know, to keep warm," Ken's eyes twinkled with mischief as he teased Chip.

"Hope not!" Chip waved as he left.

The drive to town was relaxing, with nothing indicating as to what was on the way.

"So, where are we stopping besides the gas station for kerosene, the hardware store for wicks, and, oh yea, the liquor store," Chip acted all serious waiting for Steph's reaction. Steph raised her eyebrows.

"Ken thinks he needs a really big bottle of Jack Daniels. You have plenty of wine?" he asked his wife.

Steph laughed, answering, "Then some, the Jack D isn't a bad idea. Leave it to Ken to worry about the booze for a snowy night!"

"Yeah," Chip let out a bit of reserved laughter, "and he deserves every sip he'll take. It's comforting to know someone is just as worried as I am."

Steph turned sideways toward him. "You're really worried about this one," she stated.

"Yes I am, really bad gut feeling," he said without smiling. Chip glanced at the sky to their north. He felt like she was smiling real sweet right now, but saying, "I'm coming!"

"Anyhow, back to now, yes, can we stop at the drugstore. There's a big stuffed horse in the window that I want to get for Lilly."

"How old is she?' Chip asked.

"Eight," she said, realizing he probably hadn't heard a lot that she had said about the people coming.

"Better stop at the grocery store too. I'd better get more deli ham and turkey in case we do lose power. We might be eating a lot of sandwiches," Steph said.

"What's for Christmas dinner?" Chip asked.

"Turkey, if I can cook it. Been a long time since I've cooked a big meal in the fireplace hearth, and I'm not too sure about a big turkey."

Steph's mind ventured toward a totally different direction, a Christmas without electricity.

Chip looked her way and laughed, "Just make sure there's plenty of Christmas cookies. You know the kind I like, what are they?"

"Sugar cookies," she replied.

"Are those the one's with the good frosting?"

"Yes, Chip, you'll have your cookies!" she laughed.

He loved teasing her, "Better. You know I consider them a food group!"

She returned his good mood, "That's right, I forgot!"

"What about all Lilly's stuff?" Rick asked as they were climbing into bed. Their plane would leave at eleven the next morning. They needed to be at the airport by eight thirty.

"You mean her Christmas gifts? I mailed them all two weeks ago. They're all there already," Susan answered her husband's question, thinking his concern odd.

"Steph e-mailed me four days ago confirming their arrival."

"Oh," was all Rick said.

Lilly ran into their bedroom, eyes bright with excitement. Right away Susan wanted to scold her, "I put you to bed three hours ago!"

"I'm too excited to sleep!" She started jumping up and down and rattling on and on.

Susan's heart melted for a second. It was good to see her excited, remembering that the child rarely smiled anymore.

"Okay, okay," Susan softened her voice, "Lilly, you've got to go to sleep so you'll be awake when we get there."

"She'll sleep on the plane," Rick said without turning toward them. "Go to bed, now, Lilly," he grumbled.

Disappointed that no one was sharing in her joy, she put her head down and said, "Okay," in a sad voice as she turned to leave.

Susan turned off the light and curled up on her side of the bed, far away from her husband. Lying there in thought, she tried to think positive, "A good trip and Christmas for Lilly, that's all that matters."

December 21

$\mathcal{S}$teph stood at the kitchen island, looking at her notebook and rechecking the flight times again, wanting to make sure she hadn't messed up. Mountain Time, Eastern Time, it was all so confusing, she thought to herself. The Conners' flight would arrive in Casper at two thirty in the afternoon. Since it was a three-hour drive, Steph and Chip planned to leave the ranch at ten that morning, allowing themselves plenty of time.

Kelly wanted to stay home. She planned on wrapping gifts and finishing up on her chores. Lucky's pen and her horse pens needed… picking, plus she wanted to go for a ride. Kelly was the perfect ranch kid. She'd live in the barn if you'd let her. It started way back as a toddler, she had learned how to pull on her cowboy boots at twenty-two months old and you didn't try and take them away from her. If she wasn't wearing them, she was carrying them around. "Cowgirl from the start," her granddaddy would say.

While waiting on Steph, Ken and Chip stood talking beside the truck. Both studied the sky and the northwest mountain range. The storm was brewing but was still in Canada, still dumping huge amounts of snow. Calgary was all but buried.

Steph walked up, "We'd better get on the road, Chip."

Ken smiled, "The boss has spoken. You guys have a safe trip, all will be fine here."

"We'll call if anything slows us down," Chip hollered out the window as he slowly turned the truck toward the lane. Ken waved without turning.

About twenty minutes later, they turned onto the interstate that would take them to Casper. Chip set the cruise control then leaned back slightly to relax a little. He glanced at Steph. She was going over her notes in a small notebook. His thoughts turned to the last seventeen years they had spent together, a broad smile graced his face.

"She hasn't changed one bit, still the pretty girl I fell in love with," he whispered under his breath.

"What?" Steph squeaked. She had caught Chip smiling at her, out the corner of her eye.

"Nothing, just admiring my girl," Chip said, as Steph felt her face blush.

"Seems like we never get any time to ourselves anymore," Chip commented.

"Well, we spent six hours a night in bed, by ourselves," Steph teased.

Chip laughed, "Yeah, both of us dead to the world."

Kelly and Ken had been riding for an hour, enjoying one of their long talks as they rode. Finally, she asked him what was up with the weather.

"Maybe big storm, bad one, depending on which side of the divide it comes down," Ken answered without looking at her. His eyes were concentrating on the perk of Sara's ears and the tensing of her body muscles.

"Far enough, let's turn around, guys," he said it loud enough for the dogs to hear and take notice.

"Our side," Kelly stated firmly.

"How do you know that?" Ken tried to keep the smirk on his face from showing.

"Gut feeling," was all she said, then smiling, "I got that from my granddad."

Ken smiled at her but felt a need to change the subject.

"How's Lucky?" he asked.

"Doing okay, she's due the twenty-sixth. I put her in the old barn with Jakker—but then you know that, ugh," she said, feeling stupid. "We can take better care of her in there, keep her warm, especially if that storm gets bad, and, oh yea, I plan on staying with her at night, until she calves," her words were stated in a confident voice.

Ken was quiet for a few seconds, then said, "Is that right? Your parents know about this plan of yours?" He laughed.

"No, but—" Before she could say anything else, something spooked Poco. He dropped out from underneath her to the right, straight into Sara and Ken. She instantly grabbed the saddle horn and managed to stay with him, hollering, "Whoa," at the top of her lungs. Ken leaned into her horse and was able to grab her reins, keeping him from running off with her. Trying to right herself in the saddle, she said in a quivering voice, "Glad we're headed home. There's boogers in the wind."

They rode for a few minutes then Ken handed the reins back to her, then leaned over and snapped a lead rope onto the halter that Kelly had left on him, looping the other end around his saddle horn to keep them close. Looking up at Kelly, he added, "Just in case."

Kelly smiled, concentrating now on Poco, who was still skittish. She kept talking gently to him, trying to calm him down.

"Glad you were with me," she said to Ken in a kind voice.

"Me too," he responded.

In the meantime, the dogs seemed to be acting perfectly normal. Shiloh was always the one in the lead. Dakota Breeze was the calmer of the two and perfectly happy to follow her sister.

The riders watched the dogs as they rode home for any signs. Finally Ken spoke, "Guess the spooks aren't down on their level." Kelly only smiled. Sara flicked her ears, she knew.

Kelly always enjoyed her time with her uncle, sharing her ideas, thoughts, and dreams with him. Sometimes, she felt it was easier to talk with him than her parents. She had an excellent relationship with both, but her mom tried to downplay her interest in the ranch. Steph wanted her to think about and do other things, things like clothes, girlfriends, school events and sports, anything not related to "ranching." Her mom's reasoning was for her to have a well-rounded childhood and teen years. Her dad tried listening when she wanted to talk, but he was so busy that she had a hard time holding his attention. When she mentioned the future, his answer was always the same, "We'll take care of the future when it gets here. Can't have a future if you don't take care of today." This was something that had been drilled into his head all his life. None of this reasoning made any sense to Kelly. "Isn't everything we do today for the good of the future?" she wanted to ask but didn't.

Her uncle Ken was different. He always made time to listen, really listen, then engage in a conversation that was aimed at teaching her to think out her ideas, weigh the pros and cons, and to stand up for what she believed in. He, never discouraging her in any way, said, "This country was founded on dreams, prayers, and risk taking."

He loved telling her to dream big and believe she could do and be anything she wanted as long as she was willing to work for it, for hard work and dedication made dreams come true, and to always remember no one could take her dreams away from her.

Ken wasn't always easy on her. If he felt she needed to fall on her rear, he let her. He also valued respect for everything, especially the Lord, who, in his mind, made every life opportunity possible. He felt honored that his sister and her husband allowed him to play such a big part of Kelly's "parenting." Steph would laugh and say, "This one was going to take all three of us to raise."

Kelly grew up following the men in her life. Steph used to complain that Kelly wasn't going to make much of a housewife. Kelly would bristle up at just hearing the word. If you didn't need cowboy boots to do it, she wasn't interested. Her love of horses pleased all of them: Dad, Granddad, her grampie, and Uncle Ken. The ranch was home to a top cutting horse business, with the best studs standing, the best line of broodmares and trained offering. Ben Johns was the trainer they used for finishing. The three-year-olds in training were housed at Ben's, twenty miles to the north of the ranch. To help with the board bill, the ranch traded stud services with Ben for boarding. This worked out well for both. Ben was so impressed with Kelly's horsemanship and work ethic at the ranch that he offered her an apprentice spot, teaching her along with the young horses.

Chip was more than excited, telling Steph what this meant. "If she'll stay with this, she could eventually start training cutting horses on her own. Good trainers are in great demand. If they are really good, the sky is the limit!"

Every couple of years, the Kahler Ranch managed to have a horse do well at the cutting horse trials and sold for really good money. This is what paid the bills and put the horse end of the ranch on the map. Ben wanted her to start in the spring, on weekends, and then five days a week when school was out. Chip would have to take on her chores, but he'd do so gladly. He'd also have to talk to Brenda. For the last two summers, Kelly had worked three days a week as a helper/vet assistant with Brenda. She enjoyed the work, especially riding along on vet calls. Either way, Chip was very proud of the interest she took in the different avenues of ranching.

The long drive to Casper was relaxing, it gave them the much-needed privacy to talk as life mates.

"I told you, we didn't need to leave so early," Chip teased. They had gotten to the airport with plenty of time to spare. Steph had made Chip wear a cowboy hat, to help the couple recognize them.

Chip broke out laughing, "Honey, this is the best you could do? Half the guys in the airport have cowboy hats on. It's Wyoming, remember!"

"Ha, ha, ha," was all she could come up with. He was right. Strike one, she told herself.

"We'll find them. How many couples will have an eight-year-old with them?"

"Yep, and reek money," Chip added with a grin. Steph looked at him with a frown.

Soon, passengers started exiting the plane. As their guests walked down the aisle, the first thing Chip noticed was how they were dressed. Leaning into Steph, he said, "This is not good."

She ignored him and tried to fake a smile. Rick was dressed in black slacks, expensive shoes, and expensive leather jacket. The woman, Susan, was dressed the same—slacks, cashmere sweater, a leather jacket over her arm, and spiked heels. But Lilly, the little girl was on vacation; she had drove her mom nuts until she ordered her jeans with matching jean jacket and boots, although they weren't cowboy boots.

After introductions were made and a little small talk, they waited for the luggage to be unloaded off the plane. Chip decided to "go for it." "I'm not trying to be rude, but this is for your own good. Can I ask you what kind of clothes you brought with you?"

The couple stared at them, then at each other. Susan had decided on the plane that she was going to try and be more outgoing, so she thought, "Might as well start now." Not waiting for Rick to answer, she spoke up.

"Okay, well, we have no life outside so," trying to laugh, she said, "what you see is what you get!" As soon as she said it, she wished she hadn't. "I sounded so stupid," she thought.

Under his breath, Chip said, "I was afraid of that."

"What?" Steph asked.

"Nothing," Chip said, looking directly in her eyes.

"Don't panic," Steph told herself. Needing to lighten everything up, she said, "So in other words, you all aren't cold, weather-wise," laughing lightly.

"Yes," Susan giggled. She thought she could like Steph. "That sums it up nicely!" Susan and Steph shared awkward smiles. Rick just stood there. Finally, Chip placed his hand on Rick's shoulder, for two reasons: one, to see how Rick would react to it, his temperament; and second, to break the ice if possible. The two men came from different worlds.

Rick tried to relax, a little embarrassed. "I totally understand, but what to do about it?" he added.

Steph did some quick thinking. *These people are filthy rich, so let's try this.* After a deep breath she voiced her idea, "There's a really nice western outfitter on the way out of town that I think we could get all the right things you will need, otherwise you'll freeze to death," Steph said.

Chip chuckled, "Would hate to have to bury you all up on the hill with the animals!"

"Can I see the graveyard?" Lilly asked with big eyes.

"Sure if it's not knee-deep in snow," Chip answered.

"Knee-deep?" Susan asked.

Steph quickly asked, "What's the most snow you have all seen?" Thoughts of the approaching snowstorm graced her mind.

"Probably three inches," Susan said, looking questionably at Rick. She then added, "We're both from Florida."

Steph looked at Chip, "How much on the ground now?"

"Probably six inches," he replied.

Lilly half screamed, "Can I make a snowman?" Susan quickly told the child to calm down.

"Yeah, you sure can, Lilly, lots of them, if you want," Chip replied quickly.

Susan and Rick agreed to stopping and purchasing the right clothes.

A minute later, Chip said, "First we gotta stop and eat. I'm so hungry I could eat a buffalo!"

Lilly's eyes got big again. "You have buffalo here too?"

Chip laughed again. He liked this little girl. "Yup, wild buffalo!"

"Wow," she said, trying to imagine.

Chip and Steph knew of a nice bar and grill that catered to tourists and had the atmosphere they wanted to show the Conners. Dinner was a big hit. Lilly ate Buffalo chips (french fried potato slices) and prairie chicken strips (plain old chicken). Rick tried a buffalo steak and said it was the best steak he had ever eaten. Susan was the hardest nut to crack; she wouldn't try anything Western, settling for a Caesar salad. Steph knew she'd have to work on this one; the other two were already won over. Surprisingly, Rick was relaxed and seemed to be enjoying himself. Lilly was going to be fun. *Just wait until Kelly gets ahold of her*, Steph smiled at her thoughts, *maybe this won't be so bad*.

Shopping went well. Rick was very respectful of all Chip's suggestions.

It was getting past dusk as they left the outfitters. Chip figured Rick had just dropped a thousand dollars on clothes. Must be nice, he thought.

For the next few minutes, before it got too dark to see, all eyes were on the landscape, miles of openness, lightly covered with snow.

"So this is Wyoming," Rick said in a very even tone. Neither Chip nor Steph knew the direction that the comment was to be taken. Chip started talking, just generalizing the area. Steph sat in the back seat with Susan, with Lilly between them. Susan seemed to be very nervous. Her hands were gripped tightly together in her lap. She stayed fairly quiet, only speaking when spoken to. Lilly had fallen asleep. Steph wasn't sure what she should do, so she tried making small talk, asking Susan about Florida and New York. Susan answered all of Steph's questions but had no intentions of helping keep the conversation going.

It's going to be a long week, Steph told herself.

Rick had a lot of questions about the area, "Can you tell me its history later in the week? I'd love to know about the Indians and whatever you want to tell me."

"Sure, Rick, we'll have plenty time to talk," Chip answered.

Susan spoke for the first time, "Why a retreat?"

Steph thought about how to answer, "Oh, that's a long story too, but for a quick answer, I grew up in a bed-and-breakfast environment and I wanted to see if I could pull it off."

"Oh," Susan replied.

"How long have you been doing it?" Rick asked.

"This is my first year and the retreat's first Christmas," Steph held her breath, waiting for comments, good or bad.

Rick laughed softly, "So in other words, we are the guinea pigs for this experiment!"

Chip spoke first, "Yeah, pretty much. Good one, Rick." Laughter rang out.

Susan listened intensely from the back seat. Steph was talking but she didn't hear the words. She heard herself screaming inside at Rick, *You just met them, but listen to yourself. You are being friendly, even fun to be with*. The thoughts continued as Susan's heart raced,

Why can't you be that way at home? The thoughts only lasted for a few seconds.

She forced herself to listen to the conversation, hoping Steph hadn't noticed her mind wandering. Rick commented that it sounded like this part of the country was a good place to vacation. Susan held her comments to herself but thought, *We've never gone on a summer vacation, remember, you're always too busy with work!*

"Twenty more miles," Chip stated. They had just turned onto a road that seemed smaller. It was really dark, so no one could see much, but Chip explained to Rick about the large ranches. They had driven for miles seeing very few lights, "Ranches, or I mean the main part of a ranch doesn't sit up on the road. Their lanes are usually half a mile to a mile long. The house and the barns can't be seen from the road."

"How close are you neighbors, Chip?" Rick asked.

"Well, Brian and Brenda, our best friends, are four miles west and six miles south of us. Our other neighbors are sixteen and eighteen miles away. Brenda is also our local vet."

"What is a vet?" Susan asked innocently.

Steph calmly said, "An animal doctor."

Susan acted embarrassed, "I'm sorry, I knew that. We don't have any pets."

Quick to change the subject, Susan asked, "Where is your town?"

"It's twenty-five miles down this road, past our ranch. We are really lucky it's so close," Steph commented.

"Your daughter goes to school twenty-five miles away?" Rick asked.

Steph leaned forward, talking to the front, "Yes, it's about a forty-minute ride for Kelly, in good weather. She's lucky. A lot of kids ride for two hours each way. Most of the time she has all her homework done by the time she gets home."

Chip chimed in, "Yeah, I get to put her to work then. You know I thought I needed a son, to take over this ranch, but I got lucky. This girl is one heck of a ranch kid, can hold her own against all the boys her age."

Steph hit him on the shoulder, "Bragging a little now, are you?"

"Yup, just a little!" Chip laughed heartily. "Kelly's always wanted to be a vet and breed horses. That's right up my alley. She'll inherit all this one day," Chip's voice cracked with prideful emotion.

"Did you grow up in this area, Steph?" Rick asked.

"No, on the west coast, but it's a long story," Steph answered. She wasn't one to talk about herself much unless coached.

"Go ahead," Rick said, "we have time, right, Chip?" looking at Chip. Chip smiled and nodded yes.

Steph took a deep breath, "Okay, when I was growing up, my parents ran a bed-and-breakfast. We had a big Victorian home in Napa Valley in Calif. The house had seven bedrooms, four bathrooms, three sitting rooms, and two kitchens. It was over a hundred years old back then and at one time was considered a grand hotel. I was fourth generation to grow up there. My grandma Vickie lived with us. I remember her being very prim and proper. She felt it important that I know how to run a large home. I met Chip while I was in college. I had made a trip to the ranch to visit my brother who was working for Chip. I was on break and fell madly in love with the owner's son." Steph laughed with love in her voice. Steph smiled at Chip. "We got married a year later while Chip was still enrolled in college, but by then he was doing online courses while running the ranch with his dad. We lived off the ranch until our daughter Kelly was born, then his parents decided to retire. Chip took over the sole responsibility of the ranch and we moved in to it."

"What is your degree in, Chip?" Rick asked.

"Ranch management and business," Chip replied. Chip jumped into her story, "But, I'll be the first to tell you that even though he didn't live here anymore, my dad could see every move I made. Dad always laughs and says, 'You're dang right I could,' and he still does."

Rick was listening and calmly said, "Lucky people."

Chip didn't question the comment.

Steph laughed, "Okay, I'm not done yet," then went on with her story. "The farmhouse is a cabin. It was a lot smaller originally, but as families grew over the years, so did the cabin. It's been added on to three times."

Rick spoke up again, "Where did the retreat idea come from?"

"I'm getting to that," Steph said. "We only used part of the cabin, so I had the thought about doing some sort of bed-and-breakfast since it's in my blood." Steph's memories took over now. She was the first girl to be born in the family in fifty years. Grandma Vickie was going to make sure she grew up a lady. As a child, she took piano lessons, dance, and even studied European art, making Gram proud. The minute she visited Ken on the ranch, all that was thrown out the window. All she could think about was learning how to ride—really ride—work cattle, and keep up with the men on the ranch. Gram passed while Steph was in her last year in college, but she was sure her grams was turning in her grave. Tight wranglers and cowboy boots were not on Gram's list of proper attire for a lady. Steph missed her. She still had hopes of instilling some of Gram's ways in her daughter, but so far, none of it had taken hold. Once a cowgirl, always a cowgirl. She lightly shook the memories from her head.

"I had brought the retreat idea up to Chip a few times through the years. Chip's argument was always the same and he always won out."

Chip broke in, "I didn't want the ranch turned into some kind of dude ranch. Once that stamp was put on it, it is hard to get rid of." He continued very seriously, "This ranch has stood tall with pride for over a hundred years, and in my mind the idea was demoting."

Steph took over again, "So I gave up the idea and dove into decorating the cabin the way I wanted it." She laughed heartily, "I hope you like it. I think it's beautiful. When our friends and family come over to visit, they all say the same thing—open it!"

"So why now?" Susan asked.

Chip chuckled, "There's another long story. Let's say the ranch took a big blow financially three years ago, and Steph convinced me she could make a go of it and help the ranch."

"This was my way of helping. My degree is in hotel management," Steph said.

"I just had one rule," Chip said, "I didn't want it called a bed-and-breakfast."

Rick joined in, "And that's the reason it's called a retreat."

The group was quiet. Finally, Steph spoke up softly, "I hope you find this Christmas experience one you'll never forget."

The word *promise* popped into Rick's mind.

It was dark out when they approached the ranch. Chip had slowed down and made a right turn into the lane. The headlights shone on the small pine trees tied to the rails. They seemed to be holding up okay, but the next couple of days would change that. The Kahler Ranch announced itself at the entrance. Chip drove slowly up the lane, the aspen trees had been planted in line with the pipe fencing. Their branches were lightly covered in snow. The headlights reflected off the trees, giving them a magical look. Slowly the buildings appeared. Rick seemed impressed with the surroundings. They drove past an old barn on the right, then Rick whistled slowly when he saw the new horse barn on the left. The sign in front said "Kahler Equine Center." The lane forked, and Chip took to the right. Moments later, a large beautifully decorated cabin came into view.

Lilly started screaming in excitement, "Look, look at all the lights. It's so pretty!"

"Oh, Steph, the website doesn't do it justice!" Susan raved.

Steph laughed, "Oh, you just aren't used to Christmas, country style!"

The whole cabin twinkled with white Christmas lights. It had taken Chico and his son almost a week to put up the four hundred strands of lights. As they got out of the truck, Lilly said, "Hey, listen." You could faintly hear Christmas music floating through the air. Steph had thought it added that special little touch. Ken and Kelly came out on the porch. Ken caught Susan's eyes immediately. He was tall, probably over six feet, and lanky, dressed in wranglers, she assumed. Steph had explained the importance of the brand while they were shopping—the only jeans worn on the ranch, even by Kelly and herself, she had said. Right now Susan didn't care about the brand. Ken filled them out nicely, she told herself. A long sleeved blue plaid shirt, Susan noticed the shiny snaps instead of buttons, twinkled in the lights. A worn leather vest that was left open, giving a very casual look that finished the look for Susan.

And of course, cowboy boots, old worn ones. "So this is a cowboy," she said softly so no one could hear her.

Kelly looked down toward the group, "It's about time you all got here," she laughed. "Welcome to Wyoming, Kahler style!"

Introductions were made, and Ken went down to help Chip and Rick with the luggage and the many bags of new clothes.

"You all go shopping on the way in?" Kelly laughed.

Steph left out a small sigh, "I'll explain later."

Lilly ran up the stairs, to the porch. "Hi, Kelly, will you show me everything?" the little girl was bubbling over with excitement.

Kelly started laughing. "So you must be Lilly. You're so cute, bet you'd look pretty good up on a horse," she stated with a big smile.

"Momma, did you hear? Kelly's going to put me on a horse!"

Lilly was jumping up and down now. She motioned for Kelly to come down to her level. When Kelly knelt down, Lilly whispered into Kelly's ear, "Will you show me the graveyard?" Kelly looked up at her dad.

Chip chuckled, "I told them they'd freeze to death in the clothes they brought and we'd have to bury them up on the hill with the critters."

"I think there's still room next to 360," Kelly said, laughing, then added, "Now the shopping trip makes sense."

While all this was going on, Rick and Susan were watching with blank stares on their faces.

Looking at Chip first, Lilly asked, "What is a critter, Mr. Kahler?"

Susan smiled. She had remembered to be respectful.

Then spinning around to Kelly, Lilly asked in a squeaky voice, "What is a 360?"

The ranch residents all broke out laughing. Chip sat down on a porch chair so he was close to the little girl. "Critter is a Western word for anything that walks," Chip told her.

"Oh, so I'm a critter too, Mr. Kah—"

Chip stopped her, "Yep, a two-legged one, and Lilly, my name is Chip, okay? Mr. Kahler is my dad."

She looked at her mom for approval, Susan nodded to her. "Okay, Chippp," dragging the end of the one syllable word out slowly.

"Oh, oh, oh, what's a 360?" Lilly added.

Everyone was silent. Ken spoke first, "Only the best Angus that ever walked on this ranch."

Chip spoke next, "She's famous in the Angus breed."

Kelly looked at the strangers and said, "A cow."

Susan and Rick were lost, "What are these people talking about, cows?"

"Don't worry, we'll show you," Steph said and added, "Come on, it's cold out here."

Kelly looked down at Lilly, "Wait until you see what's inside!"

The front door was huge and extra wide, made of pine, a grizzly bear standing on its hind legs had been carved into it. The door was statement piece of its own.

The group walked in, Lilly with Kelly, Susan with Steph, and then the men.

"Oh man, this is something!" Rick stated, surprised. Susan put her hand over her mouth in amazement. Lilly was running around looking at the massive room, holding on to Kelly's hand and dragging her along.

A twenty-five-foot-tall Christmas tree sat in the area near the dining table and overlooking the family room and kitchen. The cabin was open concept, so there was a lot to take in at first glance. Christmas decorations blended of country and wildlife were everywhere, as were the white twinkling lights.

"So what do you think, city slickers?" Chip joked. The combination of the sweet fragrance of live pine and spice candles, the warmth of the fireplace, and the beauty of the cabin was overwhelming. Susan looked at her husband, who had an easy smile on his face, and then at Chip and Steph, who were standing together silently, hoping these people from the city lights of New York would approve of their surroundings for the approaching important holiday. Susan held her breath. Rick laughed out loud, "I'm pretty sure we can adapt. In fact, we may never leave!" Susan exhaled.

Steph whispered to Chip, "Okay, we can relax!"

Lilly pulled on Kelly's shirt, "You really live here?" then added, "I wanna be your little sister!" she asked.

This brought laughs from everyone. Kelly patted the top of Lilly's head and with a smile, raised her eyebrows at her parents, silently transmitting her thoughts, "What have you done to me!"

Steph quickly fell into hostess mode, suggesting that the guests see their rooms, get settled, and all come back down to relax by the fireplace before retiring. Everyone agreed on hot chocolate, the sweet hot beverage winning out over wine and spirits.

Susan and Rick followed Steph up the stairs to the second-floor landing. On the right were the bedrooms, with the stair railing continuing on the left, allowing for open concept and overlooking the great room below. The railing was decorated with fresh pine and small twinkling white lights. The open hallway ended in wrapping around to the other side of the cabin, where there were more bedrooms and a library/sitting area with a large window that contained a view of the snow-covered Rockies. In the very center of the open beam log ceiling was a chandelier made out of more than a hundred deer and elk antlers. It spanned four feet wide and six feet deep. As far as Steph knew, it was one of a kind, as was the cabin, being the only one in Wyoming built like this.

Going up stairs, Susan and Rick entered their room. The massive fireplace greeted them, making the room very cozy. Ken had started a nice fire and had closed it down to hold for the night. A stack of split oak logs was piled to the left, waiting to be added to the still hot embers in the morning. The headboard of the king size bed was hand carved like the front door, with a deer scene, and was also decorated with pine and soft white lights. The room had a small live pine Christmas tree in the corner, adding warmth of the season. The master bath included a soaker tub that was surrounded by windows with the same soft lights. When the sky was clear, you could see the stars while relaxing in the tub. Susan was lost for words. Steph excused herself and told them to take their time and then to come on back down. Next she headed to Lilly's room next door. She could hear cheerful voices, so she knew Kelly and Lilly were hitting it off fine.

Lilly's room had a set of custom bunk beds with stairs leading to the top bunk that looked like a tree house. Steph had found a local carpenter to build them with a great imagination. The large window took up almost an entire wall with the view of the near mountain range. On the other side of the room was a queen size bed. The room had been decorated in horses and friendly snowmen, which wouldn't let Lilly get lonely. A little Christmas tree stood in the far corner, twinkling green and white. Kelly thought, *Mom outdid herself on this one!* loving the room.

"I'm sleeping up here," Lilly hollered from up high, as she bounced with a big smile on her face. "Where's your room, Kelly?"

"When you come up the stairs, I'm the second door," Kelly replied.

"Can I see it," then Lilly added, "tomorrow?"

"Sure, come on, let's go get that hot chocolate, and you need to meet Sugar; she's our Aussie, who lives with us in the house.

"What is an Aussie?" Lilly asked in a funny voice.

Kelly laughed, "A dog, silly!"

The girls talked nonstop going down the stairs. They were the first ones down, Lilly's parents lingering a while.

After kisses for Lilly from Sugar, the girls settled down on the bear rug in front of the fireplace, with mugs in hand.

Chip asked Kelly how her ride had been.

"Good, Dad," she replied, "but I was really glad Uncle Ken rode along. On the way back, Poco spooked and jumped out from underneath me."

Chip started to speak, but Kelly waved him off. "I stayed with him, and Ken was there to grab the reins since he jumped into Sara. I'm pretty sure he saved me from a long run." As she finished, she looked up at her uncle who was leaning up next to the rock on the side of the fireplace. He winked at her affectionately. Turning back to her dad, she said, "There's something in the air."

"It's that big storm brewing, supposed to hit right before Christmas, so no unexpected trips, anywhere. Stay close, girl," Chip said.

"Got it, Dad, and oh, by the way, I'd like to sleep in the barn with Lucky until she calves; she's getting close. Please, Ken's got the fire going. It's warm in there and I'll keep my cell with me, please." She begged with that soft look in her eyes that melted his heart.

"I'll talk to your mom, but not tonight."

"I know," accepting his response.

Finally, Rick and Susan came back down to join the group. Steph handed out the large Christmas mugs that had marshmallows floating on top and a peppermint candy cane for a stir stick. Susan was enjoying the depth of the detail that Steph had gone to. Susan loved detail, though Rick never noticed. Susan's eyes studied the cozy room, thinking how perfect everything was. Ken was standing as if planning to leave. From where Susan sat, she could look him over, really look him over, without anyone thinking that she was staring.

He was probably Chip and Rick's age, fortyish, definitely good looking, with dark mesmerizing eyes, dark wavy hair, a little long for her taste—but I can adapt. She felt like there were three of her in her head, all carrying on a conversation with each other—about Ken. Some gray hairs were trying to make an appearance at his temples, but it was the mustache that brought it all together for her. The eyes, the mustache, the clothes, "I could like this cowboy." She surprised herself with the quick approval of this man, based entirely on looks. The relaxed, interested thoughts she had actually embarrassed her. "Pull it together, Susan," she whispered to herself. Coming back to reality, she heard Chip talking to Rick.

"Hey, Rick, Ken and I are going up to check cattle on a corner of the ranch in the morning, take a couple of hours, would you like to ride a long?" Quickly he added, "Give you a lay of the land."

It only took a second for Rick to reply, "Yes, I'd love to. What time?"

Chip glanced at Ken, "Six thirty-ish," Chip said with Ken nodding.

When Ken said goodnight to everyone, Chip followed him to the front door.

"Hear anything else today?" referring to the weather.

"Nothing. Night," Ken said as he headed out the door.

"What are we going to do in the morning, Kelly?" Lilly wanted to know.

"First we need to get up early, about six o'clock, check on Lucky, feed her, the horses, and the dogs, then we'll get the four-wheeler and I'll show you around the ranch. After lunch, how 'bout I put you up on Squaw and you can learn to ride, kinda."

Lilly, listening intently, agreed with all of it.

Susan told Kelly that Lilly had never been near a horse, let alone on one.

Steph spoke up, "Don't worry, Mom, Kelly will take good care of her." Then she asked Susan, "Since everyone is leaving us in the morning, would you like to drive into town with me, see the sights and one last chance for some Christmas shopping?"

"That would be nice," Susan answered politely.

"I sure hope Santa will know that I'm on vacation," Lilly stated, very seriously.

Steph and Kelly said in unison, "Santa knows everything!"

Lilly seemed satisfied with the answer, just replying, "That's good."

The grandfather's clock struck eleven. Steph stood up and started gathering mugs, "It's been a long day, and it sounds like tomorrow will be just as busy."

Goodnights were shared, with the Conners retiring first.

"Lilly is wound up tight," Kelly said with a chuckle.

"Will you be okay with her for the stay?" Steph asked her daughter.

"Oh yeah, I love her. It's going to be fine," Kelly answered. Steph was relieved.

Chip locked the front door, then said, "Rick is a weird one, but he's okay."

"He's not weird, he's city. He doesn't know how to be any different, just give him a little time," Steph said, then adding, "I think my job is the hardest. Susan has a lot bothering her, but I'm hoping she can relax and enjoy herself for the week."

As Steph and Chip got ready for bed, they continued sharing thoughts about their guests.

"Lilly is an unhappy child, and the adults don't communicate with each other. I am not seeing much of a relationship between father and daughter," Steph said in a serious voice.

Chip chuckled softly, "And you, Dr. Phil, have figured this out in less than twelve hours?"

"Doesn't take a genius to see unhappy," she replied.

"You know the saying," Chip added as he climbed under the quilts, "money can't buy happiness."

Steph stayed quiet, thinking, then Steph being Steph said, "Well, this place reeks happiness, and I dare them to try and put a damper on our Christmas!" She jumped on the bed and kissed Chip's cheek and said, "Never underestimate a Kahler woman!"

He smiled and said, "Never have, never will, and I wish you luck. You're going to need it."

December 22

*R*ick surprised Chip and Steph by getting up early, turning the coffeemaker on, putting wood on the fire, even letting the dog out. Rick was in his glory, but no one knew it. He was definitely taking in the peacefulness of the early morning while sitting at the kitchen island with a cup of coffee.

He offered a friendly "good morning ya'll" when the two walked in.

Steph laughed, "Well, I see you are trying to adapt to our language."

"Too corny?" Rick grinned.

"Yeah, too corny," Chip responded, sitting down across from him. The Kahlers were impressed. Rick had put on the new wranglers, a flannel shirt, and even tied a bandana around his neck. Chip looked down and smiled, seeing that Rick was wearing his new boots.

Realizing he was being checked out, he said, "Do I look okay?" Jumping off the stool, and raising his arms in the air, he turned in a circle for approval.

Steph poured him another cup of coffee. Looking up with a big grin on her face, she said, "Yes, you fit right in, cowboy." Instantly, the heart of a little boy who dreamed of being a cowboy one day melted at Steph's special word.

Rick laughed, "Well, I'm glad of that!"

They heard barking and the cuffing of boots as Ken walked in the back door, with Sugar beating him in, then making the rounds, going from person to person for her good morning pats.

Ken headed for the coffee. Pouring himself a cup, he said, "Lucky's fine, but don't tell Kelly I checked her."

"Oh yeah, Steph, Kelly wants to sleep in the barn until she calves," Chip added.

"I don't know…," she said while thoughts ran through her head.

"Oh, let her guys," Ken spoke up. "She's showing responsibility and I'm close. I'll keep an eye on her," he added.

Chip looked at Steph and then back at Ken, "As long as you keep a good eye on her." Steph realized that her husband had made a parental decision for the two of them, so she stayed quiet and let it be. The three men made their plans for the morning over biscuits and sausage gravy then headed out.

A few minutes later, Kelly and Lilly appeared.

"Good morning, sleepyheads," Steph smiled to the girls as she poured them orange juice.

"Where's my mom and dad?" Lilly asked, still trying to wake up as she patted Sugar's head.

"Well, your dad has already left with Chip and Ken, and I think your mom is probably sleeping in," she said, giving Lilly a light hug.

It was six fifteen. "Eat up, Lilly, we're late. I've gotta check Lucky!" Kelly said, then looked at her mom. "She's not due until the twenty-sixth, so I'm not too worried. She's not showing any signs," she explained. "Brenda, Dad, and Ken," she said comically, "have told me what to watch for. They forget, I've been around a lot of cows calving in."

"But this is the first one that you and you alone are responsible for, young lady," Steph's voice was stern, "but it sounds like you are well informed, so don't mess it up."

Kelly looked at her with a blank face, "I've got it!"

"Good!" Steph replied, refusing to let her daughter have the last word.

Lilly swallowed a bite of food, looking confused, and asked, "Who is Lucky and what is it? What does due mean and not ready, ready for what?"

"I'll explain later, Lilly, let's go!" Kelly replied, pulling her cowboy boots on.

"Oh! I need those!" Lilly exclaimed as she stared at the boots.

Molly knew that Jamie got to the station at seven thirty. It was eight o'clock now. She tiptoed through the house, not putting her shoes on until she got to the front door. She didn't want to wake her mom, didn't want it to start again. Last night had been really ugly. Her mom had even slapped her in the face. She needed to talk to Jamie, if not this morning, then sometime today. She didn't know how much more she could take. She was hoping to use the phone at the station to call her Aunt Jane. Jane had told her that she felt bad because she hadn't come and picked Molly up by now, but her husband was ill and she was afraid to leave him alone. Molly lied when she told her she was okay until Jamie got his truck running better. Molly didn't want her aunt to worry, but truth was she needed out desperately.

The phone rang. Steph looked at the caller ID and said, "I need to take this, Susan, sorry," as she ran to answer the phone in the office.

"That's fine," Susan replied cheerfully as she ran by. Susan had slept really well, feeling more relaxed this morning than she had in a long time. She got up and started looking at the things she hadn't seen the night before. A quick thought came to mind, "Such a different way of life," then she criticized herself, "Please let me be open-minded to other ways," her thoughts coming out as some kind of prayer.

The Kahler home had almost as many cows and horses calling the cabin home as the ranch had living on it. Hundreds of framed photos hung on the walls and sat on shelves. Even cute displays were made with frames sitting on the floors near cabinets or the stairs. Chip's grandmother, Catherine Kahler, loved photography, and she instilled this love in all her children and then their children.

The bloodlines of both cattle and horses were considered the life blood of the ranch. Cow families were created with many being idolized by their ear tag numbers instead of names. 360 was considered the best cow that had ever lived on the ranch and they worked hard to merchandise her genetics. Living to the gracious age of nineteen, she blessed the ranch with ten daughters and six sons.

Each daughter was bred to a different bull, allowing the lines to go in ten different directions. The same was done with her sons. After she had died 360 had been considered the most influential cow of the breed in Wyoming and had placed in the top five of all time in the Angus breed in the USA. Two of her sons went to Canada making her a reputation in two countries. If you ran Angus cattle, you knew 360. She was buried on the ranch along with many others, respected by the generations. There was more than one framed picture of her in this room.

Chip's Aunt Maggie became a well-known Western photographer. The cabin was home to at least a hundred Maggie Kahler photos. Two Western galleries in Wyoming displayed and sold her work.

As Chip grew up on the ranch, the bloodlines were embedded in his mind. By the time he was twelve, he could carry on a conversation about a particular bloodline including all its production numbers with the best of them. Like his father, in his heart, they were all family and having them hanging in his home suited him just fine. The amazing part of the story was finding a woman who understood and cared as much as he did. Steph loved frames, and the walls displayed her weakness. Every once in a while someone would visit the cabin and say the Kahlers were crazy.

Another tradition that some questioned was Memorial Day. This day was celebrated by the whole family with as many coming to the ranch as possible.

Ever since the area out west was settled, it was custom for each ranch to bury their own, creating a cemetery for their family on their land. If you didn't own land, then you were buried in your church cemetery. The Kahler ranch claimed two resting places, one for the Kahler family and the other one for their beloved critters, as Chip would call them. The hill to the north of the big cabin was two-tiered. The first leveling was three quarters of the way up the hill and was home to the family cemetery, a small stand of aspen trees, and an old ranch cabin. The area had a nice cabin yard with a fire pit and was used frequently for gathering and cookouts throughout the years. Past the cabin, the road continued up the hill. An old oak tree stood guard over this cemetery. This was the final resting place to the special animals that had been so good to the ranch. This was the ranch's way of saying, "Rest now, you've earned it."

Every grave was marked. 360 and Chip's Australian Shepherd, Jake, his childhood pal, had special headstones with photos embedded. To this day, Chip still got emotional when he saw them. The rest had wooden crosses made of red cedar. The crosses stood strong with the test of time and weather. Each name was carved on their cross.

Since this special day was the end of May, spring usually had a good hold on things and the wildflowers bloomed across the hills. The holiday was known as Decoration Day across the country as it was on the ranch. Long ago the Kahler women decided to grow a flower garden along with the much-needed vegetable garden, ensuring enough flowers for Decoration Day.

Kelly loved flowers, especially the ones she called Easter lilies. She always made sure her great-grandfather "Grampie," had a few extra, and the animals were always graced with their share. Usually a picnic was enjoyed when the group finished the loving chore on top of the hill. The old oak tree held its own importance. It had a large burly limb that hung out a ways. It still held the wooden swing that was Kelly's favorite spot to sit. The tree held many memories on its trunk; hearts with initials of Kahler couples were carved deep. The story was if you carved your initials on the tree, you would live married, happily ever after. The Kahler family claimed that God had blessed the initials on the tree with true love, as there were zero divorces throughout the generations.

As Susan's eyes took it all in, she thought, "I could put more pictures up, especially of Lilly."

Steph's voice brought her back, "Do you like?" meaning the framed photos.

Susan smiled lightly. "Yes, I really do." Inside she realized that she truly meant it.

Steph and Susan left for town at ten. When they got to the main road, Susan asked Steph how far it was to town, forgetting the talk about town the night before. "Bethlehem is twenty-five miles," Steph answered.

"That's not too bad, at least you have some civilization," Susan stated.

Steph swallowed hard. She wasn't sure how to take the statement, so she just smiled.

"We like our little town," she explained. "We can usually get everything we need, and of course we can always drive to Casper or to Grey Bull, to the north; it's bigger than Bethlehem."

Susan was quiet, taking in the scenery. Steph only had a few errands to run, which didn't take long, so she decided to take Susan to the antique mall, just for fun.

When they walked in, Joyce greeted them with hugs, which Susan shied away from. Steph could tell that Susan was uncomfortable with the surroundings, hesitating to even look around. Finally after a few minutes, she walked down a few aisles. Steph talked to Joyce for a few minutes, exchanging Christmas wishes, then made up a quick excuse for cutting their visit short. Back in the truck, Susan made the comment that she had never seen so much junk in her life.

Steph told herself it was okay, it's not her thing, and changed the subject. Someone's junk was another man's treasure, but not to everyone.

"Strike two," Steph whispered under her breath.

Molly walked as fast as she could, which wasn't very fast. The baby was due in a week and she knew it had dropped already. She constantly said little prayers hoping that he or she was okay. She knew that not continuing her doctor appointments was putting the baby in jeopardy, but there wasn't any money.

"It's in Your hands, God," she had said the words more than once.

It was cold out and she didn't have enough clothes on to stay out very long. She hoped Jamie could talk to her for a few minutes. She walked to the door and looked in. Jamie was behind the counter, writing something down. She looked around for Jamie's boss and was relieved when she didn't see him. Now poking her head in, she called out, "Jamie," calling twice before he heard her.

The young man looked up when he heard her voice. He quickly looked around, then motioned to her to come in.

"What are you doing out in the cold? Are you okay? The baby—"

She stopped him, "We are fine, but…" He grabbed her hand and led her over near the wall furnace where it was warmer.

"Jamie, Mom's on my case bad. I don't know how much longer—" Tears slowly slid down her face; she hadn't meant them to. When she was with Jamie, she felt safe, making it harder to be brave.

"Honey, my boss said he can't pay me until after Christmas. We can't leave yet."

He felt anger building inside himself at Molly's mother. He just wished she was more understanding, but she wasn't. Jamie tried to stay calm for Molly's sake. She needed him to be the strong one. She had enough to worry about.

Jamie heard his boss talking to a customer in the back, "I gotta go, Molly. Go home, baby, just try to stay out of her sight, okay? I'm sorry."

"I know you are, Jamie, I'll try. Can you come by tonight, please?" Molly said, trying not to cry.

"Yes, I'll see you later. I've got to go," he kissed her quickly and hurried toward the repair shop in back.

She took a deep breath and patted her belly, "We'll try, Jamie—I'll try!"

The men had settled into Chip's new truck. Ken claimed the back seat, being polite.

The NY man seemed to be looking forward to his adventure today. The day was starting out clear skied but clouds would roll in for the afternoon. It was fairly cold, twenty-seven degrees. The cloud cover coming would help maintain the temps for the rest of the day.

Rick had a hundreds of questions. Chip had decided he was sincere in his interest. He liked Rick, so he was comfortable being himself, which didn't come easy for him with people. He hated it when he had to put on an act to entertain Steph's guests. His feelings about this retreat business of hers were still up in the air, but he had promised to give her and it a chance. To his surprise this morning, his gut was telling him these people were fine.

Ken was equally comfortable with Rick, telling him a couple of old-timer stories involving mountain lions and almost freezing to death.

Chip was feeling better about seeing the cows with his own eyes. It wasn't that he didn't trust Ken's judgment, but it was like, these are my girls and I need to do this. The momma cows were all between four and five months bred and in great condition, so he didn't think the cold would be a problem; it was the blizzard winds he was worried about. The winds caused cattle to start walking with the wind, leaving their natural shelter. Then, if they trampled the fences down, they kept walking as long as the wind blew. Chip was now telling Rick about the blizzard of 1880–1881, which lasted from October to April. When it was finally over, ranchers found their cattle, the ones that had lived over two hundred miles south of their ranches.

As Rick listened to Chip, he waited for him to finish, then in a very serious voice, said, "I have a newfound respect for the steaks I eat in the city. I had no idea. I guess I've never realized that your kind of life existed. It's easy to get consumed by big city life." There was a silence for a few moments, then Rick went on, "I suppose milk has a story of its own too."

Ken laughed, "Yes, and just as complicated. But it's okay, Rick, we are sure the city's challenges are just as crazy. But, don't get me wrong, you can keep your big city." Rick instantly broke out laughing, with Ken and Chip joining in. It was going to be a good morning.

"So tell me about the ranch," Rick said.

"Well, for starters, it's been in the family for over 130 years, not this big though. Pieces of land were bought up over the years as it became available."

"How big is it now?" Rick asked.

"Right at 2,500 acres, plus we rent open land from the BLM. In other words, federal land. That way we can graze the lower mountain ranges," Chip added.

"So what do you do with it, I mean the ranch? I know it really has to be diversified nowadays," Rick stated.

"Ken, you tell him. You can probably come up with numbers faster and better than I can."

Ken leaned forward, arms resting on his knees, "Let's see… livestock end of it consists of five hundred head of registered Angus momma cows, producing close to five hundred calves each year. If she doesn't have a calf on her side, she is culled, sold. We also run around thirty-five to forty bulls."

Rick seemed truly interested. Being a "numbers" person, he listened intently as Ken continued.

"Each year, we sell a hundred fifty head of yearling bulls, private treaty and exclusive bull sales. We also sell a hundred fifty replacement heifers the same way. We keep a couple of young bulls and usually fifty replacement heifers each year. Of course, conditions change yearly and so do the numbers. We also feed out a hundred fifty head—"

Rick stopped him, "What does that mean?"

"Oh, we keep them, put them on feed, and raise them until they are big enough to butcher, then we sell."

Chip broke in, "Part of them are contracted to big name restaurants back east. Ever hear of Back Road Steaks?"

"Yep," he hesitated in shock, "it's one of my favorite steak houses!"

"Well, we raise and supply some of their beef," Chip stated proudly.

"That's amazing. It really is a small world," Rick's mind was running. "What else?"

"This is your end, Boss," Ken said to Chip.

"Stop calling me that, you know I hate that!" Chip screamed at Ken.

"Yep, I know, Boss!" Ken laughed.

Chip grumpily said, "We also run thirty head of high dollar registered quarter horse mares and have three studs standing."

Before Rick could say he didn't understand, Ken jumped in, "They are for breeding. We breed our mares and also stand them to outside mares, meaning offer the stud's services to other breeders."

"I gather that brings in a lot of money?" Rick asked.

"Yep," Chip said, "they are the best of the best. We specialize in cutting horse lines. I'll show a video when we are back home."

"I'd like that."

"We sell almost all of the offspring as yearlings and two-year-olds, all privately, and finish out a handful of three-year-olds that bring good money."

Ken took over again. "Then, there's the feed end of the ranch. Without growing our own feed, none of the rest is possible. We grow five hundred acres of irrigated alfalfa, put up in large square bales and fifteen hundred or more small square bales, then there's two hundred acres of wheat for straw. We sell a lot of the alfalfa and straw. It's a big money-making end of the business. There's five hundred acres planted in various grasses, which include canary, orchard, timothy, and brome. This is our feed for the winter. Then we plant two hundred fifty acres of corn, which is put up as silage, meaning the stalk and ears are all chopped up, it's packed into ground bunkers and it's covered. Then it ferments into wonderful smelling feed for the cattle. We buy our whole corn; it's cheaper that way. All this makes those steaks you like, Rick!"

"When the corn is harvested, we go back in and plant in winter wheat, then in the spring the cows are all turned in on it. The corn and alfalfa are rotated every three to four years, depending on winter kill. Rotating allows them to feed each other, meaning the nutrients of each feed the ground so it doesn't become depleted. That's about it, I think," Ken added.

"And how many people does it take to run this operation?"

Chip broke in again, "I'm general manager, plus I oversee the horse end. Ken is ranch manager, in charge of the cattle and land management, then not counting Ken and me, there's ten full-time guys, a lot of them have been here for twenty years or more; we couldn't run this place without them. It also depends on the season. During haying season, there might be thirty to forty more. We have bunkhouses where they stay. We also borrow and lend cowhands to other ranchers, works out well."

Chip slowed the truck down, coming to the gate. Ken jumped out to open it.

Chip turned to look directly at Rick, "Then there's the wrath of Mother Nature. If she's kind to us, we do well, if she's not, it means a tough year. Too many tough years in a row and you're done. Now add that to poor market prices of a bad economy and it can be a tough life. Right now we are in our third year of losing money."

The two men sat in silence, looking at each other. Ken broke the silence when he hollered at Chip to drive on in. Moments later they drove slowly on the rough lane across the pasture toward a large tree line that ran north to south. A good sized creek ran just on the other side of the tree line.

Chip started talking again, "Three years ago, we got hit the middle of March with a real late snowstorm."

Ken coughed.

"Okay, blizzard, I'll rephrase my words. That event changed the thinking and the way ranchers did things in these parts."

"What happened?" Rick asked, almost afraid to hear the answer.

"Storm dumped three to four feet of snow and dropped the temperatures to single digits for a week. Calving season had started the end of Feb—I can't!" Chip's voice choked up.

Ken took over. "Between Wyoming, Montana, the Dakotas, and parts of Nebraska, ranchers lost ninety percent of their calf crop. This loss totaled three million head. It wiped out two hundred fifty ranches; they couldn't take the loss," Ken finished Chip's story.

"How many did you lose?" Rick asked in a whisper.

"Two hundred and fifty, the entire spring calf crop," Chip answered dryly, "the nightmare a rancher never gets over!"

Ken explained that calving time was divided, half in the spring, half in the fall.

They drove slowly in silence, then Chip added, "We and every other rancher have rethought calving season. Our first ones aren't dropping till close to the first of April now; hurts the wallet on finishing weights, but at least we have something to sell."

They drove for a few more minutes before finding the group. "Right where I want them," Chip said out loud.

Ken instantly saw a new calmness wash over Chip. The group of two hundred fifty pregnant cows were near the feeding area. The bale feeders were full with extra bales placed under some of the trees. The creek had low sides allowing the cattle to easily get to the water; it also ran fast enough that it wouldn't freeze up. The thick stand of trees on the cattle side of the creek was more than enough shelter for the group.

Chip was satisfied. He couldn't think of one reason why they would be overly stressed. The incoming storm was definitely on the bad side but was told to be short-lived.

"Things here look okay," Chip said. "Let's head down and check the south gate, then we are good to go."

Rick was impressed. He didn't know much about cattle, actually nothing, but he did appreciate a well-run business.

Jumping back in the truck, Rick said to Chip, "Nice operation," and turning to give Ken a nod.

The chains on the gate were exactly like Ken said they were. Chip didn't doubt Ken. It was just good ranch management to double-check. Ken wasn't offended.

The other group of bred cows was being kept off the cattle barns. The feeder calves had been sold late October freeing up the pens for them. This was a group of younger cows that lack the experiences of handling the strength of this kind of storm.

After riding the four-wheeler all morning, Kelly thought they had covered just about all the close-up part of the ranch that they could. Lilly had asked hundreds of questions. Kelly didn't mind; it was something kids did. Ending back up at the cabin, they decided they were hungry. Minutes later they sat, eating ham sandwiches and potato chips. Lilly wolfed hers down.

"Slow down, girl," Kelly told Lilly, "there's plenty of time."

"But I've got so much to learn," Lilly was referring to their next adventure. Back on the four-wheeler, they headed to the new horse barn. The barn was warm enough that they could shed their heavy coats. Lilly ran down the row of stalls, reading name plates, looking for a special one.

Kelly heard Lilly scream, "I found her!"

The name plate read "Squaw." Kelly had already told Lilly the mare's story.

As Kelly walked toward the stall, she saw a little girl who was transformed with love.

"Oh, Kelly, she's so beautiful and she likes me!" The mare hung her head over the half door allowing Lilly to pet her. Lilly was giggling softly.

"Squaw loves attention," Kelly told her. The mare wore a bright blue halter. Kelly took the matching lead rope off the wall and showed Lilly how to snap it on. She then let Lilly lead her out and down to the saddling area. Lilly was talking nonstop to the mare as they walked. Kelly tied the mare up and took Lilly to the tack room for the necessary tack. After a short lesson on grooming, she let Lilly place the saddle blanket on her back and then helped her lift the youth saddle over her back. The little saddle brought so many memories back for Kelly, all the way back to her first pony and her first saddle. She was only four years old and couldn't really remember, but the stories had been instilled in her mind and heart.

Kelly's first pony was a pure white Shetland pony named Snowy. Lilly had seen Kelly's pony saddle in her room where she kept it. Granddad had threatened to sell it and the youth saddle, so Kelly got the pony saddle—out of sight.

It had been her dad's first saddle, the one he learned to ride with; she had learned on it too. The leather was worn smooth, thin in places, and most of the sheep skin fleece had been worn of the underside. Now it spent its days draped over the back of an easy chair in the corner of her room where it was safe from heat and cold, the two elements that ruined leather. There it would stay until Kelly became a mom of a little four-year-old, who would learn to ride in that same saddle, then she would keep it safe until she could place her first four-year-old grandchild on it, to learn to ride.

Lilly was talking, bringing Kelly back to the present.

Now the bridle, Kelly explained the bit. Lilly was worried that the steel bit would hurt Squaw's mouth. Kelly kept explaining what she was doing, even opening the mare's mouth and showing Lilly the spot that didn't have teeth, allowing the bit to fit perfectly between the side molars.

Finally, it was time for Lilly to "saddle up."

Kelly couldn't determine if Lilly was laughing or screaming. It was kind of half and half as her rear landed in the saddle seat.

"Sit up straight, Lilly."

Kelly led her around for a few minutes, letting Lilly get her balance, then handed her the reins.

"It's just like driving a car, Lilly." The rein was single. Kelly showed her how to lay it on her neck on the left to go right and on the right to go left.

"This is called neck reining." Kelly had her practice turning in both directions.

"Now to stop her, gently pull back. Gently now, and then let up." Lilly did exactly as Kelly instructed and the mare came to a stop. The mare was so kid-gentle that Kelly knew Lilly would be fine. Kelly told her to walk next to the rail that encircled the arena, "Walk all the way around, okay, Lilly?"

With a scared grin on her face, she said, "Okay, Kelly, but what if I do something wrong?"

"It's okay, Lilly, Squaw knows what to do," Kelly told her with confidence in her voice.

"Tap your boots gently against her side and she will start walking."

Slowly the mare started walking. "Like this, Kelly?" Lilly screamed.

"Yes, Lilly," Kelly said, shaking her head.

Once Kelly saw she was on her way, she left to go get Ginger, her riding and show mare. Minutes later she loped up beside Lilly.

Lilly smiled, "I like this. Am I doing okay, Kelly?"

Kelly nodded yes as they rode side by side for a few more minutes. After the second round, they led out into a trot. Lilly was bouncing all over her saddle and holding on to the saddle horn for dear life. Kelly kept talking to her, sternly at one point, to make her pay attention.

"Okay, Lilly, we're going to slow lope, also called canter." Lilly listened.

"It won't be as bumpy, it will feel like a rocking horse, going back and forth," Kelly kept talking to her.

Lilly answered, "Okay," without looking at Kelly.

"Now quickly, kick her in the side again, now," Kelly said, as the mare responded to the command.

"Oh, Kelly, I like this. Look, I'm running!" Lilly squeaked.

"No, you are loping," Kelly replied.

"Okay, I'm loping." She was so excited.

Kelly shook her head and grinned, enjoying Lilly's excitement.

What the two girls didn't know was that the men had come back and were up in the office watching through the glass wall. A few minutes later, Steph and Susan joined them. As Susan watched, she kept fussing about Lilly getting hurt.

Finally, Rick turned to her and said, "Susan, stop it, she's fine, so just stop it." No one said a word, but Steph found Susan's hand and gave it a squeeze, then let go without looking at her.

They slow loped around the arena twice, then Kelly slowed them to a walk and turned them around to ride in the opposite direction. When they did this, it put the glass wall in their view. Lilly saw everyone watching.

"Look, Kelly, my momma and dad are watching," she waved hard, giggling the whole time. As they got closer to the office end of the arena, she asked, "Kelly, can we lope again, please!"

Kelly smiled, "Take off, two kicks."

The little girl followed her instructions and the mare responded again. Lilly was full of confidence, sitting straight in the saddle and this time taking her hand off the saddle horn. She had caught on to the rocking horse motion of the slow canter and her rear stayed on the saddle. No one would have guessed this was her first time on a horse. Lilly and Squaw had become as one; it was beautiful in Kelly's eyes.

In the meantime, the adults all came down to the arena. Halfway to the group, the girls slowed to a walk.

Lilly was beaming.

"Sit up real straight, Lilly," Kelly whispered.

"Mom, Daddy, did you see me?" her eyes were bright with excitement.

"Oh, Lilly," was all Susan could say. She had tears in her eyes and was at a loss for words. Rick took the roll of proud father, rightly so.

"That's my girl!" He laughed, "I told you, you could do it. You did fine!" He walked up to Squaw, petting her on the neck and reaching up to give Lilly a kiss.

"I'm so proud of you, Lilly girl," he smiled. It had been a long time since he'd called her that.

Teasing, Chip said, "Well now, look at that instructor. Good job, Kelly."

But Kelly wasn't going to steal Lilly's limelight. "No, Dad, it was all Lilly. She's a natural," smiling to the little girl. Lilly beamed, straightening her shoulders again.

Kelly looked at her mom. Steph gave her a wink of approval.

"Can we ride again tomorrow, Kelly?" Lilly asked.

"Sure, but we'll ride up to the cemetery," then hesitated, adding, "if the weather is decent."

Rick was listening to Steph tell the story of Kelly and Squaw's life together. Lilly sat patiently, waiting for a chance to speak.

Finally, she said in a sweet girly voice and looking at Rick, "Daddy?"

Rick and all the others looked at her. Quickly, Rick smiled and said, "Oh no!"

"Daddy, can I have a horse?" she pleaded.

Rick pointed a finger at her and said with a laugh, "I knew that was coming!"

Lilly wanted to ride a little longer.

As the girls rode off, Rick turned to Chip, "Chip, can you show us around the barn, and I'd really love to see the horses."

"Sure. Are you coming, Ken?"

"No, I think I'll finish up paperwork, still got to get paychecks for guys. Tomorrow is their last day, remember," reminding Chip of ranch business.

"Okay, Ken, we'll see you later. Ladies, are you coming with us?" Chip asked, looking at Steph.

"Sure," she didn't give Susan a chance to back out.

The guys walked down the first aisle. Chip called it "the pet aisle."

Rick was very impressed with Ken's Sara. Even a person who knew nothing about mules could tell she was a good one. At the end of the barn, there was a wash bay and the facility that he called the hospital. It contained an exam area and was full of fancy-looking medical equipment. Chip was a professional and sounded like one as he showed them around.

The opposite aisle was called the moneymakers. Chip explained in detail the value of the cutting horse bloodlines. Rick was totally amazed. At one point he stopped Chip and asked, "Do you ever let investors in?"

It took a few seconds for the words to sink in. "I've never thought about it!"

Rick was serious, "Well, can we talk more about it later?"

Chip, still stunned, said, "Sure."

Steph looked at Susan as the men talked and continued down the aisle.

"I hope you two realize that Lilly will never be the same again," Steph said, smiling, waited for a reply from Susan.

She took a few moments to find the right words. Finally, she looked at Steph with a very serious look on her face and said, "That is exactly what I'm hoping for. The little girl deserves a life."

Steph stayed silent, but she slipped an arm around Susan's waist and gave her a hug as they followed the men.

"Know what?" Kelly said. They had brushed the horses down and put them back in their stalls. It was still over an hour until it would get dark. Chip smiled and winked at Kelly.

"Anyone for taking the four-wheelers out—for a little sightseeing?" Kelly asked.

It took all of two seconds for Rick to holler, "I'm in!" Then he instantly looked embarrassed, "I'm afraid I've never rode one before."

Kelly laughed, "Oh, you'll catch on quickly, nothing to it."

Chip turned toward Steph and Susan.

"Not me, I've got to get dinner started," Steph answered.

Susan raised a hand and acted like she was warding off an attack of some kind. A simple "no" was her answer.

Everyone laughed, causing her to look down shyly.

"Okay, Kelly, we'll let Rick drive. You ride with him, help him," Chip said, then looking at Rick, "and don't hurt my kid," teasingly.

"I'm okay, Dad. I know how to bale off."

Rick was losing his confidence, "Maybe I'd better not—"

"Oh no you don't. No guts, no glory," Kelly laughed.

Lilly wasn't about to be left out. "What about me?" she screamed.

Chip looked down and patted her on the head, "You're riding with me, half-pint!"

She jumped up and down, clapping her gloved hands.

"Come on, we're burning daylight!" Chip hollered.

"How do you do that, what is bale off?" Lilly asked.

"Never mind, Lilly, come on," Kelly laughed.

They all headed to the equipment barn. A few minutes later, after a quick lesson for Rick on brake and gas, they were headed up the hill, past the cemetery toward the north open range of the ranch. Kelly thought Rick was catching on fast. She motioned her dad that all was well. The trail was actually a dirt road so Chip and Rick could ride side by side.

Boyhood fantasies took control of Rick. He was riding a horse, out on the open prairie, watching for hostile Indians.

Kelly screamed, "Hey, look," at the top of her lungs. They were about twenty minutes out from the barns when she spotted a lone buffalo on the next hill over to her left.

Chip stopped immediately. Rick couldn't believe his eyes.

Lilly screamed, "What is that?"

Looking at the rest, Chip laughed, "It's a buffalo, Lilly!"

"What is it?" Rick asked.

"A bull," Kelly answered, adding, "He shouldn't bother us, as long as we leave him alone."

"Consider yourself lucky, Rick, you don't see many of them, out like this," Chip said to Rick. The buffalo turned south and started walking away from them.

"This is amazing," Rick said in wonderment.

Chip took notice of the direction the bull was headed. He looked at the sky and decided they'd better head back toward the barns. Dark would set in fast now.

The women were in the kitchen. Steph had Mexican planned for dinner, using some of the secrets that Maria had taught her. She had put Susan to work grating cheese. They were enjoying their time alone. Susan asked a lot of questions, nothing personnel, mostly about ranch life. They heard a commotion; Sugar growled in her sleep.

A few seconds later Lilly ran into the kitchen, all excited, "Guess what, Mommy, we saw a buffalo. It was real big, but it didn't do anything to us!"

Susan's eyes showed instant fear, causing Steph to muffle a stray laugh.

Kelly came in next, laughing, "That was fun!"

"Where was it?" Steph asked.

Kelly smiled. "Up close to Wolf Ridge," she answered.

"Boy, you guys rode out quite a ways," Steph commented.

Susan's eyes were darting back and forth. Finally, Chip and Rick walked in.

Rick looked at Susan. "You hear?" he asked, glancing toward Lilly.

"Of course, sounds like you all had quite an adventure!" Susan made a big effort to sound cheerful, sharing in their fun. Steph watched her out the corner of her eye.

Rick turned to Chip and shook his hand, "Thanks, buddy, that was amazing."

Chip smiled, pleased with himself. "You're totally welcome, glad you had fun. Of course, the buffalo showed up, just like I'd planned." Eyes turned to Chip. All at once everyone started laughing.

Steph smiled, "Good one, dear!"

Rick walked toward the coffee pot. "I definitely need one of those," referring to the four-wheeler.

"Why?" Susan blurted out before thinking.

Rick turned and stared at her with a blank expression, then in a discouraged voice, said, "I don't know."

December 23

"What time does your meeting start, babe?"

"Early at nine," Chip answered in an unhappy voice. "They weren't thinking much about all the ranchers that had a long drive," he added.

"I know," Steph said, setting a plate of eggs and bacon in front of him, "but it's important, right?"

"Extremely. The new regulations they are trying to make into law will kill us," he sighed, "always from the guys that have never even seen a cow, every vote will count today."

She patted his shoulder and looked at the clock: four thirty. "Your dad should be here any minute. There's plenty if he wants breakfast," Steph added.

"There's a lot going on today?" he asked Steph.

"Yes, Ken, Kelly, and Lilly are riding out for a barn tree. I'm going to get Rick and Susan help me with Christmas cookies. Do you know when you'll be back? Don't forget we've got that cookout up at the old cabin this evening," she said, reminding him as she sat down across from him.

"You'd better keep an eye on temps for tonight. City slickers aren't used to sittin' out in the cold long," Chip said without looking up from his plate.

"You love calling them that don't you?" she said, playfully.

"Yep, any time I can," Chip said, teasing back.

Right then they heard a horn honking. "I guess Dad's not coming in." He got up, leaned over and kissed her, "See ya."

"Be careful," she hollered, then after hearing him say, "Always," she turned on the small TV sitting on the top shelf in the corner of the kitchen. She turned it to the Casper station. That was as close to local as she could get. She knew Ken would listen to the Grey Bull radio station, which was to their north. It would give them a better idea of when it was coming their way. So far it sounded as if the day would cooperate with her evening plans. She wasn't too worried. The campfire along with some wool Indian blankets would keep everyone warm and in good spirits, she hoped.

Her thoughts went back to local weather alerts they had experienced in the past. "We really do need something in Bethlehem," she told herself, thinking kindly of her small town. Bethlehem and their ranch, for that matter, they sat in the Owl Creek Valley, which was part of the Shoshone Basin. The Owl Creek Mountain Range was to the west and the Big Horn Mountains were to the east.

Most anyone would consider the town very small with a population of only four hundred, but the people that lived on the large tracts of land in the area, mostly large cattle ranches, were grateful for their town. Basically, you could get about everything you needed. Besides the antique mall, they had a doctor, an emergency clinic with six beds, a drugstore, a grocery store, a combination hardware/feed store, and two gas stations with mechanics. Then there was a mom-and-pop café that made the best cinnamon rolls, and the "Pines," an upscale dining experience.

The school was a complete K through twelfth grade and included a public library on the school grounds. Last year, the townspeople bought up an old empty building and created The Kids Zone. It was an ice cream shop with a large arcade, plus a large screen TV, a couch, and a few tables and chairs. It was overseen by volunteers as a safe zone for kids. This was the town's way to try and keep the local youth off the roads. So far, it was doing its job well.

She turned the volume up a little so she could listen while she worked on breakfast for the others.

Last night, Rick had put in a special order for breakfast this morning. Plain old fried eggs, fried potatoes with onions, white gravy, toast, and bacon. "Lots of bacon," he had said. Steph had laughed.

When Rick left the room with Chip, she asked Susan, "What's the big deal, that's nothing special?"

Susan replied, "I guess, because people don't eat that kind of food in the city. First of all, they say it's not healthy, you know, for your heart, plus no one takes the time to eat like that, always in too big a hurry." Susan was watching Steph's frown get deeper as Susan talked.

Susan finally got the courage to add more, "And no one cooks!"

Steph's frown had turned into a scowl on her face, leaning against the kitchen sink with a dish towel in hand. She looked just like Kelly.

Susan's panicky thoughts said, "Now I know where Kelly gets it from!"

Very calmly, Steph said, "Well, I'll tell you right now," her voice had a teasing tone to it, so Susan started to relax a little.

"My breakfasts are super healthy. You just have to work hard the rest of the day to work it off." Then she added in a soft voice, "This part of the country was founded on that kind of food—a hearty meal gave them the energy they needed to work hard, all day. They didn't sit at a desk." Instantly she wished she hadn't said the last part. She knew not to judge. "I'm sorry, I shouldn't have said that."

Susan found herself laughing hard. She waved her off, "No, no, you're exactly right!"

Steph stood looking at Susan. She was twisting the dish towel in her hand it was starting to look like a weapon. "So my lady, what are you having for breakfast?"

Susan looked at the dish towel, then at Steph, and smiled bravely as she said, "I'm having the same as Rick, just smaller portions, okay?" Now she waited.

"Smart girl," Steph laughed.

About six fifteen, Steph heard footsteps coming down the steps of the stairs. Cheerful "good mornings" rang out from Susan and Rick. Steph grabbed two cups and the coffee pot.

"Go sit by the fire until breakfast is ready. I waited on the eggs, not wanting them to get cold. Did you guys sleep well?"

"Like a rock!" Rick answered. "Where's Chip, did I sleep too late?"

"He and his dad left about four thirty, for Casper. They had an important ranchers meeting," she said. A few minutes later, they all heard spurs clicking on the stone floor.

Rick hollered, "Morning, Ken, just in time for a special breakfast."

Steph looked at Ken, "Not special, normal for us, but don't burst his bubble!"

Ken looked from one to the other, "Okay, works for me."

A few minutes later Ken asked, "Where are my partners in crime this morning?"

"Still asleep," Steph answered.

"Not for long. Come on, Sugar, let's go get those girls up." The Aussie responded instantly to Ken's voice, following him up the stairs. A few seconds later, everyone heard Sugar barking loudly, Kelly hollering and Lilly screaming.

"Okay, okay, we hear you!" Kelly said, trying to wake up.

When Ken came back down to the kitchen, he took the coffee cup from Steph and said, "I guess sleeping in the barn didn't go anywhere."

"No, it didn't, but that's okay," Steph replied. "Lucky okay this morning?"

"Yep. Rick, pass that plate of bacon. You gotta share, buddy!"

During breakfast, which Rick couldn't stop raving about, everyone had fun chatting. Ken got up, taking his plate to the sink and coming back to the table but not sitting down, he reached for a couple more pieces of bacon.

"I heard you say something yesterday about riding today?" He looked from Lilly to Kelly and winked, "How 'bout riding up on the ridge with me and cutting the tree for the barn, unless you've changed your mind and don't want one anymore," he said to the girls.

Instantly a reply came from both girls, "No, we want one, we're coming." Both of them started trying to talk and eat at the same time.

Ken raised his hands in the air, mouth stuffed with bacon, "Okay I got it, you're coming. Hurry up, I'm ready to ride."

Lilly was shoveling food into her mouth. "Hey, Lil, slow down, he'll wait for you," Steph commanded.

"But he—"

"Lilly, you heard Steph," Rick said sternly.

Steph followed Ken to the front door. "What about temps for this evening?" she asked her brother.

"We'll be fine. I'll go saddle while they finish up," Ken said as he walked out the door.

Susan had a concerned look on her face, but before she could say anything, Rick looked at her and fairly sternly said, "She will be fine."

Susan looked down at her plate and stayed quiet.

"I hope he's got the hats," Steph said to herself, but Rick heard her and looked questioning at her. She smiled, "You'll see!"

The girls grabbed coats and gloves and headed out the front door.

A few minutes later Rick said, "I think I'm going to see them off and then walk around a bit." With a big grin on his face, he looked at Steph, "To walk off that great breakfast. Thank you so much, you made my day!"

Susan's heart dropped. *When did he become so easy to please?*

Ken had all three horses saddled and waited for the girls at the tie rail in front of the cabin.

Lilly was jabbering at high speed again. Rick patted her on the head, "Calm down, Lilly."

Ken laughed and said, "Ain't possible!"

Lilly looked up, "What?"

"Saddle up guys," Ken hollered.

Rick's heart raced with thoughts running through his mind, *I'd give anything to go along.* His hand ran down Squaw's neck as he helped Lilly up.

"Hey!" Ken was looking at Kelly. When she looked up, he threw her a Santa hat. Next, he turned to Lilly, "Here, girly."

Giggling, she placed it snuggly on her head, pulling it down too low, making her look goofy. Rick was laughing.

Ken threw his cowboy hat to Rick, "Hold on to this for me, buddy," and placed a Santa hat on his head.

"Let's go guys. We've got a tree to cut down, and Christmas ain't waiting." Ken turned Sara and started walking up the lane. Squaw followed automatically, then Kelly.

Rick stood and watched as they headed off. His emotions were doing flip-flops.

As they started to climb the slight hill, Ken started singing "Jingle Bells" at the top of his lungs.

Kelly laughed and joined in.

Lilly screamed, "I'm coming." Squaw was a slowpoke, but would trot once in a while so she could keep up. Lilly had one hand on the saddle horn and the other holding her Santa hat on. She was lost to singing as she concentrated on the important thing, staying in the saddle.

Rick stood in place while they rode out of sight, realizing that this was the first time he'd been alone since arriving at the ranch, two days earlier. He slowly walked in the direction of the cabin. Looking their way again, they were out of sight now. He felt weird, very alone, just him. His mind wanted to retrace his memories of his boyhood dreams.

Being here on the ranch made him want to remember. Without realizing it, he had turned south and started walking. He was halfway between the old barn and the cabin with a clear view of the eastern range. The air was crisp, burning his lungs when he took a deep breath. It's a good clean feeling, he thought.

He took a deep breath and let it out slowly. "This is the life I've always wanted, the one I dreamed about all my life." As the years rolled by, the dreams and yearning faded. Now they were only a slight memory. Part of the sadness was of his own doing. He had never shared his dream with anyone. He was afraid of being laughed at. New Yorkers didn't dream of such things.

He headed back toward the cabin. As he reached the stone steps leading to the porch, he said out loud to no one, "I wish I never had to leave."

Steph and Susan were left sitting at the island. As Steph poured the last of the coffee, Susan smiled and said, "I love coffee cups or mugs. I call them cups."

Steph jumped in, "Me too. My gram said that morning coffee shouldn't be boring." She laughed now, "Of course my gram meant cups with pretty pink roses on them, not ones from the local feed store or breed association." They both laughed as Steph held up a cup covered in Angus cows grazing in a bright green pasture. The words on it said, "Shoshone Cattlemen's Association."

Susan giggled. "I got Aussies on mine. 'Life Is Better with Aussies!'" Susan hadn't had this much fun in a long time.

"But seriously, you have some beautiful Christmas mugs," Susan added.

"Yes, I've got lots of nice ones, but we have our everyday favorites. They're on the bottom shelf and that's where everyone grabs from. The pretty 'proper for company' ones are on the next shelf up."

Susan kept giggling. "Well, I'm very honored to drink my coffee out of an everyday cup," holding it up again.

As they both settled down, Steph's mind was trying to plan a schedule for what she needed to accomplish today. Tonight depended on it, but she wanted to visit with Susan. The woman seemed to be relaxing more and more.

Susan had been curious about Ken since first laying eyes on him.

"Can I ask you something, Steph?"

"Sure, anything. Do you want more coffee? I can make us more."

"Oh no, I'm fine thanks. Here it goes. What's the story with Ken, has he ever married?"

Steph leaned back on the high-backed stool. "Well, there's a long story and no." Then she added, with a slight giggle, "You want the past first or the present?"

It had been a while since she had been able to just sit and talk or gossip with another woman.

Susan had been holding her breath. She exhaled slowly and said, "Can we start at the beginning?"

Steph leaned forward, elbows on the island and hands folded together, getting comfortable for the long talk.

"Well, first, you know he's my older brother," she laughed, "by eleven months."

"Do you have others?" Susan asked.

"Nope, it's just Ken and me. Chip and Ken met in the Army, after high school. We grew up in Northern California, and Chip here. They hit it off from the start, doing a long tour in Afghanistan together. Chip got out after four years and went to college; Ken stayed in for another four years. Ken had a nickname in the Army."

Susan stopped her, "What did he do, you know, in the Army?"

"Oh, I guess I left that part out, didn't I? He was a helicopter transport medic, you know, the guys that go in to the fighting and bring the wounded out."

Susan was quiet, waiting.

"Okay, where was I?" Steph said.

"You said he had a nickname."

"The whole base called him—Guardian," Steph said.

"The Guardian, that's interesting," Susan replied.

"Not just Guardian, a name, not a title," Steph corrected.

"That's more interesting," Susan smiled.

"Ken loved the military and what he did. Everyone figured he'd be a lifer. At the end of eight years, everyone figured he'd list up again. It was Ken's life. He surprised everyone when he didn't and came home instead."

"What was his reason?" Susan asked.

"He said a voice in his head told him that he was needed at home."

Susan leaned back on her stool, intrigued. "Was something wrong at home?"

"No, nothing," Steph replied.

"Did he go home?"

"No, he came here. He said home was with Chip. Chip had made him a job offer whenever he got out. He said Chip was a brother now, cause of what they went through together in the Army. Chip came home with PTSD, post-traumatic stress disorder, from an IED that went off close by. It killed one of their friends. He died in Chip's arms."

"Oh no," Susan's hands covered her mouth.

"Ken was right. Chip needed him, then I came and we both needed him."

"So he became Guardian again," Susan stated.

"Yes, still is and will always be. None of us can imagine our lives here without him." Steph sat in silence for a short while. Slowly, a smile formed on Steph's face. "Ken is special." She jumped up and grabbed the cookie jar, bringing it to the island. She smiled. Grabbing one, she took a big bite. "Let's liven this talk up now. Where was I?"

"He came to the ranch and…"

"So, I came out that first summer to visit Ken, and, well, this"— she waved her arms around in the air—"is the rest of the story."

Susan took a bit of a cookie and said, "So, you are proof that magic does exist!"

Steph laughed, "Yes, I guess, for me and Ken both." Steph's thoughts went back to that time, the beginning. She shook herself back to the present. "Okay, now for the good stuff!"

"Wait, wait, me first. Why is this sexy man not married?" Susan asked, then after a hard laugh, she added, "I can't believe I just said that!" She laughed again.

I said that, didn't I? she thought to herself.

"Yeah, he's a cool drink of water," Steph replied.

Susan's eyes brightened. "Did you say a cool drink of water, your brother?"

She held her breath.

"Yes, it means—," Steph started, but Susan cut her off.

"Oh, I actually know what it means, and he truly is!" Susan was giggling harder than she had in years. "He definitely is!"

Steph laughed harder. "Okay, back to my story," she reached for another cookie.

"Ken dated occasionally through the years, but if he was telling the story, he'd say none of them were that right fit, you know, the fit you need to last a lifetime, kinda like that favorite pair of boots."

Susan put her hand over her mouth and giggled again. "I can even hear him saying the words."

Steph continued, "I tried fixing him up a couple of times with my single friends. Once in a while it worked, for a while, but the last couple of years have been different. Ken met Angela Sheppard at the Bear Creek Christian Church. It sits halfway between the ranch and town. Ken wasn't much of a churchgoer—his words—but it had a wood carving of a grizzly bear standing on its haunches out front. Ken said that old bear spoke to him."

Susan's eyes were full of laughter, but she stayed in control.

"So he decided to attend one Sunday. That was two Februarys ago and he's been going ever since. The town gossip says Angela was more of a draw than that old bear. Angie, as everyone calls her, is the town's librarian and a sub teacher at the high school."

Steph smiled. "Now comes the good part." She hesitated, adding drama, "She's ten years older than Ken!"

Susan raised her eyebrows. "Continue please!" she said.

"Ken said once of Angie, 'She's not the shiny kind on the outside but the shine on the inside does the rest all in.' Ken said the calm, quiet, simple life she leads is a perfect fit for him. But the biggest surprise is that neither one of them wants to get married."

"Why not?" Susan asked.

"Angie is an only child. She knows that at some point she'll need to go home to Vermont to care for her parents. She knows Ken won't go and she says she can't ask her parents to leave their home and move out here at this stage of their life."

"Why is she out here then?" Susan asked.

"She came out here to go to college years ago and stayed, but that's all I know. I do know this: she's quite a person. Anyhow, they've decided to enjoy each other while they can, with no strings attached. They love each other. Ken says sometimes love means letting go. They are happy for now, that's all that matters."

"Living happily one day at a time," Susan whispered. She looked down at her empty cup that she held in her hands. "I wonder what that would feel like."

Steph didn't think the words were meant for her.

Susan looked up. "Okay, that's all well and fine, but hasn't he ever wanted a family of his own over the years?"

"I asked him those exact words about ten years ago." Steph said solemnly, "He said he has one." Steph got up, putting the cookie jar back and grabbing a dish towel to wipe up the crumbs.

"Will Angie be here for Christmas, Steph?"

"No, she's gone home to Vermont."

Susan stood up and walked to the big kitchen window. As she gazed at the landscape, she said, "You are all lucky. You have each other. Family is important."

Steph heard a sadness in Susan's voice.

Lilly was in her glory, riding in the middle between Ken and Kelly for safety. Ken felt a calm in the air today and he wasn't sensing anything different from Sara. He thought everything would be fine, but all eyes stayed on Lilly and specially Squaw.

Lilly couldn't stop talking, so the other two just let her.

They had brought the Aussies along for exercise. They were running up ahead and watching for something to chase as usual. It was fairly cold, right about freezing, and partly cloudy. Ken looked at the sky and said, "It's coming."

Kelly replied as she looked around toward the western range, which was snow-covered, "Yes, it is!"

There was about four inches of snow on the ground, patchy in places, just enough to add some character to the surroundings.

Now Lilly was full of giggles, which kept on and on.

Finally, Ken said, "I'm going to rename this kid," pretending to be talking to Kelly.

Lilly turned and looked at Ken, "Okay, what?" She grinned.

"Giggles!" he said, returning the grin.

"Oh, I like that!" she replied, sitting up a little straighter in the saddle. "This is just the best Christmas!" she said, smiling. All of a sudden she got very serious, "Can I call myself a cowgirl now?"

Ken playfully looked her up and down, "Well, not until you get a proper pair of boots—cowboy boots, girly!"

Lilly frowned.

Ken had a feeling she'd get a pair from Santa.

The small stand of suitable trees was coming up. Both Ken and Kelly knew they could ride a little further and find a lot more trees to choose from, but Ken gave Kelly the impression that he didn't think that was a good idea. Kelly didn't question his logic. This was far enough for Lilly.

Ken was talking to the little girl, as they slowly cut back and forth through the stand. Ken was giving Lilly the chore of picking out the right tree.

A few minutes later, she stopped in front of a scrawny-looking spruce. It was probably four and a half feet tall. It lacked in what Ken and Kelly would have considered the characteristics of a nice Christmas tree. It actually looked a lot like Lilly, tall and skinny.

"Not old enough for any filling out," Ken said to Kelly, who agreed laughingly.

Lilly beamed, but not really understanding the meaning of Ken's words. They looked at each other, shrugged shoulders, and told Lilly that it was a fine tree.

"How come you picked this one, Lilly?" Ken inquired.

Looking at the tree with loving eyes, she said, "It doesn't want to be alone for Christmas. In the barn it will be warm and have its own—," she stopped and looked at Ken with questioning eyes, wondering if she was using the right word, "critter family?"

Ken smiled, "Yes, Lilly, critter is right," then added, "I think it's a mighty fine Wyoming barn Christmas tree, Giggles. Don't you think, girly?" looking from Lilly to Kelly.

She laughed, "Yep, the perfect tree. Let's get it cut, it's cold out here!"

Ken climbed down, "Here, Lilly, hold Sara's reins, and don't let go of them. I have no intentions of walking back." Taking a hand ax from his saddle bag, he went to chopping the tree down.

Kelly sat there watching her uncle. *He's sure good with kids. He should have some of his own.*

"Okay, the tree is cut," Ken said, as it fell on its side, but before he could finish, Lilly jumped in. "What now?" she asked impatiently.

"Hold your horses!" Ken said sternly.

Lilly's voice shrieked through the trees, "I am!"

Ken walked over to Sara and took a coiled-up rope out of the saddle bag.

"What are you going to do with that?" Lilly screamed too loud.

Ken looked at Kelly and said, "The impatience of youth!"

Kelly smiled, "I was never like that," and batted her brown eyes at him.

Ken just laughed.

"What?" Lilly was wound up.

Ken just looked at her and stuck out his tongue. Ken was enjoying Lilly's excitement. He tied the rope to the end of the tree trunk, then walked over to Squaw and wrapped the other end around the saddle horn, then giving it a half loop so it would hold tight. As he wrapped the rope, he talked to Lilly without looking at her, "You are going to drag your tree back to the barn."

Lilly thought about it for a few seconds and then said, "But what if I don't do it right and I hurt the tree?"

Ken and Kelly laughed and said, "You will be fine," at the same time.

Ken got on Sara and started walking off, "Come on, Lilly!"

Squaw started following. Lilly turned halfway in the saddle to watch the rope and tree. As soon as the rope stretched out, the tree started gently sliding across the snow.

She hollered at Ken, "Am I doing it right?"

Ken didn't bother to look back, he just answered, "Yep!"

Kelly laughed, as she loped passed Lilly to join Ken in the lead. Lilly, Squaw, and the tree brought up the rear. Ken started singing "Frosty the Snowman" at the top of his lungs. Laughing at her uncle, Kelly turned in the saddle to look at Lilly. "Sing, Lilly, sing!"

The off-keyed Christmas carols rang through the hills.

Rick, Susan, and Steph were in the kitchen. Steph was baking sugar cookies and had Susan and Rick attempting to frost them. The couple seemed to be having fun. Every ten minutes or so, Rick would run back to the office window to watch for the riders.

"Steph, can you come in here for a minute, please," Rick hollered to the kitchen, adding, "you too, Susan."

"Sure," Steph wiped her hands, thinking Rick must have a question about something. *It's too soon for the riders to be coming back*, she thought to herself.

Susan and Steph found him standing at the window. He turned when he heard them coming, "Come look. What are they, Steph?"

The landscape view was graced with a fairly large herd of deer heading south. Seeing them raised a flag in Steph's head. They didn't seem to be in any hurry, grazing some on the low brush as they went.

"A nice herd of mule deer," Steph said.

"They're beautiful," Susan commented.

"Is this normal, grouping like that?" Rick asked.

"Well, it depends. You usually don't get the opportunity to see them this way. I'd say that they have gathered up and are heading south because they sense the storm coming. They are looking for better cover. The only other time you'll see this is during a really harsh winter with deep snow; they'd be looking for food."

Susan got concerned, "Would they starve to death?"

"No, we have a hotline number to call when we spot groups. The ranchers all watch for wildlife. The Conservation Department will drop hay for them from helicopters and the ranches will put hay out too."

Susan sighed, "That's good."

Rick felt playful, "So Steph, this wasn't a planned part of your Christmas adventure?"

She turned and looked at him without smiling, "No, and neither is the approaching storm!"

Susan looked from one to another. She hadn't paid much attention to everyone's concerns over this storm. But maybe I should be, she thought.

Susan looked at the clock. They had been gone over an hour, and with a slight hint of panic in her voice, she mentioned it to Steph.

Calmly, Steph replied, "Ken's taking care of her, no worries." She refused Susan's concern by not looking at her when she made her statement.

They heard Rick holler from the office again, "Here they come!"

Susan and Steph ran to the window. The three riders were coming over the hill. Rick's voice was emotional, "Oh, look, Lilly's dragging a Christmas tree!"

Susan walked up to his side.

"Put your arm around her, Rick," Steph said to herself, but he didn't. They stood next to each other without touching.

"Look how good she's doing!" Rick added. Steph headed back to the kitchen to check the cookies in the oven, allowing the couple to enjoy the sight together. A minute later, they both came back.

"Do you care if we go to the barn?" Rick asked.

Steph laughed, "Of course not. Go enjoy, but bundle up, you two!"

They headed to the entrance where the coats and boots were stored. She could hear the giggles coming from both of them. Steph let out a sigh, "It sure is about time!"

She hadn't been very pleased with herself. Things between the two hadn't shaped up as fast as she thought they should have, but just maybe the tide was turning.

Looking at the clock, she was beginning to get concerned that Chip and Charlie hadn't called yet to say they were headed back. She hoped they were on the road by now and okay.

"Hey, Daddy!" Lilly screamed at the top of her lungs.

Ken looked at Kelly and said, "Sure is a good thing she's on Squaw." Kelly laughed.

"Look at me!" She was talking a mile a minute as they stopped near the barn.

"I got to pick out the tree. Oh, I hope I didn't hurt it," turning in the saddle to look at it lying there in the snow at the end of the twenty-foot rope. Ken laughed and shook his head. Kelly rolled her eyes as she got off and tied her horse to the tie rail.

"Well, Giggles, better get that tree of yours untied, stand her up, and shake off all that snow she picked up."

Looking at Rick, he said, "Think you can help her, Dad?"

Instantly Rick said, "You bet!" and handing the camera to Susan to take pictures. Rick headed over to Lilly and helped her climb down. Kelly grabbed Squaw's reins so they could take care of the tree.

Ken sighed, "I'll put the horses and dogs up."

Kelly smiled and said, "I'll help you."

Lilly and her parents had the tree cleaned off and were heading to the old barn.

Lilly stopped and turned to holler at Kelly, "When are we going decorate the tree, Kelly?"

"After lunch, Lilly," Kelly hollered back.

Quickly, a loud reply was heard as Lilly screamed, "Okay!"

Ken looked at Kelly and hugged her. They walked to the horse barn, arm in arm.

"We have a wild child. She'll sleep well tonight," Kelly laughed happily.

"Yep, good day," Ken added, reaching down to pet Breeze.

Jamie had just stopped for lunch. He was starting to worry about Molly. She hadn't walked over yet today. He was trying to stay away from her mom's house because it upset her so and she was taking her anger out on Molly.

He and a friend had changed the fuel pump on his truck. Now everyone was telling him to drop his fuel tank and clean it out. He was still having problems with the fuel lines freezing up. Their guesses were all the same, water in the tank. But payday was not until the twenty-seventh. Times were hard for the station owner. He had apologized for not being able to pay Jamie before Christmas. Jamie said it was fine, though he could have used the money. He didn't even have a Christmas present for Molly, but he was also grateful that he had a job. There weren't too many places that hired help in the little town.

He tried to stay positive, telling himself that soon he'd have a new baby. Secretly, he was hoping for a son, but he would be happy with either. He prayed for it to be healthy. Plans were to leave as soon as they could, before the baby came. He listened to the radio as he worked. It sounded like he needed to pay more attention to what the weatherman was saying: a storm was coming—a bad one.

Everybody sat at the kitchen island eating lunch, except Chip. Steph still hadn't heard from them and was thinking about calling them.

"Do we get to decorate the tree next?" Lilly asked, referring to the one she had just dragged in.

Kelly had a feeling the little girl was going to be disappointed when she announced the plans for the afternoon, but time was running out, and she was aware of her mom's plans for tonight. She still had to get her chores done.

She turned on her stool to look at Lilly, sitting next to her, "I think we need to leave the tree until tomorrow morning," then added, "I promise, we'll decorate it first thing right after breakfast. Okay, sweetie? I've got lots of chores to do yet today, but maybe you can help me. I think Mom has a surprise for dinner tonight so we need to be on time," Kelly explained.

"I like surprises," Lilly said.

"I'd like to help with chores, unless there's something else for me to do," Rick stated, looking around at the others. Then looking directly at Steph, he whispered, "I'm not much good with cookies." Everyone broke out laughing.

"I've got to go take care of the neighbors' place. They left yesterday for Christmas," Ken said.

Susan spoke up, "I've got a date with a soaker tub."

"Okay, Lilly?" Steph looked at her. Moments later she hugged Lilly for giving in so easily.

"But Kelly, tomorrow is Christmas Eve, so we have to get it decorated," she conveyed her concerns in a very serious voice, for an eight-year-old.

"I promise, Lilly, and yes, Rick, your help will be greatly appreciated," Kelly replied.

Steph grinned, "Wow, such big words from my daughter."

Kelly looked embarrassed, "Oh, Mom, stop!"

"Okay, it's settled. Everyone has a plan, but remember, be back here by four o'clock, and don't be late." Steph stared at Ken as she said the words. He replied with a wink.

Around two o'clock, Chip and his dad rolled in. Kissing Steph, he said, "Dad said to tell you 'Merry Christmas.' They are leaving early in the morning before the weather hits."

"I hope they enjoy that Florida sunshine," she said.

"Yeah, me too. This cold is starting to wear on his bones," Chip replied.

"Ken went to Jamison's. You need to be back by four."

"Yep," he said, grabbing the sandwich she held out for him then walked out the door.

Ken drove the sixteen miles to Joe's place, thinking to himself, "She's on her way." He listened to the weatherman on the radio. Calgary is buried. So far it was beautiful today and they were expecting a nice evening. "The calm before the storm," he whispered to the air.

Susan was excited to have some personnel time. Steph had come up and lit candles all around the tub, adding in a calming effect. Soothing Christmas music seemed to come out of the walls.

First thing, she needed to text Madge. She scolded herself for not doing it sooner like she had promised. Madge would be worried. She grabbed her cell phone.

Sorry I haven't text sooner, place is amazing, Lilly in heaven, Rick good too, I love it, will never tire of looking at a cowboy.

She took a long breath.

Can't wait to tell you about Ken.

Love you talk soon, Merry Christmas, ME

They saved Lucky's chores for last. Kelly handed Rick the pitchfork. The three of them were in Lucky's pen. Kelly had put a rope halter on the heifer and had tied her in a corner while she ate her grain. Her udder was filling out nicely for a longhorn, but hadn't advanced to that look that said "okay, I'm ready to calve now."

Lilly stood with the handles of the wheelbarrow and followed Rick around the pen as he picked up the few "cow pies," as Kelly called them. She told them how in the old days, pioneers collected the dried cow pies off the open prairies and stored them for winter. They were burned in wood stoves for heat when wood was scarce, especially on the Nebraska and Kansas plains where they were pretty much treeless.

"Do they smell?" Rick asked.

"No, not when they are dry," Kelly replied. When their chores were finished, they sat down on a straw bale waiting for Lucky to finish eating.

"Is there a story behind Lucky?" Rick asked.

Kelly looked down at her boots and said, "Yes, but it's kind of a long one."

Rick smiled, looking at his watch, "Tell us, we have time."

Kelly took a deep breath. "Okay, you asked for it." She didn't get to tell it often.

"Two Aprils ago, Ken had been out on BLM land."

Rick stopped her, "The federal land next to the ranch, right? Your dad told me."

Kelly smiled. "Yes," and continued.

"He was scouting for stray cattle. Anyhow, he rode up on a dead longhorn cow. After checking her over, he couldn't tell what caused her to die. Then he checked for a brand. Any cattle that are turned out on open range are supposed to be branded," she explained. "She didn't have one, then he checked her udder and saw she was in milk," again explaining her words, "a calf nursing on her. He said her udder was swollen like she had just calved, so he got back on Sara and started crisscrossing the area, trying to find a calf. Cows like to hide their new calves in the brush and they can be hard to find."

Lilly sat quietly listening on her dad's lap.

"Especially longhorns, the mammas tell their babies not to move. Longhorn babies are born with no scent. A wolf has poor eyesight and relies on scent. So a wolf can walk right by a new calf and not know it's there."

"Amazing," Rick exclaimed. "Keep going, please."

Kelly continued, "So Ken finally finds her, curled up like a black rock, at the base of a group of gnarly mesquite brush. He tore his shirt all up trying to get her out. She was brand new; he wasn't sure if she had even nursed, so he threw her over the front of his saddle and brought her home. Ken and my gramps helped me nurse her back to health. Neither one of them would let me name her until they were sure she was out of the woods."

Rick questioned again, with his eyes.

"Danger, health-wise," she said. "About three weeks later, I decided she needed some sunshine. It was good and warm out."

Kelly's thoughts of those days outran her words. The little one followed her adopted momma everywhere, so she didn't hesitate to follow her out of the barn doors when Kelly walked out. They had been outside for about fifteen minutes when her dad, Ken, and Gramps drove up, coming from a meeting in town. They all talked about how well the calf was doing. Kelly remembered taking a stand with the men in her life. She dug her heels in the ground and with her hands on her hips.

Lilly broke her spell, "So what happened?"

"Oh, well, I told them it was about time this little one had a name. Gramps looked me in the eye and said, 'What you got in mind?' I know how important names were, cause the place of honor the horses and cattle hold on this ranch. I had thought hard for just the right name."

Lilly hollered, "Lucky!"

"Wait," Kelly said, "I looked at all them and said, 'Lucky Enough.'"

Lilly sighed with an "Aw, that's pretty."

"They were all quiet. I figured they were mulling it over. Uncle Ken spoke first: 'Well, since I found her, I lay claim to her,' he said."

"I panicked, saying, 'But you gave her to me.' I remember Dad and Gramps having big smiles on their faces."

Rick was smiling too. He had caught on.

"Uncle Ken was playing with me, but I was getting mad and thought he was serious. He told me to calm down, that he wasn't an Indian giver. 'I just wanted to remind you that I have a vested interest in that critter,' he said. I remember holding my breath, then he smiled at me and said 'I think that name is very befitting for this beautiful creature.'"

"What did you do, Kelly?" Lilly asked.

"I jumped in his arms and told him that I loved him." Kelly's eyes were teary at the memory.

"And I do, then I asked him why he had to always be so mean. He said it wasn't mean, it was called a hard time." Gramps was wiping the tears from his eyes, and I remember kneeling down to her and giving her a hug, telling her she was now "Lucky Enough" of the Kahler Ranch, our first and only longhorn. Dad made it clear to me that day that this ranch didn't do longhorns and for me not to get any ideas."

Rick laughed, "That's a good story, Kelly."

"I made her one of my 4-H projects."

"What's that?" Lilly asked.

"It's a nationwide club for kids, usually on farms with livestock but other things too. We keep records and then get to show at the county fairs."

"What else have you done in 4-H?" Rick asked.

"Well, I do rodeo with Poco, mainly run barrels and poles, and then ranch and trial events with Ginger and show her at halter, and of course my dogs are a project too, and now the longhorn. Last year they added a new class, orphan calves. It was a big hit. Kids could keep records of raising a calf that had lost its momma of any breed. First place was a ten thousand dollar scholarship."

Rick raised his eyebrows. "Did you win with Lucky?'

"No, my friend Colt won. His mom is the vet, so his calf really got top-notch care," Kelly explained.

"Well, you raised Lucky Enough good too!" Lilly praised.

Kelly laughed, "Thank you, Lilly."

"Thanks again, Kelly, for sharing her story with us. It's special," Rick said, trying not to sound too emotional.

"That's okay. There's lots of stories on the ranch," she said.

"Can we go see my tree before we leave? I don't want it to think we forgot it," Lilly begged as she pulled on Kelly's coat sleeve.

"Sure, Lilly, we surely don't want it to be sad," Kelly answered in a serious voice while smiling at Rick. They headed toward the wall that the tree was propped up against.

Rick wrapped his fingers around a slim branch and let it slide down along the needles. "It has been a very long time since I've touched a real tree," he stated.

Kelly thought she heard some sadness in his statement.

"Oh, what kind do you have in New York?" Kelly asked. Anything other than a live tree had never crossed her mind.

Lilly spoke first, "It's a dead tree. Momma takes it out of a box and puts it together every year."

Before Kelly could comment, Lilly bounced around them, "This tree is real. I think it's my first real tree I've ever had. Oh, I like real ones." The smile on her face was priceless. "See you in the morning, little tree," Lilly said softly. She seemed to be satisfied now, taking their hands and heading for the door.

Leaving the old barn, they headed back to the cabin. Lilly walked in between Kelly and her dad, still holding their hands and talking in what Kelly called "Lilly style," meaning a hundred miles a minute.

Rick was thinking about the story Kelly told, "Kelly, why Lucky Enough?"

She smiled, "Because she was lucky enough that Ken found her and the wolves didn't."

Rick laughed. "You were right about that. One more question," Rick said. "What if Ken had found a brand on the cow, what would that have meant?"

"Well," Kelly started, "he would still have brought the calf home and taken care of it. Dad would have called the rancher that owned that brand. We know all the brands in this area, then it would have been up to them if they wanted the calf." Then she added, "If you find a cow without a brand on open land, you have the right to keep it. It's not a law, it's just a code amongst the ranchers."

Steph was getting antsy, "Okay guys, looking at Ken and Chip, we've got plans to put in place, right?" Steph said, wanting to be taken seriously.

"Okay, yeah, just about forgot the plan," Chip teased.

Steph laughed, "Yeah right. I want dinner at five o'clock. It's getting dark out already."

Ken looked at his watch. "Four, yep, dark."

Susan and Rick looked bewildered. Of course, they knew of no plan.

The road that led past the cabin curved around a small stand of aspens growing along the small creek. The terrain started inching upward for a quarter of a mile to a nice-size hill that leveled off. On the left of the road was the Kahler family cemetery with another stand of aspens. On the right side was a very old cabin; it was small in size but had a beautiful porch. Inside was one large room, no plumbing or electricity. A two-seater outhouse sat about twenty yards behind. The cabin was original to the ranch. It had been used as a stay-over for ranch hands checking cattle that took more than one day on horseback. The cabin contained a wood stove, a table, an empty pantry, and two roughed-out bunk beds. It had sat on another spot on the ranch and was moved to the favorable hill before Chip was born. The views from this spot of the mountain ranges were breathtaking.

Chip rode up on the four-wheeler and got a fire started in the cabin stove and also in the rock fire pit in the cabin yard area. He placed a hood cover over it for protection, before he rode back down the hill.

Ken had harnessed the two Clydesdale mares, Cinnamon and Spice; their coats glistened. Ken had spent part of the afternoon getting them ready for their part in tonight's plan. He walked them out to the sleigh, side by side. Kelly was ready to help hitch them to the rig.

The sleigh was a family heirloom that every generation of the Kahler family had enjoyed using. They all had done their part to make sure she was around for the next. The sleigh had steel runners that were very sharp from years of use. It was of an unusual style for its age, and for this area because of the double set of seats, it also contained a storage area at the back.

Steph had packed everything needed for tonight in ice chests and baskets. Her plans included everyone "roughing it," so only bare necessities were brought for the ranch-style cookout.

Susan, Rick, and Lilly were instructed to "dress very warm." "Put your long underwear on and meet them at the horse barn at four forty-five."

"Poor Lilly," Steph thought, "she's so excited." Lilly didn't handle waiting for surprises very well.

The Conners stood, waiting at the barn, alone. A few minutes later, "Listen," Rick whispered toward Lilly and grinned at Susan. The faint sound of bells slowly got louder, followed by the sound of horse hooves hitting the hard ground.

Lilly held her breath as the team of horses followed by the sleigh rounded the corner of the barn.

"Whoa, ladies", Ken hollered, bringing the beautiful sight to a stop. Lilly was quiet. She was actually so surprised that she didn't know what to say. Ken looked at her and broke the silence, "What's the matter, Lilly, cat got your tongue?" Rick and Ken laughed. Susan was overwhelmed as usual.

Kelly and Steph had walked up.

"Oh my gosh, Steph," was all Susan could say. Both Kelly and Steph smiled.

"Let's get loaded up," Ken said, "going to get cold just standin' here!"

"There's blankets on the seat to cover with," Steph said as they all climbed aboard. Lilly settled in between her parents, giggling. Chip loaded all the stuff in the back and jumped back on the four-wheeler.

"You're not coming?" Susan said to Chip.

"He's going to ride that up. That way, if I forgot anything, he can come back down for it so much faster."

Susan smiled at Steph and said, "Oh, not you!"

Steph laughed, "Oh yes, me, I'm totally capable of messing up."

Kelly climbed up top with Ken on the driver's seat.

All of a sudden Lilly screamed, "Wait, me too!" Instantly she jumped up and started scrambling her way to the top, wiggling in between Ken and Kelly.

"Everybody settled?" Ken hollered, as Susan giggled, snuggling under a blanket.

Ken handed the reins to Lilly and said, "Let's get this show on the road!"

"What do I do?" she said in a panic. Ken took her hands in his and gently tapped the backs of the mares with the reins. The mares started a slow walk. The ride would only take about fifteen minutes, but since it was twenty-eight degrees out, it was long enough. Chip had the cover off the fire pit and a good fire going. The chairs were lined around it. Luckily the wind had died down and the smoke was going straight up. That's a good sign, Chip thought.

"Dinner is ready, come on guys," Brenda hollered from the kitchen. Brian and Colt washed up before sitting down; they hadn't been in long.

They bowed their heads. "Thank you, Lord, for the food we are about to receive, and we ask you, Father, to watch over our livestock, keeping them safe, while they take on the approaching storm, Amen." Brian started passing a plate of pork chops.

"You get those bred heifers moved?" Brenda asked.

"Yes, but they didn't like it, probably not the best time to put them in a pasture they don't know," Brian's words were said with concern in his voice.

"But they are way better off there, Dad," Colt stated.

"I agree, but they don't know that," Brian added with his mouth full.

"Everybody will be okay?" Brenda asked.

"Like I said, I hope so. We are as ready as we can be, I guess," the concern remained evident in his voice. Brian had a huge pit in his stomach, to a point that he didn't know if he could even swallow his food.

"Okay, people, this is a camp-style dinner," Steph hollered as she came out of the cabin and placed two cast iron Dutch ovens on a ledge of rocks where they would stay warm.

"And the menu is…?" Rick asked as he sided up next to Steph, taking a whiff of something smelling good.

With a playful smile on her face, she said, "Cowboy baked beans, fried potatoes, steak tenders, homemade camp biscuits, and a package of hot dogs for roasting, especially for Chip and Lilly."

"And dessert?" Rick grinned.

Steph laughed, pointing a finger at Rick, "You're pushing it," then added, "peach cobbler and marshmallows for roasting."

The night was off to a perfect start. Everyone had wrapped the wool Indian blankets over their shoulders, keeping their backsides warm. Dinner was perfect, even down to Ken's homemade wine that Rick raved about. Lilly had burned her first hot dog but with Chip's help, got the second one right.

When it came time for roasting marshmallows, Susan shied away. Finally with Rick coaching her on, she agreed to try. In the end, she was laughing and having as good a time as the others.

This is just a beautiful evening, Steph thought. The moon was almost full and still coming up. The cloudless sky made the air a little colder but the brightness of millions of stars was a good trade off. Steph was sure the New York couple had never seen a night sky like this before.

"Do you allow guests to stay at this cabin in the summer?" Rick asked.

Steph replied quickly, "Yes, we do."

Susan looked surprised. "A little primitive, don't you think?" she asked Rick.

"Exactly," Rick replied, leaning forward to poke the fire with a long stick.

Chip and Steph smiled at each other. The evening seemed to be a hit.

After a bit, the conversation turned to their favorite childhood heroes. Half of them Kelly had never heard of, and Lilly hadn't heard of any of them. Everyone laughed at her frustration with their conversation.

As a child, Ken had wanted to be the Lone Ranger when he grew up. No one had a bigger smile for Ken than Chip. "That fits for sure, always the loner, saving the day!"

Rick laughed, "You're right about that, Chip!"

Susan was next. Looking at everyone shyly, she said, "I wanted to be Mrs. Cleaver from the *Leave It to Beaver* show. I always thought it would be so neat to run around the house all day in fancy dresses and high heels."

Steph started choking on her drink, "That's too funny!"

Kelly stared at her, "Yuck!"

Lilly responded, "I think that's funny too!"

Steph was rolling in giggles, partly from too much wine. "I always wanted to be Dale Evans," she added.

Rick was sitting next to her. He got very quiet, turning in his chair to look at her. Steph glanced his way.

Very calmly, he said, "You did!"

The group looked at Rick.

"What?" Steph managed to say.

Rick took a deep breath. "You grew up to be Dale Evans and you married Roy Rogers."

Chip leaned forward, putting his elbows on his knees, listening.

"This"—Rick waved an arm in the air—"is your wild, Wild West. The two of you fight the bad guys for the good life." He leaned back in his chair and waited.

Steph was stunned, realizing that Rick wasn't joking. He was being serious.

Ken winked at Steph, "Hey, Rick, if they're Roy and Dale, what's my part in this story?"

Rick laughed, "You know, the funny guy that drove Nellie Bell."

Steph broke out giggling uncontrollably, "What was his name? I can't remember!"

Chip smiled calmly and pulled the front of Ken's cap down over his face, "Pat, Pat Brady."

"That's right," Rick said, clapping his hands and laughing.

Lilly looked at Kelly with a frown on her face, "Who is Nellie Bell?"

Kelly sighed boringly, "It's a jeep."

Lilly felt a little left out. She didn't know why this was all so funny to them, so she blankly said, "A jeep named Nellie Bell."

Rick jumped up and grabbed Lilly, swinging her in the air in circles, "Yes, little girl, and a German shepherd named Bullet and a beautiful palomino named Trigger. I lived for that show when I was a little guy. Saturday mornings at nine o'clock on channel 7."

He stood still now but still held on to his daughter. He looked around the group of new friends and said, "You, lucky people, are living my dreams."

All of a sudden, Chip, Ken, and Steph pieced Rick's puzzle together—the questions asked, the interest, it all made sense now.

"But, who are the bad guys, Rick?" Kelly asked.

"That's an easy one, Kel—Mother Nature and low prices," Chip said as he turned and looked at Rick, giving him a thumbs-up.

The scene quieted down now with everyone taking everything in, then Rick started talking again, calmly repeating himself, "You all are living the life I dreamed of." Emotion could be heard in his statement.

Steph heard sadness in his voice. Slowly she asked him, "Rick, why didn't you pursue the dream?"

Rick didn't answer right off. Finally, he spoke, "I guess I never realized that it was a real life, one I could have." He laughed lightly as he talked, "Guess as a child, I was convinced it was just TV magic."

No one responded. They waited for Rick to continue. Rick sat up straight and looked directly at the fire. "I didn't know how to get here."

Rick became very serious as he bared his soul, as Ken would say.

"When you're a kid with a dream, it's important to have someone that believes in you and to help guide or make that dream come true." He looked from Ken to Chip and said, "You know." Then he looked directly at Kelly and said, "You have no idea how lucky you are."

Kelly didn't know what to say, so she smiled and nodded her head yes. Ken leaned over and kissed her on the forehead.

Steph broke in, "Rick, how and why Wall Street?"

"It was my dad's dream, the only one he understood, and it was forced on me."

Susan sat in shock. She couldn't believe what her husband was saying. She didn't know this person. She had never heard any of this before.

Maybe he thought I wouldn't understand, she told herself, then, sadly added, *I wouldn't have.*

Ken decided it was time to change the mood. He managed to slip away unnoticed to the cabin as the others talked. Returning with his guitar, he sat back down. He slowly started to strum a cord. Everyone turned his way.

"Okay, Lilly, what's it going to be?"

"'Frosty the Snowman,'" she giggled.

He turned to Kelly as she sat down next to him, "Come on, girl, you gotta help me!"

Lilly had jumped up and claimed the spot on the other side of him, snugging up to him for warmth. As Ken started playing and leading the song, Lilly sang just as loud as she could. Her enjoyment was contagious Susan couldn't stop smiling and finally joined in. Ken played for almost an hour, ending with "Silent Night."

Rick was sitting a couple chairs away to Ken's left. He poked the fire again and turned to Ken. "There was a song that Roy and Dale sang a lot on the show."

Ken smiled and broke in, "Happy Trails"?

"No, not that one, something about weeds," Rick said.

Ken and Chip looked at each other. They both had grins on their faces. Looking up at Rick, Ken said, "Go something like this." Ken slowly started singing the lyrics as he played "Tumbling Tumbleweeds."

"See them tumbling down, pledging their love to the ground."

Rick jumped up, excited, looking around at everyone as he said, "That's it!" Chip and Kelly joined in, as they knew the song well.

"Lonely but free, I'll be found, drifting along with the tumbling tumbleweeds."

Steph had turned the video camera on earlier capturing the evening. She knew Rick would be excited when he found out she had recorded the night for them.

When the song was over, Ken went right into another favorite—"Cool Waters."

"All day, I've faced the barren waste, without the taste of water, cool water."

Rick was full of gratitude. "Sons of the Pioneers," he said calmly.

Ken smiled and said, "Now join in everyone!"

"Happy trails to you, until we meet again, happy trails to you, keep smiling on till then."

Rick sang heartily. Susan smiled, totally enjoying her husband's enthusiasm.

Lilly stated, flatly, "I don't know these songs!"

As the song came to an end, Rick stood up facing Chip and Ken, and bowed to each, saying, "Thank you so much for that, for all of it," then he turned toward Steph to include her.

She spoke for all three of them, "You are totally welcome, Rick."

"Yeah," Ken laughed, "thanks for being so easy to please."

Chip joined in, "Yeah, glad you aren't a Beatles freak!"

Ken laughed hard, "Me too, but I probably could have faked my way through some Elvis."

Steph jumped up and handed out tin cups of hot coffee as everyone settled back down. Ken walked through the group and offered a little hard spirits to those who wanted. "Help fight off the cold," he whispered under his breath, but Rick heard and smiled. A falling star raced across the sky. The evening was getting colder, but no one seemed to notice.

Faint sounds of coyotes howling in a distance caused Susan to move closer to Rick. He closed his eyes, wanting to hear the sounds, wanting to remember the sounds, the crackling embers in the fire pit, the coyotes, all of it.

"Our first coyotes," Rick stated, looking from Susan to Lilly. The combination of everything tonight had the big city businessman forgetting where he came from.

With Lilly sitting on his lap, he hugged her tight, while saying out loud, "Friends, it doesn't get any better than this!"

As Ken helped Chip pack things up, he leaned into Chip and said, "It's coming, we need to pray."

Lilly came bouncing down the stairs. She was dressed in her new Christmas pajamas, a onesie with feet. The fleece was white with big black spots, with pink trim. She had the hood on exposing pink ears that stood straight up. There was no guessing; she definitely looked like a Holstein cow. She entered the kitchen where everyone was gathered. With a big grin across her face, she danced in a circle to show off her cow tail. The room overflowed with laughter.

"Moo-ee Christmas, Lilly," Ken said, speaking first.

"Do you like them?" she asked, as she tried to climb up on the cowboy's lap.

Rick, still laughing, asked, "Susan, where did you find those?"

Susan sat quietly, letting the little girl answer.

"I got on the internet and looked up cow clothes and then I found them," she smiled proudly at her mom. "I begged and begged until she said okay!" Lilly said proudly.

Kelly jumped up and went over to feel the material, "Oh, Lilly, those are so you!"

Susan sat staring at her daughter. "My gosh, they make you look so tall and skinny."

Steph, laughing, said, "Mom, she is tall and skinny. I think we need to fatten this cow up with pancakes in the morning!"

It didn't take Lilly long to reply, "Yeaaaah!"

Lilly was still sitting in Ken's lap. She looked up at him with a serious look in her eyes, as if she was thinking. Her eyes mellowed, "Can I call you Uncle Ken, like Kelly does?"

Susan started to say something, but Rick put his hand on her arm to stop her.

Steph turned her head so no one would see her big smile. She knew how playful Ken could be with kids. She thought to herself, "Oh, this will be good!"

He didn't respond to her question right away. He put a very serious look on his face, like he was thinking it over.

Lilly waited patiently.

Finally, in a negative tone, he said, "Well, I don't know!"

Instantly, her face saddened. Ken honestly thought she was going to cry. Then in a gentle voice and a hug at the same time, he said, "Lilly, I'd be honored for you to call me uncle."

She started giggling and looked around the group, "I've never had an uncle before."

Steph looked at Susan and Rick.

"Rick and I are both the only child," Susan admitted to the others.

"Boy, you sure missed out on all the extra gifts all your life," Kelly commented.

"Yeah, and no cousins to play with either!" Lilly added.

Susan laughed again, "Oh, Kelly, don't think she's gone without."

Lilly laughed, "But now I have one, and that makes you my cousin, Kelly, and"—she looked around the room, with bright eyes of contentment—"the rest of you are my family too."

December 24

*T*he lights were on in the kitchen. Ken figured Chip was up. As he walked in the back door, he saw he was right.

"Grab a cup, it's almost ready," Chip said, referring to the coffee still dripping into the carafe.

"Heard the forecast yet?" Ken asked.

"Should be on in a few minutes. How's things at Joe's?" Chip asked.

"So far so good. Since he sold the herd in October, he's only got about fifteen head left, couldn't part with those good old girls, said he'll let them die on the ranch of old age. You know his soft heart," Ken stated of his good friend, then added, "They are all up close with plenty of shelter; should be fine, boarded the dogs out." Ken walked over and grabbed the coffee, pouring two cups. "I'm headed over there shortly."

They heard footsteps on the stairs. Steph was wrapped in a long pink bathrobe, hair uncombed, and looking like she was still half asleep. Ken chuckled as he looked at her. Memories of years ago flooded his head, when they were younger, when Steph looked this same way in the mornings.

"Don't you guys ever sleep?" she said, yawning.

"Not much with this kind of storm on its way," Chip answered for both of them.

"Shhh," Ken said, jumping up quickly to turn the volume up. The weather was on next.

Warning! Storm forecast for Grey Bull and areas south. Classification upgraded to blizzard.

"That's us," Chip said grabbing a pad and pencil from the kitchen counter.

Warning! Forecast for 12/24, light snow starting between 8–9 a.m., picking up to one inch per hour by 10 a.m.; by noon—two inches per hour.

"Moving in fast," Ken commented.

Warning! Wind forecast, gusting to 40mph by 10 a.m., sustained at 30mph (visibility, less than a quarter of a mile by noon), winds increasing all day to 40 to 60mph, at height of storm—80 to 100mph.

Warning! Temperatures, currently 28 degrees, dropping this morning to 20–25 degrees, with an afternoon high of 20–25 degrees.

Warning! Temps start dropping by 4 p.m., low of 0 degrees by 9 p.m.

Warning! Full storm expected to hit area by 10 p.m., expecting 3–5 feet or more of snow overnight with huge amounts of drifting.

Warning! Governor closing all roads south of Grey Bull at noon. No snowplows out after noon—visibility zero by 3 p.m.

Warning! Do not go out, no emergency vehicles will respond until after storm has moved out of area, expected to move through by 6 p.m. (12/26).

Ken got up and turned the volume back down.

The three sat quietly for a few minutes, letting it all soak in. "Our only savior is that it's not going to get really cold," Chip said, "and it's short-lived." A few moments later, he added, "I'm going back out and check cattle."

"You'd better do it early," Ken said.

"I want both of you back on this ranch, close up, here at home," Steph said, pointing a finger down at the table, "early."

Ken and Chip both grinned, knowing the mother hen in Steph was coming out already. Ken looked at Chip. "We are loved!" Steph ignored him.

"I'll see if Rick wants to ride along. I don't think Rick and Susan really know what's coming," Chip stated.

"How could they," Ken replied.

"I'll talk to Susan today, but only going to tell her what I have to. I don't think she handles stress very well."

A moment later, they heard Rick's voice. "Rick and Susan don't know what? Morning guys," Rick said, walking into the kitchen. "Everyone looks real serious, what's up?" Rick asked, pouring himself a cup of coffee.

It was almost five in the morning. "Sit down, Rick," Steph said solemnly.

"You guys fill him in, I've got to get going. Tell Kelly that Lucky is fine so she doesn't have to run out first thing," Ken said.

"Was everything okay in the horse barn last night?" Chip asked. Animals were more sensitive to weather changes and always gave off the first warnings of impending weather.

"Well, horses seemed okay but the Aussies—"

Steph cut him off, "What about the Aussies?"

"Had them in the kennel. Weirdest thing, heard them howling, real eerie sound about one, two in the morning, got up and walked the barn, everything seemed okay. I took them both back to my place. Once they were with me, they seemed fine, slept next to my bed the rest of the night. I left them in my place this morning. They'll be happier there," Ken stated.

Steph looked at Chip but didn't say a word.

"Ken," Chip spoke as Ken was headed to the front door, "did someone get the guide rope up?"

"Yes, Chico's son, I think," Ken answered.

"Will you please recheck it? Hate to have it come loose at one end. People have been found frozen to death, twenty feet from a shelter in these kinds of blizzards."

"I'll make sure it's right. See you all in a little while," Ken said as he walked out the door.

Looking at Rick, Chip said, "It's a rope that is strung out between poles, from the front of the cabin to the old barn."

Rick looked at Chip, "It's going to be that bad?"

Chip answered in one word, "Yep!"

Chip and Steph spent the next half hour telling Rick what was headed their way and trying to answer all his questions calmly.

Rick didn't seem to be showing any nervous concerns. "I'm sure you all have dealt with these storms before, kinda like part of your life, so the storm doesn't worry me. What does worry me is that I don't want me or my family to be a hindrance. We need to do whatever we can to help."

Rick was gaining more and more of Chip's respect. "Thanks, Rick, that is greatly appreciated, and don't worry, I will holler when I need help." Chip looked seriously at Rick, "But you are right, these storms aren't new to us. Each one comes with her own special punch and we try to learn from each one so we can do better the next time. They all are to be respected."

Rick poured everyone more coffee and without looking up said, "Like breeding for later calving?"

Chip took a deep breath, "Yes!"

Steph wasn't sure she could say anything to lighten the air, so she tried to speak from her head and not her gut, "We're as ready as we can be. We may not have electricity for Christmas, but really, that just makes it more old-fashioned. I know of ranch families that turn the electricity off on purpose."

"But I think it's important to make sure Susan understands what is coming so she doesn't panic," Rick said.

"I'm telling her about the storm this morning, Rick," Steph said, trying to smile.

Chip stood up looking at Rick, "I'm headed out to check cattle, wanna ride along?"

"Sure, I'm a good gate opener," he replied, smiling.

The two men headed toward the coats and gloves. "We'll be back," Chip hollered.

"You'd better," Steph hollered without looking up.

It was still dark out when Ken reached Joe's ranch. It sat sixteen miles to the east of the Kahler Ranch toward the town of Shane.

Ken already had feed in place, but he decided to feed the stock their "Christmas grain" this morning since he knew he wouldn't be there tomorrow. All ranchers fed a little extra on Christmas morning.

Joe's wood stove was an old converted wood furnace, with a huge cavity. It would hold heat for a few days when filled. Ken checked it and added a few pieces. Just in case, he thought. Joe had left a light on above the workbench and a note tacked up above the bench, with his phone number on it, for emergencies. Satisfied that everything was okay, he made sure the barn door was closed good as he left.

As he walked back to his truck, he stopped before climbing in and looked up to the still dark sky. Something wasn't right. He wasn't sure what it was. A feeling, a sense, he wasn't sure. He didn't spend much time thinking about it. His thoughts were running. He was constantly adding to the list in his head, of things needing done this morning—before it hit.

Turning onto the main road, he glanced back at the Jamison Ranch entrance. He took a deep breath and said, "Merry Christmas, JJR, stay safe."

As Ken drove back toward the ranch, he felt a slow nervous feeling in the pit of his stomach. He'd had felt that feeling before; it was there to warn his senses.

Now he prayed out loud, "Lord, I'm not sure what this special day holds for us. Can You please send us Your protection? We are going to need it. Thank You, Father, Amen."

It was still early enough that the sunrise was just starting to peek over the eastern range. Another thought made its way across Ken's mind. "It's going to be a long day."

"Now for my day," Steph thought, "get pies baked, start sauce for spaghetti. I'll probably have to mix it up, but it will taste the same, just not as pretty, and I can reheat it on the hearth if I need to." Thoughts about losing her cooking source stayed on her mind, now thinking that she needed to have a "plan B" in place, just in case. She relaxed some, feeling a little better now. Plans always calmed her down.

Kelly got Lilly up at six thirty, making enough noise that Susan got up too.

Looking at Susan's sleepy face, she giggled, "Oh, I'm so sorry. I didn't even think that you might still be asleep."

Susan wasn't sure of how to take the comment, but smiled and said, "It's okay, Kelly, time for me to be up too."

Lilly screamed at the top of the stairs, "Mom, it's Christmas Eve day!"

Susan calmly replied, "Yes, Lilly, it sure is," then whispered to herself, "Now, the ghosts are up too."

When the girls got to the kitchen, Steph's concerns lifted some. Lilly wanted waffles, which was okay with the rest of them. Lilly talked a hundred miles an hour, mostly about decorating the tree this morning. Steph saw a special twinkle in Lilly's eyes, the one of a small child at Christmas. She missed that.

Steph looked at Kelly, "Your uncle said Lucky is fine, so you don't have to rush out."

"Thanks, Mom." Kelly wanted to ask about the storm but didn't quite know how to go about it, how to bring the subject up without alarming Susan.

As they all sat at the island eating breakfast, Steph decided telling Susan about the approaching storm couldn't wait any longer.

Kelly sat listening, thinking, *Mom, you are leaving a whole bunch of stuff out, but you know what you are doing, I guess.*

Susan listened as Steph explained, but kept her eyes on her plate.

"So technically," Steph said with a positive tone, "we are all going to be fine."

Lilly had listened intently. "Steph, how is Santa—"

Steph stopped her, "Lilly, Santa is so magical that he can fly those reindeer right through the storm that is coming."

"Won't they get real cold and even lost in the storm?" she asked with a sad look on her face.

"No, sweetie," Steph said, "Christmas magic is stronger than anything!"

Lilly looked at Kelly, who was smiling and nodding her head yes.

Lilly still wasn't sure. She looked toward her mom. Susan smiled and said, "Yes, that's exactly right, baby."

Lilly slowly started smiling. "Okay, but I think we need to put out extra cookies for Santa, because his work is going to be harder in that old storm." Everyone broke out laughing,

Steph felt the tension in the air letting up some.

She made Kelly promise that they'd get the chores done and the tree decorated and then come straight back to the house. "And keep your cell phone on you. The snow is going to start coming down heavy by ten."

The girls started bundling up. "I promise, Mom."

Lilly screamed, "I promise too!"

A little while later, Susan went back up to her room. She texted Madge again, "Worst storm in years to hit tonight, we'll probably lose signal, so wishing you a Merry Christmas now. Don't worry, we'll be fine, Love Susan."

Chip and Rick drove slowly toward the lane entrance, "Chip, is there a story behind this entrance? It's pretty grand."

Chip laughed, "Yep, but then there's a story behind everything out here."

"Kelly said that exact same thing yesterday," Rick said, adding, "She told Lilly and me the story about Lucky."

Chip chuckled, "Yeah, that's a good one." Then, with a softness to his voice, he added, "We get to lay claim to a great past."

Rick smiled. "Okay then, tell me, I'm all ears, and you can start with these," he pointed to the rock columns that stood guard to the ranch entrance.

Chip laughed heartily. "Okay, you asked for it. These rock columns were put up by my great-granddad when my dad was a boy."

"This rock work is beautiful," Rick said.

"This is the same rock that the steps to the cabin are made of and also the rock on the main fireplace in the kitchen. It was all brought down from Yellowstone before it was designated as a national park."

"What year?" Rick asked.

"1914, the rock was gathered up and hauled out before that year, even though it wasn't used for a few years, just sat here in a big pile. It's a combination of granite and volcanic rock and the only place it is found is in Yellowstone."

Rick jumped in, "Making it rare and valuable to be found privately."

Chip didn't say anything, but his face held a huge grin of pride.

"How tall are they? Looks at least thirteen to fourteen feet," Rick said as he studied the columns that they had just pulled up next to. Chip stopped the truck right behind the ironwork while they talked about it.

"Right at fourteen feet, but needed to be taller," Chip answered.

"Okay, but that arch isn't as old, right?" Rick questioned.

"You're right, it's not original. The first arch was pine and had the words Kahler Ranch, hand carved in the wood."

"What happened to it?" Rick asked.

"When I was a kid, we had a bad thunderstorm come through, bringing hundred mph winds with it." Chip continued, "It can blow pretty hard up here."

"Tornado?" Rick asked.

"No, straight line winds. I remember my granddad being real upset. He had all of us out there picking up all the pieces of the shattered wood. We took it all back to the old barn. My dad pieced it back together best he could. Granddad wanted it to have a place of honor, so my dad hung it above the double doors of the old barn, where Lucky is; that's the original barn on the ranch. I'll show you."

They slowly started driving down the road, still deep in conservation.

"My dad drew up plans and took them to Cody, to a local guy, and had this iron work done. It was a birthday present for Granddad. Turned out nice. I'm trying not to brag, but it's one of the nicest entrances in these parts."

The rock columns were square, probably four by four feet. The iron crossbar contained the words "Kahler Ranch" in capital letters. They were probably ten inches in height and welded above the cross bar. On top each column, an iron silhouette sat centered. On the left was the Angus bull, on the right was a Quarter horse. Then on the front of each column, about ten feet high, sat two iron letters—KR; the top left of the R was welded to the right leg of the K, offsetting the two letters.

"Do you ever have a problem with, maybe, a truck too tall getting under?" Rick asked.

"Yep, every once in a while we've let air out of tires to lower the load and we've unloaded the top layers of hay bales, so the load could get under," Chip replied, adding, "Where there's a will, there's a way."

Rick added, "That's right!"

Chip smiled. "I guess back in the early 1900s, they couldn't imagine that the future would include big rig trucks."

The men were enjoying their back and forth. "Never crossed their minds," Rick added, laughing.

Chip was thinking as he started driving down the road, *What else can I tell him about?*

"What is the KR?" Rick asked while taking in the landscape view.

"That's our brand. Each ranch has its own brand. They are all recorded with the state. It's considered a legal identification. All of our cattle are branded. Some ranches brand their horses too but we don't. In years past, it was done with a hot branding iron which burned the brand into it, scarring the hide."

Images of the Old West branding cattle came to Rick's mind.

"Now it's done with a freeze brand, not near as cruel. This one quick-freezes the hide, turning it white. Cattle from different ranches are all turned out on open range in the spring. Then in the fall, all the ranchers get together and have a big gather, meaning roundup—"

Rick jumped in, "A cattle roundup like in the movies." He smiled.

Chip grinned, "You got it. Then they are separated into different pens according to the brand."

"How do you know which calves go with which cows?" Rick asked.

"We use special panels that have openings large enough for the calves to fit through. Most of the time the calves stay close to their mommas, following the cows in. We try and tag all the calves when they are born, that helps a lot. We also don't rush things. If they need a couple days to pair back up again, we give it to them, then, everyone claims their cattle. Works well for everyone."

The morning sky was slowly lighting up from the east. "See how the sky looks like it has a blanket over it? That's called a snow sky, and the sunrise is very red; that's a bad sign." Chip felt himself on edge. "Sure wish I could shake this feeling," he hadn't realized he had said the words out loud.

"You okay, Chip?" Rick asked.

He chuckled, "Yeah sure. This storm has me spooked some, that's all. I'm fine. What were we talking about?"

Rick laughed. "The stormy sky!" Rick turned sideways in his seat so he could look at Chip while they talked, "Okay, let's talk Indians. Are they still relevant in the area?"

"Yes," Chip said, "Shoshone to the west, Cheyenne to the east, and Crow to the north. Probably the most active reservation is that of the Crow. It sits just across the border in Montana. This generation is probably pretty mixed up by now." Chip added, "But years ago the tribes stayed separated."

Chip looked at Rick, "My best friend growing up was an Indian."

"What was his name?" Rick's voice was full of excitement.

Chip smiled slightly as he said, "Andrew Hawk Yellowdog. We called him Hawk."

"Wow." Rick's imagination was running wild, wondering what it was like to have an Indian friend as a kid. A few minutes later, he whispered, "The Lone Ranger and Tonto," to himself.

"What?" Chip said, looking at Rick.

"Oh, nothing, just thinking that had to have been just the best childhood."

The two men drove a short distance in silence. Rick was looking out the side window. The lighter the sky got, the stormier it looked to Chip, but the gray still looked peaceful to Rick. Everything out here looked that way to him.

Without turning from the view, Rick asked, "Chip, is there any mining going on up in these parts?"

"Naw," Chip thought quickly. He didn't know much about mining. "Oh, there's always a stray dreamer panning the creeks on BLM land but never with much luck. You gotta go south some, to Colorado, then high up to find gold, or South Dakota, the Black

Hills. They're still mining commercially there. The small guys are bringing out some but they are working hard for it."

Chip was silent as he thought, "If I'm going to gamble with pay dirt, I want mine growing grass on top of it."

Rick laughed, still watching the scenery on his right. "I guess everything in life is a gamble."

Chip thought about Rick's statement, then said, "There's a lot of things in my life I'm not willing to gamble with."

This time, Rick looked at him, but had no comment.

Chip slowed down at the gate. Rick jumped out, unhooking chains, and opened the gate.

Rick laughed to himself, "I'm working on a ranch!"

The cattle were all fine, which eased Chip's concern. Looking them over he said, "You're all on your own, girls. I'll pray you stay safe."

Rick looked at him but didn't say anything.

Before getting back in the truck, Chip stopped and looked up, taking in the clouds for a few seconds. They still didn't feel right, but he couldn't put his finger on it.

"Something wrong?" Rick asked for the second time today.

"I don't know," Chip said, still looking at the sky. Then he asked Rick, "Do you care to drive? I'd like to chain the gates myself."

Rick smiled, relieved of the responsibility of chaining the gates properly and at the same time, loving the opportunity to drive the new pickup. He'd never been behind the wheel of a truck before.

"Sure thing!" Rick said happily.

Chip decided to let Rick drive back to the ranch, seeing the enjoyment on the man's face.

Chip was still trying to think of something interesting about the area to tell Rick, when he said, "Can I ask you another question?"

"Sure," Chip replied.

"Okay good. Isn't there a phrase that's used to describe land that has been in a family for years, the place that they all started out at? Hope I said that right," Rick sounded apologetic.

"You mean homeplace, Rick?'

"Yeah, that's it. I like the sound of the words. We don't have much of that sort of thing in the big city. Hard to lay claim on an apartment; not a whole lot to pass on down to your kid." Rick's voice had a sad ring to it, a sound of missing or regret. Chip didn't comment, leaving Rick to his thoughts.

A thought ran quickly through Chip's mind: there's a deeper side to Rick than the guy sitting here, a sad side.

The topic that Rick brought up warmed Chip's heart. "This country out here prides itself on the long-standing ownership of this land. Generations of families sweat their blood to make sure it could be passed down," Chip hesitated, then added, "and hoped their children would want to do the same."

"Our ranch sits kinda in the middle to north part of the state. The Big Horn Mountains sit to the east, with the Owl Creek Mountains on our west; they are a subrange of the Rocky Mountains. The highest peak around here is 9,865 feet."

"Wow," Rick said, "this is so interesting. How high is the ranch, Chip?'

"It's right at 5,900 feet, can make it a little tough to breathe if you aren't used to it," Chip said.

Rick laughed, "Yes that's for sure. I thought I was really out of shape, cause I couldn't breathe when we first got here."

Chip continued, "We sit right in the center, where the Big Horn Basin and the Shoshone Basin come together. So our weather comes right down a barrel between the ranges."

"Is this what this big one is going to do?" Rick asked.

"Yep," Chip said without either one looking at each other.

Rick didn't want Chip to think he was worried about the coming storm, so he kept asking questions not related to the storm, "I hear you have some big fancy parks out here?"

Chip grinned, turning his head to look at Rick. "Yep, the grand dam of them all, Yellowstone; she's worth seeing," he hesitated, adding, "in the summertime!"

They were almost back to the ranch. Rick wanted to ask Chip something personal, about the ranch basically, but didn't know how to go about it.

Chip picked up on Rick's silence and concern on his face. "What are you thinking?"

Rick kept looking straight ahead. "Okay, here it goes, but you can tell me to mind my own business, if you want."

Chip chuckled with humor, "What?"

"Yesterday, you said something about bad years. Can I ask what you meant by that?" Rick asked.

Chip started trying to break down the problems of ranching so a layman could understand, "There's a great deal of investment. The worst is the financial. Basically we can weather all the other things, but when the equipment needs repairing or replacing, we take a big blow. Ag equipment prices have risen three hundred percent in the last ten years, while we still get paid the same for our cattle as we did years back."

Rick listened while he drove.

"Couple years ago I purchased a new large square baler—I stole it," Chip said.

"How much?" Rick asked.

"$65,000."

Rick whistled.

Chip went on, "I can remember telling Steph and Dad at dinner one night, right after I bought it, what a good deal it had been." Chip's voice took on a sad note, "I went on to explain to them that the good deal was at the expense of another rancher. I attended a ranch equipment sale in Colorado. This was a foreclosure sale."

Rick listened, realizing that Chip's words were coming from his heart.

"This wasn't the way I wanted a good deal, at someone else's expense." Chip took a deep breath and let it out slowly. "Ranching is a gamble, a vicious circle. You need equipment to get the crops in the ground then out again. The crops feed the stock, the stock is sold, that money pays the bills. Then let's add to the financial mess, the two things that make or break ranching."

Rick looked at Chip, "Let me guess, rain and prices."

"You got it, my friend!" Chip said solemnly.

"And which one has been short the last few years?" Rick asked.

Chip answered with one word, "Both."

After a few seconds, Chip started talking again, trying to have more optimism in his voice. "We are used to hard times. They had them in the past and we'll have them in the future. We'll do the best we can, that's all we can do. We can only control so much." There was a lot that Chip left out, which he chose not to tell Rick.

Rick laughed. "Now you are sounding like the stock market!"

"Oh, don't get me started on that," Chip said with only half a laugh. "On the positive side, our diversification helps a lot. Got eggs in a lot of baskets."

A few snowflakes were floating in the air, the headlights were catching them. "It's starting to snow," Rick said calmly.

Chip could fell a slow roll in his stomach, "She's coming."

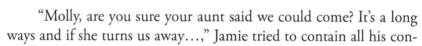

"Molly, are you sure your aunt said we could come? It's a long ways and if she turns us away…," Jamie tried to contain all his concerns and keep them from coming out in his voice.

Thoughts of his mother's rejection this morning and then Molly's mother physically kicking her out stung and were still very fresh on his mind. He looked at her, with worry in his eyes.

"Jamie, she said, 'Come,' and I know my aunt, she won't let us down. She said she would have come and got us but my uncle is ill. She said she could come next week. I told her we couldn't wait."

They stood on the edge of the road, in front of the house, where she had lived with her mother. The scene a few minutes ago was one that either he or Molly would never forget.

Her mom had stood in the open doorway, with a can of beer in her hand and a cigarette in her mouth. She took it out and blew smoke into Molly's face and started screaming, "Get out. I'm not paying to feed you and your worthless boyfriend and especially his worthless brat baby. I don't want it in my house!" Then she added, "I'm done!"

Next thing Molly knew, her mother was slamming the door in her face. It took every bit of strength the young girl had to raise her head up proudly and turn away. She took a deep breath and let it out slowly as she wiped a stray tear away and walked back to the road where Jamie was waiting.

"Let's go," she said.

Jamie took her backpack. "This sure isn't much for possession," he thought, cramming it behind the seat. He hadn't been looking forward to this day, though he knew it was coming. "Merry Christmas to us," he whispered, feeling like the devil himself was sitting on his shoulder laughing.

Brian and Colt walked in the back door. Brian hollered at Brenda, "Just a minute, I'm coming," she said, walking toward the mud room on the back of the farmhouse. "What's up?" she asked.

"Heifers went through the southeast fence. We're going out and try to find them and get them moved to a safe place to weather this storm," he hesitated, then added, "if they haven't gone too far."

"Calm down, I'll come along to help," she said, as she started pulling on her bib overalls.

"Are you sure? It's getting bad out," Brian stated.

"Six eyes are better than four," she smiled at her tall lanky husband.

"Colt, grab my bag, please, while you are in there." Colt had headed through the house to get a better knit cap.

"You really don't need it," Brian told her.

Instantly, Brenda panicked, though she didn't know why. "That's okay, it's going anyhow." She had cleaned it out last night and repacked it with some unusual items, not things she normally kept it filled with. She remembered the funny gut feeling she had, but in the end, she listened to it.

"Who you ridin', Mom?" Colt asked.

"Sugar Babe," she answered.

"I'll go saddle her," Colt hollered as he walked out the door.

"Brian, the warnings up are worse. We don't have much time," Brenda said with concern in her voice.

"Then we'd better ride. Are you ready?" Brian asked bluntly. He opened the back door and the dogs ran out, planning to go along as usual. A panic feeling washed over him. "No come, now," he knelt down and petted each one as they reacted to his command, then quickly put them back in the house. Brian gave the door an extra pull to make sure it was secure so they couldn't get out and try to follow.

Colt held three sets of reins, waiting for his parents. When Brian took his reins he stopped and looked up, staring, as if looking or listening for something.

"What's the matter, Brian?" Brenda asked, tying her medical bag onto the side of her saddle.

"I'm not sure," he turned around, looking behind himself. "Something isn't right, but I don't know," he shook his head as to clear it. "Let's head out. The sooner we find them, the better. We don't need to be out in this any longer than necessary."

Kelly and Lilly stepped back to look at the tree. Kelly had plugged the lights in; they twinkled in all different colors. They finished the look of the tree with tinsel. Lilly had never seen the shiny thin strands before. Kelly had laughed at her, showing her how to lay them on the branches, one by one.

"Oh, it's so beautiful. It's the prettiest tree I've ever had," Lilly said with a bubbly voice.

Kelly broke out laughing, saying, "I bet you say that every year."

"Well, maybe," Lilly smiled.

"We need to get to the house," Kelly said, "the snow is really coming down now."

"Can we leave the lights on, please, Kelly," Lilly begged.

"I think so," she said, as she double-checked the area around the plug-in. "If Mom thinks it's unsafe, I can come back out and unplug them."

"Can we play in the snow, in front of the cabin, Kelly?"

"Yep, but let's go tell our moms that we are back so they don't worry."

"Okay, bye, little tree, Merry Christmas Eve day. See you later," Lilly said as Kelly dragged her out the door.

Parts of the plan were in the first stages of being played out. One player was scared to death. Everything in his being said, "Don't do this!" Yet he continued forward. He was not in control on this Christmas Eve.

"Bethlehem is almost seventy miles away, but it might as well be a hundred and seventy miles. What am I thinking?" Jamie said to himself as he started the truck up.

Nothing seemed to have been working in Jamie's favor for a while now. He needed time more than anything. The truck had major fuel problems and so far, nothing he had done had helped. He couldn't do any more to the truck until he got paid and now, that wasn't happening until after Christmas. Molly's mother's timeline for Molly to get out was really messing him up, he thought, and his head told him there was nothing he could do about it. He had tried talking to Mrs. Thomas, but that didn't go very well, and now, the colder it got, the worse his truck was running. Gramps had sent him part of the money he needed, and by using the rest of his savings, he was able to replace the fuel pump, but it hadn't solved the problem. The next thing to do was drop the fuel tank and clean it out, hopefully getting rid of any water that was in it, solving the freezing fuel line problem. He'd told his gramps about the lines and he agreed, "You gotta drop that tank, Jamie Boy. Wish I was there to help you."

Jamie hadn't told his gramps about the trouble Molly's mom was causing. Jamie knew the old man would worry. He loved Jamie, but Jamie knew there wasn't any more he could do to help from afar.

The weight of Jamie's problems right now was his to carry alone, the best he could.

Jamie knew he needed to pray. He needed all the help he could get, but he wasn't sure if He was listening. He had a feeling there was a lot more in his life he should be doing to get in the good graces of God.

The talk at the gas station had been about the storm all week. The weather was definitely not on his side. He had put the chains on his tires right after Molly called this morning. When he stopped to fill up with fuel, he added double additive to the gas tank. It was used to help "dry" the gas out and keep the lines from freezing in the severe cold, he hoped. He had found an empty five-gallon gas can in his mom's garage this morning and had filled it up with gas and added the additive. He felt better knowing he'd have a little extra fuel with him. He had been going over the situation in his mind all morning. The thought of dumping Molly was not an option—he'd die first. Then he winced at the thought of trying to get to Bethlehem in a blizzard. "I just might!"

"Okay, let's get serious. Shane to Bethlehem is exactly sixty-seven miles, plus eight miles to Aunt Jane's place, total of seventy-five miles. A full tank of gas and seventy dollars in my wallet, pretty sad," he said to himself out loud, "but I don't have a choice. Molly wants to leave."

Molly got settled and turned on the radio. The stations were all giving out warnings on the approaching weather, running updated information continually. She quickly looked at Jamie she knew he didn't want to do this.

"I know there's a bad storm coming; we've just got to out run it!" she smiled at him. At this moment, she looked very immature, homeless, and scared.

"Seriously, Molly, this one can't be outrun. We'll just do the best we can and hope it's good enough," he said. Molly noticed the new tone to his voice, one she had never heard before, one of seriousness mixed with fear; it scared her.

She patted his leg and said, "We'll be fine, I know it!" She held her head high, as a single tear slipped down her face and a pain raked through her back.

Jamie swallowed hard, thinking, *She doesn't know about the gas lines.* He had decided to keep the information to himself, for the time being. A moment later, he saw her wince and try to get more comfortable. She has enough to worry about right now, he thought. "Please, baby, hold on."

He had done everything he could to talk himself out of this trip. He wanted to curse her mother, but her mother didn't create this situation, he did—so deal with it. He actually felt a little better when he was hard on himself.

A new update on the storm came over the radio. Jamie leaned over and turned it up. "Blizzard conditions by noon, heavy snow, two to four inches per hour, extreme drifting, gusts of forty-five to sixty mph with sustained winds of thirty-five to forty mph." Warnings to stay off the roads, now they were talking about the drifting snow again. Snow plows would not be out after noon. No emergency equipment either, and steadily dropping temperatures, down to zero by nightfall. Jamie felt like he was driving into the lion's mouth and there was nothing he could do about it. Thoughts screamed in his head, "Turn around, turn around!"

"Good old Owl Creek Valley," he said, heartily. "We sit between two ranges with nothing to stop that Canadian wind, just barrels on down!"

Molly sat in silence, listening. There were two sounds, the moaning of chained tires rolling on the frozen road and the windshield wipers. She wished Jamie would talk to her.

Her hand was resting on Jamie's thigh. Suddenly she gripped his leg a little harder as a pain hit. She didn't say anything but he knew he needed to drive as fast as he safely could for more than one reason, Molly's discomfort, and as importantly, to keep the additive going through the fuel lines. He was down to twenty mph. The conditions seemed to worsen with every mile. They didn't talk. Jamie hoped that Molly was praying, but he didn't ask her.

Jamie looked at the mileage, then his watch. They had been driving for almost an hour but had only gone around fifteen miles or so. His heart rate sped up. "Don't panic."

He kept telling himself to stay positive and to set his mind on closer sights right now, one mile at a time. "If we can just get to Bethlehem, to the town—even the outskirts."

"Molly honey, I'm sorry I'm not talking, but I've got to watch what I'm doing," he told her. He needed to concentrate on his driving. If he got too close to the side of the road, a drift could grab him and pull the truck into it. He knew he couldn't let that happen.

Molly put her hands on her stomach. "I know, Jamie, it's okay. The baby is really active," she told him. Her lower back was aching worse but she blamed it on the truck seat. She was trying hard not to think about anything. Maybe it would all go away.

They started out riding due south of the house and the barns, traveling with the storm made it a little easier on their eyes. The problem was, cattle moved with the storm too, walking until a fence stopped them.

Brian was very anxious to find the fifty bred heifers. The ranch had a lot of money tied up in the group.

After riding for at least an hour, they found the fence down.

"Okay, which way, Brian?" Brenda hollered.

Now it was Brian's turn to use his "cow sense." In a very loud voice, so he could be heard over the wind, he said, "If I were a cow, I would…" He left the end of the sentence blank as he thought.

Finally he said, "Let's turn west here and head for the Johnson Creek gully. That's a good shelter and they may hold up there."

They rode for another forty-five minutes before they spotted the heifers, right where Brian hoped they'd be. Hollering again, he said, "They'll be fine here." Looking around he saw the bale rings were still full from late summer. It wasn't the best feed, but it would get them through the storm. Cattle would eat snow when they got thirsty, so Brian wasn't worried about water. Then he said, "Let's ride down to the gate, south of here, to make sure it's closed and chained," quickly adding, "don't need them going any further."

The windshield wipers were having a hard time keeping up with the amount of snow that was coming down now. Jamie was stopping way too often to clean them off. The heater and defroster also seemed to be struggling. He prayed that they would keep working.

"Are you warm enough?" Jamie asked Molly.

She lied to him when she replied, "Yes."

Molly was wishing there was something to do, or at least look at. She needed something to help take her mind off the pain she was in.

Eleven fifty, ten more miles done. The snow was coming down really hard now. The roads didn't seem too bad, he thought. The six inches or so of snow cover helped keep them from being slick. He silently wished they would come up behind a snowplow, more for the company than anything. Miles and miles of fresh covered roads without tire tracks to follow left you with an eerie, lonely feeling. "We shouldn't to be out here either," he whispered.

A voice in his head laughed uncontrollably.

He felt the truck hesitate. "Oh no," he thought. He pushed the gas pedal a little harder. He caught himself holding his breath. "Breathe," he told himself. The next minute or two felt like a lifetime.

"Okay, it's leveled off, breathe," he was coaching himself.

"I don't need a coach, I need a guardian angel, one that can keep this truck running," he whispered too loud. He looked over at Molly, but she hadn't heard him.

The truck bucked a couple more times. This time Molly felt it. She looked at Jamie and saw the serious look on his face. She wanted to sound calm but she needed to ask. "What was that?"

He looked at her and said, "The truck gas lines are freezing up. It's starving for gas!"

"Can you—" He stopped her mid-sentence.

"No, I can't," he screamed at her in too loud a voice.

Instantly he said he was sorry, over and over. Molly leaned over and kissed him on the cheek, without saying anything.

Jamie suddenly remembered what his gramps had told him, "Play with the gas pedal, Sunny Boy. Hit it hard, then let up, do it a couple times." Gramps had said it might help clear the blockage. It helped, Jamie whispered, "Thanks, Grandpa!"

The truck managed to keep going, close to another hour. If Jamie's figures were correct, they had gone close to thirty miles, at least he hoped it was that many.

"Almost halfway there. Please, Lord, help us make it."

It was getting late morning when they came up on the open gate. "Good call, Dad," Colt hollered, adding, "Dad, if we go through the gate to get to the creek, we can ride back that way; it's shorter some."

A few moments lapsed as Brian thought, "You're right, son, let's do it."

They rode through, stopping while Brian climbed down and chained the gate at the top and bottom. The wind was worse. The white stuff coming down was a combination of snow and ice pellets, making it feel like BBs were hitting you in the face.

Visibility was getting bad. With the snow falling so hard, it seemed like a whiteout, you wouldn't tell ground from sky. Brian couldn't remember it ever being this bad. They were needing to holler loud at each other to be heard over the wind.

"We've got to move fast, but be careful. Basically give your horse its head so they can keep their footing, and stay close, real easy to lose each other right now," Brian told his wife and son.

Brenda was beginning to get real cold but so far had stayed dry. She had bought Brian new insulated boots but he hadn't put them on this morning, opting for his comfortable old pair. His feet were now aching with the cold.

Lilly took to the snow like a duck to water. The two girls had spent a couple of hours out in the yard playing in the snow, mostly building snowmen. They were close to the cabin, staying on the side that was blocked from the wind and were basically staying comfortable. Lilly giggled and talked nonstop, which was being referred to now as "Lilly style" by the others.

Steph had brought out scarves, hats, a handful of different sized buttons, and of course, carrots for the girls to use. They had built two snowmen, one being bigger than the other. Kelly was waiting on Lilly to say who they were. Eventually she said the little one was her and the bigger one was Kelly.

While the girls were outside, Steph and Susan had placed all the gifts under the tree except for the ones Santa would bring, then Susan bundled up and grabbed her camera.

"Rick will kill me if I don't get pictures of her," she smiled happily.

Steph let out a long breath. Finally, feeling like she could check, get Susan to relax off the to-do list.

"Mommy, Mommy, look, it's me and Kelly!" Lilly screamed when Susan walked out to where they were.

About twenty minutes later, both moms decided the girls had been out long enough and spent more than a few minutes trying to convince them to come in.

Steph had a new job for them to start on. The sugar cookies needed frosting and decorating, or they wouldn't look very Christmas-y, she had told them.

The pies were baked and the sauce was simmering real low. The cabin smelled wonderful. When Susan walked back into the kitchen area, she glanced around, taking in the fireplace, the Christmas tree, and all of the other decorations. She looked Steph's way and said, "It's all so"—she thought for the perfect words—"Christmas cozy!"

Steph got emotional, hearing the phrase. "Thank you, Susan, that really means a lot to me."

Christmas and the storm were both headed their way and nothing could stop either one of them.

Ken and Chip stayed busy all morning and part of the afternoon, doing last-minute chores, especially over at the cattle sheds. Rick had tagged along and actually ended up being a lot of help. Ken headed out to double-check paddock gates and said he'd meet them back at the horse barn. Chip and Rick jumped on the four-wheeler and stopped at the equipment barn. Chip wanted to make sure heaters were all plugged in and the portable battery charger had a full charge on it. They filled the wood furnace to max. Chip looked satisfied, so they headed to the horse barn and started chores. Chip checked outside gates and stall doors. Since the moneymaking aisle was on the north side, he didn't want any of those doors blowing open.

Rick filled hay feeders. He liked the work, he liked the smell, he liked everything about this life, even the trials of a bad winter storm.

As they headed back toward the cabin, Chip held back. "Rick, you go ahead. I need to double-check something with Ken before I come in."

Rick waved and kept going.

Ken had walked up and heard the words Chip said to Rick. "What?"

"Oh, that was just an excuse, wanna ask you something," Chip said seriously.

"What?"

"Remember when we were in Afghanistan, remember the smell that got in the air when something bad was coming down," Chip looked Ken in the eye.

Ken felt goose bumps climbing up his neck.

Before Ken could answer, Chip said, "Can't you smell it now or feel it?"

Ken held his breath as he said, "Yes, I can. I don't know what it is or what it means. This storm is different, like it has a mind of its own, a scary one!"

They both looked to the darkening sky. She had a menacing look that had swept over quickly. She looked angry, and they both had a feeling that she had left all her mercy some place way north of them in Canada.

Ken laid a hand on Chip's shoulder, saying, "Keep alert, Sergeant."

Ken checked his thought list one more time. Extra attention needed to be paid to Chip for the duration of the storm. The scenario would be prime for his trip-outs.

Jamie had spent his entire life, all of seventeen years, in the high plains, here in Wyoming, when he was small, then being raised by his grandfather in South Dakota. He had no memories of a winter storm this bad, but then, he'd never been out in the middle of one like this before. Most people hadn't. They sat in their homes and watched its wrath from the warm side of a glass window. Even ranchers with livestock got them taken care of before it hit, so they were back in the safety of their homes.

Two words came to Jamie's mind now: white hell.

The truck seemed to be getting worse. The feeling was of running out of gas, which they basically were. Working the gas pedal didn't seem to be helping anymore.

"It's going to quit any second," Jamie said out loud. He gripped the wheel harder now, the words "please, please, please" going over and over in his mind.

His eyes hurt from the strain of looking into the stark whiteness. He thought he saw something up ahead on the right, so he slowed down. On the right side of the road was a sign, on top of a post. It was hard to read being partially covered with snow. He stopped as close as he could and put the truck in neutral so he could keep the engine revved up.

"Molly, I need you to get out and see what that sign says, please, honey," his voice begged. Molly nodded to him but stayed quiet. She slowly climbed out of the truck, doing the best she could to waddle into the snow drift. She wiped the sign with her gloved hand, "Jamison Ranch-one mile," with an arrow pointing to the right. Jamie finally made out the form of a lane to the right, up ahead about twenty yards.

Molly climbed back in the truck. Jamie was laughing. He leaned over and kissed the side of her head, "We're going to be okay!" He slowly crept up to what he decided was the lane and turned in.

Molly's voice was frantic, "What are you doing!"

At the same time, the engine started stalling, lurching back and forth as it was starved of fuel. Finally, it coasted to as stop. Molly was silent, not being sure of what Jamie's next reaction would be. Jamie guided the truck to a stop as far to the right as he could, then turned and looked at Molly.

"This is as far as we are going to get in this truck," Jamie said with defeat in his voice, "but there's help up ahead." Jamie put the flashers on and grabbed another blanket from behind the seat. Very calmly now and in charge he said, "Cover up and try to stay warm. I'm going to walk up to the house—it's not far—and get help." He leaned over and kissed her again, then left.

He pulled his knit cap down low and tucked his head. The snow was a foot deep and made walking hard, but he moved as fast as he could, saying, "Thank You, Lord," over and over and over, out loud.

It seemed like they had been riding a long time. The sky was darkening from the storm, making it hard to judge time. Brian became uneasy. "We should have come out by now." Then panic set in. He turned in his saddle and looked in a circle. He didn't know where they were; he didn't recognize any of the snow-covered landmarks. He wiped his face with his arm and said, "I'm lost, we're lost, we should have been riding north and slightly east, but..." He hesitated as he scanned his eyes around again.

"Colt, where are we, son?" A few moments later, he stated," I guess I've gotten us lost. Do either of you have any idea where we are, Colt?"

Colt hadn't said anything yet. He wasn't sure. He kept turning, looking.

Brenda wasn't the panicking type. "Okay, Brian. Which way, Colt?"

When neither one responded, she added, "We are going to come out somewhere."

"If we don't freeze to death first," Colt said, the words slipping out of the sixteen-year-old's mouth loud enough for his parents to hear.

"That's enough, Colt!" Brenda replied.

He put his head down and said, "Sorry, Mom."

Brenda spoke up, "Let's keep riding this way, but watch hard for any landmarks. Surely we'll recognize something, be careful."

The girls were back in warming up by the fireplace, hot chocolate in hand, telling their moms about the snowmen adventure.

The three men had been back in for a while, sandwiches ate, coffee in hand, all three listening to the weatherman on TV.

Susan had complained that Rick smelled when he walked back in. Steph playfully walked over to him, "Yep, he's been at the cattle barn."

"My gosh, Rick, go take a shower and change your clothes!" Susan demanded of him.

"Oh, Sue, he's fine. We all love the smell," Steph said with a smile.

Rick laughed, "I'll change my clothes, that should help," smiling at Susan as he walked off.

Ken thought he could relax awhile, then he planned to head out again. Most of his list was checked off, but he still had some Santa duties to take care of. He also had to make a decision on Lucky. He'd check her later. The longhorn was his deciding factor on where he'd sleep tonight.

Jamie thought he had been walking about fifteen minutes when he saw the slight outline of a set of buildings, though he couldn't see any lights on. It was getting near late afternoon, he thought. The day was so gray and the sky was so menacing that he had a hard time guessing the time. His heart started pounding harder as he realized he was looking at a house on his left. He climbed the steps to the porch and pounded on the door. He waited a short time, then looked in the window. "No one's home," he said out loud. The rooms looked dark. He tried the door; it was locked. He turned around, thinking, hoping to see a barn, then he saw an outline.

The door at the end of the barn was starting to drift in, so it took him a few minutes to kick enough snow out of the way so he could pull the door open.

As he walked in, he immediately felt the warmth of the wood stove. The fire was in good shape, still having plenty of wood in it, but without thinking, he added more wood. He pulled his snow-covered gloves off and laid them on the stove top. Next he rubbed his hands together as he looked around the barn.

A shop light over the workbench had been left on. A note was tacked on the wall. He walked over to read it, "Thanks, Ken, appreciate you checking on the cattle. We'll be back a couple of days after Christmas. If you need me, here's my cell number." A phone number followed, then it was signed "Joe."

"Okay, what now," he thought, "I'm on my own."

He thought about going back after Molly and breaking into the house. At least they'd have shelter and heat, but a voice in his head said, "You need help—Molly needs help."

He thought about the house again, the words "it's not right" came from deep down inside him. He sighed and looked around again, this time seeing the Kawasaki side by side sitting in the center of the barn. It was set up for winter, with a canvas cab, complete with sides and a windshield. He looked inside, finding the keys in the ignition. His heart leaped.

It was like someone was standing behind him, giving him his thoughts. "No, it wouldn't be stealing," he told himself. He was only borrowing it for Molly and the baby. Right at the moment, he was convinced no one would fault him in his decision.

He started moving quickly now, knowing exactly what he needed to do. He was calm.

He found a shovel and threw it in the back, then his eyes spotted two gas cans. He held his breath until he picked them up. He started laughing. They were both full. He secured them in the back with a small rope he found. His heart was racing. He started it up, to let it warm up while he continued to look around. He found a medicine cabinet hanging on the wall. Inside were a couple of wool blankets and flares plus a couple of hand warmers. He would save those for Molly. Next, he needed to move all the snow in front of the double doors so he could get it out. Words repeated themselves over and over, in his head, "Thank You, Lord. Thank You, Lord."

When he went back in, he looked around one last time. When his eyes reached the workbench, he said, "One more thing." Walking up, he look for something to write on. Finding a pad and pen, he wrote down Joe's name and phone number on a piece of paper and put it deep in his pocket, then he wrote another note, explaining why he...borrowed the side by side. He signed his name and tacked it on top of the note that was left for Ken.

He was talking to himself now as he sat down on the seat, "There's still a long ways to go. There's still a lot of storm out there. Lord, we can't make it without You!" He took a deep breath and let it out slowly, gaining in determination.

"I guess I'd better get going." Then he hollered, so the Lord could hear him above the storm, "Lord, please guide me, Amen."

Molly was trying to stay calm, talking to the baby, trying to convince herself that everything would be okay. The truck was totally covered with snow and it gave her the feeling of being buried alive. She prayed that the blinkers were still visible so Jamie could find her. She turned the wipers on so she could watch for Jamie. She was beginning to panic. Then, a few seconds later, she saw lights coming down the lane. She patted her belly and laughed softly. A minute later, Jamie pulled the truck door open on her side. He was yelling so he could be heard over the sound of the wind.

"Grab your purse and come on," he said, pulling the blankets off her. He held her arm as he helped her get into the farm vehicle. When she was settled, he covered her up again, then he went back to the truck for her bag. He was moving fast now.

He ran around to the other side and jumped in, then continued down the lane toward the main road.

"Aren't we going to their house? This is the wrong way!" her voice was panicked.

"No, no one is home. The house is locked, I'd have to break in, and I'm not doing that!" He had more to say but she cut him off.

"Then how did you get this?" she said with a voice of concern. "It's stealing!" she added.

He took a deep breath, "No, it's borrowing. To get you and the baby to safety, I left a note and I have the phone number of the guy who owns it. I'll call him as soon as we get to Jane's."

Molly waited a few moments, wanting to cry. She said, "It's still stealing, Jamie!"

Jamie nodded his head, "Yes." He was too tired and worried to argue with her. He needed to concentrate on driving this thing. It would be harder to keep on the road, and he needed to get the feel of it. Moments later, he started talking again, feeling bad for his shortness with her, "This will sound crazy. It's like there was a voice in my head that told me to keep going."

"Your right, that's crazy!" Molly said in a stressed voice, but she was in too much pain to argue her point.

His watch said two twenty. The storm was steadily getting worse. He had it up to ten mph. It felt really unsafe going that fast. The winds had started gusting really hard, causing him keep a firm grip on the steering wheel.

"Molly, I need your help. Watch for any kind of lights, maybe we'll come across another ranch or entrance lane at least. I'm scared. It's still a long ways to town."

Just then a strong gust of wind hit them broadside. Jamie fought hard to hold it on the road. Molly had screamed, so he decided to slow down a little.

The side-by-side was a four-wheel drive and built for handling in different conditions, but Jamie lacked the experience he needed right now. The wind gusts were coming more frequent now, so his body reacted by staying tensed. The windshield wipers struggled with the heavy wet snow. Molly was quiet as she dealt with her back pain. She kept shifting in the seat.

Jamie was aware that she was uncomfortable, but all he could do was keep driving, do the best he could to keep them alive, and pray.

Susan sat at the island listening to the laughter. The girls were playing a board game on the coffee table, in front of the fire. Chip was showing Rick his arrowhead collection in the office off the kitchen. Susan looked around. "Steph?"

Steph turned to look at her. Susan's voice had sounded weird. "What is it, Susan?"

"What's that noise?" Susan asked.

Steph walked over toward the glass doors leading to the deck off the kitchen and listened.

"It's the wind, Susan." The howling was frightening, Steph admitted to herself.

Susan was showing some panic. She was counting heads. "Where's Ken?" she asked in a panic, sounding like she was ready to break into tears.

Steph walked over to Susan and put an arm around her shoulder. "He said he was going to the horse barn to check everyone and then check on Lucky before he comes back to the house." Looking directly in Susan's eyes, she said, "He's okay. He told me it was still light enough out. He could see the barns, so he'd be fine. Then he'll be in for the night. He's staying here with us."

She watched Susan to see if she comprehended what she said. Finally, Susan whispered, "Okay."

It was going on three o'clock. He still had some time before it got dark. Ken thought, "Better get these chores done while I can." He had talked to Chip a few minutes ago, then headed out to the horse barn.

The moment he walked out, he felt the heartbeat of the storm. He knew it was the barometric pressure. She was changing, and it would affect the animals. His plans involved doing chores, taking a shower while he could, and gathering up what he needed to sleep in the old barn. Steph thought he was staying in the cabin with all of them, but he had changed his mind. He had a funny feeling that Lucky would calve tonight, and she wasn't doing it by herself.

He enjoyed his work and some time alone, so he took his time. He had always preferred four-legged critters over the two-legged kind. He checked all the hay feeders again, letting the dogs go with him. When it came time to kennel Shiloh and Breeze, he sat and played with them for a while first, then decided to put them back in his apartment; they'd be happier there.

Walking back to his apartment with the dogs, on the north side of the barn, he could hear the roaring wind. He didn't let storms bother him. He didn't wish harm on any one, but he actually loved the strength that some storms contained. It was almost like they were a warning from the High, "Clean up your act, I'm still in charge."

This is the part of his personality that he tried to keep to himself.

"What else?" he thought. Now smiling, he said out loud, "Don't forget your Christmas, cowboy." He needed to grab all his gifts to take with him to the old barn. Years ago a family tradition had been born. Ken pretended to forget to take his Christmas gifts for everyone to the cabin, leaving them under the Christmas tree in the old barn. Kelly had grown up expecting this. He had a few extra gifts this year: leather riding gloves for Lilly, then there was a wooden box that contained three bottles of his homemade wine for Susan and Rick. He placed everything along with his bedding in a big green canvas bag so he could carry everything all at once to the old barn.

He checked his phone—no signal. He would have liked to have talked to Angie tonight even though they had exchanged gifts before she left for Vermont. "Merry Christmas, beautiful," he whispered.

He glanced out the window. He could still see the outline to the barn. "Good, I don't want to screw this night up by getting lost out there." He decided on a quick shower so he could get going.

The storm was getting a lot worse. Between the snowfall and the wind, it had cut Jamie's speed to five mph; he felt like he was crawling. Visibility had been zero for quite a while now and darkness was setting in. Jamie knew it would be even harder to see in the dark. The headlights reflected on the snowflakes, giving you the impression that they were coming straight at you, and that messed with your head.

They were both very cold. The heater was on full blast, but it didn't seem to make any difference. Molly had to constantly wipe the fog off the windows on her side so they could see the fence posts on the right. These were the only markers they had to follow. He was trying to judge his place on the road by watching the posts and trying to stay in what he thought was the right lane.

The voice in his head laughed at him again. *Why are you worried about the right lane? There's no one out here but you, stupid!*

The right side was getting deep in snow but was still manageable. Drifts were building against the fence on his left side and the road was filling in. It wouldn't be too long until the left lane was totally drifted in. He tried not to think about what the road would look like another twenty miles up the road.

Jamie heard a funny noise and looked over at Molly. She had her head down and her hands covering her face.

"Molly honey, are you crying?" Jamie asked in a gentle voice.

She looked at him with a scared look on her face and tears running down, "I don't feel good and my back hurts something awful." She let out a sob, "It hurts."

"I'm sorry, baby," he didn't know what else to say. He kept trying to figure the mileage in his head, but looking at nothing but white for so long was keeping his mind confused. He found it getting hard to think clearly. Suddenly, he started to panic. Is this what snow blindness is like? He was getting to the point that he couldn't distinguish the ground from the sky anymore, and now with it getting darker, he couldn't see the fence post clearly. The snow was covering the tops and far side of them, only leaving a part of the posts to rely on for guidance.

He was so tried, that and fear were starting to overwhelm the young man.

The wind suddenly brought him back to reality, hitting them hard on the right.

Jamie screamed loud, "Damn it, leave us alone!" He gripped the wheel hard. Molly grabbed the dash and held her breath. They both thought that this one was going to roll them. When it finally passed, the youth in him wanted to cry, but the man in him said, "Hold it together."

The devil on his shoulder laughed.

The snow was at least two feet deep. Now the horses were in trouble, struggling with each step they took. Before the snow had gotten so deep, they were able to high step through it. Now, out of energy, they were plodding through, like oxen breaking trail, too tired to raise their legs up. This way of travel would quickly strip the last of the energy out of them. All three riders were plainly aware of this.

The riders could feel their horses' lungs heaving, the cold air stinging with each breath they tried to take. Their heads were drooping lower and lower, unable to hold them up any longer against the wind.

The riders bent forward, trying to use the position to block the force of the wind from hitting them face on. When the hard gust hit from the north, the horses stopped in their tracts to brace themselves. It took all their physical strength to stay on their feet.

Brian was surprised by the fact that they hadn't given up and laid down. He kept talking to his gelding, even though he couldn't hear him over the wind. Brian was doing everything he could to transmit encouraging vibes to his horse. Horses were funny that way. If you were scared, they knew it. You being upset, upsets them. Brian's foot was getting worse. For a while the numbness had replaced the pain. Now it was back, throbbing hard. He questioned how long he could endure the pain, but then he didn't have a choice. He hadn't told Brenda about the frostbite; there was nothing she could do. He deemed it a small matter, considering they all might die tonight.

The whole time they had been driving, not one vehicle of any kind had come up on them. The radio had gone out at least an hour ago, leaving them totally alone now.

All Jamie had left inside of his mind and heart were short desperate prayers.

For the first time today, he was beginning to think that they were going to die.

Regardless of his trying to be hopeful, the negative thoughts seemed to be stronger. He was being honest with himself when he thought, "That road is going to be drifted in, at least two feet deep up ahead. It will stop us in our tracks, and we will die, all three of us, before anybody finds us. We are driving to our death." His mind said it's over, but his gut and heart said, "Keep praying to Jesus."

"Please help us, Jesus," the words came from his heart, loud and clear.

He had said it over and over in his mind, and now he whispered the words with his lips, over and over. Earlier, he had broken the silence between them by saying, "Molly, you need to pray."

She answered softly, "I have been, Jamie, all along."

Jamie smiled, but it was dark now, so she didn't see his face.

It was so dark. No moon, no stars, and the sky was blanketed with black hateful snow clouds.

All of a sudden, Jamie thought he saw a lightness in the sky, up ahead. Wiping the fog off his side window, he saw nothing but dark on his left side and the same when he looked right, but straight ahead...now he prayed that what he thought he saw was real and not his mind playing tricks.

His heart started beating a little faster. "Molly, does it look a little lighter up ahead?" she heard the hope in his voice.

She leaned into the windshield, wiping it hard with her glove, and then said, "I think so," unsure of what she was seeing.

Hope jumped into Jamie's heart. He sat up a little straighter and grabbed the wheel a little tighter.

As they kept driving slowly forward, the light seemed to get brighter. Jamie took a chance at hope. Laughing, he said, "We're going to be okay!"

"Okay guys, come help. These cookies aren't going to frost themselves." Steph had been trying to get this project finished all day, but here they sat plain, unfrosted, undecorated sugar cookies—so boring and beneath her quality, she thought with a slight laugh.

"Okay, we're coming." Lilly screamed, "Daddy, come help me."

"Chip, Rick, if you plan on eating them, you need to help," Steph hollered. "Here, put these aprons on so you stay clean." Lots of teasing went on, but finally, they were all around the table working on the cookies, except Steph and Susan; they were going to be the instructors.

Susan looked toward the front door, then at the kitchen clock. "I'll feel better when Ken gets back," she said, half smiling at Steph.

"He'll be here shortly." This time she memorized the time. He wasn't going to get much more before she sent Chip out after him.

Jamie was holding his breath as he drove. The light kept getting brighter and brighter. Within minutes they came up on an entrance, a ranch lane, with a light shining brightly from above the cross arch at the entrance. The light was brighter than any light he'd ever seen.

Jamie pulled to a stop as he turned into the lane. He was unable to look upward into the light. The two massive columns, one on each side of the entrance, held up the crossbar. The wording was snow covered. It looked like Christmas trees of different sizes were lined up next to the pipe fence as decoration. The wind had blown some of the snow off allowing them to wave in the wind. Red bows on the trees showed themselves every once in a while.

Jamie sat there, feeling like he was going to faint. He could feel his whole body collapsing, then a weird feeling rushed over him. He felt like someone was holding him from slipping.

Stress and fear had been responsible for keeping him going. Now he didn't know, he couldn't think.

Molly was crying and laughing at the same time. Slowly Jamie leaned toward Molly and pulled her to him. He buried his head in her neck and cried, letting it all out.

She talked softly, "Jamie, we still gotta find some place warm, maybe we'd better go."

Jamie straightened up, now grateful for the darkness in the cab that didn't let Molly see his tear-stained tired face.

"Yes, let's go." He looked around for a few moments, trying to get his bearing. The brightness reflected off the ground and the flood of snowflakes. He blinked his eyes and wiped them with his hand, waiting for them to focus.

Jamie looked ahead at the lane. "Lord, thank you for this lane light, this lifesaving lane light—Amen."

The wind had blown the snow off the center of the lane, allowing the dirt on the lane to show through, showing them the way. The snow was piling in drifts four to five feet high on the left or west side of the lane. Jamie had the side-by-side in drive once again, slowly driving under the lighted arch. Molly was crying quietly, mostly from relief. The lane was long and the drive felt like an eternity to the two young people.

Looking ahead, Jamie could finally see an image of a building coming up on his right, causing his heart to pound. As they got closer, Jamie thought it had a slight glow to it, but he didn't trust his eyes anymore. He shook his head to clear the unrealistic thoughts.

On the right a large old barn came into view. It was at least two stories high. A slight glow came from the windows. Jamie saw a set of double doors on the end near them. He pulled the side-by-side over as far to the right as he could without putting Molly into a drift. He told her to stay put. Grabbing the shovel, he walked to the doors to start digging them out. He prayed out loud the whole time that it wouldn't be barred from the inside.

Finally, he threw the shovel down and grabbed the door handle with both hands and pulled as hard as he could, saying, "Please, Lord, please, please."

The door opened so easily that he actually fell backward, ending up on the ground in the snow. He lay there, laughing.

Without taking the time to look inside, Jamie ran back to get Molly. He grabbed the blankets and her bag as she climbed out. She had found a flashlight under her seat, so Jamie grabbed it too. He took her arm to steady her while they walked to the barn.

Thoughts came to Jamie, from his heart, as they walked into the barn. He whispered the words sweetly in Molly's ear, "There's no room at the Inn."

When Molly realized what he said, she turned and stared at him but said nothing.

As they walked in, they instantly felt the warmth in the barn, coming from a wood stove near the middle. Up toward the far end of the barn, they saw the twinkling lights of a Christmas tree. Molly's eyes filled with tears, remembering that it was Christmas Eve.

The smells of the barn overwhelmed Jamie, bringing back memories of life with his grandfather, the faint sound of the crackling wood, the smells of the animals and hay. Tears ran down his face. When he felt them, he quickly wiped them away, with a snow-covered sleeve.

He quickly realized that this was where they would spend their first Christmas together.

He scanned the area near the stove and found a rocking chair. He got Molly settled in it, then he went to investigate the rest of their temporary home for the night. A lantern hung over a small workbench, with many more lined up, sitting on the bench, like they were waiting to be used. Maybe tonight, he thought.

He found the refrigerator with good orange juice and some peanut butter crackers, which he took to Molly. He checked the stove, adding one stick of wood from the large stack. Someone has been tending this stove, he thought. The barn was beautiful and very well kept. There were stalls on the right. One contained a nice quarter mare munching on hay, another one held a Longhorn cow, and the other two pens were empty. Back over near the stove, he found a medicine cabinet hanging on the wall. He located a bottle of aspirin and took it to Molly, silently giving thanks with every small find.

Molly seemed to be in some relief right now, he hoped anyway. Suddenly he was very tired. He sat down on the floor in front of the fire, closing his eyes, needing to rest them. He told himself, "Just for a minute." He had a terrible headache from hours of looking into the oncoming snowflakes. After a short rest, he'd figure out what to do next, he told himself. Surely this ranch had a house with people home since the stove was freshly tended, he hoped anyhow.

A little while later, Ken picked up the green canvas bag, quickly going over his list in his head, so he didn't forget anything. Finally satisfied, he threw it over his shoulder. He headed out into the blizzard, moving slowly toward the old barn. Just for a second, he felt like Santa Claus. Little did he know of the real gift coming tonight.

Jamie jumped up, his heart racing. He tried to get his bearings. "Okay, I must have fallen asleep." He had no idea how long he had slept. He heard something. Molly was crying, not loudly, but just the same, crying. He looked at the chair; it was empty. Quickly he turned in circles. He couldn't find her. He screamed, "Molly, where are you?"

"Over here, in the straw," she said. She had found a big pile of loose straw back by the Christmas tree. She had laid a blanket on it, then lay down and tried to stretch her back out. "Back by the tree," she added and turned the flashlight on to help him find her.

He knelt down beside her. "You scared me. Is your back still hurting?" he asked, taking her hand and brushing a piece of straw off her cheek.

"Everything hurts," she let out a sob, adding, "I'm scared. The baby is moving real hard."

Jamie looked directly at her and said, "I'm scared too," without thinking.

A second later they heard a noise. It sounded like a door creaking, somewhere near the stove. A tall shadow appeared in the darkness. "Someone here?" the shadow asked.

Instantly Jamie laughed and hollered, "Over here," flipping the flashlight on and pointing it into the straw. The figure moved closer. Fear never crossed Ken's mind or Jamie's. Ken walked closer to the intruders. Jamie decided to start talking, quickly explaining why they were there.

"Hi, mister, we were trying to get to Bethlehem and got caught in the storm, and thank God for your lane light and this barn. Molly, my girlfriend, is pregnant and hurting real bad. I'm sorry for breaking in here, but can you help us, please?"

Jamie had stood up and was pleading to the tall figure standing in front of him in the dark.

"Slow down, youngin'. I'm Ken. You're at the Kahler Ranch. You're both safe, and yes, we'll get this heifer, er, young lady some help. First, what are your names, and how old are you both?" Ken asked.

"I'm Jamie Matthews, and I'll be eighteen in March. This is Molly Thomas, and she'll be eighteen in April. Her mom kicked her out this morning and we were trying—"

"I know, Bethlehem in a blizzard. Is this baby yours, son?" he asked Jamie in a stern voice.

"Yes sir," Jamie said with his head held high. Jamie waited and wondered what would come next.

Ken relaxed and half laughed. "You weren't getting to town in this storm. You were really lucky tonight, young man—all three of you were!"

Molly spoke up in a low voice, "It was the lane light."

Ken didn't respond, but thought, *There is no lane light.* He cleared his thoughts. "Molly, when is this baby due?" Ken asked.

"Next week," she said, then adding, "but I don't think it knows that." As she spoke, she gasped with a pain.

"Okay, you guys stay put. Molly, are you warm enough?" Ken rubbed the back of his neck with his hand nervously.

Think, Ken, he told himself. "I'll be back, but it might take a few minutes. It's getting really bad out there," Ken said. Jamie watched the tall man Ken walk toward the center of the barn, not too far from the stove, and go out a side door. He quickly came back in, heading to the stove. He stoked the fire and added more wood, then quickly walked over to the longhorn's pen to look at her. A few seconds later he was gone again.

The kids were alone again, but for the first time today, they felt safe. Jamie kissed Molly's forehead, saying, "Everything is going to be fine now," and for the first time today, he felt it okay to breathe. The words "thank You, Lord" kept going over and over in his mind.

The sky was pitch-black now. "Well, it's at least five o'clock," he said. His watch had quit. Brian figured they had ridden another hour. The horses were getting weaker by the minute.

Brenda hollered for Brian to stop so she could talk to him. "My mare is trembling hard and is starting to stumble," she told Brian, quickly adding, "The horses can't take much more, Brian."

He hollered back, "Do you want to get off and lead them?" As soon as he said the words, fear pulsed through his entire body; he knew he couldn't walk.

A few seconds later, she answered, "We may have to, in a little while. Let's go a little longer." She looked from her husband to her son and said, "We all need to pray—hard!"

So many thoughts were going through her head, but none of them had a positive outcome. The realization hit her hard. When the horses quit, they were dead. She meant her husband, her son, and herself. There was no way they could track through the deep snow. Brenda was far from being a quitter, so the cruel thoughts going through her head were hard to swallow. *If only we knew where we were headed, there might be a reason to keep trying*, her mind struggled with the reality of the words.

Ken left the barn, feeling for the rope that had been tied out as a guide rope, from the barn to the cabin. He didn't think he needed it, but he wanted to make sure it was secure. "This rope is going to see some action tonight," he said out loud to no one.

He took the large rock steps to the porch two at a time. His thoughts coming fast, "Boy, this night is in for some big surprises."

The front entrance held a mud room of sorts, a place to pull off muddy boots and snowy coats. Ken ignored the area and continued in, snow and all.

Everyone was in the kitchen. Steph just about had dinner ready, a Christmas tradition of spaghetti and all the trimmings. The smell of garlic and spices floated through the air. The rest were just about finished with the cookie frosting event. Chip and Rick were right in the middle with the girls. Susan sat on the sideline, sipping a glass of wine and enjoying the interaction of her husband and daughter. Kelly and Lilly were giggling about anything and everything.

Steph and Chip recognized the sound of Ken's boots and heavy steps. Both looked up at the same time, also realizing that something was wrong. As he entered the kitchen, dripping melting snow everywhere, Steph spoke first, "What's wrong, Ken?"

By now everyone was looking at him. Kelly jumped up. "Is Lucky calving?"

He answered quickly, "No, Kel, I don't think so." He turned back to Steph and Chip. Steph had walked over next to her husband, "Well, missy, we seem to have visitors for the night and these are kinda special!"

Chip's mind was running with all the possibilities of what Ken was saying. Ken wasn't talking fast enough for Chip's brain. He hollered at Ken in too loud a voice, "Spit it out, Ken!"

Steph hit Chip on the shoulder with her dish towel and quickly said, "Stop!"

Ken started, "We have a couple of youngins in the barn. They got lost in the storm and found the barn." He hesitated.

Chip said, "That's fine."

"There's more, Chip!"

"What!" Chip said in a high-pitched voice.

"The girl, Molly, is nine and a half months pregnant, and if she were a heifer, I'd say she's going to calve tonight!" Ken said, smiling. The room was quite for one second.

Steph stepped toward him, "Say again?"

Ken looked her in the eye. "Sis, you heard me correct the first time!"

Chip stood up and ripped off the apron he was wearing and said, "Crap!"

Ken smiled at the fact that Chip had managed, somewhat, to control his response.

Susan and Rick sat silently listening and looking back and forth.

Kelly and Lilly looked at each other and giggled.

Lilly screamed at the top of her lungs, "A baby for Christmas!" her voice echoing the words through the rooms, words that either Chip or Steph wanted to hear, especially tonight.

"Hey," Steph almost shouted, "let's not get ahead of ourselves!"

Ken looked impatient, "Let's go, Steph!"

Rick was on his feet. "Can we all go?" Steph looked at him. She couldn't think.

Ken got very serious. Looking at Chip, he said, "This storm is getting really fierce, so in my opinion, everyone needs to stay together, at any time. We may not be able to get back and forth!"

Chip didn't need to think long about what Ken had just said. "Yes, all of us are going. Get bundled up good!"

Steph turned back to the stove. She had just drained and rinsed the pasta. Now she dumped the pasta into the sauce and gave it two quick stirs then headed off to the coats.

Chip was giving instructions, "And hold on to that rope. Don't let Lilly out of your hands, Rick. Kelly, go with them!"

"Okay, Dad!" she replied. Chip and Steph were out the door with Ken following quickly. The wind was still increasing, the howling was unbearable.

Chip leaned into Steph so she could hear him, "Go with Ken. I've got to go back for the others. They have no idea what they are heading into!"

Ken took Steph's hand. "Hold on to me!" They moved slowly toward the barn. It was less than three hundred yards, but seemed a lot further to Steph. She was getting more anxious with each step.

Chip reached the front door, just as they were walking out.

"It's worse than I thought, Rick!" Chip said. "Hold on to Susan real tight. I'll take Lilly and Kelly, and don't let go of that rope!"

Chip picked Lilly up and cradled her in his arms. She instantly buried her head into Chip's chest. Kelly gripped the back of Chip's belt as hard as she could and said, "Lets' go!"

They moved slowly so Rick and Susan could keep up. Kelly could hear Susan screaming at Rick. She was scared. Rick kept hollering at her to hold on!

The snow was building up between the cabin and barn, like it always did with these kinds of winter storms, but it was the wind; it blew the fine pellets of ice and small snowflakes through the air, with extreme force, making it feel like they were embedding themselves into your skin.

It probably took them ten to twelve minutes to get to the barn. Chip braced his body against the door to hold it open for Rick and Susan. He heard Rick telling his wife that they were going to be fine and he wouldn't let anything happen to her, he promised.

Chip's thoughts said, "Good job, Rick."

Ken ripped Steph's heavy coat from her and said, "Go, back of barn, straw pile."

Steph ran to the couple. She glanced at Jamie then knelt down at Molly's side. Jamie had backed out of the way to allow Steph to get close to Molly.

Jamie held the flashlight off to the side, giving them the much-needed light but not blinding anyone. The power had gone off a few minutes ago.

Steph looked into Molly's scared eyes. She spoke without thinking, "You're just a baby." Steph shook her head to clear it. "Molly sweetie, I'm Steph Kahler. Tell me how you are hurting."

Molly looked at the woman. She was younger than her mother. Steph was waiting for an answer.

Molly instantly felt relief from worry but not the pain. She started crying, "I think it's just my back, but the baby is kicking real hard and moving a lot."

"Okay, honey, when are you due?" she asked.

"Next week," Molly answered.

Steph was trying to think. *What else do I need to know?* Then she asked her, "When was the last time you saw the doctor, Molly?"

Molly hesitated before answering, knowing her answer wouldn't show personal responsibility. Finally she said, "Two, maybe three months ago. My mom wouldn't pay for it, and Jamie—" Her words got cut off by another pain. Steph looked at her watch, wanting to time the pain. She had a feeling the young woman was in the early stages of labor.

"Are you comfortable, Molly?" she asked, patting the girl's arm.

"Yeah, I'm okay. Jamie found a bottle of aspirin, so maybe they'll help soon," her voice was anything but confident, but Steph understood.

She looked in Molly's stressed eyes for a moment and then said, "I'll be right back." When Steph walked off, Jamie went right back to her side.

Chip latched the door good on the inside to keep the wind from grabbing it. Rick turned toward him, "Boy, that was something. I didn't know wind like that existed."

Rick waited for a reply from Chip, who was still brushing snow off. When he didn't get one, he continued to talk, "But nothing stops you guys, does it?"

Now, he had Chip's attention. He didn't know how to take the statement from Rick. Quickly, his mind went back to the war, with the enemy trying to stop them. Chip pressed himself to stay calm with his answer, "Rick, if she wants to stop us, she can. She's totally capable."

Rick didn't understand what Chip was talking about, but let it be when Chip walked off.

The others slowly gathered around the wood stove, trying to dry out and warm up again. Ken hurried to light the kerosene lamps and get them placed around the barn. He noticed they were putting off a different glow. It had more of an amber color to it. Maybe it's the difference in the quality of kerosene, he thought. He was very glad he had taken the time to clean the lamps all up.

Rick was nervously walking all around talking, but to no one in particular. Steph was nearby when she heard him say, "Boy, that was an experience!"

As she walked by him, she whispered in Rick's ear, "I'm afraid it's just one of many tonight, Rick."

He looked at her and said, "Okay," in kind of a questioning sort of way, wondering what she meant. Rick's mind was running, wondering if any of this was part of Steph's planned Christmas experience, the one he was paying for. Surely not, he told himself.

Ken had heard Steph whisper to Rick. Walking up beside her, he said in a low voice, "That's an understatement!" When she looked at him, he pointed to Lucky's pen with his eyes and added, "Let's just keep it to ourselves for a while. Kelly will figure it out soon enough."

Steph tried to smile, but it didn't come off very well. "Good idea. Maybe one thing at a time, or should I say, one baby at a time." Ken just looked at her. There wasn't much he could say.

It took a few minutes for everyone to get their bearings. Kelly ran to Lucky's pen first thing, with Lilly following close behind, then the two girls basically stayed there, with more interest in the cow than in Molly.

Chip and Ken were like mother hens, when it came to tending the wood stove. Chip grew up with this very one, so respect for the iron box was lifelong. Ken's stove experience was shorter, but instilled deeply. Chip knelt down on one knee in front of the stove, stoking the embers and pulling them forward, with the same poker that his great grandfather had used on Christmas Eves past. As he filled its cavity with the seasoned wood, he looked at Ken, who was standing next to the stove. "Ken, do you know where this wood came from?" Chip asked, then adding, "I can't get over the amount of heat it's putting out."

"I know," Ken said with a very straight face. "I had Jeff cutting last spring over at Cougar Creek, back up the draw." Ken glanced at the barn. "Sure staying toasty warm in here." His eyes were full of questions as he looked at Chip.

"Yep," was all Chip had to say on the subject.

Ken turned to walk. "This isn't normal, so thank You, Lord."

Steph found the two at the stove. She felt a little annoyed with both. "Hey, you two, can we talk?" She walked a little ways off from the stove. Chip and Ken followed.

Before she could say anything, Chip spoke up in a serious voice, "What did you find out?"

She instantly calmed down. "Well, I think she's starting labor." Chip showed panic in his eyes. "It's okay, she's due," Steph assured him.

She looked at Ken. "Do you have any experience delivering a baby, you know, the two-legged kind." She held her breath.

"Not really, but it can't be a whole lot different than any other baby, right?" he told himself that his answer didn't help the situation much.

She stared at both of them. "Thanks," with annoyance heard in her voice.

"Calm down, we need some time to think. We have some time, right?" Chip asked.

She took a deep breath and said, "Yes."

Ken suggested she talk to Susan. "Maybe she can help."

Steph shook her head, "Just think. We'll talk in a little while!"

They kept pushing forward. The snow seemed to be coming down harder, if that was even possible. The quietness, the lack of any sounds other than the howl of the wind and the horses' lungs, was maddening. Mental stability was being pushed to its limit, in more ways than one.

Colt had been looking ahead. In his mind, he thought the sky was lightening up. He also thought it was wishful thinking, so he stayed quiet. He tried closing his eyes, blanking his mind, but the lightness didn't go away; it was still there.

He kept rubbing his eyes. His heart started beating a little harder. He forced himself to stay calm. Finally he was convinced that he was not imagining it. Sitting up straight in his saddle, he said, "Look."

Brian stopped and turned in his saddle to look at Colt.

"Look," Colt said again, pointing with his arm, straight ahead, "the sky is lighter up ahead."

Brian turned back forward again, rubbing his eyes. It did look slightly lighter to him.

Brenda questioned in her mind that maybe they were so cold that they were all starting to see things.

Chip walked over to Jamie and Molly. "Hi guys, I'm Chip Kahler. I own this place. Jamie, can I talk to you, son?" nodding to a spot a ways off.

"Yes sir," Jamie answered, getting up and walking off with the man.

Chip studied the face and stature of the young stranger. He was a good-looking kid, clean cut, and he stood straight, with his hands together in front of him. Chip always tried to be a good and fair judge of character. So far, he saw a scared kid who had made a few mistakes in his short life, but seemed to be accepting responsibility for them, and someone had definitely taught him to show respect. Chip liked what he saw.

"Son," he started talking to Jamie in a gentle voice. He didn't want his words to sound criticizing. Chip grew up in a life of criticism. He worked hard at not being his father, but he planned to convey that he was in charge. "Jamie, can you please tell me why you two were out in this? I'm really hoping you had a good reason."

When Chip said the last part, Jamie fell apart inside. He had known, before they left, that it was a really bad idea, but youth has its way of shadowing reality and lending optimism to ideas that shouldn't even exist.

"Okay, Mr. Kahler," he started.

Chip stopped him, "No, I'm Chip. Mr. Kahler is my dad."

Jamie smiled weakly. "Okay, Chip, I'll try. First, I'm Jamie Matthews, and my girlfriend is Molly Thomas," he said, looking back at Molly. "We both lived in Shane. Molly's mom is a drunk and didn't like me. This morning at nine, she physically kicked Molly out. I really don't want to tell you what she said to Molly. It was bad."

"What she said isn't important, is this baby yours?" Chip asked.

"Yes sir," Jamie answered immediately.

"Okay, what about your parents?" Chip asked.

"I don't have a dad, and, well, my mom has mental problems. She's bipolar and has some other mental issues. She likes to drink and when she goes off her meds. Well, she is real hard to live with. She lost her job a couple months ago and I've been trying to take care of her. I work at the gas station in town. It doesn't pay much, but it's a job. It's been hard."

"Why didn't you take Molly to your house?" Chip asked.

Jamie had lowered his head, looking at the floor as he continued to talk.

"I was worried my mom would hurt Molly and the baby." He looked Chip in the eye now. "When she gets in her moods, she gets physical. I can handle her hitting me, but not Molly." They were both quiet. After a few seconds, Jamie started talking again. "Molly has an aunt in Bethlehem. She said we could stay with her, but," his voice was getting emotional, "we had to get there first." Jamie turned away from Chip.

Chip whispered, "It's okay now, it's okay."

Slowly, he faced Chip again, "Sorry about that." Chip waved him off.

"I know this sounds stupid, so stupid, with the storm, but I didn't know what else to do. Molly wanted to try, but I knew before we left that it was a bad idea. I just didn't realize how bad."

"Yes, it was Jamie. All I can say is the good Lord didn't want the three of you to die tonight, because nothing else was on your side."

Jamie tried to smile, but his legs were getting weak.

Chip thought he saw tears in his eyes, something he didn't hold against the boy. Right now, Chip thought it was important to keep talking to him. This life-and-death lesson was not to be taken lightly. Now Chip became his father. "Son, you would never have made it. The storm was upgraded at two thirty with warnings for eighty to hundred mph winds to hit between five and six, and Bethlehem is still twenty-five miles from here."

They had walked far enough away from Molly so she couldn't hear their talk. Jamie listened to Chip. When he finished Jamie responded. "I was already having a hard time keeping it on the road. I was afraid the wind gusts were going to turn us on our side."

Chip panicked, listening to the account. "What were you driving, Jamie?" Chip held his breath.

Jamie swallowed hard, "A borrowed Kawasaki side-by-side. My truck broke down outside Shane."

Chip couldn't believe what he had just heard. He turned around and walked off, rubbing the back of his neck and kicking the straw on the floor, hard.

Jamie didn't move. He didn't think he was breathing either. He could hear Chip laughing and cussing. Finally, the man walked back to Jamie.

Chip smiled at him. "You were traveling toward your death. How did you manage to find this barn?"

"Your lane light," Jamie whispered in a low voice because it was all he had.

"What?"

"The lane light, sir."

Chip took a deep breath, then gently said, "Jamie, there is no lane light."

Ken had walked up to them, but didn't engage in the conversation; he listened.

"Okay, that's enough for now, we'll talk later. Better go see how your gal is doing, son."

Jamie smiled lightly. "Okay. Thanks, Chip," he turned and started to walk back to Molly.

"Jamie," Chip hollered. Jamie stopped and looked back at Chip. "We are very glad you saw that lane light." Jamie waved with tears in his eyes.

Chip looked at Ken, "You hear?"

"Yeah, a lot of it, and I think I'm thanking the Lord—for a lane light?" Ken stated in a quivering voice.

Everyone had been in the barn for a while, Jamie and Molly had done what they could to explain their experience, but they felt like they were trying to explain a dream to someone. Ken had coffee poured into cups and motioned Chip to bring Jamie along. Kelly had Rick and Lilly helping her at Lucky's pen. Steph and Susan were with Molly.

Jamie took a sip from the cup. The hot liquid tasted good. He started talking on his own, "Molly told me after we were here for a while and had gotten warmed up that the barn made her feel safe."

Chip smiled, "Yeah, it has a way of doing that."

Jamie was nervous. He desperately wanted to convince the ranch owner that they were good people, even though they had messed up a lot lately.

Chip started talking, not knowing where his words were coming from. Ken and Jamie listened. "She's glad you found her, that you were guided to her safety."

Ken asked in a soft voice, "Who's she, Chip?"

Chip looked around the barn before answering. "This old barn." He hesitated then continued, "This barn raised me. Fell out of the loft when I was nine and broke my arm. Seen a lot of four-legged critters born in here and watched some take their last breath too." Chip shook himself out of his memories.

He stared at Jamie for a second then smiled. "Long storm, long night. I guess we'll all get to know each other a little better tonight," then he laughed lightly.

Ken hoped Chip meant those words in a good way. Jamie's face was blank. Plain old panic with some fear mixed in, Ken thought, patting Jamie on the shoulder, as he got up to get more coffee. "Everything will be fine, son."

Steph called Chip over. He looked at Ken. "You guys talk a while," then he headed over to see what Steph wanted.

Ken and Jamie sat down on a bale of straw. Ken was interested in hearing more of Jamie's story. "What happened out there, Jamie?" Ken asked with kindness in his voice. A moment later, Ken added, "You said your truck quit at someone's lane, what did you do then? Do you remember the name of the place?" Ken threw a lot at the young man. Ken already knew the name of the place. Jamison's was the only ranch between here and Shane. Ken sat quietly now, waiting. He wasn't in any hurry. They weren't going anywhere.

"I don't remember the name on the sign, but it started with a J."

"Joe's," Ken thought. "Okay, then what?"

"When I got to the house, it was dark, no one was home, and the door was locked.

I could have broken in, but it would have been wrong, so next I went to the barn. I found the Kawasaki with the keys in it. I thought if I just borrowed it, I could get Molly to safety. I was afraid the baby might come tonight and she might need…"

Jamie lost his voice for a second.

"There was a note with a phone number on it. I left a note saying why I took it and signed my name, and I copied his phone number down. I was going to call him as soon as I got to Molly's aunt." Jamie fumbled with his hand in a pocket and handed Ken a crumpled piece of paper with Joe's cell number.

"Molly got mad at me, said it was stealing. I said I was trying to keep her alive. If I had broken into the house and we stayed there, we might have lost the baby. I know I took a real big chance. We still could have died, but something kept telling me to keep going, and then there was the lane light."

Ken waved a hand to stop him, "Jamie, you did exactly what God wanted you to do!" Ken felt something wash over him, a feeling of agreement and contentment. He wasn't sure what to call it.

"What?" Jamie said, looking confused, to say the least.

Ken stood up, he patted Jamie on the shoulder and said, "You did the right thing, Jamie!"

Now Ken walked off. He wanted to end the conversation. They both needed to breathe. Jamie would have plenty of time tonight to figure everything out; they both would.

Ken needed to do some praying. He needed guidance. He realized now that there was a special plan that was going to play out tonight. He just wasn't sure who all the players were. Something inside told him there would be more. His skin crawled.

As they slowly rode closer to the shining light, the white ground and the flurry of falling snowflakes started reflecting in the light they were approaching. Minutes later, they found themselves being blinded by that same light. The horses started reacting to the light also, stepping cautiously, and not wanting to continue toward it.

"Keep them moving!" Brian hollered without turning to look at Brenda or Colt.

Slowly, images of dark objects came into sight. The columns of the the Kahler Ranch entrance stood in front of them like guards. The light centered itself directly above the arch of the entrance. They couldn't read the words because of the snow cover, but they knew where they were.

"What!" was all Brian could say. His heart felt like it would beat out of his chest.

The Kahler Ranch sat six miles to the north and four miles east of their place. When they had left their place, many hours earlier, they had headed due south.

They had been very turned around.

"Where's this light coming from?" Colt hollered at his dad, as he looked around. The light was too bright to look toward it. It was like trying to look into the sun.

Brian caught a funny look from Brenda. He sat watching her for a second. He could see her eyes in the light. He instantly felt fear wash over him. Her eyes were both were dilated and glazed over.

"Brenda," he hollered. She didn't give any response. He coached his horse a little closer to hers. "Brenda, come on, babe," he leaned over and took her reins. "Follow her, son, keep her moving, we're running out of time!"

As desperately as Brian wanted to get to the safety that he knew lay at the end of the lane, it still took another twenty minutes to ride the lane—the longest twenty minutes of Brian's life.

"Please, dear Heavenly Father, please help us," Brian had been praying all day, but none harder than while traveling up the lane.

The center of the lane was bare of snow with both sides drifted high. The center gave the appearance of a path wanting to be followed. The horses seemed to sense the end of the trail coming up too, as they tried to move a little faster.

Slowly, the image of the old barn that set on the right came into view. Brian looked at Brenda. She seemed a little more aware of her surroundings now.

"Honey, it's going to be okay now!" he hollered at her while trying to laugh.

Dull lights shown through the snow dusted glass panes of the windows. They rode up to the double doors on the south end of the barn. The snow had whipped around the corner of the barn and drifted the snow twelve feet high along the doors.

Colt hollered, "Dad, the side door!"

Brian forced his horse to move on. "A hundred more feet, fella," he told his horse, pulling Brenda's along with his.

At the present, the barn was fairly calm. Everyone had basically got over the shock of the uninvited guest and the wrath of the storm. Molly would give birth tonight, Steph had decided, but it was hours off yet. Ken watched Lucky for oncoming signs. She would calve tonight too, he was sure, but she wasn't showing any outward signs yet. He hadn't talked with Kelly about her, so he wasn't sure if she had caught on yet. Ken was also keeping a close eye on Chip. This was the kind of stress that messed him up.

Kelly was sitting on the top rail of Lucky's pen with Lilly, watching Lucky. She was standing, eating hay. Lilly was sitting next to her, telling Kelly about her New York life. Kelly was trying hard to sound interested. The pens were on the right side of the barn. There was a gap of about fifteen feet in between Lucky's pen and the next pen. A large stack of alfalfa square bales sat in that gap next to the wall.

For some reason, Kelly turned and watched the mare over in the next pen. She smiled, thinking to herself, "Dad loves her almost as much as he does me—he's loved her longer." She loved the stories her dad told about Jakker's Babe. She let her mind drift.

The mare in the next pen was comfortably eating her hay. She was Chip's pride and joy. The mare, Jakker's Babe, was twenty-eight years old now and still looked like a million bucks. The muscles in her neck and wide chest rippled as she stretched her neck out, trying to reach the tender alfalfa leaves lying in front of her, showing no interest in the stems.

Chip was in love with this animal. She had melted his heart the moment he first laid eyes on her. His dad had received the call at breakfast on a warm April day, many years ago, that the mare he was interested in buying had just foaled. Dad and son drove the twenty miles to the quarter horse ranch. Chuck would make up his mind on the pending purchase when they got there. Tomorrow was Chip's fifteenth birthday and his dad had planned to give him the new foal for his birthday, if he liked what he saw. As they quietly walked up to the box stall, Chip's dad made his mind up at first glance.

The filly was trying to stand for the first time, her long gangly legs going every which way. The mare gently talked to her new baby with sounds of encouragement. Finally, minutes later, she was standing, swaying back and forth. Thick yellow colostrum was dripping from both nipples, waiting for the filly to make her way along her mother's side. Minutes later, the instinct that Mother Nature had instilled in her took over—she stood nursing.

She was solid red with a beautiful white blaze. Chuck studied Chip. His son was mesmerized by the foal. "*It's the right thing to do,*" he thought to himself.

Chip had gone through a tough year and had been trying hard to please his father. Chuck knew he was hard on the boy. Again, he thought, "*He needs this filly.*"

Chuck leaned close to Chip, putting a hand on his shoulder, and said, "Happy Birthday, son. I know she's not much right now, but she'll grow."

Chip couldn't believe what he was hearing, saying to his dad, "What, the foal is mine?"

"Yes, Chip, she's your birthday present, but we are going to leave them here for the month."

Chip turned back to the foal, whispering the words over and over, "Jakker's Babe."

That night at the dinner table came the rest of the birthday present, the lecture of the foal's potential for Chip and the ranch. A lecture he would remember for years to come, but one that served him well.

Over the years, by breeding the mare to the best stallions available, Babe had made Chip a lot of money, enough to pay for college and then some.

Chip walked the barn. He couldn't shed the nervous feeling that overwhelmed him.

"It's too warm in here," he thought. He knew the barn wasn't capable of holding the real cold out, not with just the wood stove, but she was. He looked around. Everyone was calm and seemed to be comfortable, considering the situation. Steph and Susan were up by Molly and Jamie. Kelly seemed to be in control of Lilly. Rick was checking lamp oil levels with Ken; the two of them seemed to be deep in conversation.

Now Chip looked at the barn herself. His eyes settled on his granddad's old rocker. It sat next to the wall, not far from the stove. Chip's mind wanted to head down another road from the past. Granddad always called the barn *his office*. He loved being able to sit for a moment when he tired, especially in his last years. Chip had idolized the old man. He always felt he had learned more about life from him than anyone or anything else. At the same time, he could still hear Granddad's voice telling him why he needed good schooling. He had always wanted more for Chip than just the ranch, as he knew it. Along with his dad, Granddad wasn't happy about Chip's decision to go in the Army, but many discussions later, of listening to Chip's life plan, the two men finally gave him their blessing.

When he finally did enter college, his major was in ranch management with a minor in business, with the college he decided on, based in Wyoming. At first, they tried to talk him into going to college out of state. Both men felt he needed a different environment to open his mind, but after spending four years in the Army, Chip's response was dead set. "I've seen all the world I need to see. I'm staying in Wyoming, end of discussion."

There were phrases of Granddad that held meaning to Chip, ones that he'd never forget: "The decisions we make affect today and the future." Then there was, this one: "Always show kindness and be generous."

He wondered what advice Granddad would have for tonight. Then Chip smiled as he heard his Granddad's voice, "You've got this, son. You know the right thing to do!

Kelly was watching the mare. Ken had thrown her a fresh flake of the good alfalfa hay. He knew she didn't need it. Chip had recently complained that the old girl was getting too fat. Ken had laughed at him. In his mind, senior citizens deserved pampering, especially this one, so he always fed her the good stuff.

For no reason, Babe raised her head and perked both of her ears. She had been facing the south end of the barn where the double doors were, toward the approaching lane.

Kelly kept watching her. Lilly was still talking about something, but Kelly wasn't listening. The mare took a few steps forward. Her head was still up and her ears still perked, but now she flicked them. She gave the appearance that she was hearing something outside, other than the wind. Kelly continued to watch. The mare was starting to get anxious. Without taking her eyes off her, she hollered, "Dad."

Chip and Ken both looked her way. Both of them knew instantly that someone or something was outside.

Chip hollered, "Guardian!"

Ken was already up and grabbing a lighted lantern off the bench. They both ran to the side door. The commotion startled all the others. Kelly and Lilly jumped down and ran to the center of the barn near the door. Rick came up and stood behind them. He had heard the word that Chip hollered. He wasn't sure he heard correctly. Maybe he'd say something later, he thought.

Jamie and Steph were with Molly. Steph jumped up immediately, her heart pounding hard. She hadn't heard her brother called that in a long time. Susan had gone for coffee and was walking back toward Molly, trying to carry three cups of coffee without spilling them. She wasn't aware of anything happening.

As they opened the door, Chip used his body to brace it against the wind.

They first saw the faint glow of Brian's flashlight, then they heard the horses. They seemed to be right up on them, though they couldn't see them.

Brian hollered as loud as he could, "Chip, Ken, help!"

Both men recognized Brian's voice. Chip hollered, "Brian, ride in!" as Ken waved the lantern high showing them the way. Brian rode in first, fairly fast, then Brenda, with Colt following. All three were bent low over their horse's neck, allowing them to fit through the door. Chip struggled against the wind to pull the door closed, securing it.

As soon as the door was secured, the night knew all the players were in place. The lane light slowly grew dimmer. Within minutes, it was completely gone. The lane entrance sat in total darkness now. The snow started drifting over the middle of the lane where dirt had shown. In a few minutes it would be blended in with the rest of the landscape.

There were no more travelers needed, all His players were in place, and no one else would be on the road tonight.

The wind slowly diminished Steph's decorations to nonexistent. The constant force of the wind robbed the trees of all their strength.

Slowly, one by one, they were carried off. Shredded pieces of the red velvet bows would be found scattered across the southern prairie. In the spring, the birds would graciously include the colorful tidbits in their nest building. The trees would end up mangled in fence lines south of the ranch, creating shelter for small animals.

He did not plan for anything to go to waste on this special night; even the storm played its part.

The horses and riders looked as one. They were covered in snow and ice. Icicles six inches long hung off the rider's hats and overcoats, with the ice weighing down their arms, and it was the same for the horse's heads, necks, down their sides and bellies. The snow was so built up on the riders' right sides that you couldn't see their legs.

Brian had ridden right up on the girls and Rick. Not being able to see them, Rick had quickly grabbed both girls, the three of them rolling off to the side and ending up in a pile on the floor. His quick thinking kept them from being trampled by Brian's horse.

Steph screamed, "Oh my God!" not saying His name in vain, wanting and needing His attention.

Susan dropped the coffees, screaming. She had no idea what had just happened and she was terrified. Lilly was scared and was crying.

Kelly lay in place, unable to move, as she stared into the eyes of Brenda's mare. They were opened wide, and full of fear and death. Kelly's body started trembling as she was overwhelmed with fear. The mare's nostrils were flared and blowing blood as her lungs heaved, attempting to take in the oxygen she desperately needed.

The sound was horrifying. Kelly had never seen an animal so close to death, still standing on its feet.

Everything would happen fast now. After Chip secured the door on the inside, and he turned, his body froze in place for just a moment as he looked at the scene of horses and riders.

Ken hollered at him, bringing him back, "Get Brenda, Chip!" Ken ran to Brian.

He glanced Colt's way, "Colt, are you okay, can you get off?" He wouldn't give Colt much time to response, before he would go to him.

Ken saw Colt look up, a good sign. "Yeah, I think so. Help my mom and dad."

Before Ken could answer, Chip hollered loud to the boy, "Don't you worry, we've got them, son!"

Chip ran to Brenda. She was attempting to climb off, but as Chip reached for her, she fell into his arms. He gently tried to brush the snow from her pale face. As she tried to open her eyes, she spoke weakly. Chip couldn't make out what she was trying to say. He put his head close to hers, "Say again, Brenda," he said.

She swallowed hard and said, "She's dying, light."

Chip instantly knew she meant the mare. "Not on my watch!" he screamed with defiance in his voice. He ran to the stove with Brenda in his arms, hollering at Steph and Susan, who were right behind him.

Steph steadied Brenda as Chip sat her down on a bale of straw next to the stove. "Go, go!" Steph hollered as Chip ran to the mare.

Colt had been able to climb off and walked to the stove on his own. Chip was overwhelmed and started screaming, "We need help with these horses!"

As Ken reached Brian, his first impression was "this is not good!" Ken started talking while attempting to pull Brain's body to the left, to help him down off his horse. Brian screamed in pain, "Ken, foot frozen!"

More was not needed. Instantly, Ken let up and answered, "I've got you, buddy!"

Molly and Jamie heard Brian scream. Molly turned to Jamie, "You need to go help them, Jamie!"

Jamie looked at her and said, "Yes, I can help!" He jumped up and ran to where Ken and Brian were.

Ken handled Brian slowly and carefully now. As he tried to stand Brian on the ground, his right foot gave way. He screamed again and started to fall. Jamie had come up on the opposite side of Brian, grabbing him at the same time that Ken did. "Let's get him to the stove!" Ken hollered.

The two locked arms and lifted Brian into a sitting position and carried him to the stove. They were able to lay him on two bales that were next to each other, allowing his foot and leg to be elevated. Brian tried to talk, saying the word *light* over and over.

Kelly had looked at Lilly, who was still crying, and Rick. She placed her hand on Lilly's shoulder and said, "You're okay, Lilly. Come on, we need to help. You too, Rick!"

Brian and Colt's horses were still standing in the same place. Kelly quickly grabbed Brian's gelding and told Rick to bring Colt's horse. They moved them as close to the heat source as they could get them. Kelly started telling Rick how to take the saddle off while Lilly tried to brush ice icicles off.

Ken had a lot of things going through his head as his medic training was kicking in. All of a sudden, he stood up and hollered, "Hey everyone, this is important, absolutely no coffee for these three. Susan, get cups of warm water and get as much down to each one as you can."

Susan replied quickly, in a calm voice, "Okay, Ken." She jumped up and started gathering cups up.

Steph glanced up at Ken, then at Brenda again, and said, "Why, Ken?"

Ken answered loudly so everyone could hear, "The caffeine increases the heart rate too fast for the blood supply. The blood is too cold." He looked at Steph.

She nodded his way. "Good to know." Her heart slipped a beat, as she thought, *I would have given the coffee.*

Everyone had a job. Everyone was aware of how important that job was, in turning this night around.

No one noticed, but the barn sighed—all will be well.

Chip had ran to Brenda's mare. He walked her slowly toward the wood stove, just behind the straw bales where they had the riders. He needed her close to the heat. She didn't need to be tied; she wasn't going anywhere.

He forced his mind to stay in control. He was talking to her now, in a voice loud enough for her to hear, he hoped, "Come on, sweet girl, I'll get you warmed up and taken care of." His voice trembled, "You're going to be fine!"

He prayed silently, "Please, please help us, Lord," the words being begged over and over.

He pulled the saddle off as fast as he could, throwing it hard. He quickly looked around. He needed something to use to get the snow and packed ice off her face. Not seeing anything, he pulled off his jacket and started rubbing her head and neck with it.

Chip worked franticly on the mare, talking under his breath to himself.

Ken looked Chip's way, "Talk to me, Chip, how's she doing?"

Ken could see she was still breathing too hard, her head was still drooped, and she was not quivering.

"Well, she's still alive, stopped blowing blood—"

Instantly a cruel scene flashed through Chip's mind. He heard his voice saying, "She's dead—she just doesn't know it!" then laughing. Chip's heart screamed in defiance, *Nooo!*

Ken broke in, bringing him back, "The blood is from the air being so cold. How's her heart rate?"

"Still too fast, she's struggling," Chip added in a quivering voice.

Ken kept his eyes on Chip for a few more seconds, sensing he was becoming unstable. "Chip, listen to me, just keep doing what you're doing. Warm her up as fast as you can; it's all we can do right now," Ken told him, adding, "and Susan is warming blankets for you."

"Okay," Chip replied.

Kelly had run to a big wooden box at the far end of the barn and got out four insulated horse blankets and an armful of gunny sacks and brought them back with her. She took two of the blankets to her dad. "I figured you can double them up on her, Dad."

"Thanks, baby!" He gave her a short smile.

He quickly brushed the snow that was left on top of her back. The warmth of the barn had it starting to melt. Susan came with a warm blanket. "Thanks," he said, grabbing it and spreading it over her front end, including her head and neck, then grabbed the insulated blanket and threw that on top, the other one he placed on her back in the proper position.

Kelly and Rick had brushed the other two horses vigorously, removing all the snow and ice. She was finally ready to put the blankets on them. Rick watched her to see how it went on then placed the blanket on the other horse.

"This right, Kelly?" he asked.

Kelly turned his way, smiling, and nodded her head yes. They were beginning to shake. "On their way to recovery," she thought, hopefully.

The moment Brian was able to talk he started talking about the lane light. His words were broken, as were the sentences he attempted. He used words like *brightness*, *reflecting*, *guiding*, and phrases like *too bright to look into*, *coming from above*, then the one that hit Ken the hardest, *the light that saved their lives*—these had been Jamie's exact words too.

Ken listened, just letting Brian go on. Eventually, some time tonight, he would tell him that the light didn't exist. Ken was grateful that Jamie was staying quiet on the subject, for now.

On one of Ken's quick trips over to look at the mare, he told Chip of Brian's claims.

Chip looked straight at him and said, "You believe there was a light?"

Ken got a little snippy, "I don't know. Maybe the Rogers and those kids up there"—he pointed toward the end of the barn where Molly was—"all got together out there, in that raging storm, and all agreed to tell the same story!"

Ken didn't wait for an answer from Chip, he walked off. There were more important things that needed attention right now.

Brenda had been slower to talk, but when she could, she told Steph the same story about seeing a lane light. Steph had more courage than the men. She told Brenda right off, "Brenda, there is no lane light," as Jamie and Molly's words about the light rang in her head and heart.

As the minutes went by, Chip felt himself losing control, mentally and emotionally.

"Why were they out in this, what was Brian thinking?" The more he thought, the more unstable he became.

Finally, he turned toward the stove and looked directly at Brian. A minute later he turned back to the mare and threw his jacket over her neck, then took the necessary steps to get close to Brian.

Steph looked up from Brenda and held her breath. Ken was still trying to get the boot off Brian's foot. He looked up at Chip. Instantly his mind said, "No!" But he didn't have enough time to get the word out before Chip exploded in Brian's face.

"What in the hell were you doing out in that storm, you have a death wish or something?"

Ken jumped up, putting his hands on Chip's shoulders, backing him up, almost into Steph and Brenda.

Steph closed her eyes and put her head down, her heart breaking for her husband. She had known it was just a matter of time.

Ken quickly went into control mode, "Chip, calm down, look at me!"

Brian sat silent, not afraid. He realized what was happening to Chip right now. He had Brian's understanding.

"Sergeant, look at me!" Ken said again, this time in a military tone. He heard Chip take a deep breath, so he started easing the tone of his voice, "Brian's bred heifers got out just as the storm was starting up. They rode out to find them and got lost trying to get home!"

He physically turned Chip around now, toward the mare. "Now, you have work to do. Go take care of that mare, Chip, she needs you!" He waited for Chip to take it in.

"I'll be over there as soon as I can. *We*"—he emphasized the word to Chip—"are going to take care of everyone!" He patted Chip's shoulders gently and continued to soften his voice as he spoke.

Chip looked up past Brian to the mare.

"Chip, get Lilly to help you. She can rub Sugar's legs down, okay, buddy," Ken suggested.

Brian was still looking at Chip. Finally Chip looked down at Brian and squeezed his shoulder as he turned to go back to the mare.

Steph stood up and said, "Chip." He turned and looked at her, confusion showed on his face. She took one step and reached up and kissed him with a smile on her face, and said, "It's okay!"

"Kelly, can I have Lilly?" Chip hollered to his daughter, only walking halfway to her.

"Lilly, would you go help my dad, please?" she asked the little girl. Lilly jumped up and ran to Chip's side and waited for him to tell her what to do. He showed her how to rub the front legs with the gunny sack. Minutes later she was sitting underneath the mare, rubbing her legs as hard as an eight-year-old could. "What about her back legs, Chip?" she asked.

"No, Lilly, stay on the front ones, they're closer to her heart."

Chip started talking to himself, saying words Lilly was sure she had never heard before.

He stopped and looked at her. Lilly's eyes were big and bright. She leaned over to the side so she could see him, reminding him of Kelly, and said, "It's gonna be okay, Chip."

"Yeah, what makes you think so, squirt?"

She smiled sweetly and said, "Because it's Christmas, and you just need to believe!"

Something snapped inside his head. He instantly felt ashamed of his actions. "You're right, Lilly. Believers, that's what we all need to be." He felt a strange tightness in his chest, like someone had just given him a big hug. He knelt down and gave Lilly a hug, then turned back to the mare, rubbing her down again with his jacket and talking to her gently.

Without turning to the group, he hollered, "Ken!" and waited.

Ken hollered back, "What?" not bothering to look at Chip.

"Sorry!" Chip hollered.

Ken smiled slightly and replied with, "Yep."

Brian looked up and smiled at Ken. All was forgiven.

The clock seemed to have stopped.

The howling winds kept getting louder and louder, but something was different about them now. Even with the hectic nature of the barn, Chip heard the change. Ken also heard. The military did

169

that to you. Slowly the wind took on the form of a moan, sounding almost human.

Moments later they heard it; the moaning words were clear—*they found their way*! It kept repeating the words—*they found their way*! Over and over until they finally faded out.

Chip turned toward Ken, who was already looking at him. It was the eeriest sound the two men had ever heard. Chip's heart was already beating fast with adrenaline, now it skipped a beat in panic. Ken felt his skin crawl with goose bumps all the way up the back of his neck. Kelly had heard it too and screamed, "Daddy!"

Chip heard her voice. He flashed back to her as a child, as fear pulsed through his body. Then he heard Steph holler, bringing him back. He hollered to her, "It's okay, Kelly, the wind is playing tricks on us!" He watched her until he sensed she was okay, then turned to Steph and waited. She gave him a brief smile, so he figured his statement to Kelly pacified her too, but he knew the words wouldn't fly with Ken. Chip was afraid, but he wasn't sure of what. He had a feeling of losing control again.

Ken looked at Brian, "I'll be right back." He walked quickly to the end of the barn. When he reached the south windows, he wiped the fog off the inside glass pane. He forced his eyes to see through the snow coming down, through the darkness, looking for any signs of the lane light to the south, but all he saw was darkness.

Calm thoughts that weren't his crossed his mind: "You're not alone, I am still with you."

Steph willed herself not to think, to just react. Thinking complicated your natural responses. Susan had gone to the workbench to get the towels that were kept for rags. They were in a box on the bottom shelf. When she came back, she gently patted Brenda's face. Steph had managed to get Brenda out of her overcoat and was working on coverall hooks on her coveralls. She talked to her nonstop, trying to get her to stay coherent. Brenda wasn't answering yet. Her eyes seemed to look better, but she needed some color to come back to her face.

"Gentle with her hands, Sue, we don't know yet if she frostbit her fingers." As Steph made the statement, her eyes went to Brian.

She had a bad feeling about his foot. She could still hear his screams of pain in her head.

"Susan, cover Brenda's hands with yours gently. The body heat in your hands will help warm hers."

Steph heard Ken talking to Colt, "Colt, tell me if you are hurting anywhere."

Colt's voice shook, "I'm okay, but I can't stop shivering, Ken."

Ken smiled at the young man, "That's a good thing, son, it means that your body is working at warming you up inside."

Colt looked at his mom and then his dad, neither one of them was shaking. Ken knew what was going through his head. "They'll be fine son, just takes a little longer than you because they are older," he hoped.

Getting the snow and ice off of the Rogerses was a chore of its own. Overcoats and coveralls were frozen stiff, the zippers too.

Ken and Jamie worked feverishly on Brian. Ken, at the same time, was keeping one eye on Brenda. He was used to handling multiple traumas at one time. Steph and Susan were both working on her. Jamie held Brian's right leg still while Ken worked at removing the boot. He had lace-up high tops on that laced all the way up. The fronts of the boots had two inches of ice frozen in the lace openings. Ken feared the worst for the foot as he struggled with the boot. He kept talking to Brian. "You all got real lucky tonight, my friend," he told Brian. It was important to be in control of Brian, mentally, when he was finally ready to try and pull the boot off. "I'll try and be gentle, but this is going to hurt."

Brian nodded his head, then he locked his hands around the baling wire of the bale that he was sitting on, holding tight. Brian came real close to passing out when Ken pulled the boot off. Everyone in the barn heard the screams. There were tears sliding down more than one face.

Ken ran to the medicine cabinet and grabbed a pair of scissors, slowly cutting the frozen sock off Brian's foot. Brian's big toe and the next one were white. "I don't see any gray, so it's not as bad as it could have been, Brian," Ken was talking in a louder voice now, hoping to keep Brian with him.

Jamie looked at Ken, "How bad is it?"

"Well, the tissue is frostbitten real bad, but it's not frozen solid through, so we need to very slowly thaw it out"—Ken looked from Jamie to Brian—"and that's extremely painful." Ken had a lot of training on heat-related issues, but they were mostly at the high end of the thermometer.

"Got any Banamine, Ken?" Brian asked.

"Yes, are you going to take some?" Ken asked. "I'll give the horses some too."

"Don't think I can make it without it," Brian replied in a stressed voice.

Jamie looked toward Ken. "It's a pain medicine for horses, but people can use it too; you know bronc riders, football players, pretty strong on pain, just doesn't taste very good."

Jamie nodded.

"How's Brenda, Ken?" Brian asked.

"She'll be fine. Slow to come out of it, you know, that tiny little body of hers, got pretty cold," Ken patted his knee.

"And Colt?"

"He's okay. Got too much of his parents in him to keep him down. You worry about you right now. We'll take care of the others for you," Ken said calmly.

"Let's get you started." It was impossible to look at Brian and not see the pain he was in. Ken stood up and glanced around the barn, trying to quickly evaluate the situation again, wanting to his thoughts on the others to be current, as his medic training had taught him.

Ken was trying hard to concentrate on Brian, but the care for Sugar Babe fought him for equal attention in his mind. She was in dangerous shape. He walked quickly to the medicine cabinet and grabbed the bottle of Banamine and a 12 cc syringe and needle.

"Jamie, get a coffee cup and fill a little less than half with orange juice, please."

He brought the cup to Ken and watched while Ken threw out a little less than a cc of the drug. He squirted it into the orange juice and stirred it with the needle on the syringe. Walking back to Brian, he said, "I know how bad this is going to taste, you do too, but drink it down, Brian."

Normally, Brian would have balked, but not tonight. He drank it straight down, then shook his head. "Terrible," he said, but he also knew it would help with the pain. Without it, well, he didn't want to go there.

Ken handed the items to Jamie. "Hand these to Chip, son."

Chip smiled when he saw the bottle. He quickly withdrew 10 cc. He knew the drug could take effect faster if given IV (through the vein), but when he felt for her jugular vein, it was still collapsed, so he decided to give it in the neck muscle instead. He knew it would help more than anything else he could do.

He hollered at Kelly and waved her over. He held his arm out, waiting for her to take the bottle and syringe. "Thanks, Daddy."

He instantly got emotional. He loved her calling him that. He didn't hear it much anymore. His little girl was growing up.

Rick had been working on the gelding's legs. Kelly had explained about warming the extremities first, to increase circulation. Rick was doing exactly as she wanted; she was very impressed with his efforts.

"Better climb out while I give this shot," she said, explaining the benefits it would provide.

"Steph, can you part with Susan? I need her to help me with Brian's foot," Ken asked.

"She's up checking on Molly. I hate leaving her alone so long. I'll send her to you as soon as she comes back," Steph stated.

"You can have Jamie back now. He's been a big help with Brian and his foot," Ken told her.

"I'm going to show Susan how to make warm compresses to put on Brian's foot. Poor guy, this is going to hurt, bad," Ken added.

"I know, and I'm really worried about Brenda, Ken."

"I know, me too. Brian is okay physically, if you don't count his foot. Brenda is struggling hard, so we'll watch her. I also need to get on Sugar Babe. She's not responding like I'd like her to, plus I think Chip needs some attention, you know, to keep him grounded." Ken tried to smile at his sister but she saw through it.

"Yes, Chip needs your help too," she smiled with tears in her eye.

When Susan walked up to Ken, he gave her a polite smile. They were pretty much strangers, yet and so far she hadn't showed him much as far as fitting in around here, like Rick had, but she wasn't his to judge.

Ken pulled his jacket and sweatshirt off and sat them up real close to the stove, then he walked to the medicine cabinet and grabbed the flat box of OB sleeves, or gloves as some might call them. They were very thin plastic, arm-length gloves used for going in rectally on large animals. He explained that this procedure was also called sleeving.

"Watch me now, Susan." Ken took one of the gloves in his hands and blew into the opening, puffing it out so he could insert his arm and pull it all the way up to his shoulder. Then he repeated the step with another one, pulling it on top of the first one so they were doubled up. Then he pulled them off gently together so as not to tear them.

"Susan, get a coffee cup and start filling this with lukewarm water." Ken had three pots of water heating on the wood stove. She felt each one, finding the least warmest of the three. When half of the glove was full, he said, "Good." She watched as he tied a good tight knot in the opening. He looked at Susan with a smile and said, "Good, now we have a warm water bag."

As Susan watched, she kept telling herself, "Stay calm and watch, you can do this!"

"Brian, I'm going to wrap this bag around your toes, as gently as I can."

Susan held the bag in place while Ken grabbed his sweatshirt and covered the bag, then put his jacket over that. Brian was quiet, but Ken knew it was painful.

He looked at Susan very seriously and said, "Susan, you saw all I just did."

"Yes," she replied very calmly and with confidence.

"Okay," he smiled again, "I want you to repeat everything I did. Here's the box of sleeves, do it exactly the same way, change every fifteen minutes and fill with warmer water every half hour."

Susan stared at Ken.

"If we try to warm the toes too fast, it will do more harm than good."

Now she smiled and said, "I've got it, Ken."

He started to walk away but turned back to her. She looked straight into his eyes, "I'm right here, so don't be afraid to holler at me for anything, and watch for changes in the color of the flesh." He sounded so medically professional to her.

She nodded, thinking, "Stay calm."

Ken patted Brian on the shoulder, "You're going be okay, buddy!"

At the same time that Ken was working on Brian, he was guiding Steph with Brenda. After they got her outer clothes off, and before Susan had gone to help with Brian, she had been warming blankets at the stove for Steph to wrap Brenda in.

Ken thought Brenda was probably in the worst shape of the two adults. Colt was bouncing back like youth does. Steph pulled her own coat and coveralls off and pulled Brenda as close to her body as she could. Ken hoped Steph's body heat would help warm Brenda.

Moments later he walked to the medicine cabinet again, this time for a tin full of brown sugar. Ken mixed three heaping spoonful of sugar into each cup of very hot water and passed them out to all the cold bodies. While he mixed it all up, he explained to Susan, "Brown sugar is a good source of quick energy, but they were all too cold at first; it would have done more harm than good."

"Like coffee?" she asked.

Ken grinned, "Yep, good girl, you were listening!"

Brenda couldn't hold her cup, but she did take sips and swallowed, "That was a good sign."

Ken whispered more prayer of thanks—for the roads headed in the right direction—acknowledging that even long roads start somewhere.

Forty-five minutes had passed.

Brian and Colt's horses were trembling hard, almost to a point where they couldn't stand steady on their feet. Rick was concerned.

Kelly explained in great detail about Mother Nature and her ability to heal her own.

"So all this"—he pointed at the trembling—"is a good thing?"

She laughed for the first time in the last hour or so, "Yes, Rick, it's a very good thing. You'll see." He managed a smile as he continued to rub the front legs of Colt's horse. Rick was extremely impressed with the sixteen-year-old's knowledge.

She took a quick glance in her dad's direction, and held her breath. Sugar Babe wasn't trembling, not even a slight shiver.

Chip had to accept something he didn't want to—the mare was in shock. Susan had started warming the big insulated horse blankets for him in between keeping the bag of warm water on Brian's toes. The mare's hide felt clammy to him, a sign of shock.

Brian was holding his own. Body-wise he was better, but it would be a long slow haul with the foot.

Ken looked around for Colt. When he wasn't at the stove, Ken glanced toward the horses and found him with Kelly. He was brushing his horse's neck and talking to Kelly.

"One down, two to go, then there's the mare," Ken said out loud to himself.

Ken looked at Steph, who was facing Brenda now, holding her hands for warmth. She was wrapped in an insulated horse blanket. Steph saw Ken looking at her. She put two fingers up to her mouth to indicate quiet. Brenda had fallen into a much-needed sleep. Ken nodded his approval.

"Now for Sugar Babe," he thought. Walking up to Chip, he saw the worried look on his face.

"She's in shock!" Chip said barely above a whisper.

"She's going to need an IV, Chip, she has hypothermia," Ken stated, but he knew Chip already knew that.

"I agree, but with what, I think we have Ringer's and dextrose, but they are in the other barn." They both knew what stood between the two barns.

"Have you taken her temperature?" Ken asked.

"Yes, about fifteen minutes ago. Not good, eighty-two."

A shocked look spread across Ken's face. He couldn't figure out why she was still alive, except that he knew she had her momma's heart.

"I've got to talk to Brenda. Sure hope she's up to answering some questions," Ken said. Chip nodded in agreement as he stroked the mare's neck.

"Chip, take her temperature again for me please," Ken said as he walked to the stove and added more wood. He turned toward Brenda. She still didn't look good. He whispered out loud, "We can't lose either one, Lord!"

Kelly had walked up to her dad and held the mare's tail for him. She asked, "Dad, can I give some warm water now and then some warm mash?"

"What? Yes, sounds good, just not too much water. They'll want more, but it will cramp them if they drink their fill," Chip said, his eyes were on Ken and Brenda while thinking what it would take to get to the horse barn.

"You okay, Dad?" She noticed his uneasiness as she looked into his eyes.

"Yes, honey, just worried." He kissed the top of her head. "Go," he said.

Brenda was awake now, and seemed somewhat better out of her eyes. She was starting to talk a little. She had asked about Brian and Colt. Steph was telling her about Brian's foot but left out a lot of the detail. She wasn't ready for that just yet.

Ken walked up and knelt down in front of her. Taking her hands, he looked them over for frostbite. Seeing none, he relaxed a little. "How's my girl doing?"

She smiled slightly at her friend.

"Brenda, I need to talk to you about Sugar Babe," he hesitated. Brenda stared in his eyes, expecting bad news.

"Brenda, she has hypothermia. Chip's taking her temperature now. We know she needs an IV. I need to know with what. We have Ringer's and dextrose. I'm guessing Ringer's, but it's in the other barn."

Immediately, she looked toward the outside wall and showed a look of fear in her eyes.

"I need to know at what temperature to IV her. It was eighty-two twenty minutes ago." Brenda's eyes filled with panic, then tears.

"Brenda, do you understand?" Ken asked.

She looked past him to Chip and the mare. Tears ran down her face. "Ringer's, 82.5 degrees, temp now," she replied in a sad voice, not much above a whisper.

"Okay, okay," Ken whispered while patting her hand, then he took hold of her wrist and took her pulse. Glancing at Steph, he mouthed the words, "Try to keep her calm."

A few moments later, they heard Chip holler," Thank You, Lord Jesus!"

They all looked his way, "Guys, her temp is up to 82.5 degrees."

Ken turned, looking toward Chip. "She's gotta keep coming up real quick, Chip, or we are putting that IV in, understand!"

He looked at Brenda. She nodded then whispered, "Again in fifteen minutes."

Ken looked at Chip to see if he had heard Brenda then turned back. She was crying. He reached over to hold her, then he looked at Brian. The tears were running down Brian's face. He smiled toward Ken and gave him a thumbs-up.

The next fifteen minutes felt like a lifetime. Finally they all heard Chip scream, "It's coming up, Brenda, it's 83 degrees!"

Brenda started crying all over again.

Brenda buried her face in Steph's chest. Colt walked over, hearing a commotion. "Mom, are you okay?"

She sat up and wiped her eyes. "Yes, son," then turned to Ken, "Ken, temp again in twenty minutes and drench her with sugar water every fifteen minutes, please." Her voice was past the point of emotional.

"Will do, pretty lady!" Ken said with a big smile. "Colt, why don't you come sit with your mom for a while. I think she could use some loving."

Brenda tried to laugh as her son wrapped his long arms around her, but tears came instead.

A few minutes later, Brenda called Steph over, "I want to sit next to Brian, please."

There was only about eight feet separating them, but to the husband and wife, it felt like miles.

Steph looked at Brenda, then quickly at Brian. They looked so lonely, Steph felt bad. She should have realized that they both would response better by being next to each other. She tried to cover up her feelings by saying, "I think that's a perfect idea. Colt, can you help her stand for a minute while I move her chair." When Brenda tried to stand, she was still too weak. Her legs started giving way. Colt scooped her up in his arms and held her until Steph was organized. Brian had a big smile on his face. As Colt sat her down next to him, immediately Brenda started crying again, and Susan too.

Moments later, the whole barn was shedding tears. Colt had knelt down in front of his mom and dad, and the Rogers family huddled together, crying, each thankful to be alive.

Ken gathered himself enough to hunt for the drench gun, so thankful when he found it. Quickly he mixed up brown sugar and warm water.

"Okay, let's do this," he hollered at Chip. He inserted the slender metal neck of the drench gun into the side of her mouth at the very back and slowly pressed the plunger, letting the warm sugary liquid trickle down her throat. Chip held her head up so she would swallow. Chip and Ken both laughed, saying, "Good girl," at the same time as she swallowed willingly.

"Thank You, Lord, for small blessings!"

Chip was slowly seeing some improvement. The mare was shivering a little now and her eyes were starting to look more normal. Though, when Chip looked deep down into them, he could still see the trauma.

"I know, girl, it's going to take a while," he whispered to her, running his hand over her face with love.

Suddenly, a hard gush of wind hit the west side of the barn, hard enough that it rattled the stove pipe. Ken and Chip looked at each other, both holding their breath.

Finally it passed, but there would be more. The winds were still ramping up in strength. A war would rage tonight—the old barn against a wind from Canada, good against evil.

Ken took Sugar's temperature again. He walked up beside Chip. "84.5." He patted Chip's shoulder and the mare's neck before walking off toward Brenda.

Chip wrapped his arms around Sugar's neck and buried his face and started crying.

Jakker's Babe looked up from her pen at Chip and lovingly nickered at him.

As Ken walked up to Brenda, he noticed she was trembling hard now. Steph had a smile that showed her relief. He knelt down next to Brenda again and said, "Up to 84.5, she's finding her way out of the woods." Brenda started crying again. Brian wrapped his arm around her shoulder and pulled her close.

The mare Sugar Babe was very special to both Brenda and Chip. It was hard to tell who loved her more. She was the ten-year-old daughter of Jakker's Babe. Brenda had fallen in love with the mare and spent two years trying to get Chip to sell her. Finally he gave in, knowing she'd have the best of homes, and just as importantly, she was staying close.

Pulling herself together, she said thanks to Ken as she looked at Brian.

"Is Chip okay?," Steph asked her brother.

"He's been better, sis," Ken replied. Steph understood.

Lilly heard Chip sobbing. "Chip, is she going to be okay?" concern sounded in her young voice.

"Yes, Lilly, these are happy tears."

She bent over to the side so Chip could see her. Smiling, she said, "I like those kind!"

Finally pulling himself together, Chip hollered to get everyone's attention, "She's going to be okay!"

The whole barn erupted in cheers of relief, but none more than Chip.

Two members of this new barn family had basically been totally ignored for the last hour and a half. Molly and Lucky had both been "good girls," not requiring any attention while it was desperately needed elsewhere—they had been watched over by another.

Almost two hours had gone by. Somehow they managed to do all the right things with what they had available. People and horses all seemed to be on a path toward recovery. They had been lucky on this stormy night. Some would call it "blessed."

Ken needed a minute. He leaned against Lucky's pen, checking her a few seconds ago, deciding that she was fine, for now. Taking a long breath, he automatically re-evaluated the barn again. His heart still went out to Brian. He knew he was still struggling with the pain, but his toes were better. Susan was still putting the warm water bags on them. They had gone from white to flaming red, which was good, but painful nonetheless.

He smiled as he watched Susan. "I sure was wrong about her," he told himself, thinking back on his first impression. "No one has worked harder tonight. How do I repay a stranger for helping save the ones I love?" he asked himself.

Ken felt his heart wanting control over his mind, but his mind sent a panic signal. *Can't do, heart, you're a good thing, but right now I still need my training in control.* He scolded himself out loud, "I know better. I need to keep my heart on the back burner right now."

But his heart had a mind of its own. It turned his eyes toward Brenda, sweet Brenda. She still looked like death warmed over with the big black circles around her eyes. Next to Steph, she was the strongest woman he knew, but physically, she had met her match. The storm had come real close to claiming this small framed woman. Her eyes were closed, her head was tilted up and back as she leaned against the bench behind her. Ken hoped she was sleeping and not thinking.

Ken's eyes moved next to Steph. She was talking to Brian. A few seconds later she got up and headed up toward Molly. This told him that his sweet Brenda was okay.

He glanced toward the kids next. Colt was brushing his horse's neck as he talked to Kelly, who was working on Brian's horse again. Ken had made them stop for a while and rest, at the stove, but ten minutes later they were back at the horses. Ken figured the ranch blood in both of them had them doing what they did best.

The horses were slowly warming up and drying out. The hay they were eating would warm them from the inside out and the brushing now was basically to keep the kids busy.

Steph was coming back now, walking at a normal pace, so that told Ken Molly's baby was still on hold, for the moment.

Ken felt that called for another prayer, "Thank You, Lord, for putting Molly's condition on hold for us so we could take care of the others." Nothing was ever taken for granted by this guardian.

Ken heard Rick laugh. Rick, Rick was trying hard. He was the duck out of water that was desperately trying to be accepted. Ken was sure he was capable of handling a crisis, just one of a different nature, maybe like the stock market crashing.

Still, he was here, doing everything asked of him, but the nervous laugh showed how uncomfortable he still was. Ken knew that by the end of the night, he would be a different person.

Now, one more to check on, he had saved him for last, on purpose.

Chip was brushing Sugar Babe, gently talking to her. Ken took a deep breath, wishing he could have done something, anything to spare Chip some of the stress that he had just gone through tonight.

He forced himself not to think about Chip, given a different outcome with the mare.

"Again, thank You, Lord."

Ken listened to the wind, tuning the barn sounds out. The wind was constant. He felt her strength. A stray thought crossed his mind: *nothing happens by chance.*

Now Ken let his heart take over. "Thank You, Lord, for hearing my many prayers tonight, for answering them, then the many, many more to come, for there's a long ways to go yet tonight, but then You know that Lord, Amen."

Ken thought about his prayers and added, "Lord, I'm just a simple cowboy, with simple words." He stood a few more minutes, he still felt troubled. "Lord, everyone is claiming a lane light saved their lives by guiding them to the barn. Father, I have to believe, there is no other answer. Thank You for the lane light, Amen."

A few minutes after Chip had told Lilly that she could stop rubbing Sugar's legs, he cheerfully thanked her for her help, telling her that she helped save the mare's life. She smiled and went running to Kelly.

"What's the matter, Lil?" Kelly thought she saw a hint of distress in Lilly's face. She had her hands between her legs and was kind of hopping in place.

Lilly motioned for Kelly to come down to her level. She cupped her hands around Kelly's ear and whispered, "Where's the bathroom, Kelly?"

Kelly laughed, "Sweetie, we don't have one in the barn." Instantly Lilly said, "Oh," realizing she had a dilemma.

"Come on, Lilly, I'll show you where to squat."

Lilly didn't move. "Squat? What is squat?" she asked, very concerned now.

"Come on," Kelly grabbed her by the arm and started dragging the little girl.

"Okay, okay!" she hollered. The two walked to the south end of the barn, to the east side of the double doors. It was dark in the corner. "Nobody can see you from here," Kelly said.

"What do I do, Kelly?" sending desperate vibes now.

"Oh yeah, pull your pants down pretty far and squat, kinda like sitting, but you gotta hold yourself up." Kelly was in giggles now. "Lean back far enough so you don't wet yourself."

"What?" Her voice was squeaking, "Stay with me, don't leave me, Kelly, please!"

"I'm not leaving you, Lilly, hurry up." Kelly turned her back a little but tried to keep an eye on her. "Learning to squat can be difficult!" she told herself, instantly covering her mouth with her hands to muffle the laugh. She gave Lilly a few seconds then unrolled some toilet paper off the roll that hung on the wall.

"Here, Lilly," holding it out to her.

A few minutes later, Lilly walked out all smiles. "Sure a lot of stuff to learn on a ranch." Kelly patted her head as they headed back to the center of the barn. Lilly took off running to her mom, who was with Steph and Brenda at the stove. She walked up in front of Susan and said, out loud, in too loud a voice again, "When you need to go, Mommy, I'll show you where to squat!"

Susan looked blankly at her daughter and said, "Oh Lord!"

Steph giggled, "Yeah, we don't have a bathroom out here. There's a dark spot down in the corner where you can squat. Ken's got a roll of toilet paper hanging on the wall." Steph tried to stay serious, but it didn't work out that way and she broke out laughing.

Susan stared at her with a blank expression, then, in a mousey voice, she said, "I guess you did promise an adventure we'd never forget, and I can say that you do things a lot differently out here for sure."

This got Brenda to laugh for the first time tonight, and without thinking, she said, "You'll live!" Brenda got very quiet, realizing that the expression had taken on a whole new meaning to her.

Chip was tired. Mentally, he was trying to hold it together. After losing it once already tonight, he had to. Sugar needed him, he thought, that's what he was telling himself, anyhow. His mind would only let him concentrate on one thing at a time, so he chose the mare. He also realized that Ken had taken charge, holding the barn together, like he always did. It was the only way he knew how to be, "a guardian."

Chip panicked as he felt his mind wandering. He turned and looked at a Jakker, hoping she could hold his attention, then he tried thinking about Steph and Kelly. It helped some, but he still slipped. As his thoughts took over, he relaxed some. Memories of the animals, mainly the horses, flooded his head. He felt his body giving in to the situation that the PSTD was causing. Most of the time he called them "attacks," some friendly, some not. The military ones were the worst, but this one was okay, he welcomed it. There was no storm in this attack. This one didn't last long. Chip took a couple of deep breaths. Within a few minutes he was starting to feel like himself again. "That wasn't bad."

Ken came Chip's way again. "You okay?" he asked with a concerned look on his face.

Chip smiled. "Yep, I'm good."

Steph was keeping one eye on Brenda and going over the facts of the night so far, in her head.

Brenda was sitting up, alert, at the stove, wrapped in a blanket, and sipping the orange juice that was being forced on her.

When they moved Brenda over next to Brian, it faced her away from Molly's end of the barn, toward the horses and the south end.

Jamie had helped Ken with Brian, but that was basically while Brenda was still out of it. He had since gone back to be with Molly.

Steph didn't think Brenda was aware that the couple or their situation even existed.

Brian wasn't aware that the couple also claimed the lane light.

Ken had set some bales together, which allowed Brian to stretch out and sleep for a while. He had been keeping a close eye on Brian's toes. They had gone from the warm water bags to putting the foot in a pail of warm water, but Brian had hit his limit with the pain, so Ken backed off the water bath deciding to just watch for now. He had placed a towel gently over the foot and had Brian keeping it propped up next the stove.

Both of the Rogerses were aware to the fact that the Kahlers said the lane light didn't exist.

Steph's other eye was on Molly. She had Susan staying close by, watching for any signs of contraction.

Ken had hung up all the wet coats and coveralls up on pegs to dry out. The three kids were attempting to clean up all the saddles and tack, while being engaged in nonstop conversation. Lilly and Colt seemed to hit it right off, with Colt laughing at all her silliness. Every once in a while Lilly would run the barn, to see what everyone else was doing.

Kelly thought, *This is my chance to ask Colt some questions.* They were both on their knees. "Colt, did you guys really see a light at the entrance? You know, there isn't one," Kelly stated calmly.

Colt stopped working and looked at Kelly. "There was tonight," he said, then sat in silence staring at her.

Kelly waited to see if he would say more.

"It was so bright that you couldn't look into it. The horses were afraid of it." He hesitated, telling himself to stay calm, "I couldn't tell where it was coming from, it was just over the entrance."

"Were you scared?" Kelly asked.

"Of freezing to death, yes. I guess we were too cold to be afraid of the light." Then he added, "The light felt safe. I don't know what would have…" The words wouldn't come. "Mom's horse wasn't going much further."

Kelly looked up at the favorite mare, standing near the stove, munching on hay now. "I'm glad she's safe now, that all of you are safe."

As Colt told his story, his voice sounded a lot more mature than his sixteen years. "I think you needed to live it to understand what happened"—he looked in Kelly's eyes—"and I pray you never have to."

Kelly understood, saying, "Me too." She raised her head up, listening, as the wind attacked the barn viciously again.

Ken had just put the fourth pot of coffee on to perk, the old-fashioned way, in a stove top percolator. Everyone was allowed coffee now, so Ken planned to keep it available.

Rick had been all over the barn, making small talk. He seemed lost since everything had calmed down. As he walked closer to the middle area of the barn, the scents changed. "What is that smell?" Whatever it was, he liked it.

Ken had just walked up to him. "This smell," he waved his arms around were they stood.

"Yeah," Rick said.

"Well, it's linseed oil, wet leather, camp coffee, and a little fresh cow poop thrown in." Ken had just seen Kelly jump in Lucky's pen to clean up a fresh pile. He'd thrown that part in for fun. He looked at Rick to see what kind of reaction he'd get.

"Well, you should bottle it, it's great," he laughed.

Ken smiled and calmly said, "Oh, I'm guessing someone probably has."

The two men stood watching Kelly and Colt working on the saddles, each one knowing exactly what needed to be done.

Rick looked at Ken, very seriously. "Kids learn a lot of life out here," the words were more of a statement than a question. Ken stayed quiet, letting Rick think out his thoughts. Slowly he looked directly at Ken again and said, "They learn to be good people."

The evening was marching on, so was the storm. Chip was starting to get nervous. There were things that needed to be talked about, these talks determining which direction this night would take. He laughed to himself, "Of course I already know it's out of our hands, been that way all day."

Steph had sat down with Brenda a few minutes ago and tried to explain the situation with Molly.

Brenda let her finish, then said, "I just about froze to death, was guided to your barn by a light that doesn't exist, to deliver a stranger's baby in a barn on Christmas Eve, and oh, oh, wait, let's not forget all this during the year's worst storm going on outside. Is there anything else I need to know about?"

Brenda didn't know if she should laugh or cry. She sat motionless staring at Steph.

Steph wanted to burst out laughing. It all sounded so funny, when it was said like that, but she didn't, she knew better.

In a sheepish voice, she added, "Well, yeah, you know I love you, but Kelly's longhorn is going to calve tonight too." Steph held her breath.

Brenda threw her arms in the air, "Well, that part is a piece of cake!"

Before Brenda could comment any more, she had a quick revelation go through her head: "Be grateful, you are part of My plan." It sent a different kind of chills through her body.

Brian looked a lot better. Chip sat down with him near the stove. Brenda had gotten up to walk around with Steph a bit.

Chip spoke first, "You can tell me the whole story later, there's no time right now. I know the heifers got out, but how did you end up here?" he asked Brian.

Ken had just sat down with them as Brian started telling his story.

"Bred heifers tore the fence down. We left at ten thirty, maybe eleven, to go find them."

Chip cut him off, "Storm was starting to ramp up by then, you find them?"

"Yes, they were okay when we found them, should be okay during storm, plenty of cover, if they stay put." He continued, "We went out the south gate. Should have been a shortcut back to the house, but somehow, we got turned around."

Chip whispered under his breath, "I guess!" but both heard him.

Ken sighed, "Go on, Brian."

"Anyhow, like I said, we were turned around. We rode for hours, couldn't get any bearings or landmarks working in our favor, we weren't going to last much longer."

Ken was solemn faced, "When did you see the light?"

"Oh, I can't tell you that. We were so cold that distance and time didn't have any realization. It was just up ahead, just a lightness in the sky, up ahead of us at first. Colt was the one who saw it first. We rode toward it. As we got closer, it got brighter. Then we were sittin' under it at the entrance of your lane, and you know the rest."

They all sat in silence for a few minutes, taking Brian's account in. Finally, Ken started talking. "You know, we said there is no lane light, Brian," Ken stated.

"Yeah, well, tonight there was," Brian said in a choked voice.

Chip turned his eyes to the rafters, anticipating Ken's next words.

Ken leaned forward and took Brian's hands in his and held tight, "Those kids—you know, Jamie and Molly—they were guided to this barn by that same light, the one that doesn't exist." Ken felt Brian's hand go limp. Ken held on tighter.

Tears swelled in Brian's eyes. "We would have died tonight without that light!"

Chip looked in Brian's eyes, "That's what the kids said!"

Steph and Brenda leaned against the rails of Lucky's pen. "Brenda, do you feel well enough to go see Molly?" Steph asked.

Brenda frowned and then said, "Yeah, guess we'll see if I can comprehend anything yet." The two women walked to the front of the barn. Steph introduced Brenda to Molly and Jamie. She had already explained who Susan was and her family.

After grilling Molly for twenty minutes and asking every question Brenda could think of, Steph went and retrieved Brenda's medical bag and dug out the stethoscope.

Brenda listened to the baby's heartbeat. She held her breath with worry until she heard the perfectly healthy sound. She exhaled with a smile, telling the young couple that the baby seemed fine, for now.

Steph and Brenda walked to the stove, wanting the men in the conversation.

"We need to talk," Steph said in a serious tone.

Ken had gone to check on Lucky. He heard Steph call his name and wave him over. "What's up, sis?"

The group all sat down near the stove.

"Find out much?" Chip asked.

Brenda started talking, sounding like her old self, "Some, I understand why they were doing, what they were doing. I don't care about that." She looked around at everyone, then continued, "What matters is what is going to happen tonight. She is in labor. Course you all knew that. I haven't checked her yet. Her water hasn't broken. We are many hours off yet. The tricky part is the stuff we don't know about her, about her pregnancy.

She stopped here, to let those words sink in.

"She...thinks she's type B. She thinks her health is good but hasn't seen a doctor in two or three months, maybe longer, she wasn't sure. Sounds to me like her mom was doing more harm than good. There's no money, so I'm guessing she hasn't been eating right. I think Jamie has tried to do the best he could, considering."

"But, back to tonight, basically"—she scanned the group—"here's where we stand. If anything goes wrong, we can't get her and the baby to a hospital. We can't get a doctor here, we are it. I can't check her blood pressure."

Ken listened. There were questions he wanted to ask. "Brenda, I don't want to open that old can of worms but," he hesitated and looked at all the others, "what if she needs a C-section to save the baby?" His voice was as serious as anyone had ever heard it. Silence settled in again.

"I've thought about that some," Brenda replied, then added, "more thinking to do yet. Last night I cleaned and repacked my medical bag. Funny thing is, I put things in it that I never have with me. Don't ask me why, cause I can't answer that. I had no reason to do what I did; I just knew I needed to."

Ken heard the voice again—yes. That one word made Ken's skin crawl. He tried to listen to Brenda again. They both seemed to be on the same track, as she briefly told him what her bag contained, then his head went to the trauma room in the equine barn.

"Horses, people, medical procedures were still about the same," Ken saying his thoughts out loud. The conversation basically only consisted now of Ken and Brenda, the rest listened.

"Let's both think a bit on this, then we can talk some more, okay, Ken?" Brenda said, "I've got a feeling it will all work out. After all it's still Christmas Eve." She tried to smile, looking from one to another. She thought about the voice she had heard. Just maybe whatever it was, was here to help.

The group was silent for a few minutes, each with their own thoughts going through their heads.

Brian spoke first, "I hate to even bring this up, but Chip, how much liability insurance do you carry on this place?"

Chip replied quickly, "A lot."

"Okay." Looking toward Brenda now, Brian stated, "I think you carry enough. These seem like nice kids but—"

Steph broke in, "We don't know what kind of worms are in the can we are getting ready to open."

Ken let out a half laugh. "As long as they aren't rattlesnakes, missy!"

Chip wasn't done yet. "Okay, we still need to make a big decision," Chip said, leading out with a serious tone. He called Rick and Susan over to join them, the kids followed.

"Jamie and Molly don't get a vote," he laughed, but Ken knew his meaning. They had caused all this.

"Guys, we have a decision to make, right now—it can't wait any longer."

Ken looked at Chip and thought, "Calm down, buddy."

"There's at least three feet of snow on the ground right now, from what I can tell, and it's just going to get worse. We need to figure out if we want to go to the house or stay here."

Everyone was quiet.

"The power's out, will probably stay that way. If we stay put, we'll probably stay warm enough, so far so good."

Susan mumbled under her breath, "Probably, what does probably mean?" Rick grabbed her hand and squeezed it hard.

Chip kept talking, "We have water, we also have a heifer that may calve tonight and a mare that can't be left yet."

Ken shot Steph a quick look with his eyes, basically telling her that Chip hadn't been updated on the heifer's condition yet. Chip's wording didn't seem to alarm Kelly either.

"Someone is going to have to stay here. We can probably keep Molly somewhat comfortable if we stay here." He hesitated for a few seconds. "If we decide to go to the house, we will have a battle on our hands from the start just trying to get Molly and Brian there."

Brian's strong personality took a blow. He didn't like the fact what he couldn't take care of his family or himself right now. He wasn't used to needing to be cared for. Brenda leaned her head on his shoulder and whispered, "It will be okay."

"I doubt that either one can walk." Chip moved on, not dwelling on it for Brian's sake. "The power is out there too, and since the house is all electric and no wood stove, it means trying to heat water in the fireplace and everybody staying in the kitchen to try and stay warm. Molly would definitely be more comfortable, but here comes the important part—once we are there, this storm is going to drift that snow between the house and this barn, ten to twelve feet high, in the next twelve to sixteen hours. We can get out the back door, but we aren't coming back down that hill, maybe for a couple of days," he stopped again, letting the words sink in.

"Here, I'm close to the tractor with the snow blower on."

Everyone knew exactly what Chip was saying was true, except for Rick and Susan. They stood there with blank expressions on their faces.

Brenda broke the silence, "Chip's right. I have lived here all my life. I vote to stay in the barn. I can—we can"—looking at Ken and Steph—"take care of Molly just as well here, and we are a whole lot closer to that road out front than if we were at the house." She took a deep breath. She had stopped breathing while she said her piece.

Kelly jumped up. "I'm not going to the house," she said with enough attitude that Chip waved his hand in the air, to send the message, "calm down."

Ken stepped next to Kelly. "We need to stay in the barn," Ken said seriously.

Chip looked around at everyone and said, "Everyone okay about staying?"

Chip looked directly at Rick. "Rick?"

Susan started tearing up. Her first thought was to say no, but instead she held on to Lilly a little tighter and asked, "Are we going to be okay?"

Rick stepped a little closer to her and put an arm around her, just as a "hell yeah" came from both Steph and Kelly. Brenda put her head down and broke out laughing at her friend.

Chip looked at his two women and tiredly said, "Like mother, like daughter."

Rick and Susan still weren't smiling, but Rick spoke for his family, "We're on board, just tell us how to help." He squeezed Susan and kissed the top of her head.

Steph was engulfed with plans. "Okay people, we'd better get food and some supplies from the house before it gets any worse out there." She looked around, for Brenda. "I'll make a food list and whatever else we need. Brenda, I'll need your help with a medical list, whatever you think will help," she stared in Brenda's eyes.

Back on tract, she hollered at Kelly, "Kel, can you go?"

"Sure, Mom," she replied with a smile.

"Okay, here's your list—blankets, sheets, towels—and sweetie, we need your baby blankets, they're in Granny's cedar chest, at the foot of my bed; there aren't very many." Steph had only kept the ones that held sentimental value, but they would help tonight.

"Oh, and Brenda came up with a list of medical type stuff, okay, baby?" Steph realized she was sending her only child out into the raging storm. She swallowed hard.

"Hey, Kelly," Brenda hollered as Kelly climbed into her coveralls, "think you can bring a hairbrush back with you?" She tried to run her hand through her mangled hair.

Kelly laughed, shaking her ponytail back and forth. "Sure, I think we all could use one." She smiled at Lilly who was definitely a mess.

Thoughts ran through Susan's head, *Oh great, a community hairbrush!* By the end of this evening, she would realize that the people she called community would soon be considered family.

"Chip, here's a food list and the supplies we need. Who else is going with you?" Steph asked.

"Looks like Colt, Rick, Kelly, and me. I want Ken to stay here. I want someone who knows what they are doing with the rest of you."

Steph thought for a moment, "I'm coming too, you need more hands."

"Are you sure, honey?" Chip asked.

"Yep, just let me get some clothes on."

Chip was hollering instructions to both the ones going and the ones staying, "Ken, do not come looking for us, we will be back."

"Yeah, well, you are only getting so much time, so don't dally along," Ken said.

Chip knew he meant his words.

Everyone knew, even Rick, to hold on to that rope. Once they were gone, the barn felt lonely.

Ken made Brian move closer to the stove and prop his foot up high. He opened the door so more heat was available. Brian had a sock covering the foot now, which would allow the heat to, hopefully, reach his toes easier.

"You're going to burn a lot of wood with that door open like that, bud!" Brian commented.

"You let me worry about that," Ken said with a smile.

Lilly attempted to water horses again. Susan seemed lost as she stood in the center of the barn, when minutes ago it was so busy. Brenda walked up next to her. She looked at Brenda, "How are they going to see where they are going?" she asked, with worry in her voice.

"They aren't, that's what the rope is for. They are going to feel their way. They'll be okay, Susan." She tried to laugh. "It's not their first rodeo."

Susan had actually heard the expression before. Looking directly at Brenda, she said, "It is Rick's!"

Brenda knew she needed to calm Susan's worries fast. "Well, Rick is a quick learn, he'll be fine."

"Years ago Chip's great-great-grandpa put thick wooden posts deep in the ground, every fifteen feet, from this barn to the house. Back then, this was the only barn on the ranch."

"What were the posts for?" Susan spoke before thinking about it; otherwise, she would have figured it out without asking, "Oh, for the rope, you mean."

"When the first snow comes, they would put the rope up. They didn't have weather forecaster like we do. They never had insight on how bad a storm would be. They said only the Indians had those gifts. Now we watch the weather on TV and put the ropes up when needed, like for this storm." They walked over to Lucky's pen. "Sometimes, like tonight, you have to hold on real tight, cause the wind is so strong.

Rick held on to that rope when you guys came to the barn, didn't you?"

"No, I just held on to Rick." She smiled, realizing it had felt good relying on her husband. Then she added, "He told me he would keep me safe."

Brenda smiled. "A lot of people lost their lives many years ago by getting lost in a storm just trying to get to a barn or a house."

Brenda hesitated, then continued, "We were lost tonight, we got turned around, so we tried to follow the fence line. All we could see were the tops of the post. Thank God for the lane light." then she turned to look at Molly and Jamie, adding, "that doesn't exist."

They stood in silence for a short time. Finally Susan spoke, "I wish they'd all come back."

Brenda patted the woman's arm. Susan instantly pulled away. Brenda ignored the movement. "They will soon. The lists were long. It will take them a while to gather everything, especially in the dark."

Lilly had walked up and heard her mom's last comment. She pulled on her sleeve. "They'll all be okay, Mommy, God's in charge." A little eight-year-old from the big city was putting two and two together.

There's something about the innocence of a child that allows them to grasp on to and acknowledge ideas that adults would rather ignore or refuse to believe. This was the case tonight, Christmas Eve.

Lilly could only believe. She wasn't capable of doing anything but. She was the first to realize that a story would be played out tonight, a reenactment of the most precious story of all time…

Ken looked at his watch. He was beginning to get nervous. In his mind, he had recreated all of their steps. He estimated how long for each task, getting to the house, gathering everything up—in the dark—then the battle to get back to the barn while carrying everything. He was only giving them fifteen more minutes, then he would go looking for them.

Brenda was still standing with Susan and Lilly, but glanced Molly's way. Brenda thought Molly looked restless. As soon as Susan finished the story she was telling Brenda, she would go check on her.

Moments later, she heard Jamie call her name.

Brenda went and knelt down at Molly's side, "Hey, sweetie."

In an unsteady voice, Molly said, "I don't feel good."

Brenda felt her forehead, feeling a clamminess, "Are you hurting, Molly?'

"No, I feel like I'm going to faint."

Brenda didn't need to think long. "Jamie, when did she eat last?"

"I'm guessing she probably hasn't eaten since last night. We didn't have any food with us today," Jamie's voice was sounding shaky, fear was ramping up in him again.

"Okay, her blood sugar is crashing." She turned to Susan, "Can you see if there's any orange juice left, and bring some if there is please."

"Sure," Susan took off running, with Lilly following.

Seconds later, Lilly screamed at the top of her lungs, "We found some, Brenda!"

Brenda whispered, "Good. Thank You, Lord."

"Drink this slowly. The slower the better, Molly," Brenda said, sitting down to stay with her.

"She okay, Brenda?" Ken asked, concerned.

Brenda shook her head yes. Ken checked his watch again. "They've got five more minutes."

"As soon as they all get back here, we'll get you a ham sandwich, gotta get some food in that belly. We can't have you giving birth on an empty stomach."

Jamie's face was turning white again. Brenda wasn't sure if it was from hunger or thinking about what was coming.

Molly nodded her head yes.

Ken was listening to the wind; the sound was intensifying. "I can't stand here doing nothing," he thought. He grabbed a lantern and went to the door, opening it wide. He blocked it with his body to hold it open. Now he listened. He couldn't see anything, so he needed to rely on his hearing. Less than a minute later, he heard Chip holler. He had seen Ken's light. Slowly they all made it back into the barn.

Lilly screamed in fun, "Live snowmen!"

Brenda, with Susan and Jamie, went to help. Steph was screaming orders "No, don't throw that bag!" Everyone was dumping the bags into a big pile. Steph was horrified, picturing spaghetti everywhere.

Snow was brushed off coats and pants, and standing near the stove seemed to be popular again. Everyone survived the elements, lending the way for new stories to be shared.

"Boy, that was quite an experience. I totally understand why we are staying put. I'm in for the night," Rick laughed.

Steph walked up to him and put a hand on his shoulder. "You okay?"

He smiled at her and said, "Yes, and I was glad I could help."

Steph felt he really meant his words.

Brenda had made a quick sandwich for Molly. Within minutes, her color was better and she was smiling again.

The four and a half women went to work. Steph and Kelly on food; Susan and Lilly organized blankets, sheets, and towels, putting everything up by Molly. Brenda took care of the medical things she had asked for, knowing each item would have a part to play tonight.

Ken kept his eyes on the barn activity and his ears on the storm outside. She was demanding a big part of his attention. He worried about the barn, that she might have met her match with this one. He prayed not.

Twenty minutes later, the inside of the barn was silent for a few minutes, while everyone chowed down on warmed up spaghetti and cold garlic bread. Steph's beautiful salad had been left behind. Brenda continued to keep the pregnant girl in her sights. She was eating again and seemed to feel a lot better.

Lilly had been the first one to speak when they all sat down to eat, "This is the best food I've ever tasted!"

Susan smiled at Steph. "I think she was hungry."

Food was helping with Chip's anxiety; a full belly seemed to help a lot.

He laughed at Lilly, "Everything is better in the barn, half-pint!"

Everyone laughed in agreement. Ken felt a quiet smile.

Susan was sitting near Chip. Everyone was finishing up with the meal. "I might as well ask," she thought to herself.

"Chip, can I ask a question?" Susan asked. She was slowly getting a little braver.

Chip turned and said, "Shoot, er, sure."

Ken smiled.

"Okay, I was wondering why all the barns are so far away from the house."

"My great-great-grandfather wanted to feel like at the end of the day, he could go home. Mentally, the distance helped him separate the ranch business from his home life," Chip said in a kind voice, impressed that she asked a question out of the blue. Susan didn't talk much.

"Do you feel the same way?" Rick jumped in.

"Yes, I agree. Each is important, but in the end, the division is very important—to me. I want family to come first. They are the reason for everything else.

Neither Rick nor Susan said anything, but each knew what the other was thinking.

Rick brought his work home, every night, every weekend. Work came before family. He also knew his wife well. She would start crying soon, so he decided to change the subject to ward off a scene.

Ken had gotten up to throw his plate away. As he passed by Susan, he placed his hand briefly on her shoulder, then walked to Lucky's pen.

"Everyone get enough dessert?" Steph hollered, as she covered the rest of a pie back up. They had finished off almost two full pumpkin pies.

Rick couldn't figure out why it had tasted "better" than normal. He loved pumpkin pie, and that was a good one.

Kelly laughed. "Cause you've never tasted pie made with home-grown pumpkin. We grow them every summer, and Mom and I can the pumpkin"—she held her arms out in an open fashion—"and voila, the best pumpkin pie you've ever eaten." She took a bow as Rick laughed and clapped.

"We also grow and can green beans and tomatoes," Kelly bragged. Ken and Chip were both grinning at her silliness.

Rick loved her spunk. "What, no corn?"

Susan had never seen a bigger smile on her husband's face. He has a nice smile, she thought.

Kelly wasn't taking Rick's bait. She stood with feet planted, hands on hips. "You don't can corn," then very dryly, she added, "it's in the freezer, silly." Now with a smile, as big as his, she said, "Cream corn, kernel corn, and corn on the cob, take your pick, Rickie!"

Rick stood up and bowed to her. "You win. Best pumpkin pie I've ever eaten."

Suddenly the wind shook the barn, hard, stealing from the relaxed mood.

Rick looked toward Chip and Brian, and said, "Is she going to hold up?" referring to the barn. Instantly, everyone who called Wyoming home replied with a hearty yes!

As the evening slowly moved on, the mood at the stove was more solemn now. The talk was taking on a religious tone of sorts, as testimonies from today's experiences were told. The group was putting two and two together, which was leading them to one conclusion. This talk was stressing Steph out. She was beginning to feel like she couldn't breathe. Her personality was of a strong woman who could take charge and get things done, without being bossy. She was not in control tonight.

Now, words like "God, Lord, miracle, believe, unbelievable, and of course, baby, lane light, and Christmas Eve" were making her head spin.

She stood in the middle of the barn with a hand on her head. Everyone seemed comfortable now, warm and fed, including Molly.

Without her permission, her mind started reminding her of things. A lot had happened already tonight. Ken finding the kids—a pregnant one, ready to hatch, at that; the dramatic entrance of the pretty-much frozen Rogers family with horses near death. No one seemed to be in charge. This wasn't the Christmas Eve she had planned. But everything seemed to be headed in the right direction for now. Ken told her that Brian's foot looked like he wouldn't have any permanent damage. She was glad.

She told herself to slow down and breathe. Finally, she shook her head with her eyes closed. "Come on back, Steph, time for some answers."

"So what now?" Steph and Chip seemed to be sharing the same thoughts. Ken would already have some answers for them. He was always ahead of the game. It was an annoying trait that he possessed. Steph was unaccustomed to not being in charge. This she reminded everyone of, over and over. With everything else that had happened, the overly warm air in the barn combined with the weird amber glow from the lanterns had her on edge. She found her level of common sense pushed to its limit. Chip had already questioned Ken about the warmth, getting no reasonable answer. Steph walked up to the two, who stood a little ways off from the group at the stove. She waved them over, putting more distance between them and the group.

"Guys, don't get me wrong, I'm grateful, but why is this barn… so warm? That stove can't possibly put out enough heat for this large barn with that storm going on outside." Regardless of where you stood, every inch of the barn from the north end to the south end was toasty warm.

Chip threw up his hands and backed up a few steps. This was his defense when he didn't want to answer a question—he had no answers. He had been feeling somewhat ungrounded, like he was entering uncharted territory all night. It had been a very hectic evening. Then going out in the storm again reminded him of how helpless he could be. He wasn't about to take Steph on over a warm barn.

Knowing she wouldn't get anywhere with Chip, she turned her attention to her brother.

The moment the kids and the Rogers told the same story, about the lane light, Ken knew who was responsible. There was no other explanation for a believer.

When they heard the voice in the wind, it reconfirmed what he already knew. He was now left with nothing to question.

Steph repeated her question, "Ken, what is going on, why is this barn so warm?"

This was just the first of her concerns that she needed answers for. Her voice was squeaky, starting to crack with emotion.

"I think you'll have to talk to the Trail Boss if you are after an answer to that, sis."

"What?" Steph stood, looking at him.

"Steph, Chip"—Ken looked from one to another—"all this tonight can't be a coincidence, it's not possible!"

Chip ran his hand through his hair and looked up as he said, "Oh geez!"

Ken ignored him. Continuing, he said, "None of them could have found the lane without the light, and they would all have died." He hesitated, giving them time to absorb the statement. "Unless you can come up with another good explanation, I think we have to roll with mine."

"And what is that?" Steph asked in a defeated voice, on the verge of tears.

"Well, as I said earlier, in cowboy talk, the Trail Boss is in charge," Ken waited now.

"Please stop with the bull, tell me like it is!" Steph demanded, trying not to cry.

"Gladly, sis. The Lord has, for some reason, decided we are to be part of a plan for tonight. I have no idea why us." He kept talking, trying to calm her. "I have no reasonable answer for you," he said, repeating himself.

"I know that it's a special plan. We've already figured that much out, by the lives we saved already, and I don't think there is a way out of it." Ken took a deep breath. "I think we need to accept His wishes and do the best we can. Tonight is surely blessed," he hesitated, then said, "He's already taken the reins." Ken talked with a calm soothing voice.

"You don't really expect me to just give in or accept that logic, do you?" she asked.

Ken was sounding like a preacher on a roll to her.

He took a deep breath as he stared at her. "Why do you always have to be so stubborn?" he asked, letting the breath out slowly. He took a step forward, closer to her, placing his hands on her shoulders. He turned her around to look at Molly, then the others. "Now, do you have a better answer for this?"

He'd give her all the time she needed, as he patiently waited, while Chip stared at the rafters.

Finally she said, "I guess I don't have a good argument."

Chip knew she had hit the end of her rope, so he stepped up. "Ken, I'm going to say this for the both of us."

Chip looked at his wife. Her eyes were filling with tears, but somehow the floodgates held.

"We both believe, you know that. God and religion has always played a big part in our lives and on this ranch, but," he hesitated now, trying to find the right words, "you are the believer, you always have been. Everything about you, your love of God, has always seemed stronger than ours, more devoted. We always know we can lean on your faith for strength and guidance when it comes to things like this." He waved his arms around the barn, "You are our rock!"

Ken jumped in, "You don't need a rock—you need faith!"

"We don't doubt what you are saying; we just need a little more time for it to sink into our stubborn heads."

Steph laughed lightly, a few tears found their way down her cheek. Chip wiped them with a gentle finger, then he said, "I have a feeling we are going to have the rest of tonight and tomorrow for it to sink in."

Ken stayed silent, giving them more time for thought. It was a lot to take in. This didn't happen every day. Chip hugged Steph, who had her head buried in Chip's chest now. He held her and swayed back and forth, like you would to comfort a baby. After a few seconds, Chip kissed the top of her head and said to Ken, "You can tell the Lord we are on His side. We'll do all we can to make this night end with a good outcome. We'll do the work He has put in front of us, but...we need all the help He can give us."

Ken smiled. He laid a hand on Chip's shoulder and calmly said, "I don't have to, He heard you."

Steph was calming down now. Ken was relieved that she had stopped fighting him. She did that a lot as a child. She seemed to have a thing about her brother always winning. She backed away a little from Chip and stood tall, like the confident woman she was. "I do believe and trust Him, with all my heart. I just wish He'd let me in on some of the details."

Chip chuckled lightly and pulled her close again with his arm.

Ken looked at her seriously and said, "He did, sweetie, you weren't listening close enough. You managed to get the Conners here. They are part of His plan."

Steph's eyes brightened up. "So you are saying it was already in the plan when Susan booked Christmas week."

"No," Ken said, "it started when the other people canceled. The Conners were part of His plan, not the other people."

Chip felt playful. "You mean like kill two birds with one stone."

She took a deep breath that almost sounded like a sob, "What?"

"Never mind," Chip grumbled.

Ken continued, "And He wasn't going to make you handle everything by yourself—He sent you Brenda."

Chip frowned. "Wow, they all suffered a lot and came close to dying, just to help deliver a baby."

Steph looked around. "Let's go over by the stairs and tree. This isn't private enough for this talk," then looking at Ken, said, "I'm sure you have a lot more to say to us."

No one had paid them any mind. The laughter and loud talking told Steph everyone was fine. Glancing up toward Molly and Jamie, she saw they were both asleep.

The north corner of the barn was dark. The skinny Christmas tree had been totally forgotten. The canvas bag Ken had carried in, containing his gifts, still lay on the floor where he had thrown it upon finding the strangers in the barn.

"This is better," Steph sighed.

"As I was saying," Ken looked at them very seriously, "I'm sure there's more to their part in the story than we are privileged to know and is possibly none of our business. We each have been given a part to play we aren't to question."

"That's true," Chip whispered.

"Lilly says they're the wise men. Brenda brought the gifts. I guess you can call her skills and knowledge gifts," Ken said.

"Sometimes, God chooses to teach," Ken said, then added, "maybe His lesson is that giving is enough—do we always need to receive?" Ken looked directly into Chip's eyes. Sometimes it was hard for him to read Chip. This was one of those times.

Steph stayed quiet, looking from her brother to her husband. Finally Ken started talking again, in a calming voice. "Okay, let's talk about the Conners. Chip, you are showing Rick that there's more to being a father and husband, that there's more to life than work and money. I'm positive that family will leave here being a lot happier."

Ken took a deep breath. "Then most importantly, we are going to help that young couple bring their new baby into this world. The Lord wants that baby to live, and I have a funny feeling that He also wants these kids in our lives—it's just a feeling."

"I think He's got all the players He wanted here tonight, and now it's up to us to play out His plan."

Chip's face grew serious. "The wind, that moan, they found their way—He was telling us with the wind," Chip's voice was emotional, "and I'll bet the so-called lane light at the entrance faded out when we heard the moan; it wasn't needed anymore."

"As soon as the words faded out, I walked down to the end of the barn and tried to look out the window. It was pitch-black," Ken stated calmly.

"But that doesn't mean anything," Steph added, looking at Ken.

Ken smiled. "No, it doesn't. I believe there was a light."

Ken was getting emotional. He took Steph and Chip's hands, holding them tight. "I personally feel very honored to have been chosen to be here"—he looked toward the other end of the barn—"on this night. We couldn't ask for a better way to spend Christmas Eve."

Chip shuddered at the thought. He kind of missed spending the evening in front of the fireplace, with his family, waiting for Santa, but opted to keep the thought to himself. Then on a more serious note, he had another thought, not quite sure he should voice it, but here it goes. "I agree, it's a great experience, but let's not call it successful just yet, or in other words, not count our chickens. This night still has a long ways to play out."

Finally, Steph was able to share a laugh. "Yeah, just wait until act three starts!"

Ken turned and rested his eyes on Molly again.

"So, Ken," Steph's voice was calmer now, "if I've got this right, you are telling us all thing are possible—"

Before she could say the word *tonight*, Ken said, "With God."

Tears rolled down Steph's face.

Chip's look turned serious now, as he asked Ken, "Are we telling the others all this?"

Ken looked down at his feet for a second then looked at Chip, directly in the eyes. "Yes, but a little at a time, okay?" Then Ken added, "I have a feeling they've all figured out more than you think, especially with what Lilly has been sharing, you know, her opinion of what's happening."

"Yes, the opinionated eight-year-old," Chip chuckled.

Ken's eyes twinkled as he said, "She's right on!"

As they headed back to join the rest, Chip felt shaky. The conversation, the revelation of tonight, was going to take a toll on Chip.

A few minutes later, he felt his head start to spin. He whispered to Ken, "Stay close," as he walked off to be by himself.

Steph needed to breathe and a hug from her daughter. She just needed stability.

She walked over to Lucky's pen, feeling like she had ignored Kelly a lot tonight. She smiled when she saw her sitting in the straw, talking about school with Colt. They had grown up together and been really good friends; tonight seemed to be drawing them closer. She saw them seeing each other through a different set of eyes.

Lilly was climbing out of the pen. "Hi, Steph," she hollered in too loud a voice, then, "Bye, Steph," as she ran past.

Kelly and Colt broke out laughing as Steph walked up. "That kid!"

"Yep, she's a handful," Kelly commented. "Are you okay, Mom?"

"Can you come here a minute?" she asked her.

"Sure, Mom, what's the matter?" Kelly saw the redness from the tears.

"Oh, I'm okay, just need a hug. It's a hard night for me." Steph didn't want to cry anymore but felt tears coming on.

Kelly leaned over the rail and hugged her mom tight. "Everything is going to be great. It's Christmas Eve. Stop worrying so much, Mom." Kelly pulled back and looked into her mom's eyes. "Just wait and see." Kelly's smile was so innocent. It made her realize that Ken was right; it was an honor to be part of the night.

Steph glanced at Lucky. She was lying comfortably in an upright position, but not chewing her cud.

"Kelly, has Ken said anything about Lucky calving?"

"No, is something wrong? She's not ready yet, couple more hours, I think," Kelly replied to her mom.

Looking at Steph funny, she said, "Mom, I figured things out hours ago, but no reason to start a commotion with the city slickers—you know what I mean. There's already a lot going on tonight. I plan to surprise everyone later on. Nothing like babies for Christmas, don't you agree?"

Steph glanced quickly to Molly, then replied sarcastically with, "Of course, just a normal old Christmas Eve," then turned and headed in Molly's direction.

Kelly stood staring at her mom. "What?"

"You look tough," Brenda said when Steph sat down next to her. "Another fence lesson?" referring to Ken.

Steph frowned, "No, a lesson in faith."

Chip was losing the battle again. His life experiences on the ranch basically prepared him for all types of emergencies, but this was a first. This new critter that planned on making an appearance later tonight would only have two legs. He was present at the birth of his daughter, but that was in a top-notch hospital. This birth would include a barn, a snowstorm, cowboy boots, and straw—the nouns were endless. Oh, and don't forget the lane light that doesn't exist.

Tonight he'd take a second place roll behind the women. He'd calmly wait for instructions then do his best.

He was trying to breathe, just breathe and not think. He walked off now, to be by himself, to the far side of Jakker's pen. She walked toward him for a pat, then she went back to eating her hay. He leaned on the rails and closed his eyes, his mind was traveling back in time.

Seven years old and finding his first litter of kittens in the loft of this barn. Ten years old, standing beside his dad, holding a clean fluffy towel, waiting for the nod of his dad's head to come dry off the new set of twin lambs that Dad had just pulled, saying a ten-year-old's prayer for the one that didn't make it. The mother licking on the still little body, not understanding, and Dad removing it from the pen so the momma would concentrate on the live two. He could hear his dad's voice, "Dry them off good, son."

His heart started beating harder. The memory of that night that would be with him forever; the hard, hard lesson of a fourteen-year-old took hold. His dad had told him to check on the bred heifers that were due to calve. They were being kept up close to the barnyard, in case they needed assistance.

It was Chip's turn to check them. Being eager to watch a show on TV, Chip only skimmed his eyes over the group, not paying any attention to the heifer standing in a corner, kicking at her side and stepping backward, all signs of troubled labor.

Going back in the house, his dad asked, "You check them good, they all okay?"

As a father, he wanted to put his faith in his son and it was time to give him more responsibility.

Chip answered, "Yeah, they're all okay."

As the evening went on, something in his dad's gut told him to go check them. Chuck had been raised to follow that gut feeling every time. But tonight, he didn't. "I have to start trusting him some time," he told himself. Chuck's alarm was set for midnight for the first check. He would do this every night during calving season. This was practiced by all cattle ranchers; they checked their cattle.

As all this went through Chip's mind, he could hear his gramp's voice echoing in his head, "The good Lord gave us these critters to take care of and that's what we aim to do!"

Chip never thought about the heifers the rest of the evening. His mind was on the TV. Chuck couldn't sleep. Looking at the clock, it said eleven ten. He thought now, Chip checked them at ten. "I'd better check them," his gut feeling was too edgy to ignore.

When he got to the barn, he turned the flood light on that shown on the pen. With a flashlight in hand, he started going through the gate. He immediately heard the low moan. His heart started racing. A good cattleman knew what different moans mean. This one meant, "I need help!" He scanned the pen quickly with the flashlight. Most of the heifers were bedded down, so he needed to check them carefully. Then he saw her, down on her side in the corner of the pen. She was so tired from struggling that she had given up, stopping the birthing process. The calf was dead. Chuck cussed at himself, then started hollering, hoping Joe, in the bunkhouse off the side of the barn, would hear him. Quickly he remembered Joe was doing night duty for a neighbor, helping watch cattle. Out of frustration, he started swearing again as he ran back toward the house for help. He hollered at the top of his lungs for Chip and his wife. Once he knew they heard him, he ran back to the barn for an OB chain and the calf pullers, then back to the heifer, but as he came up on her, he stopped, realizing that she was dead.

The ranch had just taken a big blow. This group of heifers had been AI bred to a high-powered bull. The offspring of this group would bring in the money that was badly needed by the ranch.

When Chip and his mother got to his side, he looked at Chip. "I thought you said you checked them?" he asked. "Chip, this heifer has been in trouble for hours. Was she in the corner, off by herself?" Chuck asked.

Chip kept his eyes on the group of heifers. "Yes," Chip answered.

"Did you walk over and check her for signs?" his dad asked.

"No, Dad, I just looked at her from across the pen. She looked okay." Chip knew he had to be honest with his father, he didn't deserve anything less.

"How much time did you spend watching her?" his dad's voice was trembling.

Chip didn't answer. He just put his head down and looked at the ground.

Chuck was having a hard time keeping his voice level. His wife placed her hand gently in the center of his back.

"Look at me, Chip. Your greediness to get back to the house and the TV just cost this heifer and her calf their lives. You have no idea how disappointed I am in you right now. I trusted you!"

Those last three words ripped at Chip's heart, then and now.

"Go get the small tractor and the chain and get her out of here! Also," his dad added, "you'll spend the summer working until you've paid this ranch back for their worth, understand?"

"Yes, sir," Chip answered. Now his head and eyes were on the ground and stayed that way while he walked as fast as he could to the tractor shed. His mom watched her son walk off, then she turned to her husband. In a gentle, understanding voice, she said, "A little hard on him?"

Chuck took a deep breath and let it out slowly. "Martha, he has to learn. I don't ever want him to forget this night. He needs to learn that he's a caretaker of life, and regardless of how bad it hurts him or me, he will learn. This ranch's survival for the future depends on me teaching my son and then him teaching his." His voice was shaking, "This is the most important job I have." He kissed his wife on the top of her head and told her to go back in, and they'd be in as soon as they got her hauled out.

Cattle are very sensitive to the smell of blood and death. He didn't want the rest of the group anymore upset than they already were. Chuck opened the gate for Chip but stayed at the gate, letting Chip hook the chain on and drag her out. Then he walked the group, talking to them in the gentle voice they knew. He noticed that one of the heifers had her tail raised and a slight discharge, possible signs of calving by morning. He would check her in an hour. It was going to be another long night.

Walking back to the house, father and son were quiet. Before going in the door, Chuck stopped and looked at Chip and said, "Do you understand?"

"Yes, Dad." Chip knew saying he was sorry wouldn't fly; it would need to be proven with his actions. Chuck would not mention the incident again. His father had taught him to say his mind, then let it be. This Chip would do with his children.

All the memories of that night went through Chip's head now, he would never forget.

Chip held a great respect for his father, but that night would haunt him for the rest of his life. He also realized that he grew up that night, this being his father's intention.

During what he called "his memory attack," he broke out in a cold sweat.

Now he heard himself praying. "Please, Lord, give us the skills we need, then with Your help, maybe we'll be able to deliver this little critter safely tonight, Amen."

The years spent in Afghanistan, while in the Army, were life-changing for Chip and Ken. Chip was a helicopter crewman, and Ken was considered a medic transporter. He worked side by side with the medic team but lacked the title of medic, and of course the pay grade. Everyone worked as a team, so Ken learned a lot. Mental trauma was very real and widespread, affecting soldiers in different ways. Toward the end of their first tour of duty, a soldier in their unit died in Chip's arms after being hit by an IUD. Chip was behind the transport truck and had been shielded from the direct blast.

Sgt. Tim Evans from Indiana hadn't been as lucky. When Chip realized that Tim had been hit, he ran out into the open and dragged his body back to cover and held him as he took his last breath. Three months later, Chip was sent back to the States, and at the end of his four-year tour, he did not re-enlist.

Ken stayed in for another four years.

Back then, the doctors said that the bomb blast itself was part of the reasons for some of Chip's flashbacks. They said Chip needed time; it would take a lot longer to heal brain trauma than it did physical injury. That was twenty-one years ago. Chip still suffered flashbacks of the war, but they didn't happen as often anymore. The ones from his childhood were more frequent and as cruel in many ways. All the enlisted men had a name for these attacks, regardless of the cause. They called them "tripping out."

When Ken decided not to make a life of the Army, he headed for the ranch, taking Chip up on his job offer. He vowed to himself to basically take on the job of Chip's watchful big brother, even though the two were actually the same age and eventually would be a brother-in-laws.

Over the years, he learned to watch the signs coming from Chip and knew how to talk him out of a lot of the "trip outs." Right now he saw the sweat break out on Chip's face, one of the signs. Ken knew tonight was a prime situation to bring them on.

Ken walked up to Chip and laid a hand on his shoulder. "You okay, buddy?" looking directly into Chip's eyes and seeing dilated pupils.

Chip knew that Ken knew, so there was no reason to try and hide it. "I'm okay, I think," Chip said.

"War?" Ken asked.

Chip's face turned into a frown. "No. Dad."

No more explanations were needed. Ken knew the stories.

Ken wanted to lighten the air. He patted Chip's shoulder a couple times, leaned in, and said with a quiet laugh, "You know I've got that big bottle of Jack D. Let me know when you're ready to hide in a corner for a few."

As Ken walked off, Chip managed half a smile and replied, "That I just might do!"

"That was a good dinner," Ken thought. He always said the longer spaghetti sat, the better it tasted. Then there was the pie. "Sis always made good pie."

That was an hour ago and he was still uncomfortable from eating too much. Ken wandered over to the loft staircase and sat down on the third step up. The little tree that Lilly and Kelly had decorated sat in the dark, next to the staircase. He touched a branch. "Here it is, Christmas Eve, and no one is paying you any attention, you poor baby."

Ken took a deep breath. "Send me the words You have for me to share, Lord."

Ken wanted his inner self to guide his next movements and actions. He knew to follow the instructions of his soul.

He chose this dark spot in the barn on purpose. What was coming next needed some privacy, if that was even possible tonight. Steph had seen him sit down on the step. He was hoping she'd figure out his reasoning and help keep everyone away, if she saw him talking to someone.

Ken felt overwhelmed. He wasn't sure of what time it was and he still had a list a mile long in his head, of things to do. There was a lot lying on his heart, words that needed to be said, yet tonight, all part of His plan.

Ken was aware that Rick sat higher up on a step, toward the top of the staircase.

This was Ken's reasoning for setting here. He wouldn't approach him. Rick needed to come to Ken on his own free will.

A few minutes had gone by.

Susan was sitting a little off to the side of where Molly was. Brenda was with her. Steph saw Susan staring at Ken. She had a feeling that the two needed to talk, but Steph also knew Susan was shy and would need a little push. Steph was a pusher.

Susan did want to talk to Ken. She didn't know why except that she knew her heart was heavy and she didn't want it to be.

For some reason, she had a feeling that this stranger, who called himself a cowboy, was probably a good listener. Little things he had done with Lilly convinced her he was wise beyond his years, in matters of the heart.

Steph sided up to Susan and whispered in her ear. A few minutes later, she took a deep breath and got up. She had to talk to herself to keep herself moving forward, toward Ken.

Ken raised his eyebrows. "Susan—okay." His words were all planned for Rick, but Susan worked too.

Then he smiled to himself, "Smart move, Lord."

"Hi, Ken, can I sit a few minutes with you?" she asked with a smile, relaxing a little.

Working with him on Brian's foot had made him feel more like a friend.

"Sure, beautiful," he tipped his hat, "I've been wanting to thank you again for working so compassionately on Brian's foot." The woman had kept putting the warm compresses on Brian's toes until Ken told her she could stop. The toes had reached a color where Ken felt it was safe to soak in a warm water bath.

"You are a big part of their good progress. I'm praying for no permanent damage."

She waved a hand in embarrassment. "Yeah, me too, and I'm glad I could help," she answered.

"So what's up?" he asked.

"Oh, I was just wondering earlier if you grew up with animals. You're so good with them." A little voice in her head screamed in joy, "Yeah, you did it. See, you can talk to him, keep talking!"

This surprised Ken. *Okay, some small talk,* he thought.

"Well, not exactly. Steph and I grew up on the edge of town. We had a big horse ranch next door to us though and a vineyard and winery across the road, hence my love of horses and wine," he laughed, totally relaxed. "I loved the horses. My mom knew where I was if she couldn't find me, even as a little guy. By the time I was seven, the owner gave me my first job." He laughed again.

"I got paid twenty-five cents an hour to play with the new barn kittens and talk to each horse in their stall every day. My dad wouldn't let him pay me any more than that. By the time I was ten, the job got real. I made a dollar an hour to clean stalls and I kept talking to the horses."

Rick sat in the dark, with hands folded and a big smile on his face as he listened to Ken tell his childhood story.

Ken hesitated now, looking across the barn, his eyes settling on Chip. "When Chip offered me a job here on the ranch, it was a good fit."

Susan smiled, remembering the phrase when she and Steph had talked. "So it was easy to learn the cattle end of the business?" she asked.

"Yes, another good fit, but," he smiled, "I had some really good teachers and the best cattle in the state to work with." Then he added, "I'm one of the lucky ones. You know the saying, 'Do what you love, and you'll never work a day in your life.'"

She looked at him blankly. "No, I've never heard that one."

Now they sat in silence. Ken decided to take the first step. "Is this all you wanted to talk about, sis?" Ken smiled softly at Susan and waited.

The word made her heart flutter. No one had ever called her that before. "No, it's not." She looked across the barn, wanting her eyes on Lilly, so she could draw strength from her.

"I'm listening, just let your heart guide you," Ken whispering encouragement.

Rick held his breath.

"I'm pretty sure you already have most of it figured out," she said.

"I have eyes, but you tell me your story," Ken answered.

"It's not hard to see that our lives are broken. None of us are happy. My worry is mostly for Lilly. I'm a big girl. I'll deal with what comes my way, but I want more for my daughter," she hesitated a few seconds, then, continued, in a quiet but strong voice. "I have never seen her as happy as she has been since coming to the ranch. It breaks my heart to think that this happiness will end in a couple days and we'll go back to the same unhappiness we left. I can't do that to her—I won't do that do her." She hesitated now as she thought, then said, "Things needs to change, for Lilly's sake!"

Rick shifted in his spot, the words stung.

She was shaking her head and looking down at her hands, then she turned and looked into Ken's eyes. Hers were filled with tears, but she refused to let her weakness take hold. She wanted to show her strength as a woman, to show Ken she was worthy of his help.

He waited.

She looked down at her hands again, holding them in praying form. "Rick is a really good person. We've been together for twenty years. He's a good provider. We have everything we could possibly want, except…"

She went into thought, looking for the right words.

Ken was patient, giving her the time she needed.

"Rick's priorities are all mixed up, big time. Work is first to him, then money, then more work and more money, then Lilly and me. Don't get me wrong, I'll totally admit that I'm not perfect either. I'm sure Rick can come up with an equal amount of complaints about me. I realize it takes two to ruin a marriage."

Rick covered his face with his hands.

"Rick is obsessed with his job. He brings work home every night and every weekend. We can't take a vacation because of his work. He's constantly short with Lilly because she's interrupting his work." She was getting emotional as she tried to talk.

"It breaks my heart, she needs her daddy and he can't see that."

"How did you get him to come out here?" he asked. Ken hoped Rick was listening.

"I shamed him. I told him Lilly isn't little anymore, and he couldn't keep lying to her. For years he'd make promises and then not keep them. I actually stood up to him this time. He's not used to that. He got mad but agreed to come." She took a deep breath.

"Yeah, and he's having a great time and really seems to be enjoying his time with Lilly," Ken stated in a little louder voice.

"Yes, he is," Susan answered.

Ken figured she wasn't too far from breaking down. "Just breathe, Susan." Ken patted her on the shoulder.

"I finally realized I had nothing to lose."

Rick held his head in his hands, glad no one could see him.

"He says it's all for us. Well, it's killing us—our home life, our marriage. Lilly needs her dad, a regular, loving dad, like Chip is with Kelly, someone to show her the way, how to grow up to be a good person with values, other than the ones that money can buy."

Susan laughed hard. "I won't go into detail on what I need." She was serious now with some mad thrown in. You could hear it in her voice.

"That's the reason we only had one. I realized I would be raising our kids by myself. I do love him. I am his wife, whatever that means, I'm not sure anymore."

Ken wanted to stop her there, but she started talking again.

"I would gladly become dirt poor if Lilly and I could have his love and be happy," she spoke from her heart. "I want my husband back, you know, the person who is here!"

Tears silently rolled down Rick's face.

She had gathered herself again, calming down some. "It's not all Rick's fault. Both our families come from too much money. All that money has done is rot both families from the inside out. I'm not saying that money has replaced God in their lives—wait, I'm not sure God has ever been in any of their lives."

Ken had a question, "Would any of them give up the money and what it bought for God?" It was point-blank, and Ken intended it to hurt.

Susan's answer was quick and short, "No." Then Susan rocked Rick's boat, "Nor would Rick, he doesn't believe."

Susan spoke with a sad heart, "It's hard to climb out of that kind of hole when you are stuck in it, but I'm trying because I see what it's doing to Lilly. Rick, not so much. Rick shades his eyes with the dollar."

Ken pictured Susan's knife pushing deeper into Rick's heart. He was actually feeling sorry for him. Not too often did a man get the chance to hear his woman's true heart, unfiltered. Ken knew her words were not intended for Rick's ears, not in a million years.

"Those are some pretty harsh statements, Susan," Ken whispered.

"Ken," she half laughed, "anyone can look at this ranch and see there's plenty of money here. When I look at this ranch, I see love of family, of lifestyle, people not afraid of hard work, and then there's the honor. Honoring the past, people, ways, and most importantly, the love of faith. No one here is afraid to praise God for what He has given. I could go on and on, you know exactly what I'm trying to say, because you live that way." Her voice was calm but serious, "Money has a place; it just needs to be put in the right order of things, and it's not on a pedestal."

Ken had his next statement all planned out. It was more for Rick's ears than Susan's.

Lilly ran the barn. "Where's my mommy and daddy?" she said, running up to Chip and Brian.

"Honey, I'm not sure," he looked around. Ken was missing too.

"Lilly, it's okay, I think they are talking to Ken. How 'bout you let them talk. Sometimes big people just need to talk by themselves."

She stood firmly, arms crossed. "Yeah, I know, but usually it's cause they're fighting, then I'm always in trouble."

Chip's heart broke. He grabbed her and pulled her onto his lap. "Well, no one is fighting, and you"—he tickled her ribs, making her giggle—"are not in trouble. If anyone says you are, you send them to me, okay?"

"Okay, Chip, thanks. I'm going over to Lucky's pen; they like me over there." She quickly took off. Brian and Chip broke out laughing.

"You think everything is okay, you know, with Susan and Rick? I really like them," Brian asked, sounding worried.

"Oh, they're pretty normal, just don't see eye to eye. I think Ken has his…fence-mending lesson in mind for them," Chip replied, taking a sip of coffee.

Brian looked at Chip, trying hard to look serious. "Is there anyone in this county that hasn't heard that…fence talk?"

Chip grinned, full heartedly, "Probably not!"

"I agree, Susan. Chip's granddad—you would have liked him. He'd have been first to tell you that this ranch was built with the Lord's blessing. This ranch doesn't look like this because of Chip, Steph, or me. The bare land was bought in the late 1800s. It took years and years of hard work, devotion, and sacrifice to get it started. Some years were good, a lot weren't. They all put their sweat into dreams, a plan. We try to continue that dream. Their dream was the land. It was solid. You could walk away, leave it alone, come back, and it will still be here, kinda like the Lord; you can walk away and come back, and He's still there, waiting, right where you left Him. You might walk away, but He won't. Okay, I'm getting off base." Ken took a deep breath, wanting to keep going, he still had more to say.

"As anything in life, it's all about commitment, whether it's a piece of land or a marriage, but then it's a whole lot easier with a willing partner. Out here, we like to say we are married to Mother Nature. She can work with us for the common good for months then get up one morning in a foul mood and stay that way. The marriage with her still needs pampering." He hesitated, then said, "I like to use the tree example a lot when talking relationships. A tree needs to bend with the wind. Some days she'll need to bend in one direction, then at other times, the other way, not always in the same direction. She learns to give and take, if that tree can't bend—"

Susan cut him off, "It breaks, just like in a marriage," her voice quivered with emotion.

Ken patted her hand. "You got it. There's a lot of give and take in a marriage, but with the Lord's blessing and understanding, that love will have strong limbs and deep roots," he wanted her to finish the sentence.

"Then somehow it will find a way to weather the storms, like the tree. That's the kind of marriage I want."

"It won't come easy, it will always be a work in progress," Ken added.

Susan smiled, "Yes, always. I'm not asking for easy, I'll do my hard part."

"Chip, Steph, and I were lucky. We grew up in families that believed in and taught us everything we just talked about. They expected us to pass all of it down to the next generation. It was kind of their legacy to their kids."

Susan smiled. "Well, you've all done a great job with Kelly, but you seem to be getting a slow start with your namesakes."

Ken broke out laughing. "Oh, I am proud to lay claim to Kelly too," he replied.

"I know, I'm just teasing!" Susan giggled.

She took a deep breath and sat up straighter. "Okay, seriously now, is there still time for Lilly?"

Ken put his arm around Susan's shoulder and gave her a squeeze. "Sure, it's never too late, but you need God on your side. Everything is easier with God in your corner."

"I'm not sure He'll want to talk to me. I've made a lot of mistakes in my life," Susan admitted.

"Sweetie, He's been standing next to you forever, just waiting for you to take His hand."

Ken was ready to give this part of his talk, "Put God first in your life. Do this for yourself. You can't help Lilly until you have helped yourself." His words were slow on purpose, "A battle with God on your side is a whole lot easier to win, in fact, He'll ask you to let Him fight those battles for you." Ken took a long breath.

"Everything is easier and better when you accept Christ into your life," he realized he had thrown a lot out there all at once, so now he would wait, giving her the time she needed to absorb his simple words.

A few moments later, he started talking again. "Let's take tonight for example," he had raised his voice a little louder when the conversation turned toward the Lord. He wanted to make sure Rick could hear each and every word.

"You heard all the talk at the stove and about the lane light. It's real hard to think that tonight isn't anything but heaven-sent. What if we took God out of tonight, where would that leave us?"

She looked directly into his eyes as she spoke, "Tonight, as we have experienced it, wouldn't have existed, right? We are all here because God wanted us here, same with Molly and Jamie. I don't have everything figured out yet, it's all like a dream."

Ken spoke gently, his voice seem strange, like it belonged to another person, "We're all His helpers. He had a plan that needed certain players to play the parts. I guess you could call us the chosen ones," he laughed. "I also think the night has multiple purposes. This is still new to me too, and I'm sure hoping we don't let Him down. There's a long ways to go yet tonight."

Susan shook her head in agreement. It was so much to take in, kind of like watching a movie, except with this one, you were in it.

"Ken, do you think we'll figure it all out?"

Ken smiled. "If He wants us to."

Susan's mind worked at processing Ken's words. Slowly, they seemed to find their way into her heart. *He's right, it's all better with God.*

Ken looked at her. "Ready for a little more?"

She smiled and nodded her head.

"Susan, let's use the phrase 'building a foundation' as a starting point for everything. Let Jesus be the first brick you lay and He'll help you build the rest."

"If love, marriage, and family all have a strong foundation, they can't be brought down; they can withstand all the storms, regardless of how strong they are."

She seemed to have a new light in her eyes. "First I need to build my own foundation in the Lord, then He and I together can help Rick and, of course, Lilly."

"You got it, sweet lady," Ken sighed tiredly.

Rick couldn't sit in the dark listening any longer. His face was swollen from crying. He wiped his tears on his arm and started climbing down the steps, to what he hoped would be a new beginning.

When Ken heard him on the steps, he kissed Susan on the top of her head and got up and walked away. He had wondered how long Rick could stay up there. Then he said to himself, "These two have a lot to talk about, Lord."

Ken, Susan, and Rick were still missing. Steph's nerves were shot. She was worried about the Conners, probably more for Susan than Rick; she was feeling guilty. After all, they were her guests, making them her responsibility. She knew they were messed up, but when did it become their responsibility to interfere in strangers' personal lives, especially Ken? Steph felt like she was going to vomit. She was trying to stay positive. She just didn't want her brother to make things worse. Normally he didn't, but there was always that first time.

She walked around the barn. Molly was the same, very uncomfortable but not ready yet; Brenda was staying with her a lot; and Jamie, he wouldn't leave her side.

Chip and Brian were both sitting at the stove, talking.

The kids were being kids, totally capable of adapting to any situation. Lucky was basically in the same shape as Molly, uncomfortable, but not ready yet.

Kelly was doing a great job keeping Lilly happy and engaged. She'd make sure she paid her well when this was all over.

The words stuck in her head—over. All of a sudden her head went in a different direction. She listened to the wind howl, that constant howl, but for the first time tonight, she realized it would end. By this time next week this would all be a memory.

Susan looked up and saw Rick coming down the stairs. She was horrified. *He heard my words, all my words, my true feelings!* She instantly hated Ken. She had trusted him. Those words were not meant for Rick's ears. Panic set in. She couldn't breathe. She wanted to get up and run, but to where?

Then she felt a calm feeling wash over her. "It will be okay."

"You don't have to try and do anything by yourself. You have me, if you still want me. We'll do it all together, in the right order, like Ken said." Rick tried to smile. He had sat down next to her and took her hand in his. He gently caressed her fingers with his. He knew he had more he needed to say, a lot more.

Susan looked in his eyes. She needed to see that he meant his words.

He started talking again, in a gentle voice, one she had never heard before, "God first, us together, and Lilly. I am so sorry for so many things I don't know where to start." Rick continued to pour his heart out to her. "Susan, I don't want to lose you and Lilly," his voice cracked with emotion.

Susan started crying. "We need to ask God for His forgiveness and His for help—together, Rick."

He buried his head in her chest. She wrapped her arms around him and they cried together.

Ken headed over to Lucky's pen.

Steph walked up. "Are they okay?" she asked.

"Yeah, they both had a lot of soul searching to do, but they'll be fine, Lilly too." He pulled his sister close and hugged her, whispering, "God's at work."

"You think you're done with that chore?" she asked.

"Nope, next is the mending fence lesson for Rick." Ken gave her a quick grin.

"Yep, that good old fence lesson bit," she said the words sarcastically, then giggled as she walked off. "Been there, done that!"

Ken hadn't meant to ruin the evening for Susan and Rick with his talk, but it was now or later, and it was important, as it was meant to be a new beginning—it was part of His plan.

Ken hoped they could pull themselves together before any of the others noticed the stress they had been under, especially Lilly. There was still a lot of night ahead of them, and he hoped for them to experience the joy of it together as a family.

Ken's goal, the one placed on his heart, was for Rick and Susan to see clearly and realize that the wires on their fence just needed to be tightened up some.

A little time had gone by since the session that involved Susan. Rick had calmed down, getting his emotions back on track, but he didn't want to leave things where they were. He and Susan had spent some time talking. They both knew it was the first of many, but that wasn't enough. He felt a restlessness inside. He had a feeling Ken had a lot more to say, and Rick knew that he needed to hear it.

Rick glanced around the barn. Susan had gone to check with Brenda about Molly. Lilly was with Kelly and Colt at the heifer pen. A minute later he spotted Ken walking toward the stove.

"Ken, can we talk more?" Rick asked in an emotional voice as he had walked up close.

Ken turned to look at Rick. "Sure. I'm getting coffee, you want some?"

Quickly, Rick grabbed a cup and held it out to Ken. "I'll meet you at the stairs," Rick added.

"Yep, be there in a minute." Ken started talking to Chip and Brian, as Rick turned and left.

"He okay?" Chip asked.

"Will be," Ken replied, as he headed toward the stairs.

"Lord, I need to ask again, can you slow that clock down some, please? I've still got a lot to say." As he walked, he looked for Steph, finding her near Molly. He whistled to get her attention. When she looked at him, he gave her a thumbs-up and nodded his head toward the stairs. She instantly knew the meaning. She'd try and make sure they had some privacy for the talk. There was a little blond-headed girl who could manage to pop up in places she wasn't meant to be.

As Ken sat down on the stair step next to Rick, the city man spoke first, "I had a feeling you had more to say, and I had more to hear."

Ken chuckled. "Am I that much of an open book?"

"Well, I don't know about that. Let's say I see a man on a mission," Rick replied.

"Fair enough," Ken said. "First of all, I'm not trying to sound all preachy, nowhere close to it. I can name a few preachers that would say I don't know what I'm talking about. They're entitled to their opinions." Ken chuckled again, then added, "They might even be right." He took a long sip of coffee.

"I'm, as I said before, just a plain old cowboy, but the Lord has laid some heavy stuff on my heart, intended for you. I don't have a right. You can shut me down at any point. I'll understand. I'll not tread on your life."

Rick looked directly at Ken. "Keep going."

"I'm not real wise to big city life; I don't care to be. Our parents, especially our gram, taught us love and to respect all. The Army taught me more of the same and threw in some reasoning."

Ken looked up and scanned the barn in front of them. "Something deep down inside told me I was needed here, with Chip, so I came," Ken spoke solemnly, with hesitation, as he gathered the words he wanted.

"I've worked hard over the years at being the caretaker that God chose for me to be."

"A guardian maybe?" Rick asked.

Ken looked him in the eye. "Some might say." Ken continued, "Sometimes, I get confused at the message. When this happens, I get on Sara and we ride to the back country, where I can breathe, and pray—until I feel I'm back on God's path."

He looked directly at Rick now, smiling slightly. "You, my friend, are sitting right in the middle of that path. I won't go around you, so that means I'm going through you, unless you walk away. You think you might understand."

He waited on Rick's response.

Rick took a deep breath. "Yeah, you're welcome to come on."

The two men were sitting on the bottom step of the stairs. Ken bent down and picked up a stiff piece of straw and started scratching circles in the sawdust. Both sat, silent. Finally Ken started talking in a calm, level voice, but it sounded different. The tone was so gentle and soft that Rick needed to lean into Ken to hear his words.

"Out here, the land is endless, miles and miles of openness, with the biggest sky you've ever seen. You can breathe deep out here. It's not like the city, where the air is poison. We have miles and miles of fence. The fences have many responsibilities. They hold stuff in, keep stuff out; they say safety, plus give off warnings; they also mean division.—this side is mine, the other side is yours. I'll stay on my side, you stay on yours. There's an old saying, "good fences, make good neighbors." I guess you can take that in different ways too." Ken took a deep breath.

"I look at fences a little differently. I see courage, strength, responsibility, faithfulness, and love, especially the old seasoned ones, like the ones you find a lot of the time out here. They were built to last, just like a marriage should be," he hesitated again, hoping the last few words sank in.

"My fences have hearts. The heart says we have a good thing going. Sometimes we get stretched too tight, begging to be let up on, just needing to breathe some. Over the years, a fence shows its age. Some places stay strong as ever, while others places show some weakening. Staples pull loose, wires sag in tough times, even breaking a strand here and there, and sometimes, losing a post; they break or fall from weathering stress. The heart is mighty. She begs for her fence to be mended. Tighten the wires, pound the staples in deep, mend the break, or put a strong new post in, so she can do her job. It might take a lot of work, but isn't she worth it? You thought so once, and she knows she can be again." Ken stopped again, gathering his thoughts. Moments later, he continued; he wasn't done.

"It's too bad that we gain so much of life's wisdom in our older years. Just think of the lives we all could have lived if we had only obtained that wisdom at an earlier age."

He hesitated again, longer this time. Rick was beginning to wonder of Ken was finished. He hoped not.

Then Ken made a statement, with a very gentle tone of voice, "For a happy, content life, keep your fences mended." Then he laughed, "I guess that's the gist of it."

While Ken had been talking, he had been drawing circles over and over. Rick watched intently. He knew Ken had a meaning for his action. Ken had a meaning for everything.

Rick felt a stray thought come to mind—a single line with two ends, coming together, united, like a marriage, without end, always as one.

Moments later, Rick asked, "Can I ask a couple of questions?"

"Sure," Ken said.

"What if you decide you need a new fence? You think the old one is so far gone that it can't be mended, maybe it's better to start over."

Now Ken looked up at Rick. "First, there is no such thing as can't. Can't means you give up. Second, the word *new* says you aren't interested in doing the hard work to save the original one. Third, maybe you didn't deserve the fence in the first place—you let it die!"

As Ken talked, his voice was turning bitter. Rick felt like he needed to steal a phrase from Ken—to tread lightly.

"One more, are we talking fences or marriage?" Rick whispered.

Ken took a deep breath. He looked into Rick's eyes, wanting to see where his heart stood. The eyes told a lot. He saw a broken man who wanted to hope.

"Well, friend, they're one of the same. I hope this came across as a life lesson that can be applied where ever you need it. Lay it down, where it feels like a good fit. I like to say, most importantly, it will never let you down when applied, just like God."

"What if the fence has given up, of a broken heart, refusing to mend?" Rick said in a sad tone of sincerity.

Ken shook his head slightly. "Well, that was a chance you took when you let it fall in years of disrepair. There is no guarantee in life. I've never been one to gamble with a heart. All you can do is try, hard. I hope it's not too late, for all your sakes."

Then a few seconds later, Ken added, "I don't think it is."

"I hope not," Rick said, still sounding sad. "I've spent a lot of years doing what I thought was important, never caring if the ones I loved had different ideas on what that might be, you know, important to them."

Rick's eyes scanned the barn, looking for Susan. "In all the years of marriage, I never put Susan's feeling first, let alone Lilly's."

Ken felt that Rick was beating himself up pretty hard. He needed to turn the tide now. "Ever heard of second chances, Rick?" Ken smiled now.

At hearing those words, a hint of hope was visible in Rick's eyes for the first time.

"Ken, Susan told me she was willing to try, that she still loves me. I'm not sure how she could," Rick said. Looking around the barn again, he added, "This place and you have opened my eyes." Then looking directly at Ken, he said, "I want that second chance, Ken. You got any fence mending tools that I can borrow for the rest of my life?"

They both broke out laughing, loud enough, that Steph and Susan glanced their way.

Ken stood up, but before walking off, Ken laid a hand on Rick's shoulder and said, "'Love does not delight in evil but rejoices with the truth. It always protects, always trusts, always hopes, always perseveres' (1 Cor. 13:6–7)."

Rick waited a moment, then smiled and said, "Thank you, Ken, for everything. I've found my own light tonight, and I plan to work hard to make it shine bright."

Ken believed Rick. He gave him a thumbs-up and walked back to the main part of the barn. Ken was exhausted. He felt like he had been talking to Rick for a lifetime.

"I've got to sit by myself, just for a minute." Ken laughed at himself. He'd been saying that a lot tonight, but so far hadn't been able to get it done.

He thought back to what he had said to Rick. He hadn't attacked Rick by bringing up his faults. The talk wasn't meant to be judgmental in any way; it was meant as guidance and that was all. His hope was that Rick could see how things could fall apart when not tended to regularly. Then showing him a way to mend or heal. Most of the time, the heart welcomed love. She so much wants to love and be loved. She's very forgiving—most of the time.

He thought they had a chance. Ken could see the love Susan still had, though it was tucked away behind the pain, in her eyes. Rick just needed to start mending.

"Thank You, Lord, for the words. I hope it was enough, Amen."

Rick had decided to stay put for a little while. He wanted to go over what Ken had said to him, then, add it to the things he had heard him say to Susan a little while ago.

He knew he had a lot to think about, bending trees, keeping branches from breaking, building a foundation based on love and trust, one that would hold up in all situations. "Now add fences." As he was thinking, a picture came to mind, a pretty scene. It had a farm house and barns surrounded by strong fences and a large yard with lots of beautiful trees, blowing gently in the breeze. It was a picture of everything Ken talked about: the give-and-take of marriage, the warmth of a happy family home, and fences holding in and protecting all the love inside. It was confusing, thinking about each one individually, but putting all of it together made it seem like heaven. Ken had given them the greatest gift tonight, on Christmas Eve—a path to love and happiness for his family, a path desperately needed.

In a sense, he felt like he had also found the lane light in the storm and came up that long lane. Right now, New York City felt a lifetime away.

Susan had been waiting for a chance to speak to Ken again just for a moment, and it looked like that opportunity had just presented itself. Ken had walked over to the stove and poured another cup of coffee. "I'm going to have coffee coming out my ears," he said out loud to no one.

Susan walked up quickly, knowing he wouldn't be alone for long.

"Hi, Ken, can I ask you something?"

Ken quickly turned around when he heard her voice, causing him to spill coffee all over himself.

"Oh, I'm sorry, Ken." She looked around for something to wipe his sleeve with.

"Susan, it's okay, really." He tried to smile as he wiped his arm on his pant leg. "You wanted to ask me something?" Ken said gently.

She looked around nervously, to make sure Rick hadn't walked up.

Ken nodded his head toward the straw bale and they both walked over to it.

"Sit here," Ken patted the spot on the straw bale next to him.

"I was just wondering," Susan's voice was low and very insecure, "is Rick okay? Do you think he might be different, I mean think differently now that you talked to him?"

"Well, first, I'm not a miracle worker, even on Christmas Eve. All I did was show him a different way of seeing some things." He took her hands in his; they were cold.

"Are you okay?" he asked as he rubbed them.

She tried to smile, "Yeah, I'm just nervous."

"Rick's going to be okay. His path has been a rocky one. His feet have gotten sore, causing his eyes to hunt for a softer going, like the green grass off on the sides, you know, the same color as money. Still, deep down inside, he knows that the soft grass isn't the answer."

Ken looked directly in Susan's eyes. "Rick needs love, understanding, and support to help him find a way over the rocks. The Lord is beside him, waiting for Rick to take his hand. Will you offer yours too?"

He waited a bit, then added, "Rick knows the trip is worth the effort. He knows what awaits at the other end."

Ken stood up, placing his hands on her shoulders. He leaned down near her ear and whispered the Bible verse 1 Corinthians 13:6–7, as he had to Rick.

Ken kissed the top of her head and walked off.

Susan watched him walk over to Chip at the horse pen. All of a sudden, Lilly was jumping in her lap. "HI, Mommy, I missed you!"

Hearing Lilly's cheerful voice warmed her heart. For the first time in a long time, she felt she could let herself feel the love of her child, the way she needed to. Everything was going to be okay.

Rick had stayed in the dark, needing to be alone for a while. No one in the barn seemed to question his whereabouts. His mind kept going over Ken's words. All of a sudden he heard a soft voice. Rick looked up. Susan was standing in front of him. "Can I sit a while?"

Rick's eyes lit up. "I'd like that." He slid over, giving her room to sit on the same step next to him. He took her hand in his and caressed it gently. Neither one spoke for a few minutes. Finally, Rick started talking in a whisper, "Ken gave me a lesson on mending fences."

Susan waited, thinking there has to be more to this. A minute later, she asked, "A fence lesson?"

He pulled his hand away and put both of them between his knees and leaned forward. "I think it was a lesson more on life than about fixing fences."

"So, did you listen?" her voice was very sweet and gentle.

"Yes," he replied.

"Did you learn anything?" she asked, now her voice sounded shaky.

Rick looked to the floor for a few seconds, then raised his eyes to look directly at her. "Yes, I learned a lot," he hesitated, then said the words "a lot" again.

Susan had to talk to her self now, *Don't cry, please, don't cry!*

Steph was up near Molly, but close enough to the stairs that she could hear Rick and Susan's conversation. She quickly moved further away. "This is not meant for my ears," she told herself as she heard the words *foundation*, *bending trees*, and *fences*.

"Thank You, Lord, for giving Ken the words that these special people needed to hear. Merry Christmas, Conners family, Amen"

"I know I've not been in this country as long as the two of you, but I can't remember a worse wind," Ken stated.

Chip half chuckled sadly. "I'm sure if this old gal could talk," he glanced up at the rafters, listening to the wind slam every part of her, "she'd tell us some tough stories. My granddad used to tell me that when he was a boy, the winters were a lot worse than they are now. He'd seen a lot of them."

Chip and Ken leaned up against the rails of pen containing the Rogers' horses.

They had helped Brian hobble over, then sat him on a bale and elevated his foot. The horses seemed fine now, though Chip was still keeping track of Sugar's temperature. So far so good; they quietly munched on their hay. No one would have ever guessed what they had been through earlier this evening. A slight smile formed on Chip's face as he watched the favorite mare.

"I'm real worried about all those heifers that are out in this," Brian stated solemnly, concern was evident in the sound of his voice.

"Is your south gate bottom chained, Brian?" Chip asked.

"Yep, thankfully I remembered the chain at the bottom, had a hard time finding it though, had come loose and fallen on the ground it was buried in the snow."

Ken listened to Brian's worries, knowing that Chip's were the same.

None of the three men were brave enough to speak of the cattle piling; they didn't want to jinx the night.

Ken prayed silently, "Please, Lord, I know this storm has to work its way through, and I'm guessing it also is playing a part in Your plan for tonight, but can You please watch over those fine ladies, the ones we had to leave out, on both ranches? Please, Lord, keep them from piling up. You know their heads don't work real good in times like this. We pray for Your protection for each and every one of them, dear Father, Amen."

The winds pushed the cattle as far south as the fences and gates would allow them go. A few tried the gates, but the chains held. For some reason, they didn't pile; they seemed calm, as if a shepherd was walking amongst them, encouraging a sense of calm, whispering to them, "Trust Me."

Their hides were covered with eight inches of snow. Their body heat had melted the first couple layers, turning it to ice, which now hung off their bodies in long icicles. The snow continued to build up on them, as it had been coming down hard for hours. Their hides were a thick mass of white crust. The icicles also hung from their ears, noses, and mouths, even the small eyelashes drooped from the weight of the ice, making it hard for them to see. The only positive note was the fact that snow was a great insulator. They would manage to stay warm enough to handle the length of the storm. Their extra body condition also worked in their favor. The cursed wind that drove cattle was the danger. The three men were now silent, all three experiencing the same thoughts, all praying the same prayer.

Then it happened. Rick had walked up and heard the men talking about the concerns for their livestock, heard the fear in their voices. When he found a spot where he could jump in, he did.

"Can I ask a question?" Rick asked.

Ken probably reacted first, thinking, "Don't do it, Rick," but not saying the words.

"Sure," Chip said, turning a little so he could see Rick better.

"Well, as you guys were talking about the cows out in the storm, Chip, didn't you tell me early this morning that cattle piled up in storms—is piling up the right phrase?" Rick said innocently, adding, "I gathered this was a huge concern for all of you, can I ask why?"

Brian laid his head on the top rail of the pen, between his hands. Ken and Chip remained quiet.

Finally Chip looked at Rick. "It's a rancher's nightmare during blizzards. Cattle have a tendency to move with the storm, usually south. If they come to a fence with a closed gate, they can't move any further south. As they panic, the cows push on the fences and each other, finally knocking the ones closest to the fence down, and the rest keep coming. They walk on top of the ones that are down, smothering them. They also fall down in between the downed bodies, trapping them. More keep coming; they pile up, dead cows layering themselves until the pile is higher than the fence. A few might manage to go over. The ones that do might live. A normal cow weighs 1,200 lbs. They can handle the cold and snow, but not the wind. You can lose a lot of cattle in one night."

Brian looked up. "When I was about twelve, we had a late winter storm. Do you remember, Chip?" Chip nodded his head but stayed silent. Brian continued, "I remember going out with my dad the next morning. He told me it was a way for me to grow up real fast."

"Yeah right!" Ken said in a disgusting tone.

"When we drove the tractor out to check the cows, we found the whole herd piled up on the fence line, about a quarter of a mile long. What wasn't dead was so injured that my dad shot them on the spot. We lost 250 cows overnight. It was the first time I'd ever seen my dad cry like a baby, I'll never forget it." Tears ran down Brian's face.

Rick looked at each man and then said, "And this is that kind of storm?"

No one spoke. Brian stood up, wiping his face on his sleeve. "Ken, can you help me back to the stove, please."

As they watched Ken help Brian back to the stove, Chip said, "He's real scared. His ranch can't handle the loss, none of us can."

Rick stood up, tall and straight, and said, "Hey, this isn't a normal storm on a normal night, surely God will send guardians to watch over the cattle. Just maybe the safety and grace of this night will branch both ranches."

Rick stood in bewilderment. *I wonder where all that came from*, shaking his head. He had definitely surprised himself, since he claimed to be a "nonbeliever."

"Sit with me a minute, Ken." Brian had gotten ahold of his emotions but needed to talk. All of a sudden the storm was very real to him again.

"Sure." Ken smiled. "How about some coffee?" Ken poured two cups and sat down across from Brian.

"I almost let the dogs go along, changed my mind at the last minute."

"Good thing," Ken said, taking a sip. Ken could tell that Brian had a lot of things going through is head at the moment.

"I know one thing, fifty- to sixty-mile-per-hour wind and snow blowing in your face for hours on end makes it a mighty cold miserable day, even if it did get up to twenty degrees." Brian made a shuddering motion, reliving the events of the day. He laughed half-heartedly. "Not interested in doing that again!" Moments later Ken noticed a change in Brian. "I came real close to losing my wife and son, I couldn't find my way." Ken heard the shaky tone of panic in Brian's voice.

"Brian, look at me." Ken took hold of Brian's hands and shook them. "Brian, Brenda and Colt are okay, the horses are okay, buddy. You found your way to safety. You are all safe." The wind howled outside, reminding them that she was still a threat. He knew that Brian was listening too. "Don't listen, Brian, let it go."

Brian took a deep breath and looked away, trying hard to reclaim himself.

"Ken, sorry, didn't mean—"

"Brian, stop it, all is good. All is good, my friend. Brian, just breathe."

Madge walked into the break room and pulled out a chair, thinking how good it would feel to sit down for a few minutes. She had offered to work the Christmas Eve shift for another nurse, Jeanie, who had three small kids.

"Oh, Madge, you don't have to do that. My kids just need to understand," Jeanie had told her.

Madge was glad she had insisted. Besides, she figured Santa would probably bypass her apartment tonight, not that she didn't believe, or that she had been bad; she was just saving the jolly old man a stop. Thinking of Jeanie now, she whispered, "Merry Christmas, my friend."

The ER had been busy tonight but nothing major, like a gunshot wound or a bad accident. It seemed as if the city knew to be good tonight. A few minutes ago, a woman had been brought in, far along in labor. Being it would be her sixth delivery, Madge didn't think the little one would wait for the magical hour of midnight.

The TV was on, but she hadn't paid any attention to it until she heard the word Wyoming. She had received a text from Susan earlier today, telling her about the approaching storm. The weatherman was stating that the entire state was shut down now, because of the blizzard. She smiled. She could picture the Conners all sitting around a big fireplace, with Lilly in pajamas, drinking hot chocolate and something a little stronger for Susan, she hoped. She wished them a great Christmas, one they'll never forget. For a split second, she experienced a warm emotional feeling that told her this one was unforgettable.

"Well, look who I've found siting in the dark, all by herself." Chip smiled as he leaned over and kissed Steph.

She had managed to sneak off into the dark and sit down on a step at the stairs. "Just for a minute," she told herself.

"Have a seat, maybe we can get two minutes together, alone," she said happily.

"Everyone seems to be doing okay right now, for now anyhow," Chip said, adding, "as long as this barn stays up."

"Oh, don't say that, you'll jinx things. Besides, He wouldn't do that to Ken, or us, would He?" Steph's voice sounded full of doubt.

They sat quietly, just looking at the barn situation that they were responsible for.

"Rick seemed to be doing better tonight. I think Ken talked to him earlier about something. They were gone for a long time," Chip said. A moment later he added, "He seems happy tonight and then sad at the same time."

Steph scanned the barn, looking for the man they were talking about. He was at the stove, with Lilly sitting on his lap, and they both seemed to be laughing.

"I heard him tell Brian he wished he could experience tonight through Lilly's eyes. I thought that was sweet," Chip said.

Steph laughed. "Who wouldn't!"

"I think Ken caught on to some of their troubles and gave him some of his old fence lesson," Steph said in a concerned manner.

Steph snuggled closer to Chip. He put an arm around her shoulder and hugged her tight, both thinking the same thing: how lucky we are, to have each other.

"If anyone can show them how to turn their lives around, it's Ken with those fences. He's kinda gifted that way," Steph said seriously.

Chip rolled in laughter. "Is that what you call it? I guess it's all good, as long as it's directed at somebody besides me."

She turned and looked at him. "Oh you," laughing with him. She knew exactly what he meant.

A minute later, the seriousness of the night found its way back to them. "The barn is so peaceful right now. Even listening to the wind, for some reason, doesn't sound as threatening; almost makes you forget what has happened and what still has to come," Steph whispered.

Chip swallowed hard, as he said, "Yep, we still have the hard part ahead of us."

Steph didn't reply.

Rick had been talking with the other men at Lucky's pen. Steph had been wanting to speak privately with him, so now she waited to see if she could get his attention. She watched him walk over to Jakker's pen and give the mare an ear scratch.

"Now's my chance," she said out loud. "Rick," she said quietly. He heard her on her first call. He smiled and started walking her way. She patted the bale next to her, offering him a seat.

"What's up, lady?" his voice was cheerful.

"I've wanted to talk to you," she smiled.

"Is everything okay?" he asked, sounding alarmed.

"Yes," she patted his arm. "I want to refund part of the money you paid for your Christmas stay." She looked up toward the other end of the barn. "This isn't what you all expected, what you paid for—"

Rick stopped her in the middle of her apology speech, "Steph, how can I say this," he thought for a long second, wanting the words to be just right. "I'm not saying what you had planned for Christmas wasn't special, but," he hesitated, smiling, "this is an experience that can't be bought. I'm totally humbled for me and my family to have part in this….I don't even know what to call it. Ken is positive this was all planned." He looked at her with questioning eyes. "So my family is part of God's plan?"

Steph took a deep breath. This was Ken's expertise, not hers. "Is there any other way to make sense of this night, Rick?" She said as her eyes found his, "Maybe it is God's plan, all of it."

Rick shook his head in a negative way. "I've got a long way to go to believe that."

"This night has a long way to go yet," Steph replied with mixed emotions. She was troubled by his last remark. Her head told her that he didn't believe; her heart told her that she and Ken had more work to do.

Rick was talking, bringing her back from her thoughts. "What?" she said, realizing she hadn't been listening to him.

He repeated himself, "Regardless of what I believe, this is a priceless Christmas experience. I should pay you more." He laughed lightly.

Steph let out a long breath. "So, we are okay then, money-wise?" she asked.

"Yes, Steph, you promised a Christmas experience we wouldn't forget. We definitely won't forget this one." He reached over and hugged her. Rick never hugged the women in New York, but here, now, this felt right.

The barn went through cycles, some quiet, some noisy and busy. Right now it was in a quiet lull. Everyone seemed to be doing something, but quietly. Rick thought it might be a good time to just look around. He walked down along the stove wall. For some reason, he felt he was seeing the barn for the first time, through a different set of eyes. Little things on the wall came into view, noticing them now, for the first time, even down to the spider webs. He stopped in front of a makeshift bulletin board covered in burlap.

It was home to an array of award ribbons, many of them blue and red. Some of the blue ones had rosettes at the top; others were white, yellow then one or two pink. They were all indication of participating in events. Rick read the faded words on each: calf roping, team roping from Casper Rodeo Finals, barrel racing and pole bending from Shoshone and Casper County fairs. Rick wasn't sure what he was looking at. Some were dated, some forty years old, some only ten. He also noticed they had not been forgotten; the only dust lay on top of the frame. While Rick was in deep thought, Ken walked up beside him. "There's three generations of Kahlers represented there."

Rick turned and looked at Ken and started.

Ken spoke, answering the unasked question, "Blue is first, red is second, white is third, yellow is fourth, and pink is fifth." Ken's finger's gently straightened up a ribbon that had turned sideways.

"Thanks," Rick said.

Ken started walking off. Rick hollered to stop him, "Do you care if I go up in the loft? I've never been up in one before." Instantly, Ken felt a childhood memory take hold. As a child, he had climbed the ladder to the hay loft to find the kittens that he was being paid to play with at the horse farm. He had been seven.

Ken chuckled. "Sure, Rick, just don't fall out!"

The night was progressing too slowly in Steph's mind. Words from Gram came to mind for her, "All in God's timing," giving her a warm feeling. She laughed quietly and said, "As long as He looks at His watch once in a while."

The three women were sitting fairly close to Molly, who was catnapping for a few minutes. They had sent Jamie to the stove. He needed a break, even if he didn't know it. Brenda was happy that the girl was able to rest. The pain was coming on more, just as expected.

Steph looked at the other two who sat with her. "We all three have something in common—only one child."

Brenda spoke first, in whispers, "Our one and only was planned that way. Brian and I are both from big families. We both watched our parents struggle to do the best they could for each one. I'm not complaining, but Brian and I wanted to be able to concentrate on giving Colt a chance to be all he could be." Then she added, "I guess that's a little selfish." She looked at Steph and Susan, ready to take any criticism if given.

Steph smiled and spoke first, "There's nothing wrong with that." Steph thought for a second. Memories flooded her mind and heart. "After Kelly was born, to make the story short, the doctor told us to be grateful for her. If we were blessed with another, we would be lucky; if not, we were still blessed. I'll never forget those words."

Susan glanced downward as she spoke, "I had always wanted at least two. I was an only child of busy parents. I didn't want that for Lilly, but when I realized I would be raising her alone, I decided it was bad enough for one, let alone two."

Brenda didn't understand and spoke up without looking at Steph, as Steph would have conveyed to her not to question.

"But Rick seems like an excellent dad," Brenda said, but before she could comment more, Susan cut her off.

"He's different out here," Susan said in a quivery voice. Steph grabbed Susan's hand and playfully shook it.

"Well, he's being a great dad now, and now is all that matters tonight, right, Brenda?"

Brenda smiled and agreed, "Yes, it's all about tonight, and we can't forget, it's Christmas Eve."

Steph thought about what Susan had said. She knew where she was coming from. The man who got off the airplane a couple days ago was the real Rick. She hoped with all her heart, for Susan and Lilly's sake, that the Rick who was here tonight—the kind, loving, and fun one—stayed a while.

All evening long the kids had been keeping all the pens cleaned up. Colt would place the wheelbarrow on the outside of the pen, next to the rails, and then pitch the piles over. Ken told them to start a pile down at the double doors and after the storm was over, he would move all of it to the compost pile with the tractor. When things had finally settled down earlier and everyone could breathe, the kids decided to make a game out of the common barn chore, for Lilly. After explaining what needed done, they announced that a title came with the job. Colt looked at Kelly funny, as to say, "What title?" Kelly's eyes twinkled.

Lilly was very excited. She'd never had a title before. She was jumping up and down. "Come on, Kelly, tell me!"

"Okay, okay, you are the official head"—Kelly and Colt were both giggling—"Pooper Scooper," and the two teenagers rolled in laughter.

Lilly stood silent for a moment, thinking about it. Poop was a new word to her, and what did scoop mean?

She looked at both of them and said, "Wait." She ran as fast as she could toward Ken, who was looking at Brian's foot.

"Uncle Ken!"

Ken looked up. "Hey, sweetie."

"Is a pooper scooper a good thing?" she had a puzzled look on her little face.

Ken instantly glanced toward Kelly and Colt. They both waved to him, giggling.

He smiled sweetly as he looked at her. Brian turned his head so she wouldn't see him laughing.

"Sure, Lilly, being a pooper scooper is a very important job on a ranch, especially tonight."

She thought about it a moment, then said, "I'm the official one, is that good?"

Both Ken and Brian shook their heads, "Yes, it sure is, little one!"

"Okay then," and she was off.

She ran back to the kids, "Okay, Uncle Ken said that was a good job, but it kinda smells. Will I get used to it?"

"Maybe, if you're lucky enough to be around it long enough," Kelly told her, then adding, "I love the smell."

During the evening, Lilly would convince her dad to help her with the chore. It didn't take much with Lilly or Rick to change their minds from work to play. It was so comical to watch the little one's arms and hands trying to maneuver the long-handled pitchfork while Rick coached her along. Life tonight was good in the barn.

Susan called to Steph to come watch. "I've never seen him have so much fun with Lilly," tears formed in her eyes.

As the kids watched Lilly, Kelly whispered to Colt, "I can't imagine growing up anywhere but here, can you?"

He look her directly in the eyes and said, "Nope, how lucky are we!"

As the clock marched slowly along, Brenda and Steph began to think more seriously about Molly's upcoming delivery. First babies always seem to take their time, which seemed to be the case at both ends of the barn tonight.

Brenda suggested that she and Steph talk with their husbands about a few things, "Susan, would you mind staying with Molly for a little while, please. We want go to talk with Brian and Chip about a few things."

Susan smiled. "I'd be happy to. Take as long as you need."

"Come on, Jamie, take another break. You need to be rested," the last statement turned Jamie's face white again. Steph and Brenda laughed, enjoying being able to get to him.

Susan nestled down in the straw, next to Molly. She was sitting up. The pains seemed to have taken a break, for the time being. Susan liked the young girl and felt relaxed with her.

"How did you meet Jamie, Molly?' she asked, trying to start a comfortable conversation.

Molly's eye lit up, her head filling with sweet memories. "Well," Molly had a big smile on her face, "he's worked at the gas station for the past year. When I saw him for the first time, I thought he was the cutest boy in the world. It was summer. I remember hemming a pair of shorts to make them just a little shorter." She giggled at the thought.

Susan laughed, "Did you go meet him?"

Molly nodded her head yes. "I thought the shorts looked pretty good, so I walked down to the station. My excuse was to get a soda out of the machine there. I had a dollar bill, so I'd have to ask him for change. After that, it was easy for us to talk. He was going to be a senior when school started up. He and his mom had just moved to Shane, and I was the first girl he had met.

"Was that this year?" Susan asked.

"No, last year. He graduated this past June. I found out I was pregnant in May, but I didn't tell him. I wanted to make sure I didn't mess up his graduating. I've got one more year left, but I don't know now. I didn't go back to school when it started in September. We wanted to get married, but my mother said no, said he was no good. His mom has problems, which spread like fire through the town gossip. My mom wanted me to get rid of it, but I said no."

"Oh no, but what about your dad, honey? I take it he didn't live with you," Susan asked.

"My mom never married my father. He tried to stay in our lives. I miss him." Molly looked at Susan with tears in her eyes. "He always made me feel loved, the same way Jamie does now." She hesitated in thought, "My mom made my dad's life miserable. I guess it was just easier for him to leave." Molly looked down at her hands and then said, "Guess I don't blame him."

"How long has it been since you've seen him?" Susan asked.

"Five years."

Susan jumped in quickly, before Molly could get any sadder, "Well now, he sounds like he could be a good dad if given a fair chance, you know, if your mom wasn't in the picture." She laughed, shaking Molly's hand. "He's going to be a granddaddy now, that's something!"

Molly smiled as she felt a tears coming on. She wiped her eyes on her sleeve, hoping Susan hadn't seen.

"Yep, you and Jamie can find him and give him a new part in your new life." Susan felt good about what she was saying. Anything to help, she thought contently. Encouragement was always a good thing.

Susan reached for Molly's hand and patted it. "Well, I don't know you two very well yet, but I can tell you this: Jamie is a good guy, cute too."

Molly laughed.

"And he loves you and he loves this baby." She lightly rubbed Molly's belly. "I think he proved that today." She looked at Molly with serious eyes now. "And you are going to be an amazing mother, and very soon." She leaned in and hugged the girl as tears slid down Susan's cheeks.

"Okay now," Susan said laughing, "is this a boy or a girl?"

"A boy," Molly whispered with a slight smile.

Rick looked above the double doors and saw the wooden arch Chip had told him about this morning. It had been pieced or mended together. Rick remembered the story and replayed it in his mind, as his eyes scanned the large piece of Kahler history. The words Kahler Ranch were hard to read; the splintering of the words had marred the image. The wood was old, but its smoothness told a story of withstanding many years of elements. He could hear Chip saying, "Brought to you by Mother Nature." He kept studying it, not wanting to miss anything.

The "H" on the end of the word *ranch* was almost covered with a bird's nest, constructed of long pieces of straw that helped hold the nest together. Words came to Rick's mind, "Lucky birds," thinking about their ability to know they'd be safe here. He turned around seeing the whole barn and her contents from a different angle.

Rick talked to himself, as he gazed around, "Everyone has devoted themselves to a task without realizing it. Some are taking care of Molly, some are with Lucky. The content horses are faithfully being watched by Brian from his spot at the stove. Chip's filling the stove for the umpteenth tonight. I don't see Ken. I guess he's off doing Ken stuff."

Rick took a long breath, then his eyes saw Lilly, sweet Lilly. She was in her own little world. She was dancing in a large circle in the center of the barn. She was singing to herself, as her arms waved in the air, giving her a look of floating.

Rick felt his heart pounding, in a good way, with love and pride for the sweet little girl. He knew she took dance lessons back home.

Susan called it creative dance, but all he remembered about it was the big check he wrote every month to pay for it.

Shame washed over him as he watched her. "I've missed so much."

Lilly stopped and ran to Susan, breaking the spell, her image fading from his mind as he stood alone.

As Rick walked toward the stairs that would take him up top, he glanced around again. No one paid him any mind, no one seemed to miss him, but that's okay, he thought, he wanted this next experience for himself.

Ken sat on his bale of straw that he had claimed—his spot. It sat a ways from the center of the barn, closer to the south end. He had a good view of all the goings on from there. Right now he watched Rick go up the stairs.

Rick talked to himself with excitement in his voice, "I'd have given anything to have a barn to play in as a kid—anything." The stairs were built well, like everything else on this ranch. When he got to the top, he stood for a while, giving his eyes a chance to adjust to the darkest. Slowly the loft became clearer. His heart was beating hard, as he stared at it as a child. The loft spanned three quarters of the barn. Only the south end could be seen from where he stood. The floor was covered with old loose hay, at least a foot deep, making it hard to walk on. There were square bales stacked on the horse side of the barn. The floor had been swept on that side, allowing trap doors to show, about every twenty feet. You only needed to open the doors to throw hay down, landing near all the pens below.

"Wow, good thinking," he thought, "sure makes chores easier." The west or left side had a lot of boxes stacked up—used for storage, Rick thought. The north end contained a larger stack of hay. This one was stacked real high, and giving the appearance of having been there a while. The bales were covered with dusty spider webs and looked sleepy or tired with age.

Then he saw it, the old rope hanging from the rafters above, about fifteen feet in front of the old stack. It ended about four feet above the floor. It had been knotted in several places with about sixteen inches between knots. Rick walked over to it and let his hands slide down, starting high above the first knot. He closed his eyes, wanting to relish the next moments. He saw himself as a boy, swinging from the top of the stack, letting go, and falling into the deep pile of loose hay on the floor, then getting up and doing it again.

He looked at the floor, digging in with his boot to check its depth, then, he looked up where the rope was attached, following it downward. He gave it a hard pull. Next he grabbed it up high and barred his entire weight on it for a few seconds, praying at the same time, "Please, hold my weight."

Taking a deep breath, he made up his mind. He climbed most of the way up on the stack. His hands felt sweaty, so he wiped them on his pants and took another deep breath.

Moments later, Ken heard a soft thud and Rick laughing from above. Ken smiled; he had been expecting it.

All evening long, the friends would gather when they wanted to share a story. If Molly seemed comfortable and could withstand the company, they would all head up her way, sitting in a circle around Jamie and her, talking and sharing. On one of those times, the talk turned to how everyone came to the barn.

"I kinda feel like Molly and I were the lucky ones, who were luckier than you guys," Jamie was looking back and forth between Brian and Brenda. They were all sitting together. Brian's leg was out straight, and Brenda sat in front of him between his legs, leaning back against her husband.

"I guess you can say we came in luxury—a windshield, wipers, closed in cab," and Jamie got hung up on the last word. He swallowed hard before saying it, "And heater."

Everyone was silent.

Brian started detailing their experience. As he talked, the young couple kept feeling guiltier; it was painful to listen to. The reality was the fact that the Rogerses came close to losing their lives.

Lilly was too young to gasp the meaning of the conversation, but knew everyone was telling how they got to the barn. She spoke up in too loud a voice, "Chip carried me to the barn. It was scary!" No one felt like laughing at her. Susan grabbed her hand and pulled her over to her.

Ken had been listening. He spoke now, his words directed at Brian, "But you didn't, and who knows, God probably didn't intend for your adventure to be as bad as it was."

He continued looking Brian's way. "Did you follow your gut feeling or did you let your head take over?" Brian didn't answer. He just shrugged his shoulders. Deep down inside, he knew what had happened. None of it was anybody's fault but his own. He didn't follow his gut; he let his head overrule it, leading them in the wrong direction. Brian could be stubborn, sometimes his own worst enemy.

The wind howled its opinion, shaking the whole barn. Eyes turned to the rafters.

Ken made a solemn statement now, meant for Molly and Jamie too, "This plan didn't call for any of you to die."

Poor Colt, who had pretty quiet on the subject all night, spoke up, "Well, next time I think we deserve a warmer part to play."

The barn filled with heartfelt amens.

Brenda sat up near Molly, who had just finished a big piece of pie. Ken was about twenty feet away. "Hey, Ken," Brenda hollered, "how's your cat population?"

Ken looked up, as a loud "no" came from Lucky's pen. Chip had heard the word *cat*.

Ken laughed. "Well, actually, since we spayed those two old barn mommas, we're probably low. I did see a mouse the other day, why?"

Kelly had heard the word *cat* too and was all ears now, but stayed quiet.

Brenda looked at Molly. "I'll be back in a minute," and walked toward Ken with Kelly and Chip in earshot.

"Henry Bates, over on Deer Creek, brought in four little ones. I guess their momma took on a big raccoon sow, ran her off, but took a beating. He tried getting her to me as fast as he could, but she died on the way over. Said with Martha just having her knee replaced, he didn't think he'd be able to give the kittens enough attention. I told him to leave them."

Ken looked at Kelly, then back at Brenda. "How big?"

"Eating canned food real well. I've started them on dry, and Ken, they are your favorite color.

Before he could say anything, Kelly hollered, "Yellow, right?"

Brenda answered with a smile, "Yep, all four."

Another loud "no" was heard. Ken waved him off with a laugh, "Hey, Kelly, you up to helping raise some kittens?"

A voice came from nowhere, shocking everyone. Rick hollered as he came walking up, "Aw, I want them!"

About three "what!" were heard, one of them coming from Susan.

Lilly screamed, "We are getting kittens?"

All of a sudden, Rick realized he had spoken his thoughts out loud. "Ah no, that's not what I meant to say!"

Lilly stared at him with heartbroken eyes. He had to fix this, fast. "We can't right now, Lilly, maybe when we get back home. We'll see, okay, baby?" He hugged her while looking at Susan and shaking his head.

Kelly giggled at the whole situation. "Sure, Uncle Ken, always."

"I'll bring them over in a couple days. Thanks, Ken," Brenda said.

Chip walked up and playfully said, "How come no one ever asks me?"

Kelly laughed. "Because you always say no!"

Lilly danced around Kelly. "I like kittens!"

That old clock still had a mind of its own. Right now it seemed to be standing still.

Jamie was a nervous wreck. Brenda looked around the barn until she found Ken and Brian standing by the horses. Brenda came up from behind, stepping in between them. One arm gave Ken a pat on the back and the other one squeezed around Brian's waist.

"How's your foot, babe?" Brenda glanced down at the injured foot.

Ken, being Ken, had come up with a makeshift solution to the boot problem. It looked kind of misshapen, but it worked.

It was too painful for Brian to put his boot on. Luckily, he was wearing his old ones. Brenda had sarcastically made the remark that maybe his toes wouldn't have frostbite if he'd worn the new boots she had just spent two hundred dollars on.

But since they were the old pair, Ken took his pocketknife and cut out the top and side of the toe area but left the bottom. He also split the entire boot down the front. Ken had coated the toes with bag balm, wrapped them separately with gauze, then placed a piece of sheep skin in the boot before setting Brian's foot in it. Then the boot was folded back up, leaving the toe area open and without any pressure on it. The last step was to wrap duct tape around the boot, holding it in place. Brian was still in pain but said he was handling it okay. He had taken three doses of Banamine so far for the pain. Everyone who knew Brian knew they weren't going to keep him down for long.

"I'm okay," Brian answered Brenda with a handsome grin. "What do you need, babe?"

"Can you guys find a job for Jamie, or talk to him? He needs to calm down, and he's driving me crazy. I've got enough to worry about watching over Molly. How are they doing?" Brenda asked Brian, looking at the horses.

"Good. We really got lucky, babe," Brian said, with emotion in his voice.

"I know," she said quickly and walked off before either one saw the tears slipping down her face.

Ken's heart told him the word *lucky* was being used way too often tonight.

"Jamie, can I get you to give me a hand?" Ken asked the young man.

"Sure," he answered but gave Molly a look that said, "I don't want to leave you."

Molly smiled. "Go ahead, Jamie, I'm fine. Go help Ken."

Ken headed to the workbench with Jamie following. "We need to fill these lanterns with kerosene before we find ourselves in the dark, like this."

Ken showed him how to open the covers. They were a little tricky since they were made for barn use. These wouldn't start a barn fire if knocked over.

"Just pull down one at a time so we keep the barn bright."

"Okay, Ken," Jamie answered and went to work.

Ken knew his heart wasn't in it, but that was okay. Ken saw Chip and walked over to explain about keeping Jamie busy for a while. "Good, I have been wanting to talk to him anyhow," Chip said.

Chip kept an eye on Jamie as he filled the lanterns. When he was on the last one, he walked over to him. "Let's talk some, when you finish," he said, with a smile on his face. He didn't want to scare the boy.

"Sure, would you like some coffee?" Jamie asked in an uneven voice.

"Yeah, that'd be good, going to sit over here," Chip motioned to the bales off to the side.

Moments later Jamie handed Chip a fresh cup of coffee and sat down across from Chip.

Chip started with small talk, mostly storm-related, then worked into the main questions he wanted to ask. "Jamie, what are your plans to make Molly an honest woman?"

Chip came from a generation of men who spoke their minds—straightforward—even if it wasn't socially correct.

Jamie perked up at the question. "Sir, I'll be eighteen in March and Molly in April, then we don't need anyone's permission to get married. As I told Ken, my mom could have signed, but Molly's wouldn't, so we had to wait."

Chip leaned forward and patted Jamie on the shoulder. "Good enough, son."

"Sir, I didn't plan for her to get in a family way; that wasn't our plan," Jamie sounded like a young man accepting his responsibilities.

"Happens to the best of us," Chip replied. He didn't want Jamie to think he was judging him. Chip thought Jamie had been through a lot for someone his age. *Maybe I should try and raise his spirits some.*

Now, he searched for just the right words. "Well, I see a young man that loves his girl—you've proven that for sure today—and this baby is going to have a great dad." Then Chip added, "Things will get better."

Jamie managed a smile. "Thanks, sir."

Chip laughed. "And Jamie, quit calling me sir!"

Chip kept Jamie talking a few minutes longer then let him leave. He headed straight for Molly. "I tried, Steph," Chip chuckled to himself.

Ken saw Jamie leave, so he walked back over to Chip and sat down.

"Jamie made a scary decision today, to go out in that storm, with no guarantee of a positive outcome," Chip spoke quietly. The conversation was not intended for the others. Ken sat mulling over Chip's statement. The friends were close. They knew each other's strengths and weaknesses. They made a good team.

Ken looked at the floor, picking up a straw stem and rolling it in his fingers as he thought about how he wanted to respond. "I agree, but Jamie probably thinks a lot different than we might have at that age, in that same predicament. We grew up in a totally different world. I'm not saying we had everything easy, but we never wondered where our next meal was coming from or why our dad left and never came back." As Ken talked, he watched the kids. The three were sitting in a circle on the floor, talking and laughing near the stove.

"I wonder what it's like to grow up with a parent who stays drunk all the time."

Ken's voice was steady. He was trying to make a point. "You and I grew up with a foundation of love, discipline, direction, and faith, all the good things you need to be grounded. Jamie did what he thought was the best at the moment."

Chip chuckled lightly. "Yeah, well, I'm sure he thought differently about an hour down the road."

"The main thing is he took the responsibility and that's something," Ken added.

Chip's tone was serious, but Ken could hear emotions creeping into it but he held it together, "I don't think he was in control when he made those decisions, for the same reason that we are in this barn tonight."

"Maybe that was God's intentions all along," Ken said.

Chip didn't argue. "Maybe so."

The three kids were laughing louder now. "I wonder, when was the last time Jamie laughed like that, carefree, if only for a little while," Chip commented, then added, "I'm guessing about ten months ago, at least." His voice quivered but he kept talking. "We need to see if we can do something about giving him a much needed break, the one he's never got." Chip knew in his heart the Kahler Ranch needed to help these kids.

Ken's eyes moved from the kids to Chip. He smiled lightly and placed a hand on Chip's shoulder. "The boy just got moved to the top of the list."

Chip smiled, knowing exactly what Ken meant.

The howl of the wind had doubled, maybe tripled. Brenda and Steph put their foot down on the men opening the door and checking things out. They had opened it more than once. Their excuse was it helped keep the snow from building up again it.

Both women agreed it was only going to get worse.

Time was still moving at a crawl. Everyone had agreed to the unrealistic thought that no one human was in charge of the night and they just had to wait things out.

It was after ten o'clock, and Molly was progressing exactly the way Brenda predicted, and Lucky was doing the same but with more visible signs: up and down, tail out, all perfectly normal. Ken had made the comment, more than once, that the action would pick up the closer they got to midnight, with both births welcoming in Christmas, following the story.

The grown-ups seemed to be managing the slow pace well. They were still telling stories. The two teens were doing their share of talking. Lilly was another story. She was bored, for the first time since coming to the ranch. She walked over to Lucky's pen, where Kelly and Colt stood leaning against the rails. She managed to wiggle her way in between the two.

"What's up, Lilly?" Kelly asked.

"Well," she said dragging out the word, "I was thinking."

Colt raised his eyebrows to Kelly, thinking, "Not again!"

"We seem to be missing one thing tonight, you know, we have a Mary, a Joseph, a star (referring to the lane light), and the three wise men." She hesitated, trying to gather more thoughts.

Kelly smiled. "Okay, Lilly, what's missing, besides the baby Jesus, who isn't born yet."

Lilly, serious now, said, "He's coming!"

Kelly returned the serious attitude, for Lilly. "Yes, he is, so what else do we need?"

Very early in the evening, Lilly had decided that they were playing out the Christmas story. She had all the players. Molly was Mary, Jamie was Joseph, there had been a north star guiding the three wise men, which was the lane light; though, she joked about her wise men being frozen.

At one point she had tried to complain that the horses should have been camels, but instantly got shut down by virtually everyone. "This is horse country, don't go trying to change it!"

The adults didn't comment much; they just let her tell her story, which she was calling "God's Story." The approaching birth was called "God's Baby." She basically had it all figured out and was very vocal about it, something the adults were still coming to terms with.

Finally, a big cute smile showed itself. We need a Christmas barn angel!" Now, she waited for Kelly to respond. Colt looked down to mask his grin. Kelly tried to remain serious. "You know, you are right, but let me think about this, okay, Lilly?"

She answered, "Yep," and ran off to her mom and dad, over by the stove.

Kelly was sure she was going to share her angel idea with them. Kelly looked at Colt, "I'll be right back. If anyone can come up with an angel, it will be Uncle Ken."

She found him carrying an armload of wood toward the stove. Running over to him, she said, "I need to tell you something, when you're free." A few minutes later, he called her over to his special spot.

"What's going on?" he asked as she sat down next to him.

"Lilly has this idea in her head that this scenario is missing a barn angel. She says we have everything else, just no angel."

Ken had to think. He fingered the end of his mustache. A few moments later, he gave Kelly a hug and said, "Then I guess I'd better come up with an angel!"

Kelly giggled. "Not just an angel, a 'barn' angel!"

Kelly walked back over to Colt and said, "Barn angel, here we come!"

Ken walked over to the large workbench on the east barn wall. It ran from close to where Molly was nestled, to near Lucky's pen.

"Okay, Ken, think," he told himself. Looking around, he dug out a large piece of cardboard, a thin wooden dowel about two feet long, baling twine, baling wire, cotton gauze, super glue, and gold and silver spray paint. He looked toward Kelly. When he got her attention, he waved her over. "Come help me with this."

When she walked up and saw his pile of goodies, all she could say was, "Wow!"

He pulled out his pocketknife and started cutting wing forms out of cardboard.

About thirty minutes later, a set of angel wings complete with a halo were finished. "What do you think?" Ken asked Kelly.

Before she could answer, she felt a twinge of jealously, lasting for just a split second. She had never had to share her uncle before. "I love it, but I'm a little jealous," Kelly admitted.

Ken looked straight in her eyes. "Don't be. You are my angel and always will be," he kissed the top of her head, making her feel foolish.

"I know," she smiled.

"Let's get her over here, quietly if that is possible."

Kelly found her at the stove. Without saying a word, she grabbed the sleeve of Lilly's jacket and attempted to drag her toward Ken. Rick and Susan remained silent but watched.

"Now to keep Lilly quiet, while we transform her into an angel. Hope this works out," Ken thought. As he watched them walk his way, he tapped his fingers to his mouth, indicating silence.

When the two reached him, Lilly giggled and whispered, "Okay."

They attempted to mount the wings. Two loops had been formed for her arms, holding the wings like a backpack would. Then a piece of baling twine tied in front of her middle held the wings in place against her back. The halo bounced above her head about a foot. It wasn't centered with her head, but Ken said, "Beggars can't be choosers." Ken had made the halo circle by looping baling wire a couple of times into a circle, then wrapping cotton gauze around it. The wings and halo were spray-painted gold then lightly highlighted with silver paint.

Kelly thought he had outdone himself, but then she expected no less from her uncle.

Lilly, for once, was speechless. Finally she said, "Oh, Uncle Ken!" That was all she could say. Ken and Kelly took her by the hand, all walking toward Molly's end of the barn.

"Hey everyone, can we get your attention!" Ken hollered.

Instantly, everyone stopped what they were going and looked toward the trio. Rick and Susan walked up close, holding hands.

"I would like to introduce the newest member of this amazing magical night: Lilly, our new Christmas Barn Angel!"

Lilly slowly turned in a complete circle and then took a bow. Everyone clapped and hollered, "Yeah." The bubbly look on Lilly's face was priceless, Rick and Susan both had tears in their eyes. Even Ken felt a tear slide down his cheek.

The next ten minutes were spent with everyone admiring Ken's impressive handiwork and Lilly absorbing the many compliments.

Finally she ran up to Molly and fell down on her knees next to her. "Now," she said out of breath, "we are ready for your part, Molly!"

The whole barn roared in laughter, drowning out the curse of the wind.

Chip and Ken started walking back down to the pens. "I've spent many Christmas Eves in this old barn, but this is the first time it included a dancing angel," Chip said.

"Oh, they were here, you just didn't look for them," Ken whispered as they watched Lilly dance in circles.

Lilly had been an angel for a while now but that still didn't satisfy her.

But of course, nothing was normal tonight. Brenda didn't like the flushed coloring of Molly's face again.

"Molly, I want you to eat again, okay, sweetie?" Brenda asked as she felt her forehead with her hand. It was clammy, the same feeling as before.

"I'll try. I don't feel good, Brenda," Molly answered in a shaky voice. Steph walked up just as Brenda was turning. She saw the same look on Molly's face.

"Blood sugar going wacky again?" she asked Brenda. "Do you think a piece of pie will help, sugar and little protein?"

"Yes, let's try," Brenda replied.

"I'll get a small piece," Steph said.

Brenda poured a little orange juice. They were almost out.

Both women stayed with her as she ate. Chip had walked up and sat down with them.

Minutes later, Lilly came skipping up. As soon as the group turned and looked at her, she put on another gloomy face. Chip looked at her. "What's wrong, angel?"

Lilly ignored him, siding up to Steph. "Everyone has had a special job tonight but me. Angels need jobs too." The face got sadder.

"But Lilly, you've been helping all over. You've worked really hard tonight, everyone has," Steph said in a gentle voice.

Chip leaned over to Steph and whispered, "If she gets any sadder looking, her lip is going to fall off. I've seen that look before on Kelly."

Steph quickly looked down to muffle a laugh, not wanting Lilly to see. When she looked back up, her eyes, for some unknown reason, focused past Lilly, to a straw bale sitting next to the small bench between the side door and the stove.

Sitting there on the bale, all by itself, was the pine box she had purchased right after Thanksgiving. She remembered leaving it in the barn when she unloaded stuff for Chip. Until now, she had never given it a second thought. Each one of them had walked past it tonight and no one had even noticed it, until now. Steph's heart warmed. *The box does have a purpose—perfect*, she thought. In the meantime, Susan had joined them, sitting down next to Chip. Steph giggled and turned her attention back to Lilly.

"Lilly, you are right!" Steph said. Lilly immediately perked up. Steph took Lilly's shoulders and turned her around. "Do you see that wooden pine box, the one sitting on that bale of straw, down toward the stove?"

Lilly looked ahead and pointed to the box, "That one?"

"Yep, I think we have a plan for that box," Steph answered.

Lilly came unglued. "It's a manger for baby Jesus!" She screamed and ran to gather it. No one said a word.

Lilly had made enough noise that Rick and Ken had walked up. Chip stood up and hollered, "Hey guys, come see."

Kelly and Colt came running, and Brian hobbled.

Chip looked directly at Ken, who had a grin on his face. Both men were remembering the conversation they had when Ken told Chip not to use that box for his parts, which he thought Steph might want it for something special.

Lilly carried the box in both arms, dancing around in a big circle, with wings and halo bouncing as she sang, "We're having a baby, a special Christmas baby, a baby in a manger." She sang the words over and over.

Chip was losing it. "What is going on tonight?"

Steph, knowing her husband well, patted his arm and said, "Christmas magic!"

No one said a word. Lilly's voice sounded like a choir in a church. Finally, Steph called her name a couple of times, breaking her spell.

"Lilly, come, we need to make the box into a nice soft bed." Looking directly at Rick, she said, "Daddy, can you help her fill the box, er, manger with soft straw from over there?" She pointed to the pile of straw back behind Molly. "Then, Lilly, your momma can help you take a soft baby blanket for the bed cover," she nodded to Susan and the small pile of baby blankets. "Then, sweet angel, I think we are ready, don't you?"

Lilly giggled hard. "Yes, now it's all up to Mary, er, Molly!"

Everyone looked toward Molly. She seemed to be feeling a little better and smiled sweetly at Lilly's assessment.

Ken felt playful. "Well, I think we have followed the story pretty close so far, what do you guys think?" His eyes scanned the group.

Lilly screamed from her spot, near Steph, "I do!"

Ken laughed.

Molly had been pretty quiet so far tonight, but now she giggled. "Ken, I may have messed the story up some."

"How's that, sis?" Ken asked.

"Well," Molly smiles as she looked at everyone, "I didn't get here riding in on a donkey."

Ken waited for her to finish then said, "But, my dear Mary," he raised his hands up to indicate quotation marks around the word Mary, "you did come riding in on a mule."

The barn was silent with thoughts. Chip spoke first, "Well, you're here, that's all that matters, right, Jamie?"

Jamie was sitting in his spot, on the far side of Molly. The later the night got, the more of a toll it took on him. It was easy to see his nerves couldn't take much more, but he tried to be social by replying to Chip's comment. "Thank God for the mule!" his voice was sober and barely above a whisper, but the others grasped hold of the words that had so much meaning.

Steph didn't know how to help the young man, other than have Ken give him a big gulp of the JD.

Brian stood there laughing. He looked at Molly and said, "Now, Molly, don't go having a girl!"

Before she could reply, Ken said, "She won't, that's not how the story goes."

Lilly had been trying to keep up with all the back and forth. Hearing Ken's last statement, she looked at Molly and said, "Yeah, don't mess up, Molly."

Lilly, along with her parents' help, were putting the finishing touches on the manger box. Ken watched, thinking, "Steph has just the right knack for handling people. Good job, sis."

Steph had the whole Conner family working together—a win for Lilly.

Susan, Rick, and Lilly were sitting, looking at the completed project. "Steph, come look," Lilly hollered.

Steph crawled back across the straw since she was sitting nearby. "That's perfect, Lilly, I mean, Angel Lilly, good job!"

Lilly smiled contentedly. "Do you think Baby Jesus will like it?"

"Yes, I'm sure he will." She thought about correcting Lilly by saying "Molly's baby," but something inside her said, "Let it be, it's okay."

Lilly was all smiles now. "What now?" she asked.

"Well, we are going to set it right here, near all the baby things, until we need it, okay, Lilly?"

Lilly nodded yes to Steph and curled up best she could, considering her wings, in Susan's arms. Lilly's eyes glowed.

Steph whispered to herself, "This is what Christmas is all about!"

Ken had walked back to the stove and had the pot of spaghetti warming. "If anybody is hungry, I kinda think we should chow down now. Going to get mighty busy after a while!"

He raised up on his toes and glanced at Lucky and added, "Mighty busy," under his breath.

A few minutes later, just about everyone commented, "Yeah, I could eat a little something."

As they ate quietly, Ken glanced at Lilly. Susan had made her take her wings off while she ate. His heart melted every time he looked at her. She couldn't be happier. He smiled, thinking, "She's a handful, but in a good way!"

Since no one was talking, the wind seemed louder. Lilly set her fork down on her plate and looked around the group. "Can I ask a question?"

Chip glanced up. "Shoot."

"What?" Lilly responded.

Ken laughed. "Go ahead, Lilly, it means ask!"

She relaxed a little. "Oh, okay." Wiggling a bit on the straw bale, she started talking, "One of the girls at school said that a big bird called a stork brings all babies. They are wrapped in a blanket with a knot at the top and the stork carries them in his beak." Slowly, looking from one to another, she added, while shaking her head, "That's not true, is it?"

The barn was quiet, but everyone had a big grin on their face. Finally, Kelly spoke up, "No, girl, it's not, and you'll know all the true stuff by the end of the night!"

Brenda kept her eyes on her plate but quickly added, "One way or another!"

Susan's head popped up, her eyes wide. "Lord, help us." She didn't mean to say the words out loud, they just slipped out.

Ken smiled, and said, "Yes, definitely Lord."

Very calmly, Kelly looked toward Susan and said, "Really, it's no big deal, we do this stuff almost every day here on the ranch," then added, "Brenda does for sure."

Brenda started turning red in the face. "Well, it's not exactly the same, Kelly."

Chip choked on the bite of food he had just swallowed and said, "Some of it."

Ken felt he needed to bail Brenda and Chip out of this one before Lilly could ask any more questions. "Lilly, Kelly, eat!" He used a stern voice, sounding like a parent. Rick looked Ken's way and gave him a thumbs-up and laughed.

"End of conversation," Ken added with a smile.

Kelly and Lilly were picking up all the plates and rest of the trash while Steph put the food away. The men had gone back to the stove—to rest their full bellies, they said.

All of a sudden a gush of liquid was heard. Kelly turned quickly and ran to Lucky's pen, the others followed. Lucky had turned toward the soaked puddle of slimy straw and had begun licking it up. A slight mooing sound could be heard, as if she were talking to it. Her tail was out and all wet.

"Brenda, her water broke," Kelly hollered loud enough to be heard at the end of the barn and over the howling wind.

Lilly had jumped up on the rails next to Kelly. "What's that?" she asked with the emphasis on the word *that*, as she looked in horror at the wet straw.

Colt laughed lightly. Lowering his head down close to hers, and in a very calm voice, he said, "The baby calf is in that sack of embryonic fluids." She looked at him with eyes that said, "I was following you until now."

Colt laughed again. He replied, "Water, the baby has been in that sac of water the whole time it has been growing." He waited to make sure she was following him, then added, "It's time for the calf to be born now, so it doesn't need the water anymore."

Lucky had the mess cleaned up pretty well but kept talking to it and turning in circles with her tail held out.

Brenda headed toward the pen, leaving Molly with Steph and Susan. She stood between Kelly and Colt, placing a hand on each shoulder.

"Looks like we'll have a new calf soon, you okay?" she asked looking directly at Kelly.

With plenty of Kahler confidence, she replied, "Yep!"

Looking across the pen to the men standing there, she laughed. "Anyone want to take bets on who shows up first—baby baby or calf baby?" No one spoke. Brenda broke out laughing.

Chip didn't handle her joke well. He turned and looked at Ken, his face turning white. Ken tried not to laugh. Rick sat down on a bale; he was choking on a sip of coffee.

Brian grinned, mostly at Brenda. "His girl was back. Thank You, Lord."

"No takers? Okay then, I'm leaving."

Before walking off, she turned to Kelly. "Hey guys, this heifer needs some peace and quiet."

Kelly responded, "Got it, Doc."

Next, Brenda turned to Chip and pointed a finger at him with a stern look on her face.

Chip stayed quiet but raised both hands up, meaning, "I give up." Satisfied that he got her message, she walked off.

Ken whispered, "What was that all about?"

"She was telling me to stay out of this birth; it's Kelly's to handle."

Ken patted his shoulder, "She's right, leave her alone."

"Boy, talk about being ganged up on!" Chip stammered, walking over to Jakker's pen.

"Come on guys," Kelly said, walking to the south side of the pen. A big stack of alfalfa square bales was neatly stacked about ten feet high. The back side of the stack was the side being fed out. The bales had been pulled down from the top, which left a tiered stack. Kelly started climbing up, turning to look at the others. "We need to leave her alone. We can climb up on top and watch from there."

Colt let Lilly climb first, then he followed. Kelly heard Rick's voice, "Can I come too?"

Kelly smiled at the city man. "Sure, come on up."

Chip, Brian, and Ken stood next to the stove, looking up at the top of the stack. The four of them lay on their bellies, whispering back and forth.

"Boy, if that's not a sight!" Ken said with humor.

"How long are we staying up here?" Lilly whispered to Kelly.

"Until she gets started. She's a ways off yet."

"Have either one of you ever seen anything born?" Kelly glanced from Lilly to Rick.

Both shook their heads no. Then Lilly made a funny, as Ken would have called it. "I've believed in the stork until tonight, remember." All four of them laughed so hard and loud that the men at the stove looked up.

Chip hollered, "Hey!"

Kelly knew what it meant and quieted her group down. Kelly looked at Colt and said, "I guess we should get into teacher mode."

Colt replied, "That would probably be good."

The next half hour was spent with Kelly and Colt giving Rick and Lilly step-by-step details of what was going to happen. In the meantime, Lucky had lain down but hadn't started pushing yet; she was still a ways off.

Another hard gust of strong wind hit the west side of the barn. The three men turned toward the wall, holding their breath, again, as they had many times tonight. Chip swore the wind was splintering the wall boards on the outside, at least it sounded like it was. Ken and Chip had been checking the walls and rafters after every hard hit. Both of them were concerned as to how much the roof joists could take. They both had accepted the fact that their favorite old barn wasn't going to look the same on the outside after taking this beating.

Up on the hill, the old cabin battled the storm, trying to stay on her feet, but her age was against her. Around ten thirty, she started losing the battle. The old tin on the roof had been working loose all evening, the nails being pulled up and out against their will.

The next hard gust would take the tin roof with it. By morning, she would also lose her west wall, it being found after the storm, crumbled on the ground. The tin would be scattered far south, caught in the fences, along with Steph's trees.

The clock was on the move. It was after eleven now. Ken was thinking that a lot was going to happen within the hour. He wanted to talk with Brenda. He walked halfway to the end of the barn and whistled to get her attention. She spoke to Steph then walked over near the Christmas tree, where Ken waited for her. Sitting down next to her friend, she said, "What's up, Ken?"

"Nothing, I just thought we should touch base before everything starts coming down." He waited for her response, but added, "I've got the easy end."

Brenda knew what he meant.

"Well, I can't tell you much, because I have no way of checking anything. Sure wish I knew how her blood pressure was. Her pulse is real good. Baby's heartbeat sounds good to me, little fast, but babies beat a little faster."

"How dilated is she?" Ken asked.

"I'm guessing she's a five or six," she responded, "ways to go yet. Seems to be handling the pain good for a youngin'."

Brenda got serious now, looking directly in his eyes. "I'm worried, Ken. I don't have anything I can use as forceps. I've racked my brain and haven't come up with anything." She took a deep breath and held it. "I'm afraid I won't be able to grab on to the baby's head and guide it. Do you think you can make a pair out of, oh, I don't know!"

Brenda's voice showed the stress she was under. A moment later, she said, "I need your help Ken."

Ken wasn't used to seeing Brenda worried. This made him uncomfortable. "I'll do the best I can, but sweetheart—no promises."

She stood up, leaning into him for a hug. She whispered, "Please try," and walked off quickly, before he could see her tears.

Ken whispered, "Lord, I need some help with this one."

He walked toward the long workbench. "I managed an angel, how 'bout forceps." He hadn't meant to say the words out loud, but they came, then added, "Think, cowboy!" louder this time on purpose. He stood with his hands on his hips, looking at the bench and thinking of its contents.

Chip watched him from across the barn. "Well, something's up and it's not angel wings," Chip said to himself.

"What's up, Ken?" Chip said as he walked up beside him.

Ken had a serious look on his face. "Brenda needs me to come up with something she can use for forceps."

"Dang!" Chip said scanning the barn.

"They need to be solid, won't bend with pressure, but at the same time be gentle on the baby's head," Ken explained.

Both men were silent for a few minutes while they thought, then Ken starting laughing lightly and doing a little gig with his feet.

"What you thinking, bud?" Chip's voice sounded hopeful.

"Up in the loft is a stack of boxes, you know, the stuff for the barbecues and picnics."

"Yeah, so?" Chip replied.

"There are some large plastic bowls I think Steph used to put cut-up watermelon in, if I remember correctly," Ken said with a questioning smile.

"Yeah, maybe we can cut narrow pieces out of them; the sides are right. Brenda probably needs some curve to them, doesn't she?" Chip was getting excited.

"Yes, I think so. If we can get it cut, might work just right. Let's go!" Ken was already heading toward the stairs, and Chip followed closely.

Brian had been watching the two. *I wonder what they are up to.* He prayed quickly as he saw them going up the stairs, "Please don't let it be the roof!"

His first thoughts were to go help, but he decided to stay put because of his foot. He wasn't sure he could maneuver the stairs. *They'll holler if they need me.*

It didn't take long for the two men to make a big mess in the loft. They had to open two-thirds of all the boxes before they found what they were looking for.

There were two of them—big, red, hard plastic bowls, thick enough for what Brenda would need. They brought both of them back down to the bench.

They worked together, speaking in whispers, as if a loud voice would jinx their efforts. They managed the cuts and filed down the rough edges. Lastly, they used sandpaper to accomplish the silky smooth edges that were needed. The end product actually looked like large melon scoops. They were eight inches long and one and a half inches wide, with a gentle curve. If Brenda didn't think they would work, they had enough material to make a pair with different dimensions.

They went together to show Brenda. She looked up as Ken held out his hands toward her, showing her the homemade forceps. She didn't say anything. She took one of them and felt the smoothness of the edges. Still without saying a word, she took the other one, feeling it the same way.

Time seemed to stand still for Ken and Chip as they waited. Brenda put the two pieces to her heart and started crying. Ken and Chip didn't know what to do, what to think, as Brenda sobbed harder, as if all the night's events had come down on her at this moment.

Steph crawled over to her, wrapping her in her arms and whispered to her. Slowly, Brenda calmed down. Steph looked to the men and said, "Give her a minute."

Ken and Chip moved off over by the tree and waited.

A few minutes later, Steph called them back. Brenda looked up at her two friends and said, "You guys probably just saved this baby's life." Her voice cracked with emotion.

Chip had to turn away. His knees had gone weak, and he knew he was losing control. Brenda's crying had wiped him out. Tears rolled down his face that he didn't want the others to see.

"So okay, Brenda?" Ken asked.

She nodded yes, still clutching the pieces to her heart.

He walked up to Chip, pushing him ahead, saying, "Why don't you and me go see how that old cow is doing."

"Maybe, we'll do okay yet," Chip said in a choked-up voice as they walked toward the pen.

Ken gave Brenda some time to calm down, but he still wanted to talk to her. A few minutes later he walked back to her end. "First things first," he told himself.

"Are you letting Jamie stay?" Ken asked Brenda.

"No, not much longer, he's a total basket case, and I don't need the complication."

"Okay, just send him over whenever you want. I'll give him to Brian. He's good at keeping the calm."

Steph walked up. "How's Chip, is he holding together?" she asked.

"So far, but that's not saying much," Ken answered truthfully.

Ken was getting anxious to get his words out. "Brenda, the heifer will be fine. If you need anything, don't hesitate to holler. I plan on keeping one eye in your direction. Have you got a suction bulb and suture?" Ken asked, concerned.

"Yes, for some unknown reason," Brenda looked up, "I put both in my bag this morning." They shared thoughts for a few more minutes. As Ken turned to go, he looked at Brenda and said, "God knows all."

Brenda sent Jamie to get Molly a fresh bottle of water. She wanted to talk to Steph and especially Susan without him present.

"Susan, I'm going to need your help. I need Steph with Molly. She knows how to coach Molly firmly, to make Molly work."

Susan broke in, "I understand," then waited for Brenda to continue.

"I need you next to me, handing me whatever I need and taking the baby. We'll be moving fast, so hear me the first time I say it. I don't mean—"

Susan waved her to stop, "Brenda, I absolutely know what you are saying." Then, in a confident voice, she said, "I won't let you down!"

Brenda swallowed. "Good." She was too serious for niceties.

"Now, Molly, I need you to listen too." Brenda went on to explain to the three women what was expected to happen and also to let them ask whatever questions they needed to. When she was done, they all joined hands and said a quick prayer for guidance, safety, strength, and blessings. Brenda looked at each one ending with Molly, and with a smile, said, "We've got this, lady!"

Ken was putting more wood on the stove. He kept watching the pile get smaller. His brain told him there was plenty. His heart prayed, "Please bless us with enough."

Chip walked up. "Ken, do we have some tarps somewhere? There's a draft over near Mary."

Ken straightened up. "Over by who?" he mumbled, sounding like a grumpy old man.

Chip grinned. "Oh yeah, the mother-to-be, I've nicknamed her Mary. You know, Lilly's thing—Mary, Joseph, no room in the inn, Baby Jesus." He laughed, "Come on, Ken, it's Christmas!" He waited.

"You've been hitting my bottle. You sound like Lilly," Ken said with a straight face.

"No," Chip said bluntly, "tarps!"

Ken shook his head. "Over here." They grabbed a fairly large one and headed to the spot Steph pointed to. A good stream of cold wind mixed with light snow was finding its way between two wall planks. Once they had it tacked up, Chip knelt down next to Steph and Brenda and asked, "How's it going?"

Brenda spoke without taking her eyes off Molly, hoping to catch a sign of the next contraction, "All is well here, how's your end?"

"Fine," he said, "Kelly's staying with her. Feet not showing yet, but she went in. Everything's in place."

"Good," Brenda said. "Could be a while, give her time to do it on her own, if possible."

Chip managed a smile. "Yes, madam."

Then in a soft voice, Brenda said, "Remember, Chip, let her do it."

Sounding now like a little boy, he replied, "I know!"

Steph's heart melted, "Awww!"

The group hadn't been up on the stack of hay very long before Lilly found excuses for why she needed to climb down then up and so on. Kelly made the decision for everyone to go back down.

It seemed like the later it got, the more energy Lilly had. She was carefully pacing the barn now, from cow pen to "God's baby." That was her permanent name for the soon-to-be-born-in-a-barn-on-Christmas-Eve baby.

Susan commented to Brenda and Steph, "I guess she was listening in Sunday school last Christmas." She went on to explain that they didn't attend church very often, but Susan insisted that they went on Christmas.

Susan was praying that all would go well with both deliveries tonight. She was worried about Lilly being traumatized if something went wrong with either birth.

Lilly quietly climbed up on the rail. Kelly looked at her. *Good girl.* The poor kid had been hollered at so many times tonight for being too loud.

"Kelly," she waited for Kelly to look at her, "do you want a boy or a girl?"

"A girl of course. You don't want to be born a boy on a farm or ranch," Kelly answered.

"How come, Kelly?"

Kelly realized she had just opened another can of worms. "I'll tell you later, okay, Lilly?"

Lilly smiled. "Okay," she said and jumped down and ran off.

Colt busted out laughing. "Ha-ha, you dodged that one, Kel."

Kelly laughed back. "Thank goodness."

Chip tried to stay busy, trying to stay in the present. He looked at his watch. It was finally after eleven. He was so ready for this night to be over. As he glanced around the barn, he noticed how quiet it seemed. No one was filling the air with talk. His heart needed to hear the normal everyday barn sounds that he loved. He worked at drowning out the howl of the wind, that ever-present howl. He closed his eyes and listened. Finally the sounds came: the horses munching on their hay, the crackling of burning wood from the stove, even the swallows in the rafters, though they seemed quieter now; they weren't used to this much action in their barn and had been pretty vocal earlier. These sounds helped calm him down. He breathed them in right now. As Chip's thoughts turned to the barn, he felt himself relaxing some. He welcomed the effect.

Moments later, Kelly's voice brought him back, "Dad, I've got a bubble."

Before he could response, Lilly was back up on the railing, screaming, "What's a bubble?"

"Lilly, what were you told about screaming? Talk softly. Remember, we need to keep Lucky calm," Kelly used a stern voice to get her meaning across.

Rick had walked up and flipped her on top of the head with a finger. "You listen, young lady, or I'll ban you from the pen, you understand?"

"Okay!" she said, not happy.

Lucky was lying on her side and hadn't paid any attention to Lilly. Chip had walked up and was standing next to Lilly and Rick.

Kelly started answering Lilly's question, "The bubble has the calf in it." Kelly looked at Lilly, "Climb over quietly and come over to me."

Lilly scaled the pen railing and knelt down next to Kelly.

"Give me your hand. It's going to feel warm and slimy." Kelly guided the little thin fingers toward the bubble and pushed down on the little hoof that was present, just inside. Lilly gasped as she felt the tip of the hoof. She quickly pulled her fingers out of Kelly's hand, wiping them on her jeans. Rick and Chip laughed.

"That's the tip of the hoof or foot on the front leg, and right behind that a little ways is the head."

"How come it's not coming out?" she asked.

"It is slowly, the way Mother Nature intents it to. It moves when she has a contraction."

Lilly looked at her funny.

"Okay, a pain, the pains cause her push the baby out, but it takes time."

"What if she can't?" Lilly looked concerned.

"It's okay. My dad, Uncle Ken, and Brian know what to do, and Brenda is the animal doctor, remember?"

Lilly broke in, "But Brenda is busy. She has to born Molly's baby."

"You mean birth," Kelly corrected. "Everything will be okay."

Chip smiled at Kelly when she looked up at him and nodded his head.

Lilly was done. She climbed out and ran up to Molly's end.

Brenda had just checked Molly then looked at the time: eleven thirty. "Not long now," she thought.

Lilly flopped down on the straw next to Brenda. "Will Molly have a bubble too? Can I feel the hoof when it starts coming out?"

Steph looked at Susan. Her mouth was wide open, in shock, not knowing what to do about her daughter. Steph and Brenda started giggling. Molly had no idea what was going on and didn't care.

Brenda coughed, trying to act serious. She placed an arm around Lilly and pulled her close to her. "It's not exactly the same as a calf, sweetie. The calf comes front legs first with the head lying between the legs." Brenda put her arms over her head to show Lilly. "Like this."

Lilly listened and watched. "But not Molly's baby?"

"No, Molly's baby is going to come head first with its arms at its sides," Brenda said.

Lilly jumped up, placing her arms at her sides.

Brenda smiled. "That's right, Lilly."

Lilly giggled. "And he doesn't have hooves—they're feet!" Brenda nodded.

"Can I watch?" Lilly asked.

Brenda looked at Steph and Susan, who was shaking her head no. Brenda giggled.

"Honey, it's okay for you to watch the calf being born, but a woman having a baby is a very personal thing, so only your mom, Steph, and I are helping, no one else. Even Jamie is going to go sit with the men. Do you understand, Lilly?" Lilly nodded her head yes. "Molly is going to be in a lot of pain, but it's a good pain, but she will cry and maybe even scream. It might be kinda scary for you."

"I don't want to hear her scream," Lilly said with a sad tone.

"Okay, sweetie, you won't," Brenda reassured.

"Can I see it as soon as it's born?" Lilly asked.

Brenda kissed the top of her head. "Of course you can."

Lilly wiggled out of her arms and said, "Okay, I'm with the cow," and took off back to Lucky's pen. She must have told Kelly what Brenda had said, because Kelly hollered, "Thanks, Brenda."

The three women laughed.

"And thanks, Brenda, you handled that better than I could have," Susan said with a smile.

Brenda laughed lightly. "Hey, I wasn't going to be responsible for an eight-year-old having nightmares about watching a baby being born on Christmas Eve—in a barn."

Steph sat shaking her head, thinking, "This is an unreal night for sure!"

"Besides, seeing the calf born will be bad enough for her." Brenda was quiet for a few moments, then added, "You city people, how do you survive?"

Susan didn't know if she should smile at Brenda's statement or not, but took a chance and smiled shyly.

Steph went looking for her husband, finding him in a pile of men by the stove. They all held cups of hot coffee in their hands. Her first thought was, "Typical men, letting the women do all the work!"

"Chip, can you come over here, please?"

Chip walked up smiling at his wife, "What's up?"

"Can you find something to put over Lilly's ears, like the things you wear when you mow? I'm afraid for her to have to hear what might be coming."

She glanced back at Molly who was beginning to pant. Chip didn't smile. A serious mode had taken over.

"Sure thing, babe," he said, walking toward the long workbench. Moments later, he found a set of earplugs that he thought she would be comfortable wearing and also a headset that was fairly bulky. He would let her choose.

To his amazement, she chose the bulky headset. He placed them on her blond head and laughed.

"You look like an alien!"

She smiled and ran off to her dad and the others. "Chip says I look like an alien," she said with a big grin on her face. Playfully, they all agreed.

"Now we have an alien angel," Brian whispered.

"Oh, don't go telling her that," Rick warned quickly, "you'll start something new!"

Jamie, looking totally exhausted, walked over to the stove, staring blankly at them. "They said she's real close and told me to leave!"

Ken handed him a cup of coffee and poured just a little whiskey in it. "Drink this, son."

Steph had taken Jamie's place next to Molly, continually wiping the sweat from her face. Susan was next to Brenda. The supplies were spread on top of a sheet, in the order that they would be needed: clean towels, forceps, suction bulb, clamp, shoestring, scissors, suture thread and needle, more towels, and finally, baby blankets. The shoestring was resting in a cup of alcohol. A large kettle of warm water sat waiting, covered with a lid and a heavy towel draped over to hold in the heat. Ken had two more kettles on the back of the stove, staying warm, until needed. Brenda thought about the items she had placed in her bag this morning and then Brian telling her that she didn't need to bring her bag along. She remembered the fear she felt when he said those words. Right now, she thanked God for giving her the gut feelings that she followed; she didn't know what else to call them.

The clock was ticking the hour away.

Molly's contractions were coming closer and harder now, but she wasn't dilated enough yet. Brenda wouldn't let her push yet. She was doing real well with the pain, only screaming a few times. Susan glanced Lilly's way, but she wasn't responding to the sounds coming from Molly. Susan told herself to concentrate on her job at hand.

"I've got feet," Kelly hollered at Ken and her dad.

Chip responded by saying, "Finally, we can move on with all this stuff." Ken laughed lightly, knowing the stress that Chip had been under tonight. He knew Chip was more than ready for the pace to pick up.

Lilly was up on the rail next to Chip, with her headset in place. Rick stood on the right side of the pen with Ken. Rick's eyes were on Lilly. He was seeing her right now for the first time, through a different set of eyes. This little girl of his was beautiful, smart, and amazingly fun to be with. His feelings were all mixed up. *Where have I been, what have I missed?* Moments later he had an overwhelming feeling of sadness wash over him.

Ken had been watching Rick. "You okay, buddy?" he asked, placing a hand on Rick's shoulder.

"Yeah, sure," Rick answered without looking at him.

Rick glanced up toward Molly, looking for Susan. He was wondering how she was holding up. He knew her as an insecure woman, who usually didn't handle stress well.

"Hang in there, Susie, they need your help," he whispered. He hadn't called her that in a long time.

"You say something?" Ken asked.

"Uh, no," Rick replied, trying now to focus on the heifer.

Lucky was doing fine, Kelly thought. Chip agreed when she asked his opinion.

She had lain down in the perfect position, her head pointed toward a corner of the pen, leaving the important end in the center, leaving lots if room if they needed it.

Ken had put a rope halter on her but she wasn't tied. Her contractions were getting harder now. Minutes later, she gave a good push, the bubble came out completely. Kelly took two fingers and poked the bubble hard, breaking it. More fluids escaped, exposing two small black hooves and about three inches of legs.

"Can I come closer, Kelly, please?" Lilly begged.

Kelly waved her on. Lilly quickly scrambled over the rail.

Rick spoke to her as she went over, "Lilly, you don't get in Kelly's way and do exactly as she tells you, okay, baby?"

Lily gave him a quick smile and said, "Okay, Daddy."

Lilly touched the tiny feet. The hooves were soft. Ken explained to Rick, "That was Mother Nature's way of keeping momma safe. If the hooves were hard, they might puncture the uterus," then he added, "being exposed to the air will harden them up."

Rick listened closely. "Well, I'll be. She really does have it all figured out!"

At eleven forty-five, the heifer was constantly in pain now and starting to push harder. Her moans were fairly loud, but Lilly couldn't hear. Rick was showing concern, but Ken kept talking him through everything and trying to keep him calm.

Ken kept looking toward the front end of the barn, keeping an ear in their direction, but so far, so good.

Jamie was a nervous wreck. Brian had made him sit down. Every few minutes he would stand up, looking up toward Molly. Brian stood up next to him and placed his hand on Jamie's shoulder. "She's fine, son, let the women do their work," then he added, with a smile, when Jamie looked at him, "you'll know when it's here."

Susan was surprising herself with her calmness. So many things were going through her mind, memories of her prissy mother, who would have been totally disgusted with the events of tonight. The way her mother treated her father, but Susan knew in her heart he was partly to blame, letting her walk all over him; they were both gone now.

Her thoughts jumped back to the present. "I can't think about this. I won't do this," she told herself. "I need to keep my mind clear. Nothing matters now except helping Brenda. I can't think about Lilly or Rick either."

She shook her head and listened to Steph talk to Molly. She smiled slightly, feeling Molly's pain in her heart, but also knowing that the outcome was worth it.

The heifer was stretched out now, on her side, back legs as stiff as she could get them, the top one was high in the air.

"Watch, Lilly, here comes its nose." The black shiny nose made its appearance with a long gray tongue hanging out to one side of its mouth.

Lilly drew back. Kelly said, "It's okay, Lilly, it's fine. Tickle it's tongue with your finger."

When she did, the tongue moved inside the mouth. Lilly laughed.

The color of the tongue was good, so they would give her a few seconds.

Lucky gave another hard push along with a good scream and pushed the rest of the head out. It was steaming from exiting a world of 101.5 degrees. The head was shiny black, slimy of course, with a perfect white star on its forehead.

But the biggest surprise for Lilly was that the eyes were wide open and blinking. Kelly stuck her hand in its mouth to make sure it was clear of mucus. Lilly couldn't contain herself. "Oh, oh, oh, it's so beautiful, oh, oh."

Kelly and Colt laughed, Rick had tears in his eyes, and Ken smiles while glancing to the front of the barn. He was silently praying for help for Brenda and was ready to head that way if he heard anything unusual.

Brenda had just checked Molly again. "Good, fully dilated," she told Steph and Susan.

"Okay, Molly, it's time to bring this baby into the world." Brenda had no idea what time it was. It was eleven fifty.

"Now on the next pain, I want you to push. Steph is going to count. I want you to keep pushing till she tells you to stop, then take a deep breath and pant, the way we showed you, okay, honey?"

Molly gave her a nod.

Brenda whispered to Steph, "Count to ten." Steph nodded.

As the next pain took hold, Steph started counting and held on to Molly's hands, giving her something to bare down on.

"Okay, relax, that was really good, Molly. On the next one, I want you to push as hard as you can, okay, honey?"

Molly screamed hard and loud this time. Jamie jumped up and started moving toward the front.

Brian hollered, "Chip!"

Chip came running and grabbed Jamie, physically hauling him back to the stove. "Gotta relax, buddy, gotta stay here."

"Ladies, it's time to start praying," Brenda said in a whisper, "we need all the help we can get."

Then she looked at Susan. "I'll need the forceps after this next push."

Brenda and Steph kept talking to Molly. She was doing great but getting tired. Brenda told her that she could see the head, so it would only be a few more pushes, but she needed her to push harder than ever with this next contraction.

"Here it comes. Push, Molly." Molly wasn't crying at all, but her screams flowed through the barn.

"Okay, Susan," she held her hand out for the red plastic forceps. The next push produced enough of the head that Brenda could grasp onto it and guide with the next push. "One more, Molly, come on now!"

Almost immediately, the head slide out all the way. Brenda cleared its airway and literally screamed at Molly, "You can do this. Give me one more hard push, Molly. It's almost here."

The next few seconds seemed like a blur to Susan. This was nothing like the childbirth she had participated in. This was truly a Christmas miracle.

Colt whispered in Kelly's ear, "What do you think it is?"

Kelly giggled. "A heifer of course. You see the size of those feet and legs!"

Kelly made Lilly step back near the rail, next to Ken, who patted the top of her head. He looked at the clock—eleven fifty-seven—then glanced toward the front. He had just heard Brenda holler pretty good at Molly, so he was guessing they were getting close to bringing that critter in.

Lucky gave another hard push. This time most of the body slid out, with steamy fluid going everywhere.

Kelly looked at Colt. "Let's get this over with."

The two teenagers got up. Each grabbed a front leg and gently pulled the rest of the calf out. Lucky instantly sat up. The kids pulled the calf over in front of her so she could start licking on it. It wobbled around, flinging its head, until it got itself into a sitting up position.

Kelly reached over and picked up the top back leg, giving her a view of the underside. Excitedly, she screamed, "Merry Christmas to me, it's a heifer!"

Lilly had been quiet, so surprised by what she had just witnessed. Now she jumped around. "Kelly, what does that mean?"

"It's a girl, Lilly!"

Kelly wiped its mouth off again and picked up a piece of stiff straw and stuck it in the calf's nose. It sneezed hard.

"What are you doing, Kelly?" Lilly asked.

"Making sure she's breathing good!"

"Oh, that's good, can I pet her now?" Lilly asked.

Kelly looked at her dad. "You stand next to her head so she can't hit Lilly," Chip said. She nodded to her dad and moved to a different position.

"Okay, come here, Lilly." As soon as she walked over, Lucky looked up at Lilly and tried to lick her. Lilly screamed and jumped. Kelly grabbed her. "It's okay, Lilly, calm down."

A moment later, Lilly was down on her knees near the new calf's head, talking softly to her and looking into the bright black eyes. Lilly was mesmerized with the eyes. She smiled up at her dad. "Daddy, I want one." Of course, everyone laughed, even Rick.

Molly had done it, gave birth to a beautiful baby boy.

"It's a boy, Molly!" Brenda was crying as she placed the baby face down on the palm of her hand and rubbed his back. She didn't want to spank him unless she had to.

A few seconds later, he let out a loud wail. Steph laughed. "He's got healthy set of lungs!"

Brenda laid the new baby on Molly's stomach so she could cut the cord. Susan pulled the shoestring out of the alcohol cup, handing it to Brenda on a sterile pad.

"I was wondering what that was for," Susan stated, as she watched Brenda tie the cord with the shoestring before cutting it.

"Can I see him?" Molly asked. Brenda held him up for Molly to see, then said, "Let us get him cleaned up real quick, sweetie."

Susan held a warm baby blanket in her outstretched arms, waiting for Brenda to lay him in it. Steph and Susan worked together quickly, cleaning the little guy up before he got cold, while Brenda finished up on Molly.

Brenda's tears continued to flow. "Sweetheart, I've never been prouder of a young woman than I am of you right now!" She wiped her tears on her sleeve, trying to get ahold of her emotions. "The composure you showed all of us by handling all that pain puts all of us to shame!" Brenda was babbling now, overwhelmed with emotion.

"You did it, Molly, congratulations!" Susan said. She was crying again.

Steph glanced from the baby to Susan, smiling. She said, "Good job, Susan, we couldn't have done it without you!"

Susan smiled shyly through her tears. "Glad I could help!"

Brenda looked up at all the women and said, "Ladies, we make quite a team, but let's not plan a repeat performance next Christmas." Agreement came from all, especially Molly.

December 25

*A*s they wrapped a fresh blanket around the baby, a commotion was heard coming from the center of the barn. The women turned toward the noise, only Molly's eyes stayed on the baby.

Ken was standing on a wooden crate in the center between the pen and the stove.

He had a hammer in one hand and an old bucket in the other, banging the bucket with the hammer, his way of ringing in Christmas. The banging got the attention of all. "It's twelve o'clock, friends—Merry Christmas!"

Steph instantly stood up and cupped her hands around her mouth so her voice would carry further, screaming, "It's a boy. Mother and baby doing fine!" Then she added, "Merry Christmas everyone!"

Jamie had been standing, looking toward Molly. When he heard Steph's statement, his knees buckled. Brian caught him, setting him gently on a bale.

Lilly was jumping up and down, clapping and screaming, "It's Christmas, it's Christmas!"

She was still in the pen when she jumped and screamed. It startled Lucky, causing her to jump up.

Colt grabbed Lilly, getting her safely out of the way and laughing, "That is one way of getting a cow up!"

"Mom, it's a heifer. Woohoo!" Kelly screamed to the front of the barn.

So much was happening all at once. Chip and Rick laughed. Jamie swallowed hard, looking at Brian, and said, "I've got to go!"

Brian slapped the young new father on the shoulder. "Yes, you do, son!"

Ken had stepped down off the crate and looked Brenda's way. In a silent prayer, he gave thanks.

"Ken, can you help the kid get to his new baby? Not so sure he can walk by himself!" Brian laughed hard.

In two steps, Ken was at Jamie's side with an arm around him, holding him up. "Kid's got lungs. We can hear him from here!"

Chip sat down on a bale, watching all the others. He needed to breathe. "Lord, I don't know what to say. The words 'thank You' don't seem enough. Ken says You planned this night out. Maybe so. All I know is You kept Your word like Ken said You would. We did it. We made it, all because of You!" Chip leaned forward, laying his head in his hands, and cried. Moments later, he pulled himself together, like he needed to.

Brenda had finished up her care on Molly and was cleaning up around her.

Molly was holding the new baby in her arms. When Jamie knelt down at her side, he kissed Molly's forehead and then took a finger and gently brushed the tiny pink face. As Molly softly whispered and cradled the baby, his cries silenced. He knew who had him and he knew he was home.

Everyone had gathered close. Lilly had come running, first to hug her mom, then crawling over next to Molly.

"Please, can I see?" she asked in a calm voice. Molly pulled the blanket back giving Lilly a better view of his head. The baby's eyes were wide open. Lilly didn't know he couldn't see yet, but as he turned his head her way, she talked gently to him, "Hi there. God sure made you a pretty little boy!"

Lilly teared up and started to cry.

Susan laid her hand on daughter's shoulder. "Are you okay, Lilly?"

"Yes, Momma, I'm just happy," she said between sobs.

Chip and Ken shared concerns for Brenda. Brian had just talked to her then backed out of the way. The two moved closer. She looked totally wiped out. She tried to brush the wet hair back away from her face as she tried to smile.

"Everything go okay?" Ken asked.

Brenda nodded her head, then said, "Yes, as far as I can tell, she did good, perfectly normal delivery, but I did need the forceps." She took a couple of deep breaths before continuing, "I'm guessing him at nine pounds, more or less."

Susan had walked up beside her while she was talking to Chip and Ken. When she finished, Brenda turned and wrapped her arms around Susan, saying, "We did it, Thanks so much for your help!"

Susan started crying again. In a half laugh, half sob, she said, "I'm crying now whether anybody likes it or not!"

Rick had walked up, looking worried. "Why are you crying, honey?"

Susan looked in his eyes and managed one word—"Happy!"

When Lilly was done looking at the baby, she managed to slip off. She headed toward the workbench, where the angel wings waited. She looked around and saw Ken watching her. She grinned full-heartedly as she waved him to come help.

It was time to be the barn angel again.

As much as Brenda would have liked to let the couple enjoy their new son, it was time to take him again. He needed to be tended to. She moved closer and took him from Molly. Steph and Susan cleaned the baby up with the perfectly tempered water and wrapped him in one of Kelly's soft baby blankets.

Susan looked at Steph, "May I?"

Steph smiled. "You may," giving Susan the honor of handing the bundle to his father for the first time. Steph sat thinking, "This is truly a different woman than the one who came to the ranch a couple days ago."

Soft beautiful sounds were faintly floating through the air, causing heads to turn toward it. Barn angel Lilly was singing to herself as she danced in a circle. Her wings and halo bounced in a magical way. She seemed to be making the words up as she sang:

> "Oh Christmas light, guiding all to the barn,
> Helping to keep all of us safe tonight,
> He brought us babies with big bright eyes and
> strong cries,
> You did good, God. Merry Christmas, God,
> Merry Christmas!"

Tears rolled down all who listened, but none more than Ken. The little barn angel had just turned the Army medic turned cowboy into mush.

"Can I get a hot cup of coffee and some cookies? I need sugar," Brenda said, walking up to Brian, adding, "I'm pooped!"

Brian laughed as he wrapped an arm around her. "I've got a cup with your name on it, and maybe I can find a cookie or two, if cookie monster Chip hasn't eaten all of them."

Ken sat off by himself again, trying to regain composure. Angel Lilly had just wiped him out emotionally. He listened to the wind. It sounded like it might have let up a little right now—maybe.

He felt himself praying quietly, in his head. He figured he'd been doing it all night without thinking, "Lord, so much could have gone wrong, but so much went right. You have truly blessed this night." He felt so much relief, but at the same time, knew they weren't out of the woods. A lot of problems could still pop up. "So I'll keep praying, Lord, along with all we still need. Please keep a roof over our heads."

He had a gut feeling that the storm wasn't done with them yet.

As Jamie slowly walked back to the stove area carrying his new son in his arms, pride exploded from his face. Everyone came up to congratulate him and see the new baby again, including the barn angel.

Lilly had come running, followed by her dad. "Jamie, I want to see him again, please."

Jamie sat down on a bale so she could see the baby easier. His eyes were open and his mouth was moving. He had a little bit of hair; it was dark brown like his daddy's and very fuzzy.

"He's hungry already!" Lilly said firmly, hugging her dad. "I'm so happy," she commented to the group with bright eyes. "This is just the best Christmas ever!"

In just a few minutes, Brenda and Steph had Molly sitting up. Everything was cleaned up and moved, leaving the new mother in a clean bed of straw.

Jamie handed their new son back to Molly. Everyone else backed away for a few minutes, allowing some private time for the couple.

Brenda had walked up to Kelly and gave her a pat on the back. "Good job, lady."

Kelly smiled and said, "Piece of cake!"

Colt turned his back to laugh, whispering, "Cow did all the work!"

Lilly was headed up near the front to see her mom. Just as she reached her parents, the strongest gust of wind of the night hit the west side of the barn. All conversations stopped and eyes of all looked to the rafters. The barn shook hard. It felt like the storm was consuming the entire barn. The sound was deafening.

Lilly was on the verge of tears, clinging tight to her mom. Rick wrapped his arms around Susan. The horses could be heard in their pens, getting more nervous by the second. Brian talked to them in a loud voice as he stood near them. Chip and Ken stared at each other, both silently praying the same thing: "Hold it together girl!" Twenty to thirty seconds felt like a lifetime. Molly was crying. Brenda worked hard trying to convince her that everything would be fine. Susan couldn't breathe, still holding onto Rick and Lilly. Kelly and Colt huddled in Lucky's pen, with their heads low.

Finally, the hard gust subsided. Chip looked toward Kelly. She smiled back as if saying, "I'm okay." He then walked to the main group of people and said in a solemn voice, "We were just reminded of how very lucky we are." No one said a word.

Kelly and Colt knew it wouldn't take long for the calf to start trying to stand. Lilly was nestled close to Kelly with her arms around Kelly's waist. "Someone is starting to wear down," she whispered to Colt. The calf had flopped from side to side, attempting to stand, but kept getting her legs tangled up under her.

"Is she going to get hurt?" Lilly asked.

"No, sweetie," Kelly answered as she bent over and talked Lilly through the calf's attempt to stand. Lucky had done a pretty good job of cleaning her up but she was still wet. After fifteen minutes of trying, the calf managed to stay up on all four feet, though a bit wobbly.

Lilly pulled on Kelly's sleeve. "What?" Kelly asked.

"She needs a name. The baby already has one," Lilly answered.

Kelly laughed out loud. "Yes, she does, missy. So what are you going to name her?" Colt stood smiling and waiting.

"Me? I get to name her?" Lilly's voice squealed.

"Yep, you get to name her, but remember, her name needs to start with the same letter as her momma's name."

Lilly proudly stated, "L."

Kelly nodded.

Lilly climbed up on the pen rail and screamed at the top of her lungs, "I get to name the calf!"

Lucky jumped, knocking the calf down. Scowls came from every direction of the barn, and Kelly frowned as she looked at Lilly and said, "Not good!"

"Oh!" Lilly responded, looking around at the group then saying, "Sorry."

Two seconds later she put on her sweet act, trying to get back in Kelly's good graces.

"I know what I want to name her. It's a really special Christmas Eve name!" Kelly couldn't stay mad long. The little girl just had that effect on her.

"Okay, Lilly, what's the name?" Kelly replied.

Rick and Ken had walked over. Everyone patiently waited to hear.

"I want to name her Lite, and her whole name can be Lucky Lite," Lilly said. The whole barn was silent.

Kelly smiled. "I like it, Lilly, it's a really good name, and it fits." Kelly looked up at Ken for his approval.

Ken looked at Lilly with soft eyes. "Why Lite, Lilly?" Rick had gotten the others' attention and waved them over.

Lilly smiled when she saw everyone waiting to hear her answer. "Well, it's because of our story, I mean the Christmas story. We have a barn, Mary and Joseph, I mean Molly and Jamie were headed to Bethlehem and couldn't make it and found the barn because they saw the shiny star that guided them, which would be the lane light, then the three wise men got lost and real cold, and they found the lane light like a star. Brenda brought all the things needed to help deliver the baby Jesus, er, I mean Joshua Luke. That was the gift she brought them. God made sure that both of our babies got born safely. That was a real special gift." You could hear a pin drop. Even the wind was silent while Lilly told her Christmas story.

A moment later, sounding very mature, she added, "Our light tonight has been very special, in more ways than one!"

Everyone in the barn was impacted by her words. "Then Uncle Ken gave a real special gift when he named the baby. Joshua in Hebrew, well, it's one of names for Jesus! We even had a special manger box for the baby to sleep in." Lilly looked around the group, smiling.

She wasn't used to adults allowing her to talk all she wanted. "So the name I choose is Lite, our second light of the night. Both are very special and both are very lucky," her voice sounding very serious.

Ken started a slow clap. Soon the others joined in. Kelly hugged Lilly as Rick spoke, "That was a really good story, Lilly, reminding all of us what tonight is about." Rick's voice quivered with emotion catching a few eyes.

Lite had been on her feet for a while, attempting to find a source of warm milk that Mother Nature told her was waiting for her. As she nuzzled a teat, Kelly called to Lilly; she came running at first then quietly stepped up on the rails.

"There she goes," Kelly said as the calf latched on and started nursing.

"Awww, is she getting milk now?" Lilly asked.

"Yes," Kelly replied.

"Watch her tail, Lilly. As soon as she gets this all figured out, her tail will wag back and forth."

"Why?" Lilly asked.

"Because she's happy," Kelly answered.

Lilly beamed. "That's real good!" Lilly said as she jumped down from the rail, "Gotta go tell Mom."

Kelly and Colt shook their heads.

Ken headed back to his spot, the bale of straw sitting a ways off from the busy area around the wood stove. Everyone teased him about it, saying he was being a loner. But he liked it, just tucked far enough away to be peaceful but not too far away to keep an eye on everything; from here he could see the entire barn. Chip walked by earlier and whispered in Ken's ear, "The guardian watches." Ken didn't respond.

Right at this moment, Ken was just plain thankful; everything had turned out good, on both ends of the barn. Both critters arrived safely. The electricity from tonight's events still flowed through the air. It would be quite a while before any settling down would begin.

"Lilly sure has her Christmas story down pat," he said to himself in a whisper. He laughed, letting his mind wander back to the events of the last hour.

"Lord, you couldn't have sent a more special little girl to share this night with, thank You for that."

Ken let himself continue to relive the special moments of a little earlier. Lilly had been running around talking about boy names as if she'd be the one to have the final say-so in naming Molly's and Jamie's new baby. As she got near Ken, he called her over. She climbed on his lap and waited.

"So, here's a name that might raise a few a few heads." She looked at him strangely. He smiled, "A name they may like."

"What is it, Ken?" He had her full attention now. In a soft voice he started talking, "Since there are many different languages and each one has their own translation." She was starting to squirm. He realized his answer was taking too long for an eight-year-old.

"Hold on, Lilly, listen," he said firmly, "in other words, in Hebrew, one of their names for Jesus is Joshua."

"Oh, that's pretty, so they should name him Joshua because it means Jesus, and tonight is Christmas Eve, the celebration of the birth of Jesus." Her eyes lit up. Ken nodded his head. She kissed his cheek and started to get up.

"Wait, Lilly, there's more," Ken said. She settled back on his lap.

"The Christmas story, the birth of Jesus, is found in the Bible in the book of Luke." He waited for her response. She didn't say anything, and so he explained further, "Joshua Luke."

"Oh, I get it. Luke is the part of the Bible where Jesus is born," Lilly said proudly.

Ken smiled. "Now, go."

She kissed his cheek again and ran toward Molly and Jamie. Lilly walked up quietly to the new family. Molly was holding the baby. Lilly's angel wings were removed earlier so now she was just a sweet but energetic little girl again.

"Hey guys," Lilly was bubbling, "I have the most perfect name for the baby." Her little voice was full of delight. "Well, Ken has the perfect name," now proud of herself for coming clean about the name. Molly smiled at her, as they had just made the decision to name him James Junior.

"What did Ken come up with, Lilly?" Jamie asked softly.

In a soft but excited voice, Lilly said, "Joshua Luke!"

Seconds later she went on to make her case for the name. "Joshua is one of the Hebrew names for Jesus, and Luke is the part of the Bible where you find the Christmas story," she turned to look toward Ken, needing to be reassured. It came as he nodded his head and smiled. Now she stood quietly, waiting their response, but she didn't wait long. Waiting and being quiet wasn't high on Lilly's list.

"It's Christmas Eve, in a barn. We had a star, the lane light, the three wise men; of course, they were frozen," she was rattling now, and the couple let her. Looking at Molly and sounding very grown up, she added, "I can't think of a better person to name him after!" She pointed to the baby, "This is our Jesus!" Quickly, she added, "Oh, oh, don't forget I'm the barn angel, but my wings...," her voice trailed off as she turned, trying to remember where Ken had put her wings.

Molly and Jamie smiled at each other.

Jamie raised his eyebrows as to say, "What do you think?"

Molly replied to his look with a big smile and said, "We know what we need to do."

Lilly turned back, hearing Molly's voice, "What?" Realizing she missed out on something.

"Well, Lilly, would you like to announce our son's new name to everyone?"

"You mean Joshua Luke?" Molly nodded.

Lilly quietly hollered, "Yeah," and went running to the calf pen.

Molly looked at Jamie with tears in her eyes. "It's beautiful," she whispered.

Jamie leaned over and kissed the baby's head. "It's meant to be."

"Quick, somebody!" she shrieked toward Kelly and Colt, "I need my angel wings, it's important!"

The teenagers laughed as they climbed out of the calf pen. "Okay, Lilly, we're coming, what's up?"

Lilly jumped up and down. "You'll find out real soon, it's really good!" She covered her mouth with her tiny hand to hide her big smile.

Kelly looked at Colt. "She's definitely excited about something!"

As soon as Kelly finished tying the knot in the twine that held the wings in place, the barn angel was gone. A minute later she was dancing and singing in the center of the barn.

"He has a name. God's baby has a name," she said over and over.

Her arms waved through the air as if she were truly an angel. Ken got up and slowly walked toward her, with the others following. Steph turned and glanced at Molly and Jamie. They both had big grins on their faces.

"Okay, giggle angel, what kind of name did that little critter get saddled with?" Ken's eyes danced along with Lilly.

"What?" Lilly stared at Ken.

Ken laughed. "Lilly, what did they name him?"

Running up beside him, she whispered, "You know!"

When she realized all eyes were on her, she made her announcement, in too loud a voice, of course, "His name is Joshua Luke Matthews!" Again, going into mature mode, she added, "He is named after the real Jesus and the real Christmas story!"

The barn was silent. A few moments later, she started talking again. "Uncle Ken named him. It's really special." Slowly everyone turned to the new family and started a slow clap.

Lilly beamed, as Ken watched her. "She's a lot like Kelly," he thought, "she'll be okay when they leave at the end of the week." He just had that feeling about her.

Ken shook his head and smiled to himself. "Good memories made."

"Now focus on the now," he told himself. A moment later, a complete feeling of contentment washed over him. Thoughts ran through his head. "What a night. The worst storm of the year blowing outside, all stuck in a barn with some good people, one needing some special help, some really good horses, an old special longhorn, and not to forget a handful of city slickers." Picking up a piece of straw and putting it in his mouth, he made a statement meant for the heavens, "I can't think of another place I'd rather be."

Moments later, Rick sat down next to Ken. "Did you say something?" he asked.

Ken thought on the answer he wanted to reply with. Finally he said, "Oh, it's just a barn thing." Rick looked at him strangely but decided not to question. All eyes were back on Lilly as she danced around the barn.

"She's so happy," Rick said.

Ken nodded. "So am I!" Looking at Rick, he added, "Merry Christmas, my friend!"

The baby was almost an hour old. Brenda thought, "It's time, let's get this little guy fed." Jamie wanted to stay and watch, but Brenda noticed an uncomfortable look on Molly's face. Brenda took Jamie by the shoulder and walked him off, explaining that Molly would be more comfortable without him there. "Give her a chance to figure this all out," she gently instructed. Brenda felt sorry for the young girl, too young to become a mother in Brenda's eyes. Brenda's heart battled her mind. Her educated mind said "too young," but deep down in her heart, the message was, "She'll be fine," and her faith was saying, "They just need a little help along the way and that's why I have you here, my child." Brenda's heart skipped a beat.

Jamie walked back to Molly, kissed her forehead, and said, "I'll be back in a little while." He winked at Brenda as he walked toward Lucky's pen.

Steph and Brenda were quietly talking Molly through the steps. Lilly came running but Susan got her stopped. She told her mom about the calf nursing and asked if she could watch Molly feed the baby. The answer was a simple no. "Little at a time," Susan told herself. Susan felt a form of confidence starting to build, a feeling of being a stronger woman, that told her that her voice mattered. Her daughter stood frowning, not liking her mom's answer.

Moments later, Molly smiled with relief it only took Joshua a few try's to figure things out.

"Good baby!" Steph said out loud.

As Brenda sat watching the baby nurse, her mind was going on to the next step—diapers and clothes. Currently he was wrapped in a thin receiving blanket, then a heavier blanket. They weren't going to stay dry long. Brenda giggled as she had a flashback of Colt as a baby. "Gosh, can baby boys get wet!"

Scanning the immediate area of delivery supplies, the towels, sheets, and few baby blankets that they had brought from the house had mostly been used up, only a few clean unused items remained.

She walked toward the stove. "Hey, Chip," Brenda hollered. When he walked up, Brenda asked, "What have you got lying around that we can use for diapers; needs to be something real soft." She waited patiently.

"Oh gosh, let me think a minute." He turned a complete circle to take in the contents of the barn. "Nothing, we keep everything in the horse barn." He looked straight at her, a thought came quickly, "In the horse barn, I've got probably six new rolls of cotton leg wraps." He waited.

"How thick are they, do you know?" Brenda asked.

"Oh, probably the half-inch ones." He waited again.

Her voice was serious now, "Can you get them for me?" Then she added, "I realize what I'm asking, please."

Between the two barns was a raging blizzard.

Steph took the baby from Molly to burp him. Susan let Lilly come closer now. Joshua gave Steph a hardy burp and Lilly laughed. All of a sudden her eyes lit up, turning toward Molly. Now in her sweetest voice, the one her dad called "her want something" voice, she started her speech to Molly.

"I'm eight years old and really pretty big and strong for eight. Can I hold Joshua? I'll be ever so careful and you can watch me, please Molly, pretty please."

The women all giggled. She was being so cute. Molly quickly glanced at Steph, who gave her a slight nod yes. Steph was still holding the baby. He had gone to sleep against her chest. Molly smiled. "Sure, Lilly, you can sit next to me, cross your legs Indian style."

"Like this," Lilly said as she carefully sat down.

"That's perfect." As Steph started to place the infant in Lilly's arms, she explained the importance of supporting his head.

"Okay, is this right?" she asked without looking up.

"Yes, Lilly, that's perfect!" Steph answered softly.

Lilly laughed, keeping her eyes on the baby. "Boy, baby calves are way ahead of baby people. Lite is already walking around!" Instantly, the women all smiled at Lilly's assessment. Lilly immediately started talking to the sleeping baby, telling him how lucky he was to be God's baby, born on Christmas Eve.

Steph prayed in a whisper. "Thank You, Lord, for the sweet innocence of children."

Brian had been watching Jamie. As he got closer to the pen, Brian hollered. Jamie turned, seeing Brian wave him over. The two sat at the stove alone. Brian thought it might be a good time to lay out what had been on his mind.

"Son, I know this is none of my business, but what are your plans for tomorrow and the day after?"

Jamie's mind ran. "There's seventy dollars in my pocket, a broken-down truck, and a new baby." Brian handed Jamie a cup of coffee, then waited respectfully. Right now, Brian wanted to find out the maturity level of this young man, even though he knew it wasn't fair to ask so much so soon.

Jamie sat up straight toward Brian a bit. Brian liked what he saw, strong shoulders and a good heart.

"Sir," he started bearing his heart to Brian. "Molly and I were trying to get to Bethlehem, to her aunt's house. Her mother kicked her out early this morning," Jamie hesitated, looking at Brian. He said, "Boy, this morning seems like a lifetime ago!" He took a deep breath, "I was trying to work and get my pickup running enough to go get her and get her to her aunt's before the baby came. Money's tight, my mom is, er, an alcoholic and can't hold a job, so I've been paying the rent, trying to keep the lights on and then food. Anyhow, all that hasn't left me much to work on the truck with or help Molly."

"Could you take Molly home with you?" Brian asked.

Jamie put his head down. "I was afraid to. You see, Mom can get real abusive when she's drunk." He raised his head now and looked at

Brian. "I won't have her hurting Molly or the baby. Then there was this storm." Brian heard the boy's voice starting to crack. It was time to change the direction of the conversation.

"We don't need to talk about the storm, I understand. Do you have anyone who will help you?" Brian asked.

"My gramps, but he's in South Dakota. He helped raise me. I grew up on his small cattle ranch. We can go live with him, as soon as I can get us there."

"So you know ranch life, son?" Brian asked, feeling encouraged about his plan.

"Yes sir, all of it, well, I mean a lot of it, Mr. Rogers."

"It's Brian, remember."

Brian did some quick thinking. He knew Brenda would go along with it. Satisfied with his gut feeling about the young man, he decided to throw his plan out there.

"I want to make you a proposal. I have a small house. It's not much, but it would keep you guys warm and dry. No one has stayed in it since last summer, so it needs some sprucing up, but it's yours and Molly's if you want it." He hesitated for a moment to give Jamie a chance to process all of it. Then Brian added, "Along with the house will come a full-time job on my ranch. I'd expect hard work out of you, but it would give you a chance to get back on your feet." Brian held his hand out to Jamie as an offering.

"Brian, I, we appreciate what all of you have done so far for us." Now shaking Brian's hand, he said, "Yes, yes, thank you, sir, I won't let you down." A million thoughts ran through Jamie's head.

"Jamie," Brian said calmly.

Jamie looked at the man, "Yes, sir?"

"You can let go of my hand now," Brian laughed hard for the first time tonight.

"Oh, okay." As he pulled his hand free, Jamie held it in the air, as if not knowing what to do with it now.

Brian kept laughing. It felt good inside to be able to offer the help.

"Now listen, Jamie," Brian was trying to get his attention again. Jamie was still struggling to take everything in. "As soon as possible, we'll get you all settled into our house. You can stay with us until we get the small house cleaned up." Jamie started to speak, but Brian stopped him, "I'm not finished. Then we'll go get your truck and throw it in the shop where you can work on it." Jamie listened. Brian's voice seemed more serious now, "But I want you to do a couple of things right away."

"Yes, sir," Jamie replied.

"You will call your mother and tell her where you are and we'll see about getting her some help." Tears slowly leaked out of Jamie's eyes. "Then call your gramps, and Molly needs to call her aunt; they will be worried. We'll let her mother wonder for a while." When Brian finished, Jamie broke down crying. Brian pulled him to him and held him. Jamie had a lot of stress that needed relieving. As if something told the others to keep a distance right now, Jamie was allowed the time he needed to be able to pull himself together.

As he wiped his tears on a jacket sleeve, he said, "Thanks, Brian, for everything," then he added, "the kindness."

He took a deep breath, "Is it okay if I go tell Molly now?"

Now was Brian's turn to choke up as he said, "Sure, go tell your lady the good news."

As Jamie started walking off, Brian hollered, "Son!"

Jamie stopped and looked back at Brian, "Merry Christmas, son!"

Jamie couldn't find his voice, the emotion was too great. A moment later, he whispered, "Merry Christmas, Brian!"

Brenda heard the news that Jamie had to tell Molly. Molly started crying and softly caressed the top of the baby's head. She looked at Jamie and said, "God is watching out for us, Jamie!"

"He has been all day, sweetie!" Jamie replied as the tears ran again.

Brenda sided up to Brian, who was now standing next to the stove. "Are you cold, cowboy?" she asked.

"No, it just seems like a good place to stand, been sittin' too much," he answered.

"I just heard about the offer you made the kids," Brenda said softly.

"You mad? I should have talked to you first," his voice sounded worn out, but he still had that sparkle in his eyes that she loved.

She reached up on her tiptoes and kissed his cheek. "Are you kidding? I'm so proud of you!" Then she laughed, "But your buddy Chip is going to be very upset you beat him to it!"

He smiled as he said, "You know, that never crossed my mind, but you're right!"

Brenda now had a serious look on her face. "Now we have to figure the diaper thing out. Chip is planning to go to the horse barn."

New concerns showed across Brian's face.

A lot of things were going on in the barn right now. Kelly and Colt waited patiently with a pitchfork in Lucky's pen. They wanted to be there when she expelled the afterbirth. Rick was standing on the outside, talking to them.

"It's normal for cows to eat it," Kelly explained to Rick. "The afterbirth attracts predators like wolves, which would put the new calf in danger if it was left lying out in the wild." Kelly smiled at Rick who seemed to be trying to visualize all this.

"She got everything figured out!" Kelly stated.

Rick looked at her. "Who's she?" he asked, then quickly, he said, "Oh I know, it's that Mother Nature thing, right?"

Kelly laughed. "Yes, Rick, you're catching on! Mother Nature, another one of God's perfections." She laughed lightly. "I'm spending too much time with my uncle. I'm starting to sound just like him!" Then she made a statement that Rick did understand, "Lilly doesn't need to see Lucky eating the afterbirth!"

"Thank you, Kelly!" he said in a short manner, not planning on being around to watch any of it. The kids shared a good laugh.

Susan and Steph, sitting with Molly, talked about baby clothes. All of a sudden Molly got a big smile on her face and started giggling.

"What?" Steph asked.

Excitedly, Molly told the women that she had a set of sleepers and a cap for the baby in her backpack, then in a sad voice stated, "This is all I have for the baby."

Jamie jumped up. "I'll get it. It's over by the stove!" When he got back he dug the clothes out and smiled as he held them up.

Susan teared up, "Oh, how cute!"

Steph laughed and said, "And small. I guess I've forgotten!"

"And cold!" Jamie added.

Steph got serious now, knowing Chip was planning to go out in the storm. "He's okay right now," she said. "We'll warm the clothes once we get diapers made."

She looked around the barn until she found the group of men planning. "Lord, we need your protection again," she whispered.

"Brenda thinks those rolls of cotton leg wraps will work perfect for diapers. I think there are about six rolls, don't you think, Ken?" Chip stated.

"Sounds about right, but you're not going out in that storm without some kind of safety line," Ken said in a serous voice. Ken was guessing the storm was at her height right now with winds blowing at least seventy to eighty mph or more. The barn had been constructed with oak; the older it got, the stronger it became. Brain told the others earlier, noting it was probably the only reason it was still standing. The horse barn sat about five hundred yards to the north of the old barn and just on the other side of the lane. Chip would only have one chance to get it right.

All of a sudden a holler came from Ken. Eyes turned his way; he was doing a jig in place again, but the moment was too serious for anyone to laugh.

"What?" Chips voice shrieked.

Ken headed to the workbench near Lucky's pen. Underneath were a couple of unopened cases of round bale twine. He grabbed one box and ripped the top off. Inside were two bales of orange braided plastic twine.

Brian hollered, "Yea-woo!"

"But is it strong enough?" Rick asked.

Brian, Chip, and Ken all answered at the same time, "Yep!"

Chip relaxed some. "Yeah, that'll work, should work good!"

Brian knelt down pulling the ends from the center of each bale. They unwound easily. "Better double them just to be on the safe side," he said.

"Okay, what's the plan, can I go with you?" Rick asked. The answer came quickly from all of them—no!

Ken took charge, talking directly to Chip, "We'll tie this off around your waist. Once you get to the barn, go inside the south side door. Hopefully it's not drifted."

Chip broke in, "Shouldn't be."

"Once you are inside, the emergency lights might still be on. You are going to have to cut the twine off your waist, because you won't be able to untie my knots. Make sure you tie it off to something on the inside of the barn. Then you have to find your way to the other end to the hospital supply cabinets. Just make sure you retie the twine around your waist really good, not the cowboy way, the Army way, understand?"

"Yes, sir," Chip saluted Ken, which caused him to frown.

"How's he going to find his way back?" Rick asked.

"We'll keep our end tight. He's going to have to keep it tight on his end too and gather it up as he walks back. It's going to be tricky, Chip," Ken said, answering Rick's question, but talking to Chip. "You are going to have to rely on your Army training, concentrate on the direction from the pull of the twine. Probably easier to do with your eyes closed."

"Might as well close them, won't be any good out there anyhow," Chip remarked. "How much time you giving me?" Chip looked directly at Ken. The others knew to stay silent.

"One hour, then I am coming after you!" Ken answered.

Chip thought for a moment, "Probably sounds about right. Better get going."

Brian hobbled off, then came back. "Chip, take this flashlight. Might help in the barn." Chip tucked it in an inside pocket.

Brenda walked up carrying a plastic bag folded small. "For the cotton wraps."

"Is there anything else you can think of I can get for you?" Chip asked.

"Not that I can think of. Please be careful, my friend." She hit him in the shoulder before walking off, not wanting him to see her tears.

Kelly hollered from the pen "You got this, Dad!" with a big smile. He sent her a thumbs-up.

The men concentrated on where they wanted the bales sitting and how they would feed the twine out. Ken was tying the twine around Chip's waist over coveralls. Steph stood next to him. "I'm not giving you a lecture, you know, just make sure you come back to me!" she said.

"I plan on it. See you in a little while. Love you, girl!" It was hard to smile, but he did.

As soon as Chip walked out the door, the strong wind hit him, actually catching him off guard. He knew it would be strong but had definitely underestimated its strength. He had his head tucked as low as he could get it and still watch where he was going. He could only take one step at a time. He needed to plant his feet and brace himself after every step. He knew he needed to go to the right in a northerly direction. It was important that he kept his mind on his path. "Don't think about the storm," he told himself. He also knew he only had a certain amount of time. When that ran out, Ken would come looking for him. He didn't want him and Ken both out in this. He'd move as fast as he could.

Brian and Rick had a plan in place, to partially block the door open allowing the twine to be controlled without too much cold air being allowed in. Jamie manned the wood stove, adding to it as soon as there was room in order to keep it roaring; they all needed all the heat they could get right now.

Chip closed his eyes. He forced his mind to draw a map in his head the way the Army taught him. He counted his steps north and to the right. The image traced in his head, one step at a time. All of a sudden he bumped into something. He realized it was the sign out front of the main barn doors. He made another image in his mind.

As he felt the sign with his hands, he tried to take a deep breath. The extremely cold air stung his lungs.

His head wanted to think about Sugar Babe—this is what she felt. He quickly reprimanded himself. *Stay on task, Sergeant,* he heard the words in Ken's voice. He started walking in the direction of the barn. A few minutes later he bumped into the barn wall. Now he turned south to the corner, then west, feeling his way to the south doors. The south wall and door were open, meaning no snow drifted in. Once he got inside, the twine would stop pulling out from the old barn. They wouldn't know he made it into the barn and was inside or if he was lost. They would be unsure until they felt the twine being pulled on again. All anyone could do was pray that it went the way they intended.

The air in the barn was full of tension except for Lilly. The scary situation with Chip going out in the storm escaped the child. She was babbling to her mother about dressing the baby. All of a sudden Susan panicked. She realized that she couldn't wait any longer. She was standing a little ways off from Molly and asked Brenda if she could talk to her for a moment. Brenda said sure and walked over to Susan. "What's up?" Susan looked upset, scaring Brenda. "What's the matter, Sue?" Brenda's nerves were on edge with Chip still gone. Four thousand and one things went through her head in two seconds. "Tell me!" was all that Brenda could get out of her mouth.

Susan leaned into Brenda and whispered, "Lilly doesn't know about boys and girls!"

"What?" Brenda stared at her, not catching the meaning of Susan's words, causing Susan's nervousness to go sky high.

"You know, plumbing!" Susan said shyly.

"Oh!" Relaxing some now, she thought about what Susan was trying to say.

"Dear Lord, what else are you going to throw at me tonight?" Then feeling ashamed, she said, "Sorry, God!" Brenda looked around for Steph. Chip had been gone for a long while. Brian, Ken, and Rick were at the door with the line.

Brenda hollered at Steph, starting to giggle. "I've got to share this. It's too good to keep to myself!" she mumbled the words out loud, still giggling. Susan stood beside her, still not knowing if Brenda had understood her or not.

"He should be back soon I hope!" Steph said as she walked up.

"Okay." Brenda found herself losing control, as she told herself that everyone needed a good laugh some time tonight. "This is too good to pass up," she laughed inside again. Brenda found Susan's problem hilarious. Steph looked at Susan. Her face was beet red and she definitely was upset. Brenda worked at trying to stay straight-faced.

"What is going on?" Steph asked, looking from one to the other. Luckily Lilly had gone over to Kelly. Brenda probably should have taken a different tact, but she didn't—she couldn't, to Susan's dismay.

Brenda stood up tall and straight as she said, "Lilly doesn't know about wee-wees!" Brenda was now in full laughter, covering her mouth with her hands as she doubled over.

"What?" Steph said, and then all of a sudden, bells went off in her head. She turned to Susan, knowing that she needed to calm her, but a smile still managed to appear on Steph's face. "You've never told her? She's never seen Rick?" Susan's eyes were bugged out in horror. She was at a point that if she tried to talk she'd bust out bawling, so she just shook her head no.

Brenda had turned her back to Steph and Susan and accidentally let a loud laugh escape. Steph automatically took her foot and gave Brenda a big push in the rear, sending her stumbling forward, still laughing. Steph turned back to Susan patting her on the shoulder.

Brenda managed to get it together and walked back up, finally acting concerned. Susan made an attempt to explain, saying, "It just never came up," which sent both women into spasms of laughter.

Steph pulled Susan into a hug with Brenda. "Relax, Mom, it's not the end of the world, but Lilly is going to be wiser to the world by the time this night is over!"

Susan looked at her new friends while wiping the tears in her eyes and weakly saying, "Okay."

Brenda was trying to regain her composure. Steph frowned at her and said, "Bad Brenda for picking on Susan." Brenda returned the gesture by sticking out her tongue out.

"Are you telling her or me?" Steph asked Brenda.

"Oh, this one is mine!" Brenda smiled back.

Chip secured the bag of rolled cotton wraps inside his jacket as he tied the baling twine back around his waist and headed back out in the storm. He remembered Ken saying to gather the twine as he walked. "Try to feel the direction of the pull." Chip closed his eyes, trying to concentrate.

"It's not working," he told himself. He thought he'd probably walked out about twenty yards. All of a sudden he felt turned around, and he could feel himself starting to panic inside. "Breathe, think," he told himself, "stay calm."

He stood in place. The winds pushed at him, confusing his head, confusing his direction, giving him a lost feeling.

All of a sudden the howl of the wind changed. "Follow me, follow me."

Chip tried to breathe, tried to stay calm. He heard Ken's voice in his head, "Follow the voice!"

"He's out of time, I'm going after him!" Ken screamed as he started pulling his coveralls on. A moment later, the door flew open. Chip stumbled through the door and fell down, tripping on the twine under his feet. Ken took a deep breath. "Thank You, Lord!"

Lilly screamed, laughed, and danced. No one could even imagine how or why she still had this much energy at this late hour—it was after one.

"Chip's a snowman!" she hollered.

He held up the plastic bag, "I bring diaper material." He made an attempt at a laugh but he didn't have enough breath.

"He's melting fast!" she added.

Chip was covered in more ice than snow. Going into the warmth of the horse barn had slightly warmed him, then going back out in the cold froze him up good. He looked at Ken and said, "The wind is so cold out there you can't breathe!"

All of the others were trying to brush the ice of him and get his outer garments off.

"Rough going out there?" Ken asked.

Chip looked right into Ken's eyes and said, "I got turned around and lost my way on the way back." He needed to breathe. "A guardian in the wind led me to the barn." Ken held his breath. Chip was acting totally normal, but his eyes were totally dilated and glazed, and the statement wasn't Chip's. Ken patted him on the shoulder and turned and walked off to be alone.

"Well, the men have something new to talk about now, should keep them busy for a while," Steph thought, referring to Chip's trip to the barn. They all gathered around the stove. She was sure the coffee they were drinking had an extra spark to it at this late hour.

Back at the baby end of the barn, Brenda was back in charge, ordering people around. Kelly and Colt were holding baby clothes above the stove to warm them and taking some joking at the same time. Rick laughed telling them that they were getting the experience of babies a little early. Colt's face turned red, but Kelly wasn't rattled; she could handle Rick.

Brian was digging the scissors back out Brenda's medical bag. Steph and Susan had a cotton wrap laid out, unrolled on a clean sheet. Brenda carefully cut the material into squares the size of newborn diapers. Lilly was quietly listening as her mom explained why and what Brenda was doing. Earlier, Brian had found an old brick, and now they had it warming up on the stove. They would use it to warm up the diapers before putting on the baby.

Brenda called Lilly over. "Give me your hand. You are going to be my tape girl." Brenda cut small pieces of green duct tape and stuck one end of the pieces to Lilly's wrist and then told Lilly to stay close.

She took a deep breath. "Okay, we are ready to roll," Brenda said.

"Are we going somewhere?" Lilly asked.

"No, no, it's just, never mind, Lilly!" Brenda added.

"Kelly, wrap the sleepers. Colt, wrap the brick," Steph hollered to the kids. Colt had donated his T-shirt to be the brick cover. Quickly Kelly folded a towel around the warmed-up sleepers and cap. They headed to the baby end of the barn. Brenda took the brick, setting it on top of a diaper square and wrapping the rest around it then covered with a towel. Steph took Joshua from Molly and laid him in front of Brenda. She had Lilly slide over close. She started talking to Lilly. Jamie and Molly listened intently, along with Susan.

"You know, Lilly, kids on a ranch know a lot more about life than city kids, because they see Mother Nature at work, especially in the spring when all the babies are born."

Lilly cut in, "Like tonight with Lucky and Lite?" she asked.

"Yes, and baby Joshua," Brenda added.

"What is Mother Nature?" Lilly asked.

"It's the Lord's way of all things living and reproducing, like flowers, birds, animals, even people. It's the cycle of life, do you understand, sweetie?"

Lilly nodded her head yes.

Brenda continued talking. "God only made two sexes in all of creation, one ends up being mommies and the other are the daddies."

"Boys and girls," Lilly added, "just like Lucky is a girl and Lite is too."

"That's right, Lilly, and God made boys and girls different. Why isn't important right now, you'll learn that when you are older."

Lilly cut Brenda off, "But it takes a mommy and a daddy to make a baby, not a stork." Laughs were muffled quickly. Susan covered her mouth, but her eyes smiled.

"You got it, Lilly," Brenda giggled. Brenda slowly unwrapped the baby boy. "See, Lilly, he's different than you because he's a boy!"

Susan held her breath, waiting for Lilly's shocked reply.

"Aw, it's cute," was all Lilly said, then seemed more interested in knowing why there was a piece of shoe string on his belly button.

Steph quickly took the diaper off the brick. "Toasty warm," she said to herself.

Brenda talked to Lilly, explaining the diaper, "Okay, lady, I need a piece of tape right here."

Lilly took a piece off her wrist and placed it where Brenda pointed, patting it down secure, then she repeated the act on the other side. Looking up toward Molly and Jamie, she hollered, "He's diapered now, for a while!" Brenda had told her how much little boys peed.

"Clothes, Kelly!" Steph held out a hand. Steph got to dress him. The sleepers were white with blue ponies on them. The cap matched. Lilly giggled at the little feet of the sleepers.

Looking at her mom, she asked, "Was I that small, Mommy?"

Susan's heart melted. "Yep, in fact, you were quite a bit smaller. You were only six pounds."

Lilly smiled at her mom as she said, "Awww!"

All wrapped up in clean blankets again, he was handed to his dad.

Lilly went running back to Lucky's pen. Kelly and Colt were perched on the top rail, talking. Lilly jumped up on the bottom rail and leaned in next to Kelly. Looking up at Kelly, she said, "Did you know that boys and girls are different?"

A big smile graced Kelly's face but she tried to act serious, "Yes, I did, Lilly."

"Okay," was her response; jumping again she ran off to the men. Kelly's eye twinkled at Colt and told him, "She's probably going to ask them the same question." Colt laughed.

Susan looked at Steph and Brenda, and said, "I'm so sorry for making such a big deal of that."

Steph laughed at the woman. "Oh, you're fine. I guess we don't think it's a big deal. Our kids are born to it. It's a way of life out here. I remember Kelly running in the house at four years old telling me that 360 was going to have a baby. I asked her why she thought that, and she said Daddy told her what that old bull was doing to 360. That was the only time we mentioned the facts of life to her."

Susan covered her mouth again as she laughed.

Brenda stepped closer. "And I'm sorry about the way I treated the situation, especially you, Susan!" She hugged Susan, then pulling back said, "I so needed to laugh, and I couldn't pass it up!"

"Brenda—wee-wees, shame on you!" Steph laughed.

Brenda responded quickly, "Well, I can think of a lot of other words to use, but that sounded the kindest at that moment!"

Steph was worried about Chip. She hadn't been able to talk to him alone since he came back. She knew he wouldn't talk to her in front of anyone. Steph managed to get Ken off to the side. "How is he?" she asked.

"Okay, I think, seems okay except for one thing." He had a puzzled look on his face.

"What?" she asked, her heart started beating a little faster.

"Well, as he was getting out of his clothes, I asked if it was rough going out there and he answered that a voice in the wind led him back to the barn; he had gotten lost."

Steph felt her skin crawl.

Ken went on, "His eyes were dilated and glazed over, said he couldn't breathe in the wind."

She didn't say anything right off. Finally she said, "Ken, that doesn't sound like him."

"No, it doesn't. One more thing, as he retraced his story for the others, he left that part out." Ken laid a hand on hers. "I wouldn't mention what I just told you, wait and let him tell you when he's ready." She nodded and hugged him.

She searched the barn with her eyes for her husband. He was sitting alone, so she headed over. "Hey, my hero, how'd it go?" she asked with a fake smile.

"Piece of cake, well, a cold, windy piece of cake!" he answered while running his fingers through his hair.

Steph felt his nervousness. "Well, it worked out, thank God!" she said without thinking about her choice of words.

His only reply was, "Yep." He shook his head to clear it. "Anything good happen while I was gone?" he smiled genuinely now.

"Well, Brenda told me that Brian offered the kids their little house on his spread and a full-time job."

Chip just looked at her, then looking around the barn until he found Brian, said, "The turkey beat me to it!" He kicked the shavings on the floor with his boot.

Steph laughed, saying, "I'm sure we can find ways to help them out too." She kissed him and turned to walk back up front, leaving him to stew. She was about twenty feet away from him when she heard him holler at her. She turned and walked back to him. Chip had a strange look on his face.

"What is it, babe?" she felt her heart beating faster.

"God used Brian and Brenda for more than just the baby; he used them to help with the future for the kids."

Steph didn't comment but reached for her husband. The two held each either.

Some of the pieces of tonight's plan were slowly coming together in their eyes.

Ken had walked down to the end of the barn, and he stood by a window. The darkness outside combined with the heavy falling snow refused him any chance of seeing the heavens that he looked toward.

"Lord, it's me again. I know I've done my share of bothering You tonight, but I just needed to say thanks one more time for the protection You graced upon this old barn and all of us critters on this special night. I hope we are doing our part, hope we haven't let You down, Father. Amen."

"Praying?" Kelly asked as she placed a hand on his shoulder and snuggled close to his side. He wrapped his arm around her waist and pulled her tight.

Still looking out the window, he said. "Yeah, baby, for the millionth time tonight." He turned and looked at her.

Her big brown eyes met his. "Me too," she said, laying her head on his chest. She had taken her pony tail out earlier, so now her long brown hair flowed down her back, reminding him of an angel.

"Gosh, I'm tired. Guess I'm getting old!" Ken said out loud to himself. He wandered toward his quiet spot, adding, "But old is good. Maybe I can just get a few minutes to breathe."

He glanced around. Everyone seemed content doing their own thing. His eyes settled on Lilly aka "Angel Lilly." She still had her angel wings on. She stood on the bottom rail of Lucky's pen talking to Kelly. Lilly turned, scanning the barn until she found Ken. She spoke to Kelly again, then jumped down and briskly walked his way, her angel halo and wings bobbing with each step. There was no way Ken could look at her without smiling. When she got close, he opened his arms and she willingly climbed in his lap. Kelly glanced their way and smiled, giving Lilly a thumbs-up, then turned back to her conversation with Colt.

Now's my chance, Colt thought. He'd been trying to ask Kelly something but couldn't seem to find the right time. "Lilly sure could be a pest at times, but a cute pest," he told himself, smiling.

"Hey, Kelly, would you maybe like to go get pizza some Friday night, you know, when the weather is a little better?" He was nervous and didn't know what he'd say if she turned him down. They had been close friends all their lives, but now, well, he felt something different.

He hadn't looked at her when he started talking, so he didn't see the smile form on her face.

"Well, Colton Rogers, I'd love to go get pizza one night," she hesitated then added, "yeah, that would be fun!"

He still hadn't looked her way, so she slugged him in the shoulder and giggled quietly.

With a funny kind of smile, Lilly looked at Ken.

"Uncle Ken, I've got a question."

"Okay, what is it, angel?" he replied, waiting.

"Kelly and I talked, and she said I should talk to you, cause you are a really good pray-er," she had a questioning look on her face. "A person who prays is a pray-er, right, Uncle Ken?"

Ken perked up, thinking, "This will be interesting!"

"Yes, Lilly, a pray-er," saying it the way she did.

"I think I want to pray, but I'm not sure how to, and do I pray to Jesus or God?" She started looking more confused than ever. Before he could answer, she had more to say, "Uncle Ken, God is a lot older than Jesus, right? He's Jesus's father." Then she followed with another question, "How old is He, Uncle Ken? You know God."

Ken got serious for Lilly's sake. "Well, I think you can pray to either one," Ken replied.

"Okay, I think it should be God. This is His night, because Jesus wasn't here till He got born."

"Okay, Lilly, that's good. God would like that." He smiled, enjoying their conversation. "As for how old God is, I can't answer that. All I know is that God is our Creator. He made everything. There was nothing before God. I think God is Infinity."

She jumped in quickly. "What does that mean?"

"It means no beginning and no end, forever," Ken replied.

"And ever," Lilly added.

Ken was pretty sure she was catching on. Ken hoped that would satisfy her. It was a hard one to explain, and he wasn't sure he had explained it correctly, but then she was only eight.

"Okay, do I pray out loud or in my head?" she asked.

"Oh, out loud. God likes to hear your pretty voice," Ken answered.

She took a deep breath. Smiling at Ken, she folded her little hands and said, "Okay, here it goes. I hope God likes it."

Kens heart melted. "Whenever you're ready, cause God's listening, honey." Ken bowed his head and pretended to close his eyes, but kept one eye on Lilly.

She closed her eyes and looked toward heaven. "Hi, God, I'm Lilly. I don't know You very well, but I want to. I just wanted to tell You thank you for everything tonight. We've got new babies, oh, You know that!" she giggled. "And they got borned safely because You sent Brenda to help Mary, er, Molly have Jesus, I mean Joshua." She opened her eyes and looked at Ken. "I sure get confused!"

Ken smiled as his heart continued to melt. "God doesn't care. Go ahead, angel."

She took a deep breath. "Okay, and Brian's foot is going to be okay cause Uncle Ken knew what to do. You know, God, Chip cried when he knew Sugar would be okay because he loves her. Because of You, some really great things have happened tonight, and this is just the best Christmas Eve ever. Merry Christmas, God!" She waited a second then added, "Oh, and two more things, God, I want to thank You for making my momma and daddy happy tonight, and for my new uncle Ken, I love him so much. That's all, God!"

Ken opened his eyes. She was looking directly at him, her eyes twinkling, full of love.

"Amen," Ken said quietly.

Lilly giggled, covering her mouth. "Yes, Amen!"

"A lot of people pray, don't they?" Lilly asked, looking in Ken's eyes.

Ken nodded his head yes, and waited, trying to get a handle on his emotions.

"How does God hear everyone's prayers? It must be awful noisy up there with all those prayers going to heaven at the same time!"

He hugged her tight as he said, "Because He's a wonderful God and He can hear each and every prayer. They are all important to Him."

Lilly's eyes got big. "Boy, He is really busy, but He sure took good care of all of us tonight."

Ken's heart was a puddle of love. "Yes, He did, Lilly. Yes He did!"

She smiled sweetly at him. "Thank you, Uncle Ken, for teaching me how to pray. I think I can do it all by myself now."

Ken swallowed the lump of emotions in his throat, smiled, and whispered in her ear, "You always could, Lilly—you always could."

"I should probably get up and wander around," he thought to himself, then decided against it. "No, I'm going to stay right here with You, Lord, if that's okay?" Ken continued to sit on the straw bale, on the sideline again.

My spot, he smiled to himself. "A guardian's place" entered his thoughts from somewhere. "But not my thought," he whispered. He looked up toward the other end of the barn; the special end, he called it. Thoughts came again: "Go talk to them."

Ken got up and headed in the new family's direction. The kids were alone; the others all visiting near the calf pen or the stove. Ken had decided he'd probably be there awhile, so he sat down on the straw Indian style facing the couple.

As soon as he got settled, Jamie looked into Ken's eyes, searching, hopefully for the answers to some of questions that had been weighing on his heart. "I don't understand what has happened, Ken," Jamie's voice quivered as he spoke. "Logically, we should have died, froze to death out there." His eyes darted the outline of the barn, remembering what was on the other side of the simple wooden walls.

For a few seconds, Ken could see the subconscious fear in his eyes.

His voice took on a calmer tone as he stared into Ken's eyes. "Everyone, including you, is telling us that we are special. Ken, are you a preacher or something?" Jamie laughed lightly. "I can guarantee that we are not special!" Jamie fell silent, waiting.

Ken picked up two pieces of straw. As he held them, he twisted them together until they formed a cross. Molly sat up a little straighter with her eyes on Ken's hands. Joshua slept soundly in the wooden box between his parents.

"Kids, I'm just a plain old cowboy," he hesitated, then added, "but, this cowboy totally believes that God made a decision tonight. He didn't want the three of you to die in that storm. I have no explanation why these things happened. That's not something I've been privileged to know, but I can give you my personnel opinion. I think the plan started way before this morning. In my heart, I think he wanted the three of you in our lives."

He hesitated, looking down at the cross, gently running his fingers across it. "When you are older and look back at this night, it still won't make any sense. There still won't be answers. You just have to have faith. He knows what He's doing. God felt the both of you special enough to control this night and give you your lives, your futures, and especially Joshua's. He wanted this baby to live. I'm sure He has plans for him."

The words exhausted Ken he started to tremble.

Jamie was listening to each one of Ken's words, but in his heart, the words were only being transmitted by Ken. They were being spoken by the Lord Himself. "What about tomorrow?" Jamie asked, staring in the cowboy's eyes.

"He gave you a tomorrow," was Ken's calm reply.

Silence followed. Molly's eyes teared up and she reached for Jamie's hand. Just then Joshua threw his arms out in a stretch and gave out a peaceful yawn. Ken took it as a sign. He was funny that way. He believed that you could see God a hundred times a day, if you just looked for Him.

Lilly came running up. Looking at the three, she stopped short. "What?" she said in a squeaky voice. She felt they were looking at her kind of funny.

Ken smiled, realizing the special moment had been broken. He took a deep breath and said, "What yourself, Giggles!"

With her hands on her skinny hips, she reminded Ken of Kelly at that age. "Steph wants to know if anyone is hungry yet."

Molly sat up even straighter. "Yes, I'm starving!" Ken and Jamie relaxed in laughter.

When Ken got up, he looked at the straw cross he still held in his hand. He leaned over Joshua's box and placed the cross in a slight split in the wood at the head of the manager. It stood up straight and strong. Then he touched his fingers to his lips and then touched Joshua's forehead.

Molly stared at Ken. He smiled slightly to her and winked before he walked off. The couple looked at the cross. It would stay where Ken had placed it for the rest of the night, standing strong over the child. The lamp above their heads casted a shadow of the cross over the baby. Jamie felt the hair on the back of his neck raise and a funny feeling washed over him.

No one really started the next line of talk. It just happened. Brian seemed to start it with his comment, "You know, guys, if any one of us had done anything different today, it could have changed tonight's outcome. I tried to talk Brenda into staying home, and then I didn't want her to bring her med bag." Brian leaned back as if the statement had worn him out.

"Hey, Ken, remember when you brought the loader full of wood into the barn and I asked you if you were expecting to need all that?" Chip let out a scary laugh.

"Yeah, Boss, and I kept unloading it too, didn't I!" Ken replied.

"You all have no idea the fighting I had to do to get Rick to agree to come out here. Now look at him!" Susan laughed. All eyes turned to Rick, making him feel embarrassed.

Rick smiled as he looked at all. "And now I don't want to ever leave!"

Lilly had gotten lost in all the back and forth and didn't seem to be hearing all the words. "Are we going to live here, yeah!" It was kind of a question.

"No, honey, I was joking about us staying here." Now Rick felt really bad.

"All I know is I thank God for that light, guys. You can't even imagine how bright it was," Brenda added.

Lilly managed to get into the conversation, "Well, God didn't make even one little mistake. Everything turned out perfect. He even made sure that Uncle Ken had everything he needed to make my angel wings," she smiled contently.

Ken coughed and cleared his throat. "We will all spend the rest of our lives sharing tonight's story, even the what-ifs. I think we can even say that it looks like we might have been handpicked for this plan of His."

Everyone sat in silence, the true meaning of those words having a little different meaning for each one listening.

Steph had a personnel feeling of winding down. She sensed a much-needed calmness in the air. She studied the barn, trying to think of what was left to do. It was getting late, or early, depending on how you wanted to look at it. The clock said almost three o'clock. Molly and Jamie were both asleep. She was sure the baby was too.

Looking toward the stove, she realized that all the others were still sitting in a group. Her eyes caught a slight movement. She saw that Chip was trying to get her attention, waving her over.

"What you all doing?" she said, smiling as she glanced at all the special faces.

"Well, we've all been sitting here, sharing thoughts and revelations, I guess you might call them. Anyhow, its some amazing talk and we didn't want you to miss out," Ken stated.

She wiggled her way through the tight group, finding room next to Chip. He instantly placed an arm around her shoulder.

"Okay, it's my turn," Rick said. He looked around until he found Lilly, nestled in between Kelly and Colt. "I love you, little girl!" he said with a big smile.

"I love you too, Dad!" she shrieked.

He took a deep breath and let it out slowly. "Here it goes. Before tonight, I was not a religious man. You might even say I was a nonbeliever."

Susan's hand flew to cover her mouth but she remained calm.

"We were talking about what-ifs. I can honestly say that I cannot come up with even one logical answer for any of the events tonight. Every time I think I can argue a point, it fails. I'm forty years old and I am ashamed to say it has taken me my entire life to be able to say the words I'm about to say."

Rick stood up and moved to the front of the group, facing them all. He took a deep breath. "I don't need anyone to tell me that God doesn't exist because I have all the proof I need—that He does!" Tears formed in Rick's eyes.

"I saw God tonight—I saw His power and strength. I saw His kindness and His protection for all of us, His children, and most of all, I saw His miracles!" He took another deep breath, looking around again, seeing each face, as he said, "I now believe in the Father, the Son, and the Holy Spirit, and in front of all you, I asked for Jesus to forgive me of my sins!"

The tears slid down Rick's face; he welcomed them. Both Susan and Lilly got up and went to his side. Susan wept openly, and Ken closed his eyes and whispered, "Here's another one, Lord!" The rest of the group was totally overwhelmed. Soft laughter of happiness graced the barn air, as the storm continued to voice her opinion on the other side of the wooden walls.

Chip gave Steph a big hug, whispering, "Yeah, we did it!"

Brian spoke next in a soft voice, "Rick, I think I can speak for all of us, we are so happy for you, and welcome to our family, because we also all believe and that makes us family."

After everyone told Rick how happy they were for him, Kelly decided to take over. "Okay, people, tell us one thing that each of you is grateful for tonight." Kelly said happily, "You first, Colt!"

Colt looked around shyly. "The lane light!"

He turned and looked at his dad. "I'm grateful for warmed-up toes!"

Rick laughed. "I bet you are!"

Brenda was next. "For safe deliveries on both ends of the barn!"

Steph shook her head back and forth. "I don't think I can pick one thing!"

"Come on, Mom, just one!" Kelly said.

"Okay, everyone knows I like a good plan, so I'd have to say 'His perfect plan'!"

Ken smiled and winked at her as her eyes teared up, her heart accepting his approval.

"The fact that we did it, people, it all worked out. Thank You, Lord!" Chip's voice rang through the barn. No one was more grateful than Chip for the night's turnout.

Susan was teary-eyed again and afraid of losing control of her emotions. Her words were simple but meant so much, "For everything!" placing both of her hands over her mouth again.

Rick actually stood up again. "For finding the Lord, I am grateful!"

"Okay, Lilly, you are next," Kelly laughed, thinking this will be good!

"Well, I've got lots." She knew if she talked fast, Kelly couldn't stop her. "For the lane light, the frozen wise men, Mary, Joseph, the manager box, my angel wings, baby cows, er, calves, and, and our baby Jesus—Joshua—and diapers and the storm, cause without the storm, none of this would have happened, and oh, baby Jesus. Oh, I said that (giggle, giggle) and pretty big eyes!" No one spoke. She said so much so quickly and she was right. She was all smiles now. "Kelly, it's your turn!" Lilly stated.

Kelly thought for a moment and then said, "I am grateful for a Christmas that no one will ever forget!"

Steph looked toward Ken. "Ken, your turn!"

Ken had more he wanted to share tonight, so he felt it might fit in now real good. Ken stood up, getting everyone's attention. "First, I am grateful for angels," he smiled at Lilly," but I have a little more I'd like to say. You know, an old cowboy couldn't have asked for a finer Christmas Eve, but I have a feeling that we are all so wrapped up in our own special miracle that we needed to be reminded of the true miracle that happened on this night many years ago. Let's not forget the true meaning of Christmas. That night birthed the Savior of the world, that's kind of worth remembering. Without that birth, we wouldn't have this night."

"But?" Lilly's voice had a confused sound to it. "But, this was our own special miracle. God sent it, didn't He, Uncle Ken?"

Ken picked her up and hugged her, realizing the words he was trying to get across upset her. "Of course, Lilly, everything tonight is truly heaven-sent, especially Joshua." Then he tickled her and added, "Even you, angel."

He knew the others understood.

Finally, the excitement was whining down. Steph stood up. "I hate to break this good time up, but it is very late on Christmas Eve, and Santa will not come if a certain little girl is still awake!"

Kelly had walked over to her mom. "You think you and Colt can get Lilly to go down?" Steph asked her daughter. Ken was already shaking out straw for beds.

"I'm sleeping with Kelly and Colt!" Lilly screamed.

Susan pointed a finger at her. "You'll wake the baby!"

"Oh, sorry," she said as she continued bouncing around. Ken had a triple-sized straw bed made right in front of the stove. He felt kind of bad for Colt as he was being roped into something Ken thought the young teenager wasn't too happy about. Kelly dug out three sleeping bags, shocking Ken when he saw them. "Where'd you find those?"

"These? Oh, the big box under the medicine cabinet."

Ken felt bad. "We sure could have used those earlier!"

"Yeah, I just remembered them," Kelly replied sadly to Ken's statement.

Steph had walked off a ways and called Rick, Susan, and Chip over.

"We've gotta come up with Santa's gifts for Lilly," Steph said. "I think the rest can be left under the tree at the house. We'll just have to celebrate Christmas when we get back there."

"Oh, you mean open gifts. We are celebrating Christmas, we have been all evening, Steph!" Rick said proudly.

She smiled. "You're right, Rick!" She tried to gather her thoughts again. Rick had knocked her off track with his statement.

Looking at Susan, Steph said, "Kelly's too old to care, so Susan, Rick and Chip need to bring your Santa gifts out here. Are the rest under the tree?"

"Yes, Steph." She turned to Rick and said, "Honey, Lilly's Santa things are in the back of our bedroom closet and under the bed."

"Anything else you need, baby?" Chip asked.

"Just check Sugar's water and food," she replied.

"You got it."

"Wait, one more thing," she turned to look for Kelly. "Kelly, can you come here a second, honey, please." Kelly walked up and waited. "I have a thought, Kelly, but it's up to you."

"What, Mom?"

"I was thinking we need a gift for Joshua from Santa and—"

Kelly cut her off, "what about my baby lamb?"

She was attempting to smile. The lamb was her first baby gift when she was born from her great-grandfather. It still looked brand new with its soft white fleece. She cherished it. She also knew it was the right thing to do.

Steph looked into her eyes. "Are you sure, baby?"

"Yes, Mom, I want this special baby to have my special lamb." She turned to look at her Dad, "It's on the shelf above my doll cradle, the white stuffed lamb."

"Okay, Kel, I'll grab it. You ready, Rick?" Chip asked.

"In just a minute, Chip, I need to say good night to Lilly," Rick replied.

"Sure, take your time, Rick," Chip smiled.

The kids laid the sleeping bags out. Lilly wanted the middle one. That seemed to be fine with the other two. She was just about to crawl in when her mom said, "Lilly, don't you have something to say to everyone?"

"Oh yeah," she jumped back up. "Thank you all for giving me the best Christmas in the world. I'm so lucky. My friends aren't going to believe me when I tell them all this!"

Ken chuckled, "She's right about that!"

"I love you all. I might be an only child, but I sure got a lot of new family now. Merry Christmas!"

Susan teared up again, very proud of her daughter at this moment.

Lots of good nights were shared as they settled into the sleeping bags. Ken walked over and knelt down, kissing Lilly on the forehead. "Sweet dreams, my beautiful barn angel." As he walked near Kelly, he rubbed her back with his boot. When she looked up, he whispered, "I love you, sis."

"Me too," she said with tears building in her eyes.

Ken went back to making a double bed for Rick and Susan. It was a short ways from the stove; he wanted them to have a little privacy if that was possible.

Chip and Steph walked up to the kids to tell them good night, but it was too late. All three were sound asleep, turned on their sides, facing the same direction.

Kelly's arm was over Lilly, and Lilly's arm was over Colt. It was so sweet. Steph whispered, "Sleep tight, kids."

"Are you ready to head out, Chip?" Rick said as he pulled on his gloves.

Chip hollered, "Ken, we are heading out."

Ken's head popped up from the spot he was shaking out for Brenda and Brian. "You've got forty-five minutes, tops, you understand?" His orders contained that serious tone he'd used a lot tonight.

"Got ya, buddy," Chip hollered back as he struggled to open the door. Brian hurried over to help, securing it good but not barring it, so they could get back in easily.

Steph glanced the barn. Ken and Brian were finishing up with the beds. Susan was tending the stove. She had made Rick show her how earlier. Steph found Brenda standing at the nativity scene. "I can't believe no one has used those words all night, especially Lilly," Steph said. She liked the sound of it and was a perfect fit for the scene in her eyes. Brenda stood completely still, not hearing Steph walk up. Her eyes were closed. Steph had a feeling that her friend was praying, so she stood next to her quietly. Finally, Brenda stepped back and realized that Steph was there.

"Hey, friend, you okay?" Steph whispered. Mother, father, and baby were sound asleep, creating a very peaceful scene.

Brenda laughed lightly, "Oh yeah, I'm fine, dead-on-my-feet tired, but fine." Her voice was cheerful so Steph believed her.

"Just needed to say one more personal thank you to you know who," Brenda added in a choked voice this time.

Steph hugged her. "How about we go thank Susan for all her help one more time, then my lady doctor, you need to hit the straw," she stared in Brenda's eyes, smiling, "literally!"

"You got it, let's go. I'm so ready, but," she stopped and looked at Steph, "Joshua will be waking up soon for another feeding and diaper change."

"You are going to bed. I can handle baby duties just fine. Besides, I'm still waiting for Chip and Rick to come back. I've still got Santa duties. Everything will be fine. You're going to bed." As they walked toward the stove, arm in arm, Brenda whispered, "Long day, long night, perfect night!"

Brenda walked up to Susan with arms wide open. Susan still wasn't used to all the Midwestern hugging. Her first response was to shy away, but her heart overruled her mind this time.

"Thank you again, Susan, for all your help. First with Brian's foot and then with the baby. I don't know what we would have done without you!"

Brenda spoke truly from her heart. Susan had an odd feeling wash over her, a feeling of having been needed, of being appreciated, and mostly importantly, a feeling of belonging. The three stood talking for a few minutes. Finally, Brenda said goodnight.

Ken looked at his tired friend and pointed to the straw on the ground. A pair of folded up coveralls were being used as a pillow and there was an extra thin sleeping bag to cover with. They would sleep on the bare straw. She was so okay with that; a pile of straw had never looked so good.

She walked over to Ken and wrapped both arms around his neck. Staring in his eyes, she said, "I love you, you know that, there aren't words to express—"

Ken placed a finger over her mouth. "Shhh, Merry Christmas, sweetheart, sleep well!" Of course, she started crying, and Ken laughed as he turned her around and gave her a push toward her bed.

Ken's next job was to find Brian. He was at the horse pens again, throwing out more hay.

"Brian, it's time to hit the sack, er, straw!" Ken waited for Brian to look at him, then he pointed to Brenda.

Brian laughed. "I'm coming, but first I've got to say goodnight." He hobbled into the pen containing the Rogerses' horses.

Ken teared up as he watched Brian tell each one what they meant to him. As Brian latched the gate on the pen, Ken asked, "How's your foot, think you can sleep some?" then adding, "I'll want to unwrap it in the morning and see how it looks."

"I'm tired enough I think I can doze some. Thanks, Ken, for everything." Brian's eyes looked wet.

Ken gave him a big hug, laughing. "It's too bad we can't make some money off all the tears that have been shed tonight, we'd all be rich!"

"We already are, Ken," Brian said as he stared in Ken's eyes, "we are rich in friendships."

"You are absolutely right. Merry Christmas, Brian," then looking at the horses, Ken added, "and to all a good night." Ken's love for his friend and the horses was easily heard in his voice.

Brian struggled some with his foot trying to lie down on the ground next to Brenda. She was already fast asleep. He chuckled and kissed her lightly, then pulled her into a hug next to him.

Ken heard the door opening and the rush of cold air barreling in. "Good!" He ran to the door to help Rick and Chip.

Both were panting hard, trying to catch their breath. Ken busted out laughing. Chip had Sugar in his arms. She was covered in snow and was wide-eyed, as to say, "What?" Chip looked at Ken. "Us family all gotta stay together, especially on Christmas!"

Steph had walked up and heard his statement. She kissed him and took the bags from him. "Go warm your dog up, softy!"

"It's over four feet deep, Ken. Good thing that rope has held. It's still up good. It's the only way we could find the house and then the barn again."

Ken tried to be funny. "At least I didn't have to go searchin' for your sorry—"

"Hey! That's not much of a welcome back!" Chip laughed with a light heart, as he brushed the snow off Sugar. It felt good for them to let go of all the seriousness that they had taken on tonight.

Steph and Susan took bags of gifts and spread them around the Christmas tree that sat in the dark corner. Steph had found paper and markers in a drawer at the bench, probably left over from Kelly's kid days, and made a name tag for the lamb since it wasn't wrapped.

"The barn tree is so beautiful, even in the dark," Susan said, her voice was quivering.

"Yep, even in the dark," Steph said, repeating Susan's words.

They both heard Joshua cry and then Molly's voice calling Steph.

"I think he's hungry again," Molly smiled.

Steph handed the baby to his mother, noticing that Jamie had slept through the crying. She smiled. "Sleep tight, young man, you've earned it. Molly, I'll be right back," Steph said.

"Time for bed, Susan." Steph looked toward the stove and found the Chip and Rick still warming up.

"Molly, good night. Sweetie, I'm so proud of you, and Merry Christmas!" Susan said before walking off with Steph. The women walked over to the stove.

"These two need to go to bed," Steph commented, looking at Rick and Susan.

Rick looked at the Kahlers with serious eyes. "I don't know what to say. Thank you doesn't seem fitting, it's definitely not enough!"

Chip looked at each before speaking, "I think I can speak for the entire Kahler ranch when I say we are honored to have been able to share Christmas and this experience with you and your family. You are all amazing people."

Steph's heart melted hearing Chip's words. She whispered in her head, "Good job, babe!"

"And we are a better family because of all of you." Rick laughed through his tears that appeared out of nowhere, then trying to laugh, he looked at Steph and said, "What you got planned for next Christmas, Steph, I'd like to book next Christmas week with you now!"

Steph started laughing and quickly added, "Sure, but let's tone it down a bit. I don't think I'd survive another one like this!"

Susan smiled. "Yes, a little milder on the drama end for me too!"

Rick seemed to struggle saying good night. He wiped a tear, adding, "I don't want it to end!"

Steph hugged him. "Oh, it's not going to end. You can't get rid of us that easy!"

Rick laughed, "Good," but he was too emotional to say more.

Ken heard Steph's words to Rick, "not going to end." They sent goose bumps crawling across his flesh, scaring him, and he didn't know why.

Rick and Susan headed for their bed. Ken had spread out a blanket on top of the straw explaining that sleeping on bare straw took some getting used to.

"Thanks, Ken, but as tired as we are, it wouldn't have mattered. Merry Christmas, Ken," Susan whispered on the verge of tears. Then she kissed him on the cheek.

He replied with a big hug for her, whispering, "It will all work out, pretty lady, that's my Christmas wish for you!"

"Yes, I know that now." She looked in Ken's eyes and smiled, "Because of you!"

As Susan and Rick got comfortable, Susan laid her head on Rick's shoulder when he opened his arm for her. It's been a long time, she thought, but it felt right to snuggle.

"Can I ask you something, Rick?" she whispered.

He bent his head down and kissed the top of her head as he said, "Sure, babe," and then waited.

"Why haven't you ever told me your dreams?" She waited for him to reply, not pushing. This was a new Susan.

"Cause I didn't know how." He took a deep breath then added, "My Christmas promise to you is to be a better person, in every way possible. Ken told me that a man's word is everything. You have my word, sweetheart. I love you and always will." He had a lot more to say, but there would be time.

She told herself not to cry and managed to get her words out in a calm, loving voice, "Me too, babe, Merry Christmas."

Ken spread some straw up close to Molly and the baby, knowing Steph would want to be within ear shot. Joshua was finished nursing and Steph was waiting for a burp as she patted his back gently.

She smiled at Molly. "I'm already in love with your baby!" Instantly a stray thought came to her—Nana. She had no idea of its meaning.

Ken and Chip stood at Lucky's pen. Mom and daughter were both curled up next to each other. Lucky was already showing the signs of being a good mom.

"Well, we made it!" Chip stated happily without looking at his brother-in-law.

Ken grinned. "Yes, we did good with the grace of God!"

"That's for sure, Ken, I'll never doubt you again. You were totally right about tonight, you know—about God." Chip still didn't look at his friend as he spoke; he knew he didn't need to.

Chip watched Steph finish up with the baby, laying him back in the manger box. He had already gone back to sleep. Steph assured Molly that she would stay close by and shared good night and Merry Christmas with her.

Chip had walked over to Jakker's pen. She nickered at him and walked over. He talked gently to her like the old friend she was.

"Are you going to bed, Ken?" Chip asked as they went around turning lanterns off.

"Yeah, in a minute, think I'll walk down to the end and see if it's clearing any yet."

The wind had quieted down quite a bit in the last half hour.

"Okay, buddy, see you in the morning." He started walking off but stopped and looked back toward his brother-in-law and said, "Merry Christmas, Guardian."

Ken wiped the inside fog off the glass window pane. The snow had built up on the outside, only the upper left corner of the pane was clear. Ken's heart started racing as he gazed up to the sky. The snow had let up, only coming down lightly now, and the clouds seemed to be thinning. The stars were showing in the few clear patches of sky.

Then he saw it, a bright star, so big and bright that Ken could see and count the eight points, just like the star in the church's stained glass window. He turned quickly to holler at Chip and Steph, the only two still awake, when a thought washed over his entire being, "*No, this is for you, my son, you alone.*"

Ken felt odd. He could feel his legs getting weak. He shook his head to try and clear his mind as he looked up at the star again. All of a sudden he realized that this bright star had been the lane light, the light that guided the lost travelers to where they were meant to be on this night, just like it guided the wise men to the birthplace of our Savior, over two thousand years ago.

Time seemed to stand still now while Ken's mind ran. He wondered if it was possible that this was the same star. His faith told him "*yes.*" He also wondered what it would have felt like to have been part of that special night a long time ago.

Tonight seemed to have followed along the same lines. Why, Ken wouldn't question—the Lord had His reasons. He prayed out loud, "Thank You, Holy Father, for allowing me to be part of Your special plan." Then he started singing.

"Silent night,
Holy night,
All is calm,
All is bright."

The barn was quiet and peaceful. The bright star was sending beautiful rays of light directly over the barn engulfing it as if the Lord was holding it in His hands.

Ken was overwhelmed with feelings of God's love for the world on this night. Slowly more clouds moved over the clearing, blocking his view, but in his heart, he knew it would remain there above the rest of the night.

"We had nothing to worry about tonight, He was here."

In a white landscape, a weathered old barn stood alone. The wind kept the snow clear of the roof, allowing Him sight, allowing Him to feel the heartbeats that rested inside; hearts that had been saved, hearts that had been changed. He was content. The players he placed on this night did not let him down—the plan played out as He intended.

Ken decided he wouldn't share his experience, the vision, with the others, realizing it had been a special gift for him. He slowly turned and looked to the other end of the barn. In the faint lantern glow, he could see that Chip and Steph were still up, sitting together and talking. His eyes scanned the sleeping groups. All was calm. Lastly, he looked in the direction of the new babe and his parents. The manger was glowing slightly. This did not surprise him; nothing would tonight. Ken smiled and whispered these words, "Our holy night."

Though the wind continued its howl, the barn silence was welcoming. Only two lanterns remained on. Both were turned down low, one was near the stove and the other near Molly so she could see the baby easily.

Steph did one last baby check. Joshua was sleeping soundly in the box between his parents.

She walked over and sat down on the hay bale next to Chip. He put his arm around her and pulled her close. With his other hand, he gently turned her face toward him and kissed her long on the forehead.

"Tired, babe?" he asked.

"Oh, I guess I'm okay. What about you?"

"I'm very glad this night is coming to an end," he said. He reached down and ruffled Sugar's fur. She was curled up at his feet.

Steph added to his statement, "A perfect end."

Chip smiled, "Amen."

"Amen," she said with a big yawn.

"I know one thing, next week, when all this stuff is over, you and I need to sleep for a week." Chip laughed lightly.

"And how much does Ken get?" Steph asked.

"Oh, he gets two weeks. You know, baby, all this God stuff is really hard work!" Chip added with a quiet laugh.

"Yes, the Lord worked him hard tonight, but he's fine. One thing about my brother, he is one of God's chosen. His strength of faith is always true and everlasting," the words were said with love and admiration for Ken.

"Yes, for sure, I thank God every day that He put him in my life," he looked at Steph, "but you already know that. There's so much in my life that I am grateful for." He looked upward. Steph didn't say anything; she understood.

They sat together in silence, looking at the peacefulness of the barn.

"Merry Christmas, everyone," Steph whispered.

"Listen," Chip said.

"What? I don't hear anything," she replied.

"Exactly," he said. "I think this is the first time tonight that you haven't been able to hear the storm or Lilly," then he added a heartfelt laugh.

Chip pulled his arm away, turning on the bale to face his wife. "Okay, one question, tell me about that manger box," as he pointed to where the baby slept.

In the darkness of the barn, you could see the faint glow coming from the pine box.

"Where did it come from?" he asked, then added, "I started to take it one day to put tractor parts in and Ken said I shouldn't, that you had just brought it home and that you might want it for something special." Then he laughed. "That was some understatement if you ask me!" shaking his head in disbelief.

Steph calmly started telling her story, "Right after Thanksgiving, you sent me to town and I had some extra time, so I stopped at Joyce's. I found it there toward the back of the store. I had no idea why I wanted it, I just did. Guess I thought I could do something with it. But what's weird is I didn't take it to the house. I left it here in the barn and then didn't give it a second thought. I remember thinking though that I'd use it for something special!" Then she added with a slight laugh, "I'm thinking that's another understatement, but that box sure came in handy, don't ya think!" She tickled Chip in the side.

"What did you pay for it?" Chip asked.

"Twenty bucks," she said, smiling.

"Pretty good deal for a glowing Christmas manger!" Then he looked at her very seriously, "You can see the glow, can't you?" Chip waited. He needed a serious answer now.

"Of course I can," Steph whispered then added, "but I think the glow is heaven-sent."

"Yeah, tomorrow it will be an ordinary box again," Chip stated.

Steph corrected him, "Nothing in our lives will ever be normal or ordinary again."

The Grey Tribune, December 31

Christmas Baby Born in a Barn
by Marcie McColm

The Kahler Ranch, twenty-five miles east of Bethlehem, experienced an unusual Christmas Eve during last week's blizzard. Stray travelers Jamie Matthew and Molly Thomas, both of Shane, were stranded in the storm while attempting to get to Molly's aunt's home in Bethlehem (Jane Stillman is Molly's aunt). Thanks to the lane light at the Kahler Ranch entrance, they found safety from the storm at the barn. At the same time, the Rogerses of the R Bar R Ranch got lost in the storm while checking cattle. They also were saved by the same lane light.

Later that evening, Doc Rogers, the local veterinarian, would deliver a healthy baby boy (at midnight) to the young couple. On December 27th, the mother and baby were checked out at the Bethlehem Community Hospital; both were doing fine.

When this reporter interviewed Chip Kahler, owner and manager of the Kahler Ranch, he was asked to make a comment about the event.

He calmly replied, "There is no lane light."

May 1

"Thank You, Lord, for the blessing of a beautiful sunny day. Please watch over this young couple and their son as they make a commitment to You, Lord, and each other, and Father, thank You for believing in me enough to allow me to have been a part of that wonderful night and also today, the rest of Your plan. In the name of the Father, the Son, and the Holy Spirit, Amen."

Ken placed his cowboy hat back on his head. He was sitting on Sara, who had stayed perfectly still while he prayed. He leaned forward and lovingly patted her neck, talking to her softly. The mount and rider sat at the top of a special hill; it was toward the north corner of the ranch's open range. Ken liked this spot, his special spot he called it. He didn't think the others knew of it, as he had never mentioned it, but when he needed to be alone and pray, this is where he found himself. God understood.

He scanned the view and said out loud, "This is my church!"

It was very early. The sun was just now creeping up over the eastern range. Ken had taken his time coming up in the dark, though Sara knew the way.

Ken reached into the front pocket of his shirt and pulled out a folded piece of paper. As he sat quietly on Sara's back, he read the note again.

A few days after the storm had moved on, Ken and Jamie returned the mule to Joe's barn.

Ken listened to Jamie re-account his story to Joe, trying to find the words to explain his reasoning for the actions he took on that day.

Ken knew Joe to be a kind and religious man and knew he would go easy on the boy.

With a heartfelt handshake, Joe accepted Jamie's apology, saying, "No harm done," assuring the young man that he'd probably done the same thing. Joe wished him and his family well.

Ken and Joe attended the same church and saw each other every Sunday. No more had ever been said about the Christmas Eve event. On the Sunday before the kids were to be married, Joe walked up to Ken. They shared in a short conversation and then Joe made apologies for not being able to attend the wedding. Before walking off, he patted Ken on the shoulder and handed him a folded piece of paper, a note.

Now, he closed his eyes for a second and let out a long breath. He folded the note back up and placed it back in his pocket. He looked over the landscape and said, "Will do, Lord."

He sat in silence for a few more minutes, then talking to Sara, said, "Well old girl, we'd better head back. Steph will be running around like a chicken with her head cut off!" He smiled to himself as they slowly started back down the hill. "It's aiming to be a blessed day!"

Brenda had invited the Kahlers and Ken over for dinner one night in late February. Molly and Jamie had finally set a date for their wedding, and all the plans needed to be updated.

"We picked May 1ˢᵗ," Molly said with excitement. "I was hoping that was late enough for the wildflowers to be in bloom."

Brenda and Steph both said, "It should be!" at the same time.

There would be no lack of conversation tonight.

"The Conners are definitely coming," Jamie said. "It wouldn't be the same without them!"

"Steph is making my dress," Molly stated proudly, looking around at the others.

"Fortunately," Steph laughed, "my gram taught me to sew. Got pretty good at it in my younger years. I've never taken on this big of project, but I want to," looking sweetly at Molly, "it's my wedding present to you!"

Kelly asked, "Is it going to be long, Molly?"

"Not in front, I want my cowboy boots to show. I'm in cow country now!"

Steph's head was running. "Plans, oh how I love a good plan!"

Jamie spoke next, "Chip, is it still okay to have the wedding in the old barn? We want to be married at the spot where Joshua was born."

"Sure, that works!" Chip replied.

"And," Jamie waited now for everyone's attention, "with Ken marrying us, it couldn't be more perfect!"

Brian leaned over laughing and patted Ken on the shoulder. "Only Ken could get wrangled into that, such a nice guy!"

Steph couldn't sleep. The clock said four thirty. Moving quietly so not to wake Chip, she slipped out of the bed. She stood at the top of the stairs for a moment, breathing in the quiet and saying a quick prayer for a day that went according to the plan. She headed to the kitchen, finding Sugar was ready to go out. She stood at the open door looking out. She could see the sun rise making a faint attempt to climb the mountain range. Chip's granny graced her memory.

"Every morning the sun comes up and tries to climb that mountain so she can shine on the other side. Always remember, she never fails.

So you climb that mountain, and no matter how hard it gets, you keep climbing, because if the sun can do it, you can too."

She felt tears sliding down her cheek. Chip's granny called them memory tears.

"I miss our grannies," she said out loud to no one, thinking of her gram too.

Steph considered herself to be a strong woman, but right now she questioned her ability to hold things together today. She put the coffee on and sat down at the island, reminiscing now about all the news that had come from the Conners last week.

Steph had promised Rick that she would get everyone together as soon as they arrived at the ranch. As it turned out, Brenda wanted everyone to come to their place for dinner that first night.

Everyone was chatting together while they ate. Finally, Rick stood up and tapped his wine glass with his fork to get everyone's attention.

Smiling, he said, "I or we have an announcement, people!"

Lilly covered her mouth with both hands to contain the giggles. Her parents hadn't been sure if she'd be able to keep their secret until they could get everyone together.

Ken laughed. "Well, Rick, you'd better spit it out, otherwise Giggles is going to burst!" which made Lilly giggle even harder.

"Okay, okay, I'm very happy to announce that we, the Conners, are the proud new owners of a twenty-two acre farm in Connecticut!" Everyone screamed and hollered at once. As soon as everyone calmed back down, Rick had a story to tell, though it was mainly for Ken.

"When I was explaining to the realtor what I was looking for, I used these phrases." He hesitated then slowly said, "A good strong foundation to build on, lots of healthy trees with branches that can withstand all the back and forth bending they will need to do, and probably the most important, fences that can hold all our love in and stand years of mending."

The room was quiet. Finally, Rick laughed. "Of course, the guy thought I was crazy!"

Everyone laughed, but as Rick's eyes met Ken's, he nodded to Rick and held his wine glass up, thinking, "He listened. Thank you, Lord." Ken looked toward Susan and winked at her.

Before anyone could say anything else, Lilly exploded, "And I'm getting a horse and daddy is too, and I'm going to take riding lessons!" She turned to look at Kelly, sounding apologetic, "Because you aren't there to teach me!"

Kelly smiled. "It's okay, Lilly, you'll learn fine!"

Lilly was bouncing around the table, now at Kelly's side.

"And guess what!"

"What, Lilly?" Kelly smiled and waited.

Lilly's smile was contagious. "Mommy and Daddy said I could have one of Breeze's puppies when they are born next month!" She took time to breathe, then added, "A girl, and I already have a name for her!"

Ken laughed, "Someone is sure wound up!"

Rick and Susan smiled but stayed quiet.

"What are you going to name her, Lilly?" Kelly ramped up Lilly's excitement by responding equally.

"I'm naming her Kelly," her voice was full of love. The room was in awe. Ken had to turn away as he choked up.

Eyes were all on Kelly now. Kelly looked around the table. Steph saw the ornery tease in Kelly's eyes. She grinned and waited.

"You realize, Lilly, if you name her after me, she'll probably be headstrong and defiant."

Rick responded first, "Yes, Kelly, and smart, bright-eyed, and never being afraid to tackle anything—we want her to be just like you!"

Lilly had no intention of giving people time to response. She was off on her next agenda. "Hey, Chip!" Lilly's voice squeaked as she hollered at Chip. "Daddy is naming our farm, er, ranch!" Turning and looking from Chip to her dad, she asked, "What did we buy?"

Both men laughed. Chip smiled. "You have a farm, Lilly."

She was confused, "But you have a ranch!"

"Yep, most places on the East Coast are called farms because they are usually small. Places out West are usually referred to as ranches because they are big."

"Well anyway," Lilly stated firmly, "Daddy wants to tell you himself. I don't know why—"

Susan stopped her, "Lilly, enough!"

Finally, Rick got to talk, "I didn't have to think long on what I wanted to call the place."

"Well?" Chip wasn't good at waiting, kind of like Lilly.

"Homeplace," Rick said proudly, "it's a new beginning for our family."

Brian raised his wine glass in the air. "Welcome to farm life, Conner family!"

Ken whispered in Chip's ear, "Rick's working on making those childhood dreams come true."

Chip nodded and replied, "He's going to get to see those dreams through his eyes and Lilly's. I'm happy for him!"

"Me too," Ken added.

When everyone settled down, plans started coming together. Ken had to fly out right away. Rick informed all to check out the barn and fencing situation.

"And we'll need help finding the right horses for Lilly and me," Rick bubbled.

Ken looked at Chip and with a straight face, said, "Well, I know who she gets her giddiness from!"

On the other end of the table, Susan was talking a mile a minute to Steph and Brenda. She wanted Steph to come out and help her make decisions about the house.

"It's a hundred-year-old farmhouse. The stairs creak awful, but Rick says that's character and there's a wood stove in the kitchen. Rick can't wait to build his first fire, says he has a little experience thanks to the barn stove," Susan was rattling now. Brenda and Steph shared glances, both thinking the same thing: she's happy!

"Mom, I can fly out when the puppy is ready," Kelly smiled, looking at Lilly.

Steph broke out laughing. "Well, guess we can squeeze all this in. Sounds like it's going to be a busy year!"

Ken had been fairly quiet, just listenin', he called it, when Rick spoke up, "Oh, one more important matter," Rick said, looking at Ken, "can we have two of those half-grown kittens?" Rick smiled as Lilly screamed at the top of her lungs, "Oh, Daddy!"

Then she turned to Ken. "Can I have Sunny and Honey, pleee-ase, Uncle Ken?"

Lilly didn't know about Rick's kitten plan. Looking at Ken again, he said, "I'm pretty sure we've got a mouse or two."

Chip laughed hard. "I'll bet!"

Ken laughed quietly. "Oh, we can probably share, don't you think, Kelly?'

Kelly smiled at Lilly. "Yeah, we can share."

After moving into the living room to relax, Steph noticed that the Conners seemed too quiet. "Susan, is everything okay?"

She didn't answer but instead nudged Rick's arm.

Rick cleared his throat and said, "We have more news to share. I'm guessing it's better than the farm news!"

Instantly heads turned toward Lilly, expecting her to be in full giggles, but instead, she calmly walked over and climbed on Rick's lap. Ken had taken notice and sat up straighter, holding his breath. He had a lot at stake with this family.

"While we were looking around Connecticut for property, we found the area we liked and decided to focus our search there, that's where we ended up finding our farm. But that's not all we found. Two miles down our road, which is dirt, by the way!"

The room fill with laughter. This was becoming hard to picture, Chip commented.

"Anyhow, sitting on the edge of a small patch of woods with a creek running next to it is the prettiest little white church you have ever seen." Lilly stayed quiet, but with a big smile on her face, she shook her head yes.

"You can tell them, Lilly," her dad said. "It's called the Little Church by the Water, and it's so pretty!"

Quickly Chip said, "Sounds Indian."

"Yep, anyhow, we knew it would take two months between closing and the people moving out, so we decided to drive up every Sunday to attend church."

He whispered to Susan and Lilly. The three of them stood up, all holding hands.

Ken was still holding his breath.

"We were all baptized Easter Sunday!" Rick said happily.

Ken exhaled slowly. Before anyone could commit, Lilly turned back into the kid everyone knew.

With bright eyes, she started telling her story, "It was in a river and, man, was that water cold!" Her voice filled with enthusiasm,

"And the preacher told me to hold my nose, but I guess I didn't do it right, cause it got full of that cold water!"

Rick started laughing, "Yeah, she came up fast and fighting, it was quite a sight."

Ken was afraid he was going to cry right in front of everybody.

"But seriously, it was the best moment of my life, especially sharing that special experience as a family," Rick said, as he pulled Susan closer. He looked around the group of friends. "I am proud to say we have asked to be forgiven of our sins and have accepted Jesus Christ as our Savior."

No one had ever seen Rick look so content.

Ken stood up, eyes full of tears, and calmly said, "Amen, thank You, Lord!"

Brian was next, shaking Rick's hand. "We couldn't be happier for you all!"

Steph sat quietly in shock. She now realized what that night back in December truly meant for these people, "Thank you, Lord, for giving me a part to play in Your story. I wouldn't have missed it for anything."

It was still early. The wedding wasn't until noon, but Steph and Susan had been up for a while. The two went over what still needed to be done while drinking coffee then planned to head out to the barn. The flowers had been left in coolers overnight so they would be crisp for this morning. The big south doors were blocked open with straw bales. Lilly had been left in charge of decorating the entrance. It was now the temporary home to all of Kelly's stuffed animals and the wildflowers the girls had picked the day before.

As Ken was stringing lights up over the entrance, Lilly tugged on his shirt wanting to ask him something. "Does this look ranchy, Uncle Ken?"

Ken smiled at her efforts. "It couldn't be ranchier, Lilly!" Satisfied, she ran off. Ken laughed. "That's my girl!"

Steph had dug out some Christmas lights for Ken to string up front, where the kids would stand. She loved the magic that the lights added. The guests would be sitting on bales of straw. Jamie had laughed the day before when he was sitting the bales up in rows. "We definitely can't get married without some straw." The rows were set up on each side with an aisle coming up the center. Susan was making small bouquets of wildflowers tied with yellow ribbons that would be placed on the aisle end of the bales.

The kids would be married in the exact spot where Joshua was born. The manger box sat off to the side a little, full of wildflowers and yellow roses.

Steph was happy with the way everything was coming together.

Everyone who had been a part of that night would be there. The Conners had flown in from New York the week before so Susan could help put the wedding together. Lilly had a part in the wedding; she was the flower girl.

It was going to be a small wedding. Molly's Aunt Jane was coming, as she was bringing Molly and the baby. Jamie would come with the Rogerses. His mother was coming. The relationship between Jamie and his mother was on the mend. She had accepted Brian's help to deal with her problems. Jamie's grandpa had come up from South Dakota and was staying with Jamie. He had come out to the ranch a couple of times to visit with Chip and Ken. Both men said they could see some of his wisdom had rubbed off on Jamie, especially when it came to faith and family.

Molly's mother was still refusing to have anything to do with her and hadn't even seen the baby yet. Brenda had told Molly that "one day she'll come around, so do not to give up hope." Molly and Jamie hadn't been successful at tracking down Molly's dad yet, but they weren't giving up.

The kids had a few friends coming plus Ken's Angie. That was about it. The kids didn't seem to mind. They said the important people in their life would all be there.

Back in early January, Jamie had gone to Brian to talk about something that had been bothering him and Molly.

"Brian, Molly and I aren't comfortable living together. We aren't married yet and it's not right." He hesitated a moment, then added,

"We have already made a lot of mistakes and have been given a second chance." He took a deep breath. "We want to do things the right way from now on."

Aunt Jane had suggested that Molly and the baby move in with her until the wedding.

Brian listened while Jamie talked, then told him that they were doing the right thing in the eyes of the Lord. Brian couldn't be more proud of Jamie and planned to tell him so when the time was right.

As Ken rode closer to the barns, he started getting nervous. "I sure hope I can do this without messing up," he thought.

Months before, Molly and Jamie had come to Ken—to talk, they said. They had decided that they wanted Ken to marry them.

"What?" Ken said, caught off guard. "Did I hear you right?" he asked, hoping he was wrong.

Jamie and Molly were very calm. "Yep," was all Jamie said, silence followed.

Ken told himself to calm down, then he asked, "Why me?"

Molly looked at Jamie and nodded for him to do the talking for both of them.

"Because of that night," Jamie said emotionally.

Ken started to say something, but Jamie stopped him, "I'll explain." He took a deep breath as Molly took his hand in hers then he continued. "I don't know a lot about church. My mom didn't care, but my gramps did, made me go to church some, so I do love the Lord, so does Molly. Joshua has his name because of you. We could have, no, we would have died that night, but we didn't because God sent the lane light. Everything that happened on Christmas Eve was because of God. Everyone played a part that night, but you..."

He stopped for a moment, trying to find the right words. He looked at Molly again, then back to Ken, "This is going to sound crazy, but, it's like Jesus took your form, telling you what to tell us and how to guide us. You don't understand what your presence was that night."

Ken was trying to take all of it in, trying to remember if he'd done or said anything special that night. *"Why are these kids saying this?"* he thought.

Ken laughed. "Kids, I'm just a plain old cowboy." He looked down at his worn-out old boots and shook his head. He was sitting on a bale of straw in the old barn where everything happened that night. His elbows rested on his knees with hands clasped in praying form.

He raised his head and looked at Jamie.

"You weren't that night," Jamie said calmly.

"I appreciate your feelings, but I can't. I'm not a minister or anything, don't have the right," Ken stated firmly.

The day had been cloudy and cold. At that moment, the clouds parted, allowing the sun to shine. A bright ray of light came through the barn window near them. The rays beamed across the floor, reflecting on the insides of the barn.

Molly broke out laughing. "There's your sign, Ken. You gotta do this for us!"

Ken sat looking at the light and heard a faint whispering that said one word—*believe.*

The kids were quiet, waiting for Ken to reply.

Finally, he said, "I can't make any promises."

Molly smiled as she said, "That's good enough!"

The kids jumped up. As they headed out the door, they ran into Chip. "Hi, Chip. Bye, Chip!"

Looking at Ken, he asked, "What was that all about?"

"I don't even know if I want to tell you." He sighed. "They want me to marry them!"

"What, you can't!" Chip replied in a stunned voice.

"I know, this is total craziness!" Ken answered.

"What did you tell them?"

Ken threw his hands up in the air, exclaiming, "I don't know anything, and how do I get myself onto these things?"

The next morning, Steph poured her brother a cup of coffee. "Figure out what you are going to do yet?" she asked with a big grin on her face.

Ken looked at Chip and said, "Big mouth!"

Chip shrugged his shoulders and smiled.

Steph leaned over and kissed Ken on the cheek, whispering, "Where there's a will, there's a way."

Ken stood up and pushed his stool back. "Do without me today, I'll be back."

Ken drove the ten miles to the Bear Creek church. The pastor's car was in the parking lot. Good, he thought. Hat in hand, he walked through the parish, back to the office area.

"Good morning," Pastor Eric said when he saw Ken, "what can I do for you this fine Lord's morning?"

Ken grabbed a chair, turning it backward, and he sat down.

"Help," he said and started telling his story. Eric listened patiently until Ken was finished.

"What do you think?" Ken asked in a defeated voice.

"Well, I can't make you a minister, but I know you are blessed in the Lord, if you can get the mayor to give you some kind of authorization to make it legal. I think the Lord himself would be honored to have you partake in this blessed union, so you have my permission and my blessing."

Ken didn't know what to say. He stuttered around with his words, said goodbye, and left. Next stop was the mayor of Bethlehem, who he considered a friend.

Finding him in his office, Ken told his story for the second time, when he was finished, the major started talking, chuckling at the same time.

"Out here, in the Wild, Wild West," he looked at Ken. Seeing he was not amused, he tried to act a little more serious, for Ken's sake, "We get to be a little lax on the rules and laws I guess, so I can see no reason we can't do something since the pastor has given you his go-ahead. I wouldn't want to offend the Lord."

Ken still wasn't in a joking mood, so he continued, "Get me the date when all this is coming down and I'll make you temporary mayor for the day, making it all legal," then adding "no problem."

Quickly he pointed a finger at Ken and in a gentler tone, said, "You owe me a hunting trip for this."

Ken relaxed, "You got it, friend!"

Now, one more stop. Next he drove to the library. As he walked in, Angie smiled at him. "Needing a book, stranger?"

She melted his heart. "Well, not today. Hey, Angie, you remember the kids who had the baby in the barn last Christmas?"

Before she could answer, he started talking, "They want me to marry them. I know it's crazy, but Eric said okay and the mayor too." Now he waited.

"Okay," she said in a questioning way.

Looking like a schoolboy, he asked, "I guess what I'm wanting to know is, would you be my date for the wedding? I need to know there's a kind and loving face feeling sorry for me in the onlookers."

She broke out laughing. "I'd be honored, cowboy."

Ken took a deep needed breath and smiled. "Good, see ya, beautiful," and turned to leave. Driving back to the ranch, he was content with himself, whispering out loud, "With You, there is always a way. Thank You, Lord."

"Sit still, Lilly!" Kelly said as she tried to get the crown of white and yellow daisies secured to Lilly's hair.

"You look beautiful, Lilly!" Molly said. The combination of the wild flowers in Lilly's long blond hair and the pale yellow dress were perfect.

"Where's my basket?" Lilly screamed. The little basket was full of yellow rose petals that matched the bride's bouquet. Molly couldn't make up her mind on her maid of honor, saying both Steph and Brenda played such an important role in her life, so she asked both of them to stand up with her.

Jamie had asked Chip to be his best man because without the Kahler ranch, none of this would be happening. They wore new wranglers, very pale yellow long-sleeved Western shirts with new black felt hats and, of course, cowboy boots. Ken was decked out in Ken style—his favorite black shirt topped off with his old leather vest, making the statement, "This is me."

Jamie would hold his son. The baby wore baby wranglers, a yellow plaid cowboy shirt and moccasins because they couldn't find boots small enough for the four-and-a-half-month-old.

The little bit of hair he had was slicked down little boy style.

Steph had added one last special touch for the barn. George Strait's "I Cross My Heart," played softy in the background.

Lilly slowly walked up the aisle, gently throwing the rose petals out. The women had made her rehearse over and over. Their main concern was that she wouldn't walk slowly enough. They decided to have her count, "One, two, three, step, one, two, three, step," throwing the pedals out on "step."

Susan turned to watch as Lilly started down the aisle. Her heart was melting as she watched her. All of a sudden, a half-grown yellow kitten came scampering out from between two rows, leaping playfully in the air, as it attacked a floating rose petal. Its fluffy tail brushed against Lilly's leg, getting her attention. She stopped walking and knelt down. Everyone watched smiling.

Petting it gently, she told it, "Cutie, I can't play right now. We need to get Molly and Jamie hitched." Slowly she started down the aisle again with the kitten following.

"Where in the world, did she get the word hitched?" Susan whispered to Rick.

He laughed lightly. "Where do you think?"

"Ken!" no other words were needed.

When Lilly reached the front, she scooped up the kitten in her arms before sitting down. She looked up at Ken with big eyes, thinking she might get scolded. He smiled slightly and gave her a wink.

Molly had asked Jamie's grandfather to give her away. As they walked slowly down the aisle, Jamie's heart skipped a beat. "So this is what an angel looks like," he whispered.

Molly was a beautiful bride. The dress that Steph had made was stunning. Molly had told her that she couldn't wear white, it wouldn't be right, so Steph had picked a pale cream. It was short in the front, so her new cowboy boots would show, but long on the sides and back. She wore the silver cross earrings that the women had bought her as a bridal gift.

Everyone was in place now, waiting for Ken to start the wedding sermon. He looked over the group gathered in the barn, then started talking.

"Friends, I'd like to say a bit before we start this get-together." He slowly pulled a folded piece of paper from his vest pocket.

"Most of you were part of that Christmas Eve. If you weren't, I'm sure you have heard the story, probably more than once. Joe Jamison was the rancher who owned the Kawasaki mule that Jamie had borrowed." Ken winked at Jamie, then, continued, "He and his wife weren't able to attend today, which he felt bad about, but his granddaughter is also getting married today. Anyway, Joe gave me a note that he wrote, especially for Jamie and Molly, but he felt all of you might just be interested in its contents, so I'll read it now."

Joshua was starting to fuss, so Steph reached her arms out for him, settling the baby immediately when she took him.

Ken read the note slowly. It was a lot to take in when you added it to everything else about that night.

Ken,

I'd appreciate if you'd read these words at Molly and Jamie's wedding. I'm sorry I can't be there, as I would have enjoyed telling my part of their story.

Thanks, Ken.

Your friend, Joe

Steph's heart started beating a little harder, as did all the others.

I have told no one of this. I've spent many hours thinking about what happened that night. That morning, before we left on our trip, I was in the barn. As I looked over everything, I took the keys to the mule out of the ignition to hang up in their usual spot. You see, I never leave them in the ignition. There is a cubby hole on the wall, out of sight, where I keep them. It would have been very hard for someone to have found them.

While I held the keys in my hand, a voice in my head told me to *leave in place*.

I have heard this voice before and through the years have learned to follow its guidance, with trust and faith. I took the word *place* to mean in the ignition. I did as the voice instructed and put them back in the ignition. You see, I have never questioned this voice—ever.

I now believe that I was part of His precious plan. The keys played an important role. Without them, the couple could not have gotten to the lane light.

As I grow in age, my love and faith in God grows continuously. He amazes me every day.

I am honored and humbled to have been a part of His plan for all involved.

I pray for happiness for Jamie and Molly and especially Joshua Luke, as he is truly a blessed child.

Sincerely,
Joe Jamison

As Jamie listened to Joe's words, his knees went weak. Chip grabbed his arm to help steady him. Tears rolled down Ken's face as he folded the note back up and handed it to Jamie. Jamie didn't put it away; he kept it in his hand and took Molly's hand so they could both hold on to it throughout the ceremony.

Molly dabbed her tears with a tissue Steph handed her.

The emotional air that flowed through the barn was traumatizing. Memories of what had just happened would not be easily forgotten.

Ken had one more thing to add, "Joe and I agreed the key wasn't a missing puzzle piece, it was a piece of sheer detail that showed us the completeness of God's plan." He closed his eyes and said, "Thank You, Lord!"

Ken heard Lilly's voice. He wasn't sure she had meant for everyone to hear her when she said, "God is perfect!"

He pulled a handkerchief out of his pocket and blew his nose. "Okay, friends, we need to get this show on the road!"

The ceremony was beautiful. Susan cried her eyes out while Rick had his own tears to deal with. Lilly had missed the whole gist of it, being too young, plus the kitten kept her busy. It had been hard for Ken to stay in control. The kids had asked him to write their vows. This he had taken very seriously and hearing each one repeat his words had emotionally drained him.

As he presented the two as Mr. and Mrs. James Matthew and son, he had a mixed feeling wash over him. There was something different about it. It was a feeling that he had never felt before and it scared him.

He raised his hand that held the worn Bible high in the air. Eyes were on him as he said, "Thank You, Lord, for this, the second beginning of Your special plan, Amen."

Ken had meant to use the word *perfect* at the end as Lilly had. Something deep down inside of him wouldn't let him. His skin crawled. This feeling told him there was more.

About the Author

 C andee MacQueen and her husband, Alan, spent the past thirty years in the dairy business as owner, breeders of registered Holsteins, under the name of Alandee Dairy. After the loss of Alan in 2013, Candee returned home to Missouri from Maine and now shares her home with her beloved family of Aussies. As owner/breeder of "Hearts on Fire" Australian shepherds, her breeding goals are geared toward improving the breed by producing puppies with compassionate hearts and personalities.

She claims no writing experience, only a deep-seated passion to write that has been with her since childhood.

The Lane Light is her first work that lends itself toward the things she loves—Aussies, barns, cattle, mountains, storms, and the Lord.

She is currently working on a sequel to *The Lane Light*, as the story needs to continue.

CPSIA information can be obtained
at www.ICGtesting.com
Printed in the USA
FSHW010343171020
74818FS

9 781646 707980